# DIVE SMACK

# DIVE SMACK

## DEMETRA BRODSKY

TOR
TEEN

A TOM DOHERTY ASSOCIATES BOOK • NEW YORK

DIVE SMACK

Copyright © 2018 by Demetra Brodsky

A Tor Teen Book
Published by Tom Doherty Associates
175 Fifth Avenue
New York, NY 10010

www.tor-forge.com

Tor® is a registered trademark of Macmillan Publishing Group, LLC.

The Library of Congress Cataloging-in-Publication Data is available upon request.

ISBN 978-0-7653-9695-2 (hardcover)
ISBN 978-0-7653-9697-6 (ebook)

Our books may be purchased in bulk for promotional, educational, or business use. Please contact your local bookseller or the Macmillan Corporate and Premium Sales Department at 1-800-221-7945, extension 5442, or by email at MacmillanSpecialMarkets@macmillan.com.

First Edition: June 2018

Printed in the United States of America

0  9  8  7  6  5  4  3  2  1

*For Pumpkin*

# ACKNOWLEDGMENTS

I would like to thank my agent, John Silbersack, for believing in my writing and this book enough to sign me. I don't know what I'd do without your consummate professionalism and calm, which consistently ran counter to my debut author anxiety during parts of this process. You've had a string of excellent support staff in your assistants and I'm so lucky to have worked with them over the past few years. Jennifer Johnson-Blalock, thanks for pulling my book out of the slush pile and putting it into John's hands. Hannah Fergesen, thank you for helping me shape this story for submissions into something I love. (Hannibal and Will forever. We ship it.) Caitlin Meuser, thanks for answering all my ridiculous questions about the process so quickly and enthusiastically. Sometimes I think you can read my mind.

A million times thank you to my editor and champion, Bess Cozby, for loving my story and characters enough to offer this book a home at Tor Teen. I'm forever grateful for your vision, the support provided by you and the entire team at Tor, and the laughs we shared in-between all the hard work. Slay, slay, slay.

Special thanks to Nikki Katz, critique partner of dreams and stellar friend. Going through this journey in tandem with you has been a wonderful adventure filled with tears and laughter. Here's to the unfortunate felling of many more trees in the pursuit of putting books into the hands of readers, both reluctant and voracious. Without them, we are nothing.

I would be lost without the friendship and support of the truly extraordinary Gretchen McNeil who is both an incredible mentor and cherished friend.

Writing a book is a solitary process but it doesn't happen entirely alone in the proverbial cave. A huge amount of gratitude goes to the following people who cheered me on, offering support, friendship, laughter, and incredible notes (sometimes in real life and in person): Elle Jauffret (ma soeur), Robin Reul, Jennifer Bosworth (reality-check advisor and guru), Ara Grigorian, Jennifer Keenan, Debra Driza, Lisa Ritter Cannon, Holly McGuire, Elaine Garrett, Caroline Tyler and Amy Rose Thomas (Texas forever), Miguel Camnitzer, Edith Cohen, Julia Collard, Amy Del Rosso, Matthew MacNish, Jessica Siblaugh-Cowdin, Luvina Jean-Charles, Jenny Peterson, Rachel Harris, Stephanie Monday, Sian Preston, and the incomparable Electric 18. Much appreciation and respect to Jennifer Laughran and Eric J. Adams, my mentors at the 2011 Big Sur Writing Workshop for instilling belief in me early on and teaching me a few tricks I still keep up my sleeve.

Heartfelt thanks go to Michelle Zink and Lois Duncan (may she rest in peace) for providing thought-provoking editorial notes and encouragement simultaneously that continue to help me grow as a writer.

I'm in awe and indebted to the amazing authors who agreed to read a prepublication version of this book while their own lives and deadlines loomed: Carrie Mesrobian, Stephanie Stuve-Bodeen, Gretchen McNeil, Christa Desir, and Michelle Zink.

I can't thank my friend Karen LaFace—a USA Olympic springboard diver in the 1992 games in Barcelona, Spain—nearly enough for reading this book and providing editorial notes on all things springboard diving. Any and all liberties taken were mine for fictional purposes.

I would be a sad and lonely recluse without my non-writing friends who meet me for happy hours and brunch, running dates, and movie nights. You know me, listen to me moan about my fears and deadlines, and still invite me to your parties. Thank you for making my life so fun and rich: Michelle Yoho, Alexandra Gerritson, Alison Stanton, Jessica Thorndike, Katy Fryer, Lorenza Tupaz, Marissa Weir, Cherry Hernandez, Megan Luce, and Kristen Fay.

Chrissy Weir, I don't know what I would have done without the delicious, healthy meals you provided every time I ordered from Food Made Fresh during deadlines. Tammy Lawler, the world's most awesome bartender, thanks for lifting my spirits (pun intended) every time Mike and I showed up at the bar for a pint at the end of a very long day. You rock.

Special thanks go to my parents, Vasilios and Vasiliki Kouvaros, for believing me when I told them I won a puppy in a spelling bee (sorry not sorry for lying). My love for storytelling began that day. Thanks to my extended family The Mariano, Schwalbe, Tranakas, and Brodsky clans. Look at me, still the same weirdo going against the grain that you've always known. There's something to be said for consistency. And to Barbara Brodsky, my resolutely supportive mother-in-law, who always let me know she believed in me. Every single day I wish you were here to share these special moments. I know you're proud. I know. Still, I miss you.

Thanks aren't enough for my daughters, Zoe and Ava, who provided encouragement and cheers through revisions and deadlines, giving their thoughts on plot and characters, while eating whatever was in the house when I was too busy to cook. I hope this book makes you proud of your strange, sometimes absentee, mother.

And last but never least, all my love and thanks to my incredible, irreplaceable husband, Michael, for enthusiastically reading every single draft of this novel and offering usable, intelligent feedback. It's nothing short of a miracle that you know me, and all my characters, so well and love me anyway. *Would that it were so simple.*

# DIVE SMACK

The truth is always an abyss. One must, as in a swimming pool, dare to dive from the quivering springboard of trivial everyday experience and sink into the depths, in order to later rise again, laughing and fighting for breath, to the now doubly illuminated surface of things.

—FRANZ KAFKA

Your vision will become clear when you look inside your heart. Who looks outside, dreams. Who looks inside, awakens.

—CARL GUSTAV JUNG

# ONE

**Heavy Entry:** Entering the water with a lot of splash.

**EVERY HUMAN** reaction has to be silenced before doing a single twist. Then it's go time. The more twists the better. That's why I like to chuck it at the break of dawn when no one is watching or keeping score. Once the school day begins, I'm Theo Mackey, Ellis Hollow springboard diving captain. People expect me to behave a certain way in the classroom, at home, on the diving board. Especially on the diving board. But out here, I can blow as many new dives as I want before bringing them to the team. Like the 5337D I've been working on for the past hour.

The Reverse 1½ Somersault 3½ Twist was my mom's favorite dive, the one she claimed got her into Stanford. Adding it to my dive list this year isn't optional. Not in the official sense. Voluntary dives are required at meets. Optionals are a diver's choice. Don't try to wrap your head around voluntary dives being required or your brain will explode. Just trust that diving has some strange rules. The important thing to know is that the dive has a high degree of difficulty. A 3.5. That's still lower than the dive I'd call my own favorite. But the reverse entry will help set me further apart from the rank and file and secure my position for a scholarship, which is the only way I know how to honor my parents now that they're gone.

So far it's not going great.

My thoughts keep shifting from my dad, for good reason, to

the fucked-up dream that left me sleepless for most of the night. I'm not sure *dream* is the right word since I wasn't fully asleep at the time. Maybe I never was. More like in a trance, trapped between awake and sleep, watching my actions unfold in another space and time. I saw myself running down this long deserted hallway under humming fluorescent lights. Pushing open doors that lined both sides while fresh dirt spilled in alongside me. My goal was to get to the last door but my Uncle Phil slithered around the corner like a snake and blocked my path. A heart-pounding urge to clobber him with the garden shovel in my hand took over my senses. But as soon as I lifted the tool to strike—bam—I was right back to staring at the ceiling in Chip's room.

I wipe my arms dry with a shammy and rub my feet across the springboard's pebbled surface. Diving is also like slipping through a door into another world. Everything goes hush quiet after entry, and for a few seconds I can pretend life is back to normal. Mom is watching, Dad is watching. And all is right with the world. But reaching that door in just the right way takes practice, hours of twisting and turning just to whoosh through that addictive portal for less than a minute.

"You need more height," Chip announces.

I didn't see him coming and the surprise of his voice makes me circle my arms for balance so I don't fall into the pool. "I'm already six feet tall."

"Hilarious." He straddles a lounge chair by the edge of his family's pool and takes a seat. "You need another six inches on your flight if you want to make the last twist."

"How long have you been out here watching?"

"Long enough to see you eat shit on your last two dives. Where's your girlfriend? You know my mom would freak if you got hurt."

I fling the shammy over a diving rail and search for his dog from my 3-meter height advantage. "She was here a minute ago.

Maybe she saw you coming and gave up her post to look for a bone."

"*Or* she got tired of watching you almost crack your skull open."

I know what Chip's getting at. Flying solo is a diving no-no—a safety issue—but I wasn't entirely alone. The Langfords' black Lab was looking out for me, the way she's done for as long as I can remember. Chip's mom trained her to follow us to the pool and bark like hell if anyone is floating facedown in the water. It's a cool trick I'm glad I've never seen used in a real emergency. But now, I can't hear a dog barking without thinking something is wrong.

Belly comes running to the sound of our voices, paws muddy from digging holes in the yard, and leaps into the pool with a giant flop, true to her name. Water splashes everywhere. Not that it matters. The rain last night already left everything slick, and the air heavy with the stench of fresh dirt and dusty old basements.

"Why didn't you wake me up?" Chip shields himself from Belly as she shakes dry. "I could have kept an eye out and done some laps with the snorkel to power up my lungs."

"I needed to get my head straight before school."

Chip nods.

He understands. For the most part.

My dad died a year ago today, making me an orphan, more or less. Chip and I talked about it on the way home from practice last night, what it would be like if one variable had changed. But I live with my grandfather now, who I call GP. He used to be a hero, the Ellis Hollow fire chief, but he fell into a bottle of whiskey after my dad died and hasn't been the same since.

I get it. And I don't.

It's not like he's the only one who lost people.

"What do you think The Mack Attack would say if he saw you balking every other approach on the board today?" Chip asks.

Good question.

My dad, Mitch Mackey, was a sports psychologist known as The Mack Attack by his clients because he attacked whatever problem they were having. He usually had plenty to say to me when things weren't going my way. But it's not my dad's words that haunt me today. It's Mom's. When I first started diving she said, "Your mind will betray you before your body; acknowledge your fears and do it anyway." I get that now more than ever. Diving is as much mental as physical. She was selective with how much she'd coach me unless I asked for help. But she also had a way of knowing when I needed her before I ever said a word.

Drove my dad nuts.

He used to call Mom The Diving Whisperer, like it was some big joke. Dad made his living fostering excellence in others, but it was Mom who had a knack for spotting which of his clients would go to the big leagues. And she was usually right. But I could tell something about those coincidences drove him a little crazy. That's what killed him in the end. Not the accident—work—his obsession with being able to pick the right athlete after Mom died. He had a heart attack while driving to see an important client. I kind of saw it coming. He was on edge after Mom died, flying off the handle without much provocation. I wish I'd said something about the way he was acting when I had the chance. But I didn't. In a way, I guess that's my fault too . . . It's complicated.

"Never in your father's life was silence an answer."

Right. I almost forgot the question.

I clasp my hands behind my neck and squeeze. "He'd probably ask something obvious like, 'What did you learn from your last mistake?'"

"And?"

"I need more height, like you said. I'm coming in short and fast."

"Then take it up. Girls don't like a guy that comes too fast.

Take it up, then slow it down, but speed it up. Control is the name of the game."

"Sounds like a personal problem, Chip."

"If you don't believe me you can always ask Iris. Inquiring minds want to know."

"Idiotic minds want to know. Maybe you should take it up with Amy."

"No can do, brother. I already know the answer to that question, and I value my life."

"You mean your sex life."

"Potato. Po-tah-toe."

I flip him off and walk back to my starting position.

There are lots of things I'd like to ask Iris Fiorello, but none of them have to do with how she likes it from a guy. Not that I wouldn't want to know if ever I got that lucky. It's just that I lost whatever ask-a-girl-out nerve I had the minute Mr. Malone assigned her and Les Carter as my sociology partners for our family history project. Chip likes to call me the King of Avoidance. Especially when it comes to girls. But I disagree. Sometimes caution and self-preservation are warranted.

I crack my neck from side to side and twist my trunk to loosen up my muscles.

When we talk about inertia in diving, this isn't what we mean. The moment of inertia happens inside the dive when we interrupt rotational motion, controlling the speed of somersaults by lengthening or shortening of our bodies. A serious screw-you to gravitational pull I'm usually on board with (pun acknowledged, not intended).

What I'm doing now is stalling.

Chip says, "What's our mantra?"

"I got this."

"You got this. Visualize the dive and chuck it."

I haven't been able to see myself nailing this dive yet, but I'm willing to give it another shot. I close my eyes and envision myself leaving the board. This time it looks good. I've got the height, the rotations. I take three big steps to the end of the board and lift my right knee for the hurdle. When I come down I land the perfect ride. The board springs me higher into the air this time and my flight is perfect. I rotate backward for the reverse somersault, and twist. Once. Twice. Third time's the charm and—

Chip yells, "Yeah! *Chinga tu madre,*" as I end the final half twist and I crimp the entry.

When I surface his eyes are bugged out like he can't believe I screwed up. "What happened?"

"Fuck your mother," I tell him. "That's what you yelled. I'm pretty sure that's not a regulation call-out."

Chip sucks at Spanish so I'm never sure if he understands what he's actually saying.

"Oh." His eyes go wide. "That's some disrespectful shit, especially today. I meant to say *for* your mother. Like an homage."

"That's *para tu madre.* Don't stress about it too much. I doubt Señora Torres will put the verb *chingar* on our midterm."

"I like it, though," Chip says. "*Chingar!* It packs a punch."

I flick my eyes at the house. "You do know your folks have the windows open, right?"

"My mom doesn't know Spanish," Chip says. "Not that kind of Spanish anyway. And my dad already left to pick up his crew, where *I'm pretty sure* he's heard worse."

Mr. Langford owns a pool company. He uses their backyard to showcase his work to clients, but really went to town on the lap pool once Chip showed promise in swimming, adding special year-round heaters and extra lighting. He put the 3-meter board in for my birthday after Mom died. I'd stay here forever if I could.

"You don't give your mom enough credit," I tell Chip. "If your dad knows, she knows."

"You're probably right. But that's your job, son. Especially since she's in the kitchen right now making a special memorial breakfast just for you. A situation I'm inclined to let slide under today's circumstances. Because nothing says I'm sorry for your loss like a pound of bacon."

I chuckle and shake my head. Mrs. Langford likes to show us she cares through food, no matter the occasion. And since my dinners at home usually consist of either pasta and jarred sauce or sandwiches, who am I to look a gift horse in the mouth?

I'm glad Chip isn't walking on eggshells around me today. Not that he ever does. The best thing about having him as a friend is I never have to guess what he's thinking.

"You want me to hang out while you rip that dive one more time? I swear I won't say a word."

"Nah. I think I'll just do a 305B and meet you inside."

"Why not try the Triple Lindy instead," he says. "Maybe you'll finally get some respect."

"If it were that easy, everyone would be doing it. Leave me some bacon."

"I make no promises I can't keep."

I wait until Chip reaches the sliding glass door before inching back up the ladder. He knows I don't like leaving the board on a bad dive because the failure sticks with me all day. I think it's a side effect of having trained under the nonstop motivational maxims of my dad. I still find *maxim* the SAT word more inspiring than any of my dad's psychobabble, but thinking about him that way today is also some disrespectful shit.

I breathe deep, visualizing my Reverse 3½ Tuck. I approach my hurdle and hit the end of the board, shooting up and backward, hugging my thighs to create a tight fold. My pike is clean. Core tight. Toes pointed so hard they might cramp. All my rotations are good. I come-out and grab the top of my right hand, thumbs interlocking, and rip the entry with zero splash.

That's how every dive should be done. Without distraction, paying attention to the dive during every twist and turn until there's nothing but the rush of water and silence.

But the conditions are never perfect. I think that's what my mom was ultimately trying to say.

# TWO

**Lead-Up:** Practicing the beginning portion of a difficult dive before attempting the full dive.

**I TAKE** my morning Adderall with a glass of juice, then stuff the last piece of crispy bacon into my mouth with a grin aimed at Mrs. Langford.

"You better hurry," she says, handing me my letterman's jacket. "Before he—"

Chip blasts his horn and we cringe. I've told him a million times it sounds like a mutant duck being—

*Hooonk.*

"Jeezus."

He never listens.

I slide into my jacket and head outside where Chip's white Dodge Dart sits in the driveway shaking like it's terrified. It should be. Chip is by far the crappiest driver I know. The guy may be my best friend, but I only ride with him when I have to, or it makes more sense to carpool.

Chip cranks the passenger window down by hand. "Let's go, genius. This is what you get for letting Bumblebee die."

Case in point. I left the lights on in my truck yesterday, killing the battery. After surviving an intense practice we were both too tired and hungry to stick around and jump-start the engine.

I slide into the passenger seat and buckle the narrow, vintage seat belt.

"Hey, you think roadside assistance will update Bumblebee's voice box when they come give you a jump? Get some new tunes going in that bad boy." Chip does the robot in his seat and I can't help but laugh. He'll never let me live that joke down.

When the last *Transformers* movie came out, he made some wisecrack about my FJ Cruiser that got a huge uproar of laughter from the team. Now it's his standard dig. He used to call my truck Velveeta. If he's going to riff, I'll take Transformer over processed cheese any day. Plus, deep down, Chip knows my truck represents: Monarch orange, Bose stereo, four-wheel drive. My last gift from Dad before he died because he didn't want me driving his car. He would have been safer in mine.

"For all the shit you give me about my truck, you didn't seem to mind when Amy Sloan thought Bumblebee was yours. In fact, I specifically recall you leaning against the door with serious pride of ownership."

"Didn't matter, though. Did it, numbnuts? Amy liked my Dart's black racing stripes and I scored anyway."

He waggles his heavy eyebrows and jerks the Dart's long shifter into reverse with a thunk, backing out of the driveway without looking. I hold my breath as we roll over the curb and bump the recycling bin into the street. At least he didn't overcut his wheel and take out the mailbox. Again.

"Do me a favor," I say, checking my watch. "Take Quarry Road to Mount Pleasant the long way."

Chip stomps the brake pedal and I jerk forward. "Mom said I should take you to the south side of the cemetery."

"I'll stop by there after school on my own. Otherwise it'll mess with my head. If you take Mount Pleasant Road to Whiptail Loop we'll still drive past the south side and you won't be lying if she asks. Not technically."

"Whiptail Loop again?" He shakes his head. "How many times do we have to go over this, bro? It's talking not stalking that'll get you what you want with that girl."

"I know. Just drive. I'm trying to sort something out."

"Something cruising by Iris's house will solve?"

"Maybe."

"All right. It's your funeral."

"Theoretically, it's my dad's."

Chip's eyes widen slowly. "Shit. I didn't mean—I wasn't thinking."

"I know," I say. "Gotcha, though."

"Dick."

Chip hits the gas, spinning the Dart's tires against the wet asphalt, and I shift in the seat and stare through the passenger window, watching patches of yellow and green trees zip past.

A few weeks ago, Iris caught my eye at the quarry. Not for the first time. And not the way other girls have by sprawling themselves on the large, flat rocks in bikinis, loud talking to grab everyone's attention. Iris was standing at the edge of the second highest cliff wearing a yellow one-piece as blinding as the sun. But her quietness and one-piece swimsuit weren't the only things that set her apart from the other girls at the quarry. At first, I thought she was just taking in the view of the nearby dam, because she turned and walked away, leaving me gaping at the empty place where she'd stood. I didn't expect her to come rushing off the cliff's edge a moment later, her dark hair rising above her like a raven taking flight. I felt so many things at once. Awe. Admiration. Seeing that sent me over the edge alongside her. A complete goner. I jumped into the water in two seconds flat to see the look on her face when she surfaced. Making that plunge the best decisions of my summer.

Cruising by her house isn't about stalking, no matter what Chip says. I'm working on my lead-up. That's what divers do. We practice portions of dives to build up to the ones we plan to attempt later. I can't just chuck this one.

"You okay?" Chip asks. "You went stone quiet."

"I was just thinking about the quarry." I turn partway in my seat. "Don't you think it's kinda weird Malone made Iris and me partners?"

"Don't forget Les. You know how he loves to help."

"Don't remind me."

"It's kind of good, though, right?" Chip says. "Her mom died in a car accident. Your dad died in a car accident. You two can relate to each other."

"Death is kind of a shitty thing to have in common."

"True. But it's not nothing."

That's debatable.

If I hadn't already been through my mom's death a few years ago, my reaction to Dad's probably would have been more noticeable at school. I definitely got quieter around people the second time around, but I kept doing what was expected of me. Even if that meant listening, if not exactly following, whatever crazy shit GP dictated about who and what he deemed off-limits.

When Iris got back to school after her mom died, she went from the most outspoken girl in any of my classes to this empty shell of her former self, walking the halls hugging books like a ghost.

Seeing her jump from the cliff this summer blew my mind because I knew her pain. I also know what it takes to make that jump. And believe me, it takes next-level guts.

"So according to your dumb logic, Malone set me up with the perfect take-off position. All I have to do is feel her out."

"Now you're talking," Chip says. "*Feel her out. Or up.* Gotta start loading the bases sometime."

"Easy for you to say. Amy's a swimmer. Trying to date outside of our circle takes a different skill level. I'm telling you, the whole thing is weird."

"What's weird is watching you make goo-goo eyes at her in class with your thumb up your ass," Chip says. "If you ask me, Malone did you a favor."

Some favor.

Talking about my family with Iris will be hard enough, given our similar histories. But rehashing my parents' deaths with someone on my team would be a huge step backward from the Theo I've worked so hard to become.

Chip cranks the radio and starts singing along with that Rolling Stones song about how you can't always get what you want.

*Subtle, Chip. Real subtle.*

He semi-speeds toward the turn for Mount Pleasant Road. Since I'm used to Chip's driving, I assume he'll slow down. But it's never safe to assume anything when Chip's driving. He jerks the wheel last minute and we hydroplane onto Mount Pleasant Road, narrowly missing a utility pole as we come out of a fishtail.

"Easy, Speed Racer. You're gonna get us killed."

Chip stops bobbing his head to lower the volume. "Almost forgot stalker patrol."

"You might want to check your tires."

"You might want to check your nads," he says. "I think you left them at home in your man-purse."

"That's right. I put them next to your chlamydia medication."

Chip snorts out a laugh. "Nice. You're King of the One-Liners today. New moniker."

Could be worse.

We can only talk serious about girls for about five minutes before circling back to giving each other shit.

No one else is on the winding road, so I dare myself to face my fear and close my eyes. I listen to The Stones song and think about what I need for my project. Since I can't have what I want in the form of parents who are around to tell me all about their families, I have to settle for the documents and photos I can get. Along with the balls I need to talk to Iris about it without sounding like a pathetic asswipe.

Chip smacks my arm. "Hey, isn't that Dr. Maddox?"

He slams his brakes and I lurch forward, bracing myself against the dashboard as we come to a complete stop. My Uncle Phil is standing on the road's narrow shoulder behind his charcoal Escalade.

"Maybe he got a flat or something on his way to work," I tell Chip. "The backside of Green Hill runs along this road."

"Hey, Dr. Maddox," Chip says loudly as he rolls down his window. "Almost didn't see you there. Rolling Stones." He points at his ear like music is his best excuse for distracted driving. And with Uncle Phil, it might be. The guy is a total audiophile. My love of rock music definitely comes from him.

"No harm, no foul," Uncle Phil says, flashing back Chip's grin. "I'm always willing to extend a little 'Mercy, Mercy.'"

Chip turns to me. "You smile the same as him. It's kind of freaky."

"My dad used to say the same thing." Only it seemed to bother him.

"Nature versus nurture," Chip says. "What can you do?"

Not a damn thing.

Mr. Malone talked about that in class. How we're shaped not only by genetics, but the environment we're raised in. But Mr. Malone wasn't the first person to introduce me to that concept. That honor belongs to Uncle Phil.

"I'll be right back." I jump out of the car so I can talk to him without yelling through the window.

Uncle Phil takes off his trench coat and tosses it into his trunk. Before it lands I swear I see the handle of a garden shovel lying inside. My stomach twists into guilty knots. If you know anything about me at all, you know clobbering my uncle with a garden shovel is probably the last thing I'd ever do, whether I saw it in a dream or not.

"What are you two doing over this way?" Uncle Phil asks. He pulls me in for a quick hug and pat on the back. "Are you headed to the cemetery?"

"Theo's stalking a girl who lives around here," Chip shouts.

I shoot him a shut-up look.

"We've all been guilty of that at one time or another," Uncle Phil says. "The heart wants what the heart wants."

"Never been an issue for me," Chip says. "The ladies flock to this like bees to honey. I wield an irresistible power over them."

Uncle Phil releases a short puff of laughter through his nose. "If that were actually true, Langford, I might consider you a specimen worth studying."

"He's definitely one of a kind," I tell him.

"A legend in his own mind if my idiopathic analysis is correct."

I glance at Chip and see him air drumming to whatever song he's listening to, completely oblivious. "You got the idio part right, Uncle Phil. Fits him to a *T*."

He grins back at me and reaches into the pocket of his discarded trench. The silver Zippo lighter my dad gave him tumbles onto the ground as he pulls out his keys. We both pitch forward to retrieve it but I get there first, reading the words engraved on its case before handing it back.

*My best man. My brother. My friend.*

The fact that he carries this around shows how much he still cares about Dad.

Dr. Phillip Maddox isn't really my uncle. Not in the biological sense. GP adopted him right before he aged out of the foster care system. A shitty upbringing is something he and Mom had in common, even though she didn't like to talk about her past. Come to think of it, he doesn't really talk about his either.

"What's with the shovel?" I ask, tipping my head to the trunk. "Did you get a flat or something? Chip probably has a jack in the back if you need one."

"No, it's nothing like that. I like to patrol the grounds for leaks periodically," he explains. "In a state-run facility with budget constraints it's best to try and stay ahead of problems before they arise."

"If you say so." The guy I know is a white-collar neatnik but I take him at his word. "Are you gonna be around this weekend? I wanted to come by and talk to you about a couple of things."

He hits me with the practiced look of a psychiatrist. "Anything in particular?"

"Information mostly. About Mom. For a family history project at school. Since GP is usually too tanked to help me with anything, I was hoping you might be able to help with Mom's side of the family. I don't really know anything about the Rogans."

"Neither do I. Your mother was adamant about erasing them from her memory. But I'll do what I can to help."

"Great. My Adderall supply is running kind of low too, and since I'm going to need maximum focus for the next two weeks, do you think you could hook me up with a refill?"

"I thought I gave you a two-month supply?"

"You did. But there were days I needed to double up to make it through training and homework." Truth is I've tripled up, especially on weekends, but keep that part to myself.

"Has doubling up helped?"

"Yes and no. I can't really get into it or we'll be late for school."

"Fair enough. Come by on Saturday and I'll see what I can dig up between now and then."

"Not with that, I hope." I gesture to his trunk again. "I'd be the only kid in class to show up with a relative's skeleton. Could get me an A if it were the right relative. You know, a skeleton from the family closet."

I thought that would get a laugh even if his normal state does bend toward stoic, but he only stares at me with the slight smile mirrored back in my direction. In his defense, today is probably the wrong day to joke about corpses. That was my bad.

"Okay, so Saturday. That's tomorrow. Tomorrow's great."

"Tomorrow it is," he says. "Just don't expect a tableau of your deceased relatives."

"Understood."

I hop into Chip's car, feeling like a jerk for the joke. And dumb for not hinting at wanting to talk to him about my weird dream since he helped me deal with something similar after the fire, which made sense at the time. But why now? Maybe I should try to figure that out before I go confessing to seeing stuff while I'm semi-awake again.

"Did he say mercy twice?" Chip asks. "That's an old Rolling Stones song, isn't it? 'Mercy, Mercy.' You think he meant it that way, like a play on the band? Probably. The guy never says anything off the cuff, am I right?"

More than right.

Chip used to call him Moriarty back when we were in our Sherlock Holmes phase. But I'm not sure whether Uncle Phil saw the humor in that either.

"I'm glad I saw him," Chip says. "Imagine if I ran the guy down while I was fucking around with the radio? We'd be screwed. Good thing we're near the hospital."

"That's a psychiatric hospital."

"So?" Chip says. "They practice life-saving measures, don't they?"

"They probably would for him."

"What's that supposed to mean?"

"I don't know. Nothing. It's just, there's a lot of lonely, forgotten people in that place."

Green Hill Psychiatric Hospital looms on our right like Frankenstein's castle atop Ward Hill. A building completely out of time among the ranch houses of the surrounding neighborhood. I've only been inside a couple of times, when Mom took me to visit Uncle Phil at work. But that was enough to freak me out for a lifetime. I can see why he isn't too keen on tableaus in that respect. The place is rife with them.

Chip flips around on his iPod. "'Mercy, Mercy.' Bam. I knew I had that song on here." He sets it to play and hits the gas, spinning the Dart's tires against the wet asphalt.

I slump down to listen and the seat belt pulls uncomfortably tight. The song is about loss and forgiveness, which is appropriate for today because according to my dad what happened the night of the fire was unforgivable. It was all harm, all foul. There wasn't any room for mercy. He and Uncle Phil fell out after Mom died, like the trauma of losing her was too much to take, too heavy to keep their friendship afloat. But her death didn't change that relationship for me. If anything, it made Uncle Phil and me closer, especially after Dad was gone, because I needed to talk to someone about what I'd done that night, and where I'd been.

"You better jump on the highway," I tell Chip. "Abort stalker mission."

"You sure?"

"Positive. We're running out of time." I chew a hangnail on my middle finger, conflicted again. "You think Uncle Phil already went to the cemetery? Maybe I should have asked him to go with me later." I rip the hangnail out with my front teeth so hard blood seeps up the side of my finger.

"I wouldn't be surprised if he was the first person there," Chip says. "He and your dad were like brothers. Just like us. Only . . . aww, hell, Mackey, you know I can't never quit you."

"That's right, Chip. We'll always have Monarch Night. Now fuck off and drive."

Chip laughs again. "I knew you cared."

He makes a right for Route 12. The farther we get from the cemetery the better I feel. Because Chip is right about one thing. Uncle Phil and my dad were like brothers.

Until I lit the match that made all of our lives go up in flames.

# THREE

**Break in Form:** A break in position that results in a deduction from the judges.

**THE FIRST** warning bell rings as we pull into the packed parking lot of Ellis Hollow High. Home of the Monarchs, as in butterflies not kings and queens, and I'm back on the E.H.H.S. stage. Captain Springboard. New banners sway from the light posts.

GO MONARCHS!

STATE CHAMPS.

MONARCH PRIDE.

32ND ANNUAL MIGRATION CARNIVAL.

"Check that out. The PTA finally gave us props. You ready for this weekend?"

"Hell yes, I'm ready." Chip glances at me sideways. "You better be ready, too, 'cause we're gonna nab that title again this year or die trying."

I give him a fist bump, but take a hard pass on dying since there aren't that many Mackeys left to go around.

In less than thirty-six hours, the entire team will head to the quarry for Monarch Night where we'll take turns diving off the cliff at Pikes Falls. In years past, guys have quit the team before willingly diving into what they saw as a blind death trap. But it's been a Monarch tradition—and the way captains have determined how they'll seed divers at meets—for decades.

Sometimes keeping secrets is warranted too.

When Coach Porter made Chip and me captains of the swim and diving teams, respectively, a few of our friends were pissed. But we didn't ask for it; our performance at regionals junior year clinched his decision. We went big and came home bigger. Coach calls us his strong finishers. Now that we're seniors, though, the pressure for scholarships is on. Full-blast.

We catch sight of Amy jumping to catch our attention as we trudge through the parking lot. Her platinum hair is bobbing like a jellyfish in the sea of students migrating toward the main entrance. Several people are pointing toward the football field. Smiling, nudging people they wouldn't normally acknowledge in the social pecking order so they'll see the rainbow arcing across the sky behind the goalpost.

I'm not one to believe in leprechauns and pots of gold. But today, I'll take it as a sign of something promising. The Mackeys *are* Irish, after all.

"I better catch up to her," Chip says, backhanding me in the chest. "Live to dive another day, bro. Know what I mean?"

I get it. Things can always be worse.

I hang back to make a call to roadside assistance, hoping they can send someone out here to give Bumblebee's battery a charge while I'm in class. The call center's robo-recording gives me my estimated wait time. Seven minutes is cutting it close. I keep my ear to the phone and head toward the space where I left Bumblebee parked.

There's an orange flyer flapping under one of the wiper blades on top of our school newspaper, wrapped in a plastic sleeve. Not surprising since the PTA fells multiple forests going crazy for all things E.H.H.S., including the Migration Carnival, but especially the football game. Then again, they did give us props for being state champs on the banners.

I have no *P* to speak of, so I don't have an issue with the PTA specifically. But if any one of the guys on the football team were capable of doing a somersault over another player, and then kept running for a touchdown, not only would I attend every game, I'd understand why all the T&A shows up too.

I prefer my puns intended.

I hate to admit I never read the newspaper, considering Iris is on the editorial staff, because that right there would be a perfect conversation starter. But the hours of homework on top of practice and looking after GP don't leave me much time.

The flyer on Bumblebee is for the game, as expected, so it's safe to assume the newspaper is full of articles about the football team, as well. But I think I'll hang onto this edition, in case Iris asks. I'm about to crumple the useless flyer when I notice a handwritten note from Les on the backside. Every letter has been scribbled over multiple times in purple pen.

> We should talk.
> THE SOONER THE BETTER.
> —Les

Christ.

Why couldn't he just text me like a normal person?

*The sooner the better . . .*

The words run through my mind in my mom's voice seconds before I sense myself disconnecting from the parking lot with an unexpected memory.

*I'm standing at the top of the stairs in our old house, squishing my toes into the carpet to keep from running to my room to light matches until the yelling stopped. Wiped after a day of swimming at the quarry with Mom and Uncle Phil, my limbs weak as jellyfish tentacles, but I kept listening. I was always listening. Especially on days when fun ended in a fight between my parents.*

"I need to know," Mom said. "The sooner the better. Without proper guidance . . . Well, you know how that turned out for me."

"He's my son, too, dammit. Don't I have a say?"

"Yes, of course. But he will see the truth on his own—it's only of matter of when—and without proper guidance . . . Well, you know how that turned out for me."

"Even if he is like you, Sophia, he has a family. He's not some orphan."

"Don't be merciless, Mitch. It's ugly. And it's unfair."

"Do you want to talk about what's fair?" Dad spat. "Or should we start with mercy?"

"A little mercy might be nice."

"For me or him? I never thought I'd say this, Sophia, but you might actually be delusional."

"You know that's not true. You can't blame anyone for this but me."

"Because you're addicted to the power of your own mind. If you do this you're on your own. There won't be any room for mercy."

"You don't mean that."

"We've been here before and you made your choice, Sophia. You can't have us both."

I creaked down the steps, terrified he meant me.

Mom stepped away from the harsh light of the fireplace and smiled, but it didn't reach her eyes.

"Hey you. I thought you were asleep. You want to come for a ride with me to Uncle Phil's?"

"Is Dad coming this time?" I looked at him, hopeful, but he kept staring at Mom.

"No. Not this time. Go grab your shoes."

As I turned to run back up the stairs, I saw my father sigh and hang his head.

THE SHRILL peal of the second warning bell rushes me back to the parking lot, my heart racing from running up the stairs because the return of this memory felt entirely real. Not real the way people say when they mean it abstractly. But a total mind-trip. I felt like I was standing on those carpeted stairs, the soft fibers squishing between my toes, while my parents' anger and disappointment hung in the air alongside my fear that they were arguing about me this time.

I knew this could happen, Uncle Phil warned us, but having it hit me out of the blue leaves me a little unhinged.

After Mom died in the fire, I started having bizarre dreams and night terrors. Dad tried everything in his arsenal to help: sleep aids, guided meditation, Adderall. But he couldn't do it alone. He wasn't trained that way. And eventually he called on Uncle Phil for the heavy lifting, even though they weren't on speaking terms. He told us I had PTSD and offered hypnosis as treatment with one stipulation. Dad couldn't be in the room. Uncle Phil warned I might lose random pieces of memory from around that time, as well, that might come back someday, triggered by certain words or objects, a familiar scent. But not like this.

A disembodied voice echoes from another dimension and takes me by surprise until I realize it's coming from my phone.

"Hellooo? Mr. Mackey, are you still there?"

"Yes. Yes, I'm here." I put the phone to my ear and swoop down to save the flyer from soaking through in the puddle at my feet.

"And are you still in need of assistance?" the woman asks.

"Yes, I am."

*The sooner the better.*

I unlock my door, tossing the flyer and newspaper onto the backseat, forcing myself to answer all the required questions about Bumblebee: location, spare key, number of my parking space, membership identification. Then I take off across the parking lot to beat the late bell, still struggling to shake off the memory of my parents' argument until I can talk to Uncle Phil.

The hallway that leads to my physics class reeks of pencil shavings and nervous sweat. The gross but comforting constant helps put me back on track until I round a corner and zero in on Iris, her long black hair, the stacks of beaded bracelets circling her wrists.

Crap.

Sooner isn't always better.

I skitter to a stop. My wet running shoes squeak against the linoleum and heads turn, including hers, which makes me freeze. I wasn't expecting to see her until Monday. We don't share classes on odd days because of E.H.H.S.'s block scheduling, so it's not like I was purposely avoiding her or anything. I just thought I'd have more time to get my shit together.

She sends me a broad smile and I realize there's nowhere to hide. I breathe in deep through my nose and pull it together before I have to dive in. Resistance is futile.

"Hey you," she says, backtracking in my direction on quick feet. "I've been looking for you everywhere since yesterday."

"You were?"

"We were supposed to exchange phone numbers after Malone's class."

"We were?"

She nods, examining me like I'm as out-to-lunch as I feel. "I turned around to get yours after class and you were already gone. Malone thought you might be sick. Were you? You did leave fast. I got Les's number, but he seemed like he was in a rush too." She digs through the slouchy, canvas bag at her hip. "I can never find my phone in here. Or my favorite pen. Some journalist I am, huh? It's a miracle I have a pad of paper."

"We had practice," I blurt while she's still digging.

It's not a total lie.

I had to get some air after Malone announced that the first part of the semester-long project was due in two weeks. He was still yammering about interviewing our families about their lives and the importance of creating extensive family trees when I bolted in search of a noose I might use to hang myself from the single branch I have left. I won't tell Chip this because he loves when he's right, but I'd probably call that avoidance. I haven't even visited my parents' graves yet. Interviewing them would take an act of necromancy.

I reach into my letterman's jacket for a pen and pull out a Sharpie. "Will this work?"

Iris pulls her eyes from her bag and smirks. "Black Sharpie, huh? A pen says a lot about a person, Theo. Especially the color."

"Oh yeah? What does my black Sharpie say about me?"

I tend to put this type of assessment in the same realm as those online quizzes that determine what breed of dog you are. I'm a pit bull, by the way. Definitely a misunderstood breed. But it's just a dog. And this is just a pen. Plus, it's not even mine. Chip dropped it after writing his event, heat, and lane numbers down the inside of his arm at a swim meet a long time ago and I forgot to give it back. Still, I rock back on my heels and wait for Iris to analyze me as fuzzy or thick—thickheaded might be true.

"I'd say you either have issues with impermanence or you're the type of person who doesn't intend to make mistakes. Black isn't your color, though. You should stick with Monarch orange."

Iris winks at me and I get this . . . I don't know what to call it, but whatever it is she does it to me. For me. Big time.

"What's your color?" I ask. "I mean, of the pen you're missing."

"Violet. I special order them by the dozen."

"So, you like purple pens." I remember the note left on my truck. "Maybe Les took it by accident when he was giving you his number."

"Oh. Maybe. He was sitting next to me in class. But to answer your question, I like violet. There are lots of shades of purple: lavender, orchard, grape. Violet has something special."

So does she.

I bring up something that might sound less moronic to fill the awkward silence.

"Did you know violet isn't actually a color in the rainbow? Isaac Newton called it violet but he was actually seeing dark blue. It's a physics thing. Supernumerary circles." I draw an invisible circle with my finger. "The blue and red overlap."

"Does something about me make you think of rainbows?" Another smirk makes a dimple pucker in one corner below her mouth.

"Not *you* specifically. I saw one this morning. Over the goal-post. I mean, I was thinking about you; it's not like I was distracted by thoughts of leprechauns and rainbows with pots of gold at the end or anything. I was headed to physics before I ran into you. I have refraction on the brain."

"Sounds serious. Does it hurt?" She tries not to laugh and I realize I just springboard-diver physics-geeked the hell out on her.

Asswipe status achieved.

"Do you have your phone?" she asks, when I stand there mute. "I'll give you my number in case we need to talk. Les told me he's already in good shape for the project and finding more than he needs. Did you have a chance to pull any of the stuff on the syllabus together?"

"A little." I hand her my phone with another lie. "You?"

"Personally? No. But my dad is all over this project. Our living room looks like Memory Lane. I'm sure you know what I mean."

"Totally." I swallow hard because the lies are piling up in my throat.

Getting help from GP will be about as easy as nailing Jell-O to a tree. Believe me. I've tried to bring up the night of the fire before. Timing is everything for me, in my home life and in diving.

"I was a little worried when you bolted yesterday that you

might not to want to partner with me." Iris shakes her head and punches her number into my contacts. "It doesn't matter. I can already see I was wrong. I wish we had more time to talk now. I have to get to journalism class. Lots of high school news to report. But it sounds like we'll be in good shape for the field trip on Monday."

"The field trip?"

She hands me back my phone. "To the county clerk's office? Are you sure you're feeling all right, Theo? You seem a little muddy."

"Yep. I'm good. I just forgot for a second. County clerk. Info. Monday. It's a date."

"A date, huh? All right, Theo Mackey. Text me so I have your number. We'll see you then."

I pat myself on the back for a job well done. Saving that conversation from complete failure after diving blind in the middle was tricky. And then I realize *we'll* means Iris and Les Carter, tagging along like a third wheel.

Iris peers at me over her shoulder with a smirk, confirming my delayed grasp on the Les situation.

I try what we call a *save* in diving. "Hey, what if I drop my phone in the pool? How will we get in touch with each other?"

She turns and walks backward toward the newsroom. "Worst case scenario, you know where I live."

Yes. Yes, I do.

I'm still smiling like an idiot when the inference in her words clicks. Iris has seen me drive by her house. Probably more than once.

*Smooth, Mackey. Real smooth.*

# FOUR

**Moment of Inertia:** The property of a body that makes it reluctant to speed up or slow down in a rotational manner.

COACH PORTER bursts through the double doors to the pool complex and blows his silver whistle. Three ear-piercing shrieks that take the headache I've been riding all day to a new level. I'm not sure how he does it exactly, but Coach Porter uses that whistle like an extension of his personality with all the associated emotions. This time it says we have to get a move on.

"You know what day it is—Chuck-Your-Luck-Friday—the day you chuckleheads get to show me something new. Start warming up with lineups." He looks around for a specific target and finds Chip. "Langford, take the swimmers to the far end and get them running one-arm catch-up drills."

I scramble to line up with the rest of the 3-meter divers to practice entering the water with zero to little splash.

"Not you, Mackey," Coach says. "Over here. I need a word."

I step out of line and jog toward him. "Yes, Coach?"

"Rocco Bennett was made a co-captain for the Andover Sharks."

"Wait. *What?*"

There's no such thing as a lead-up in conversation with Coach. He's staring at me like he's trying to gauge whether or not I'm faking surprise. I'm not. Rocco defecting to Andover to dive for our longtime rivals wasn't only a blow to our team, but a kick in the teeth to our friendship. The news of him becoming an

Andover captain isn't something I saw coming, and the betrayal I felt when he decided to leave unnerves me all over again.

"You didn't know?" Coach asks. "Close as you two were."

"Rocco and I haven't talked that much since he left."

"Hmm." Coach scratches his chin. "The added secrecy must be part of Coach McGee's strategy since we added another promising Bennett to the team this year."

I didn't know that either.

"You know what this means, don't you?" Coach asks.

"Claiming the title this season might be a cakewalk?" I give him a crooked grin to cover how I really feel. Andover may be our rivals, but we've beaten them every year. It's been close a few times, but we usually bring it home in the end. That's the reason they hate us, and the reason Rocco's loyalty got thrown into question. Also complicated.

"I like the confidence," Coach says, grinning. "But no. It means our dive lists are garbage."

"Garbage? Wow. Okay. So you want to switch things up?"

"That's right. Starting with you."

"With *me*?"

"Stop repeating everything I say, Mackey. You're starting to sound like a parrot."

"Yes, Coach."

"Since Rocco had access to the dive list for every guy on our team, they may be looking to take out my top divers first. Starting with you, then Trey, Ace, Sully, and down the line. What they don't know is we have Les Carter bringing something to the lineup this season."

"Seriously?"

I don't bother hiding my shock because I'm two for two. Les and Rocco were both peeved when I made captain, but only one of them was bothered enough to ditch the team.

"We'll see," Coach says. "But that doesn't change the fact that I need my captain to go big." He pokes my chest twice when my eyes wander. "Listen, if any of my top divers fail, Andover will have a shot at beating us out of our ranking. Understand?"

"Loud and clear. Should we tell the team?"

"About Bennett? Not yet. Let's see what we're really working with here first."

"I have something to add to my dive list that might help," I tell him. "I've been working on the 5337D in my free time."

"Attaboy," Coach says. "I can always count on you to bring your A-game. Get up there and show me something I can brag about at the coaches' banquet this weekend." He cups his hands around his mouth and shouts, "Make way for your captain."

"Oh captain, my captain," Sully says, stepping aside with an exaggerated bow.

I scratch the space under my nose with my middle finger out of Coach's view.

Truth is I'm not ready to rip this dive. But if Coach is putting any stock in Les Carter, I need to bring my A-game.

Everyone steps aside to let me pass. Everyone that is, except one pimple-faced freshman who pauses to look me in the eye for an extra beat. I don't know his name, but future-captain wannabes surface every year. And this kid, like so many before him, needs to get in line (pun intended).

Halfway up the ladder I pause and give a sharp whistle for Chip. He hands a set of goggles to one of the swimmers and looks my way. I make a twirling motion with my index finger three and half times so he knows what dive I'm about to chuck in front of everyone.

He gives me a thumbs-up and shouts, *"Chinga!"*

He still doesn't get it. That verb packs a lot of meanings.

Chucking a dive I haven't perfected in front of the team is a huge risk, so a lot of those meanings probably apply.

I stand on the board and take a deep cleansing breath. Some people like the smell of freshly mowed grass, barbecue, even gasoline. I swear this one kid in my English class loves the smell of his own armpits. But for me, it's chlorine. Which is a good thing because the smell never really leaves my skin. That's what happens when you dunk in it every day like a tea bag.

I visualize Mom's favorite dive and approach my take-off. One, two, three big steps to the end. I throw my arms hard after my hurdle, rotating backward. I'm a little swingy, flying farther out than I should for a reverse, but I manage to get enough height and come-out straight as a board. My layout is close to spot-on, and I rip the entry without causing too much ripple. It's not perfect. But at least I didn't eat shit.

The water rushes past me and washes away some of the weirdness from this morning. Every time I come up for air after a dive, I'm reborn. It's my sanctuary. The only place I can escape from all the stuff in my regular life that bothers me.

When I surface, some of my buddies are standing around the edge of the pool, eyes wide.

"Holy shit," Chip says. "That was it. A little swingy at first, but it'll be fucking beautiful once you tighten it up." His eyes flick to Coach before he lowers them. "Sorry about the language, Coach, but I had to come over and give props for that dive. If Theo pulls that off at the meet we're gonna get *paid*."

"I'll let the offense slide this time seeing as I agree. But don't start counting our wins yet. We've got some work to do." Coach nods at me. "Not bad, Mackey. If you stop sailing out as far as Christopher Columbus, I think you've got something."

Chip laughs so hard he snorts. "Good one."

"You still here, Langford?" Coach says without looking his way.

Chip makes his oh-shit face and jogs back to the swimmers.

I clamp my hand around my buddy Ace Coburn's heavily freckled forearm for an assist out of the pool. The Flying Ace might be all of five-foot-six but he pulls me up like I weigh a feather ounce.

"Nice flight, Big Mack," Ace says. "You thinking of chucking that dive at the demo on Saturday?"

"Don't you dare," Coach warns. "That's top secret."

I smirk like I might disobey, just to get a rise out of him, and he gives me a serious warning look.

"Carter," Coach says without looking at Les. "Take the board."

"Me?" Les tugs a dark curl at the base of his neck.

"Yes, you. We got another Carter I have to worry about now?"

"No, sir."

I get Les's hesitation. I wouldn't expect him to follow my dive either. He's always been one of the guys we use to seed up front to fool other teams before unleashing the big dogs, so I'm anxious to see what he's supposedly bringing to the table.

"What are you waiting for," Coach barks, "a sparkly invitation? Get up there."

"I'm not sure I want to do that dive we talked about," he says.

"Why the hell not?" Coach asks. "You told me you had something big."

"I do. It's just . . ."

Les flicks his eyes to a group of freshman and I start to feel a little sorry for him. Nobody likes to chuck a dive with a big buildup, then smack. But I want to see what he's got that's so great so I say, "Don't sweat it, Les. We all know the mantra."

As soon as the words leave my mouth the chanting starts. "Les is more. Les is more. Les is more."

Les is usually *less* in my opinion. The guy has never brought anything extraordinary to the team. He's what I'd call a cobbler, taking a little something from this diver, and a little from that diver, with no real style of his own. But camaraderie is a big part of being on this team, and expected, especially from me as captain.

The chanting is enough of a boost that Les pulls his shoulders back and climbs the ladder. When he reaches the end of the board and turns, I'm a little surprised. Back entries are tough for everyone and Les struggled with his at regionals last season. His low scores cost us, but not enough to spoil our win. Trey and I made sure of that, along with Chip who scored big in butterfly for the swimmers.

Les rises onto his toes. The only sound in the room is the hum of the pool filters and Coach Porter's raspy breathing. He takes one more breath before doing a perfect backward press and take-off, rotating into 1½ somersaults, then 4½ twists with flawless execution and entry.

*No fucking way.*

My brain feels like it might explode.

I did not see that coming. A 5239D has a 3.7 degree of difficulty. It's simply not done.

There's no doubt this is a championship team, especially now. I just hope I can defend my own ranking. I scan the faces of the other divers, wondering if anyone else is holding out. The freshman that blocked my path earlier pesters me with a crooked smirk that I can't take seriously. There's no way in hell a freshman would ever be a threat to me.

When Les surfaces, Coach says, "I may have underestimated you, Carter. Remind me what school you have your eye on again?"

Les glances at me before answering. "Stanford, sir."

Every combination of curse words known to man runs through my head as Les climbs out of the pool and grabs a shammy from one of the guys.

Coach flicks his eyes at me and I swallow the giant lump rising in my throat. I never in a millions years thought Les-freaking-Carter would be the guy I'd have to beat.

A scholarship to Stanford is my ticket out of Ellis Hollow. Not because I don't have any money saved for tuition. But because I want to get there on my own merits, like my mom, and finish what she couldn't, because she had me.

I compare the degree of difficulty of Les's dive to some of my own. My best dive is a 3.8. And his grades, as far as I can tell, are solid for the few AP classes we share. The only difference that matters is Les's dive was perfect.

Adding a fourth twist to my mom's favorite dive would raise the degree of difficulty to 3.9, but it's unheard of in high school diving on a 3-meter board. Not only do I have to keep my grades up, I also can't afford to screw up a single dive this season. And Les-freaking-Carter is tied to both problems.

# FIVE

**Killing the Spring:** When a dive has poor timing during the take-off that results in stomping the board and killing its spring.

**THE REST** of practice went downhill from that point, at least for me. I messed up nearly every dive because I was thinking too much about the wrong things, and that's the enemy of diving. I didn't catch enough air to even try doing four twists, but I do catch Les in the locker room.

My impulse is to punch him in his smug face, but I opt for congratulating him on his dive because that's what's expected of me as his teammate and captain. But then, when I ask Les who he trained with to get that fourth twist his face goes beet-red. One of the freshmen blurts that Les's dad sent him to Masters Diving Camp in Boston over the summer, which tells me everything I need to know. Masters is a game changer. College coaches from all over come out to train the springboard divers in that program.

"I heard Rocco went to Masters over the summer too," Ace says to Les. "You see him?"

Les nods quickly. "Yeah, I saw him." He gives us a one-shoulder shrug, then walks away.

"That was kinda weird," Ace says.

"Agreed." Especially since the note he left on my truck made it seem like he was hell-bent on talking to me.

Rocco going to Masters doesn't concern me as much as Les because Rocco's grades were never that good, even if the extra training is what helped him snag the co-captain spot at Andover.

I don't realize I'm staring at the empty place where Les was standing until Chip hits me in the back with his duffle bag. "You coming over for pizza night?"

I have never missed a Friday night pizza night at the Langfords'. But today is different.

"I have to stop at the cemetery and check in with GP first, but I should be able to make it over."

"Cool. I'll catch you later," Chip says. "For real if you plan on doing any dryland training on my trampoline."

"I wasn't," I say. Though I probably should keep working on getting enough height at the apex of my dive because that would result in a higher score.

Even higher than whatever score Les might pull.

Chip looks at me like he's suddenly keen to my thoughts on Les's dive. "You totally nailed that reverse by the end of practice, bro. Keep doing that and you'll be more golded than Louganis. That shit is in your blood."

"Nobody is more golded than Louganis," I say. "But yeah. Not too shabby. It went a hell of a lot better than this morning."

"True, Sir Smacks A Lot," Chip says. "Too true."

"Give me a break." Sully groans from his locker. "*Not too shabby?* Since when are you so modest?"

Craig Sullivan has been part of our circle since grade school, but right now he's looking at me like I just drank the last beer on Monarch Night, which for him would count as a major sin.

"I have to clean it up," I say. "You heard Coach."

"Just don't make me look bad at the carnival demo. Do something *less*." Sully grins and scratches the scar that runs from his left nostril to his lip, a thick vertical striation he got when his youngest brother accidently whacked him in the face with a golf club. Girls love Sully's scar. But what he really means is do something *Les*. As in one of his other dives. To shake him. I know he's just messing around, but the truth is I can rip all of Les's dives better than anyone. Except that Backward 4½ Twist.

I reach into my locker and pop an afternoon Adderall, later than normal, too late to help me with practice but I always have mounds of homework.

"If I were you," I tell Sully, "I'd be more worried about Trey Dumas. I hear he's perfected his Inward 2½ in pike."

"Shit," Sully says. "Seriously? That's my best dive." He walks away yelling, "Dumas, where you be, brother? We need to talk."

Five minutes later, I'm winding my way to the student parking lot with pictures of Les Carter wearing the Cardinal jersey flooding my head. The idea of him going to Stanford on my coveted scholarship makes bile rise up in my throat. Not because I believe my dive was weaker. But because his was as good as mine. Shit. Better. I imagine Les turning in his perfect family tree. Complete with parents who are alive and well, beaming at him because he got into his school of choice. *My* school of choice. I rush the last dozen or so steps to the exit because I think I might hurl. For real.

The push-bar handle clacks like a shotgun being loaded as I exit the building, and my chest heaves like I took a hit. A cool September breeze hits my face and I lift my chin, taking a deep breath so my nausea subsides.

"There he is."

Coach Porter's voice startles me. Usually, he stays in his office until the last diver is gone, but today he's outside, pulling photos and trophies from a cardboard box and arranging them inside a glass case. Iris is standing beside him with her notebook and purple pen at the ready.

I pull my head out of my ass. "Were you waiting for *me*?"

Iris smirks like hanging out with Coach Porter is part of her normal. "Waiting? No. I was just here bribing your coach for your address and phone number since you never texted me."

My face goes slack. "I was meaning to," I say. "Tonight. Once I looked over what I have." Or don't have in my case.

"I'm kidding, Theo. Relax. I only gave you my number this

morning. I'm actually here because I have to write an article about one of our sports teams. The editor put me on athletics because she thought I was writing too many dark pieces. I told her I was the cemetery sexton's daughter. Writing dark stuff sort of goes with my territory. She wasn't swayed *or* impressed."

I didn't know that about Iris's dad, but now it makes sense that her house sits on the edge of Pleasant Hill Cemetery.

"I was explaining to Coach Porter that since I'm working on a sociology project with you and Les, I picked springboard diving. Two birds, one stone."

Coach raises his eyebrows like he thinks I might be in over my head with this girl.

"Did Coach Porter tell you that you'd have access to his best diver?" I try not to smirk because, really, I'm probing for what Coach made of practice today.

"Actually, he told me to go to the dive demo and make that assessment for myself."

"You should."

"You're welcome," Coach inserts, giving me that good-luck-with-this-one look again.

"I think I will," Iris says. "But only if you promise to put on a good show."

"I'll do my best." I scratch the base of my head and shift my eyes to the trophy case. "Are those for this weekend?"

"Yep. We're finally hosting the coaches' banquet, thanks to you and the guys on the team. There's one from your mom's big year," he adds.

"Theo's mom was a diver? I want to see." Surprise shoots Iris's voice an octave higher.

"I'd actually love to see that myself," I tell Coach. "Pictures of my mom from her diving days are few and far between, since . . ." I stop. It's still hard for me to say *since the fire.*

Coach Porter pats my shoulder and crouches to dig through the framed photos in the box.

"I swear it was here this morning," he says. "I came in early and put the box on top of my desk so it would be ready to go after practice. I had every intention of pointing it out to you. The 1988 Individual Springboard Diving First Place Winner, Sophia Rogan, Andover Preparatory Academy. Not that I'm ever proud when E.H.H.S. takes second place. But your mom. That's hard to forget, considering you went against legacy by coming here."

"That was more about districting. But I'm bummed your photo is missing. Not because of the sociology project we're doing for Malone, but for me. I never even thought to ask what you might have."

"It's a family history project," Iris explains.

"I see." Coach says, and the sympathy I've seen so many times before creeps into his eyes. "Well, don't give up hope, Mackey. People aren't erased from existence when they pass on. They always leave traces behind for us to remember them. I'll check my desk for that photo before I lock up."

Truth is, erasing my mom from existence is exactly what I did. The fire burned so hot and long they weren't able to recover a body. We put an empty casket in the ground, leaving whatever scant ashes remained to blow on the wind or get picked up by bulldozers.

I glance at Iris, trying to keep any elements of guilt or grief from surfacing on my face. She smiles back like she understands, completely unaware that I've never gone back to try and dig memories out of the rubble at the old house. But now that I'm starting to remember—*if* I'm starting to remember since the parking lot may have been a fluke—then I want to believe Coach Porter is right about traces left behind.

"Sophia Rogan? I feel like I've heard her name somewhere before." Iris turns her attention to Coach Porter. "Did you say she went to Andover Prep?"

I've seen Iris do this in class, put together smaller pieces of information to make a whole. It might be a journalism thing for her, but my mom being a former diver for Andover isn't something I talk about openly. Even if that shit *is* in my blood.

"Isn't that something?" Coach says to Iris. "We're happy Theo chose to dive for us, especially with rival champion blood in his veins. Just wait until you get him talking about his dad. Theo might just give you the story of the year."

"I look forward to hearing about every member of Theo's family," she says. "Thanks to Mr. Malone my article for the paper may have just gotten a more interesting angle." Her eyes stay glued on me like I'm a blue ribbon–winning science exhibit at the county fair.

Zero thanks to Mr. Malone.

"Do you need a ride home?" I offer. "I'm headed that way."

Maybe I can convince her to drop whatever angle she thinks she's picked up for a story. The Twisting Mackeys, a tale told in motivational maxims that ends in tragedy.

"To the cemetery?" she teases. "Those are your big Friday night plans?"

"Something like that. It's the first anniversary of my dad's death, so I should probably swing by and—I don't know—say something."

"Oh. I'm sorry, Theo. I didn't realize. I should have been paying more attention."

Everything that's been coming out of my mouth has this girl staring like I'm an alien. I told Chip it was weird. He didn't believe me.

"Why didn't you say something, Mackey?" Coach asks. "You could have taken the afternoon off from practice to be with your—"

"Grandfather," I say, letting Coach off the hook. "But then I would have missed the opportunity to see Les's new dive."

"You did pretty damn well yourself in that department today."

"Thanks, Coach. I appreciate that." I rock back on my heels. "So how about that ride?"

"My dad is on his way to pick me up for dinner. Can I get a rain check?"

"You can have an all-weather pass. Anytime. Day or night."

"Christ," Coach says. "You two flirty-birds are starting to make me feel old."

"Don't listen to a word he says, Iris. Coach can still rip dives better than every guy on the team."

"Including you, hotshot, so keep your mind on that 5337D and play it safe this weekend. Don't try anything stupid." He gives me a long look meant to serve as a Monarch Night warning. Coaches can't mention it outright, but they know all about the team's cliff jumping tradition.

"Understood, Coach. I'll see you Monday, Iris." I flick a good-bye wave with my phone in my hand, then send her a text.

*Aren't phones also impermanent?*

After several seconds my phone buzzes. *Yes. But field trips are forever.*

*That's very Hallmark greeting card of you.*

*I do what I can.*

I'm feeling a little better about my shitty day when my phone buzzes again. I expect the text to be from Iris, an emoji or something. Instead, I find one from Les.

*You need any help with your family history project?*

Jeezus. Why didn't he just talk to me in the locker room?

*Nothing you can help me with*, I reply.

Then I text *Thanks* to be polite. Because I am team captain.

People like to say the struggle is real about everything. But for me, the real struggle has always been maintaining expectation, even in crisis.

# SIX

**Inward Rotation:** A backward take-off with forward rotation where the diver begins with their back to the water and rotates toward the board after take-off.

**I DRIVE** to the cemetery rehearsing the things I should say when I reach my parents' graves. *Sorry. I miss you. Wish you were here.* All of that sounds dumb, like something written on the back of a postcard, which is one reason I never come here. Not that every one of those sentiments isn't true. It's just talking to a grave feels weird. Knowing one of those graves is empty, even weirder. Because I know what's really permanent and not very Hallmark greeting card at all. Death. So how about I start with *Hey, sorry I burned the house down and Mom died inside. If it's any consolation, I think I had one of those fucked-up dreams again. The Adderall isn't really helping. I can't nail Mom's favorite dive. And, oh yeah, do you know if you left any traces behind, because I'm starting to remember stuff again and could use some extra help?* I mercifully leave Uncle Phil out of my diatribe because my dad would probably roll over in his grave at the mere mention of his name.

The closer I get to their plots the more I change my mind about stopping. At the last minute I blurt "Sorry" out loud and keep going. It's an a-hole move, I know. But I'm not ready to stand there between two headstones and bare my guilt.

Instead, I do something I haven't had the balls to do, return to the last place we were all together. The site of our old house on Eight Moon Hill. Talking to Coach Porter made me want to come back and see if there are any tangible traces that might help me regain another memory.

My grandfather is holding the property in trust for me until I'm twenty-five. Then it's mine, complete with the ghosts and guilt of most family homes only turned up by a thousand degrees.

GP hasn't done anything with the place past having it razed. The lot is overgrown with knee-high, dying weeds and patches of bare, muddy dirt. I get out of Bumblebee and stand on the sidewalk, picturing our yellow house as it once was, with its stone chimney and asymmetrical second-story windows that made it easy to sneak in and out with friends.

I step into a patch of gray, ashy earth where our house once stood and kick around at the dirt, looking for something. Anything. The ground is littered with scraps of other people's lives. Receipts that got blown here on the wind, an empty fountain drink cup, several discarded beer bottles like this lot has become a hangout to throw back a few with friends. I close my eyes and take a deep breath to regroup, then walk farther into the invisible rooms by memory, starting at the stairs where I'd stand silent as a statue and listen to my parents fight. I make my way to the spot that used to be the downstairs bathroom, then turn and head for the kitchen where I step on a purple juice box. It compresses under my foot like an accordion, hissing out a puff of air that steals my breath.

"Where are my parents?" I tried to dash around Uncle Phil, but he held me back by the arm. "Where's Mom?"

"I don't know. They'll find them."

"Mom!" I yelled for her but my voice cracked and I coughed up a lung. I tried to jerk out of his grasp. "Let me go! I'll find her myself. This is all my fault."

*"Do it," Uncle Phil hissed.*
*But he never let me go. He wasn't giving permission to me.*

THE MEMORY stops and I turn my head to look for someone I know, instinctively, was standing behind me on the street the night our house burned down. But it's not the street view I'm facing. It's the back of the house, all the way to the tree line of the infamously haunted Blood Woods. For a split second my heart almost explodes because I swear I see my mom looking back at me, as washed out as a watercolor painting and then she's gone.

"Do what?" I ask out loud.

But the only response I get is the wailing of a police siren, answering a different call, miles and miles away.

Maybe the reason I never stop and talk to my parents' graves is because I've been hiding the truth about how the fire started. Not from Uncle Phil, but from them, and my grandfather who knows everything there is to know about fire. Because it's one thing to light a match, and another to survive when someone you love died.

I jump back into my truck and rest my head on the steering wheel until my breathing slows. I don't understand why all the memories from that night are coming back now, choppy and out of order. The argument between my parents after the quarry happened when I was ten, the fire when I was thirteen. I know Uncle Phil said I'd lose pieces of my memory from around that time, but those were three years apart. That's a huge gap.

I take the back roads to my grandfather's house, the same house my dad, and for a while Uncle Phil, grew up in together. The shake-shingle saltbox sits at the end of Willow Lane, one of the oldest and longest streets in Ellis Hollow. All the blinds are drawn when I step inside, which is never a good sign. I'm still feeling a little what-the-fuck-ish when I walk in to find GP sitting in his favorite chair with a nearly empty bottle of Jack Daniel's on the side table.

"The prodigal grandson returns," he says in his usual gruff way.

"Have you been drinking all day?" I scan the room for evidence of solid food, but don't see a single dirty dish.

"Why? Were you hoping you'd come home today and find all the B.S. in your life was one long dream?" He slurs the ends of a few words, answering my question by default.

"Not a dream," I mutter, "but I'm getting tired of this nightmare."

"What in the hell is that supposed to mean?"

"Nothing."

He coughs a bunch, and I hope he isn't coming down with something on top of all the drinking.

I pick up the bottle of Jack Daniel's and GP clamps his hand over mine. Up close his dark brown eyes are red-rimmed, like he might have been crying, and it makes me feel like a world-class asshole.

"What do ya think you're doin'?" he says.

"Cleaning up." I resist accusing him of anything this time.

"Did you make it over to the cemetery today?"

"Did *you?*"

"Curtis took me this morning," he grumbles. "You plant those damn flowers up there? Waste of money if you ask me, flowers. You pick 'em and they die. Every beautiful, full of life thing in this world dies if it's picked by the wrong hands, kid. Remember that."

Depressing thought, but I didn't leave the flowers. I don't even know what flowers he means since I never made it to their headstones.

"It wasn't me," I tell him.

"Guess that sonofabitch can't leave well enough alone," he mutters into his whiskey tumbler.

"Who?" I ask. "Curtis?"

It's a legit assumption on my part and his. I've heard him call the guy who's been his friend for as long as I can remember an SOB right to his face.

"No, not Curtis. Jesus H. Christ, kid. Ain't you paying attention?"

"Oh. You mean Uncle Phil." I should have figured that out when he said flowers. The guy does have a penchant for them, and he did have a shovel this morning, so two plus two.

GP's mouth wrings in disgust. "For the last time, he ain't your goddamn uncle. Didn't I make my feelings clear?"

I raise my hands in surrender before he goes off on a tangent. "Crystal." I'm gonna make myself a sandwich. You want one?"

He coughs, grunting something I think counts as a yes, so two ham and cheese coming up. A snack for me, dinner for him. If he bothers to eat it this time.

I take the whisky bottle with me. I'm thinking about downing what's left when a knock at the front door interrupts me.

"Go away!" GP yells. "We don't want any."

I look through the peephole before opening the door for Curtis Jacobs. He's standing on the stoop dressed in firehouse blues, holding a brown paper bag in one hand and two extra-large coffees in the other.

"Heya, kid! I brought over some food from the station. You hungry?"

"Starving. But I'm heading over to the Langfords' for pizza night."

"Sure. I get it. Maybe next time."

Thankfully, there's always a next time with Curtis. I couldn't do this on my own.

"Thanks for taking him to the cemetery today," I say.

"Least I could do. He was in no condition to drive. Did you get a chance to go over there yourself, 'cause I'm happy to go with you, too, if you want."

"I just got back." I bite the inside of my cheek even though it's only a half-lie.

"What is it?" Curtis asks. "And don't lie, halfway or whole. I investigate liars for a living."

"I thought you fight fires?"

"Other guys fight them. I look into who started them. And those guys are always liars."

True enough.

I lower my voice. "I know today would be bad timing, but I need to ask GP some questions for a family history project at school and I'm not sure how to bring it up."

Curtis chuckles. "Carefully, kid. Your grandfather decided to put the past behind closed doors a long time ago."

"My only other option is to go to Uncle Phil and we both know how GP feels about me talking to him."

"He's not your uncle," Curtis says evenly. "So I'd tread carefully there, too, if I were you."

Curtis always has my grandfather's back, but my fucked-up dream has me wondering if he means behind doors literally or figuratively.

When I moved in with my grandfather, one of the first things I discovered was the door to my dad's childhood bedroom was locked. And stayed that way. The first time I saw GP slip behind the door he mumbled he was going into his office. Didn't matter that my grandfather's been retired for three years. When I asked about it he told me there were things I needed to know and things I didn't, and that a man sometimes needs a private place to think. None of that stopped Chip and me from picking the lock a couple of weeks later. We didn't think there was much more to see than stacks of papers and a row of empty Jack Daniel's bottles on his heavy desk. Until we opened the top drawer and saw his gun. That's when I knew for sure his drinking and his grief were worse than I thought. Maybe worse than my own guilt if the gun meant he was contemplating the value of his own life. I left him to his man cave after that, too scared to mention it or go inside again.

"Who you talking to in there?" GP yells.

"Your one and only friend, you old cranky bastard," Curtis yells back. "I brought you dinner, but if you don't quit barking at everybody like a junkyard dog I'm gonna chain you up and make you watch me eat every bite myself."

"I'd like to see you try."

Curtis pats my shoulder. "Go on, kid. Get out of here. Your grandfather and me have some talking to do that may put a stop to his drinking for a while. Probably better if you're not around for that."

Curtis to the rescue.

"Thanks, Curtis. I owe you one. Let him know I'll be back by ten."

GP stumbles into the small kitchen and leans against the oak-cased doorway as I'm grabbing my keys. He used to have a huge presence, even when sloshed, but last year has wrecked him. He's been balding and losing weight like crazy. Probably because he never eats.

"Where the hell you running off to?"

"The Langfords'."

"The Langfords'." GP swipes a hand over his mouth. "You better hope the *Langfords* are willing to take you in if things go south. Even if they ain't your family, you treat 'em good. Better than good. You hear me? Don't ever bite a hand that feeds you."

"Unless it's mine," Curtis says. "Isn't that right, Bruce?"

GP waves his hand dismissively.

"And here I was thinking he'd name me as your guardian or something of the like," Curtis says.

"You want him? Take him. You've always been a glutton for punishment."

I sigh and shove my hands inside my jacket pockets with my keys. "I can stay."

"Nah. He doesn't mean it, kid." Curtis pushes GP back toward the living room. "That's just the booze talking."

"What the hell you whispering for? My drinkin' ain't some big secret in this house."

"You heard that?" Curtis asks. "I thought you lost your hearing when you gave up on common sense."

"Lucky for you all my senses ain't fried, yet."

"Good. You're gonna need 'em."

Curtis jerks his head at the door and I take my cue to leave, fully aware of what the big secret is in our house.

# SEVEN

**Feel:** The spatial orientation a diver sense while in the air. Referred to as cat sense or kinesthetic awareness.

**WHEN I** saunter into Chip's house it smells so good I want to lick the air. But first I have to crouch and scratch Belly behind the ears before she wags herself cross-eyed. Chip's mom is at the stove, stirring a pot of sauce, and I'm struck by how completely normal it is compared to the train wreck I walked away from at my house.

"You managed to get out," Chip says. "Window?"

"Front door. Thanks to Curtis."

Mrs. Langford sighs. "That man is a saint. A pillar of the community."

"He's definitely a pillar in my life with GP."

She turns away from her big aluminum pot to smile at me with the same deep dimple she passed down to Chip. "Beside the getaway, how was the rest of your day?"

"Long," I tell her. "And strange. But mostly long. What are you making over there?"

"Yeah," Chip says. "I thought it was pizza night."

"Lasagna," she answers. "I thought I'd change it up. It's been a while."

A smile as wide as the length of their pool stretches across our faces. Pizza would have been great, but this—this puts a Band-Aid on everything.

Mrs. Langford points her wooden spoon at us. "That's exactly the reaction I was hoping for. Lasagna is always good on . . . well, on unfortunate days like this."

"It's better than good, Mom," I tell her. "You're the best." I put an arm around her and squeeze.

"Flattery will get you everywhere, Theo Mackey."

"You mean Eddie Haskell," Chip says.

Mrs. Langford insisted I call her Mom when I started to spend more time at their house than my own. I miss my own mom more than I let on, but as far as stand-ins go, Chip's mom is pretty perfect.

I give her an extra squeeze and she lifts the spoon to let me taste the warm pasta sauce. As the spices pass over my tongue, a memory of my own mom comes out of nowhere.


*She handed me half a meatball sub in our old kitchen. "Eat something hot, Theo. Before we go. It's a big hike to the cliff."*

*"Is Uncle Phil coming?"*

*"Yes."*

*"Is Dad?"*

*"Not today. He's with a client."*

*"Big surprise."*


CHIP PUSHES past me to try and taste his mom's sauce and she swats him with a dish towel, just past my face, flicking the memory away. I chuckle awkwardly like it's no big deal. Completely normal. When in reality this isn't the first time a memory has come back to me today. It's just the first time where I wasn't alone.

"I put all the photos and stuff you'll need on your bed, Chip." Mrs. Langford gives me a gentle smile.

Family history photos. She understands my dilemma without me having to say a word.

"Cool, Mom. Thanks," Chip says adding, *"You're the best,"* to mock me.

I pull him into a headlock and drag him to his room where I finally release my grip.

Chip's twin bed is covered in photo albums, scrapbooks, and shoe boxes. My bed—the one I claimed in fifth grade—sits six feet away, bare. The only thing on the plaid comforter is the hoodie I left here last week that Mrs. Langford washed for me. I pick up one of the Langfords' scrapbooks and flop onto the bed next to Belly. Photos of Chip and me cover the pages. We're nine or ten. I can tell because his front tooth is still chipped. His parents didn't take him to get it fixed until right before middle school. That's how he and I became friends, a fistfight on the playground that resulted in his chipped tooth. Lewis Langford: forevermore known as Chip.

There's a gold medal around his neck in one of the photos. I read the words, glued around the pictures in multicolored letters. *Age 10. First Place Butterfly Stroke.* Taken around the same time he started obsessing over Michael Phelps, while also telling me everything I needed to know about Greg Louganis, the greatest diver of all time. Everybody needs a hero.

"Look at this," Chip says, flipping an old black-and-white photo my way. *Frederick Langford, 1932.* "Check out that suit, man. My Great-Grandpa Freddie was a snappy dresser. I bet he was a hit with the ladies. See, that's the shit in *my* blood."

"Your problem is keeping the blood in your head from always rushing to your johnson."

"I don't see it as a problem so much as an ability to please the masses."

"Right. I forgot. You're an idiot." I Frisbee-toss the photo back with a laugh and pull out my phone.

"Who are you texting?" Chip asks.

"Nobody. Just seeing if I got a text from Iris."

"You got her number?" He looks impressed.

"Didn't think I had it in me, did you?"

"Nope."

"I didn't. Not technically. We had to exchange numbers for Malone's class."

"Bonus. Unless you're just gonna add it to your stalker collection of unused girls' numbers? 'Cause I gotta be honest. I worry about you, bro. I don't want to walk into your room one day and find a pinboard full of photos of all the girls you never called."

"We already texted."

"So Malone *did*, in fact, do you a favor."

"I still have to deal with Les outside of my responsibilities to the team."

"True."

I put my phone down and shuffle through another stack of old Langford photos. There are so many, I wonder if I could pass some off as my own. Truth is, the Langfords look nothing like me, though. Chip is five-ten with brown hair and hazel eyes and I'm topping out at six feet, blonde and green-eyed. Not even close.

"Too bad we don't look more alike. I could use some of these." I hold a photo of one of his uncles next to my face. "What does your mom's side of the family look like?"

"Like my mom," Chip says. "Short. Brown hair."

"They have light eyes, though, don't they?"

"You know I consider you family, bro, but we're in the same class." He gives me a sympathetic look and his resemblance to his mom is even clearer.

I can handle a little pity from Chip and his mom, but that's about it. I was hit with enough soft looks and "poor things" from strangers after my parents died to last a lifetime. And the first time around was way worse than the last.

"I know this project probably has you freakin' out over what happened," Chip says. "But it wasn't your fault."

"Maybe it was." I drop a shrug and look away. "There are limits on my memory since the fire."

"You sound like a shrink."

"I'm just saying you have all these photos to jog your memories. The project has mine coming back to me all choppy."

"So what's really bothering you? That you don't remember every detail of everything that's ever happened to you, or that you don't have anything for the project?"

"Both."

Chip taps his temple. "You just haven't unlocked your mind castle, Sherlock."

"My mind *palace*. Thanks for the advice, my good Watson. But it's not like I haven't tried."

"You've made honor roll every year. Trust me, broheim. There's nothing wrong with your memory. Haven't you ever watched one of those hypnotists on TV? There's always a trigger."

I don't need to watch a hypnotist on TV to know about triggers.

"Plus, you have Dr. Maddox. Who could pass for your real uncle and said he'd help you with pictures and stuff."

"Good. If I had to rely on GP alone I'd be screwed."

"Look at the upside," Chip says. "His booze has come in handy for us a few times. Living with him isn't all bad."

"True. He might even help with the Mackey side if I ever catch him sober enough." I drop the stack of photos on the bed. "Screw it. I took a beating at practice and could use a soak in the hot tub."

Chip narrows his eyes. "I have a better idea."

"I don't like the way you're looking at me."

"Yeah, well, I don't like the way you keep avoiding shit. You'll have to trust me on this."

Chip is one of the only people I do trust when I think about it, despite his crappy driving. He's also the only person I've told about the hypnosis I got for PTSD after the fire, because admitting I needed that much help makes me feel weak.

"All right," I tell Chip. "I'm game. What's your big idea?"

TEN MINUTES later, we're hanging ten over the edge of the pool in Chip's backyard.

"Here's the deal," Chip says. "You win, I'll help you with the project—no matter what. I might even consider giving you Freddie Langford as a last resort. But if *I* win, you swallow your dumb pride and push your grandfather for help on the issue. The man is a high-functioning alcoholic, not a dead-end. Shadowboxing around this thing cant go on forever. Besides, what's the worst that can happen: he helps you with the family history project and fills in some blanks in your memory? Sounds like a win-win to me."

To him, it's a win-win. Chip's always been the stronger swimmer. For me, losing means dredging up things I've avoided talking about. Not to mention how hard GP would flip a nut if he ever found out I'm getting help from Uncle Phil. If I win, I'll be lying to everyone, including myself. Sounds like a lose-lose to me, but I'm short on options and family. Freddie Langford and Uncle Phil might be my best choices.

"No matter what?" I ask to confirm.

"That's the bet," Chip says. "Take it or leave it."

"I have one stipulation."

"Name it."

"No butterfly. We have to do the same thing. Freestyle."

Chip grimaces. "Fine. A hundred meters. Take your mark."

I take my position as the sun dips below the horizon. I'm ready. Because I might actually need his help.

The automated pool lights flicker on, bouncing across the top of the water like camera flashes, leaving me temporarily stunned.

"Prepare to have your ass handed to you," Chip says, curling his toes over the edge of the pool. "Just remember. A bet's a bet. I'll call it. On your mark. Get set."

*A bet's a bet.*

"GO!"

I cut into the water before the vowel sound is cut from Chip's mouth. Air bubbles travel along the sides of my cheeks and past my ears. I surface and start digging deep. My competitive instinct takes over in a few strokes. I have a slight height advantage, but Chip is no longer human once he hits water. His parents should have named him Gills. When I rotate for a breath, I see him pulling ahead of me and give it everything I've got.

I flip before I reach the wall and push off hard, gliding ahead in smooth dolphin kicks. My height gives me the lead again, but my mind starts drifting to a race I had against my mom, clouding my vision. I struggle to focus on the here and now. I flip again, but fail to keep the memory that started in the kitchen at bay.

*Mom and I had a race at the end of the day, and I won. She laughed and swore she didn't let me win on purpose, but when she climbed onto the rocks and looked at me, her eyes were sad. That happens sometimes. One minute she's smiling, and the next minute her eyes are downcast, like her happiness can't make it all the way out.*

*Still, a bet's a bet, and she lost.*

*Her punishment was jumping into the water from the rocks. She hesitated, sighing. Seeing Mom sad was the thing I hated most, so I puffed up my cheeks and ran full speed to the edge of the rocks and jumped, yelling, "Bonzai."*

*Mom screamed my name.*

*But I was fine. The rush was incredible.*

*I surfaced before I had a chance to think about what I'd done. I looked up at the cliff and saw Mom standing with Uncle Phil. She dove in after me and it was the most amazing thing I'd ever seen.*

70

*When her head broke the surface of the water, she was smiling. She swam over to me, breathless. "What made you do that? Do you realize that's a 10-meter drop?"*

*"I knew I could do it because I saw the girl do it first."*

*"What girl, Theo?"*

*"The teenager girl with the black hair and body tattoos. I told Uncle Phil about her when we got here."*

*"Are you sure you're not remembering something from a movie me and Dad watched?"*

*"No. I saw her. She jumped in after me when the sun disappeared and it went all-dark outside."*

*Mom treaded water beside me and looked around nervously. Uncle Phil was still on top of the cliff where we left him. "I didn't see a girl, Theo. And the sun didn't disappear. But it is darker under the surface."*

*Mom smiled again, but it was sad this time and didn't go all the way to her eyes. "You're so much more like me than I ever imagined, which makes me incredibly happy, but you have to be careful what you say to anyone but me. Don't blurt out everything you see, okay? Not everyone will understand."*

*"What won't they understand?" I asked.*

*"You." Mom ruffled my hair. "If you see that girl again, promise you'll let me know, okay? I'll be looking for her too."*

I PULL hard through the next few strokes, desperate now to keep the memory going, to connect what happened between our time at the cliff with Uncle Phil to the fight between my parents, that I lose sight of my position in the pool. My hand reaches for the concrete wall too late. My elbow collapses and I hit my head. Dull pain radiates from my skull into my shoulders and I bounce back, gulping water as I pull myself up to for air, then coughing it back out. My head is pounding inside and out, blunt and throbbing.

"You okay?" Chip asks, wide-eyed.

I press the butt of my hand against the top corner of my head, nodding. Lying. A monster headache is making it hard for me to think.

"Were you planning on swimming straight through the wall?"

"I, um, I remembered . . . A few minutes out I started to realize—"

*Iris reminds me of the girl I saw standing on the cliffs.*

"That you know better than to race me by now, you fool?" Chip interjects. "If I thought you'd brain yourself trying to win I might have let up."

"No you wouldn't."

"True," Chip says. "I enjoy watching you try to beat me too much."

"Will you help me with the project anyway? Even though you're not on my team." I look at him with one eye closed against the pain in my head and drop mentioning the memory.

"I'm always on your team," Chip says. "Plus I feel obligated to help uncover whether you actually have an extended family or were hatched from an alien pod and raised as a human by evil scientists." He chuckles. "Dude, maybe that's why you're not good with girls. The whole women are a different species thing might be true in your case."

I make a grab for Chip over the ropes, but he's too fast. "You still have to talk to your grandfather, though," he says, backstroking away. "Your loss might be a win."

The optimal word there was *might*. But a bet's a bet and I lost this time.

# EIGHT

**Press:** The downward press of the springboard before its upward recoil.

**GP WAS** in a stupor when I came in from Chip's so I spent the rest of the night finishing a ridiculous mound of homework, while intermittently staring into space, trying to make sense of the memory from the cliff. Especially what Mom said about being like her and not blurting everything I see. But Uncle Phil isn't just anyone. He's the only person I can talk to about any of this stuff. My grandfather is the one who wouldn't understand.

I hear GP coming toward the kitchen and I fumble a bag of much-needed coffee, knocking over the glass of water I poured to take my morning Adderall. The dark roasted grounds and water swirl together and cascade over the oak cabinets like mud, drizzling onto the dingy, yellowing tiles at my feet. I stare at the mess through eyes that sting from lack of sleep, semi-frozen, because for a split-second I thought I felt the memory crawling forward again from the deepest part of my brain.

I crouch to mop up the grainy mess and stuff the sopping wad of paper towels into the trash bin under the sink. As I stand my eyes land on the kitchen window and I jump a freaking mile. GP is standing right behind me. Not super close. But offset like a pair of playing cards, our side-by-side reflections a study in genetic anomalies. Different heights, different builds, different hair colors, though his is mostly gray now. I look more like my mom than the Mackeys who all have brown hair and eyes.

"Caught you off guard, did I?"

Yeah. You could say that. But I don't. "I was just making some coffee."

"Looks like it got away from you."

Not as much as the bottle got away from him last night. "You want a cup?"

"I suppose I should."

And I suppose he's right, as long as he doesn't substitute Jack Daniel's for half-and-half. If I'm going to get any help from him, I need him relatively sober.

*Adapt or perish.*

That's what Mr. Malone said about survival of the fittest during sociology before he assigned us our partners. He was talking about it in context to our family histories. Ancestors immigrating to the United States, taking control of their futures, when they had no reason to trust the process. Truth is, unless I'm on the springboard, taking control was never my strong suit. But that has to change.

I take two mugs from an upper cabinet and restart the coffee making process under the weight of GP's presence. He won't apologize for being drunk last night. I doubt he even remembers half of what he said. From the corner of my eye, I see him staring at my sociology notebook. I try not to stiffen.

"How are your classes going?"

"My classes?" Now I know he's sober. This is the first time he's shown interest in my academic status in ages. "Okay, I guess. For the most part." I flip the knob on the coffeemaker and face him, keeping my back against the sink.

"For the most part," he says. "You guess."

"Not as good as they should be," I clarify. Even though I hate when he responds in question-statements. My dad used to do the same thing. Nature versus nurture in full effect.

GP scratches the gray scruff on his chin. "I hear there's something you want to talk to me about?"

Curtis must have mentioned the family history project to him last night. I root through the cabinets for sugar, avoiding his stare. Then I take a deep breath, the way I do before every big dive, and let it rip.

"I know you don't like talking about the night of the fire," I say to the inside of a cabinet, "and that the subject is sort of off-limits, but my sociology class is doing a semester-long project that explores the family as a social institution. We're supposed to start with our nuclear families, conducting interviews and gathering information, then work our way out to mini-biographies of other relatives."

"Social institutions, huh?"

"I can show you the synopsis." I start pulling up School Loop on my phone, but have to wait for a stupid app to update. The little progress bar, running red, is an accurate measure of my patience. It turns over to green and I hold my phone out for GP.

"I don't need to see that damned thing. Just tell me what you need already, before I'm dead from old age. Or worse."

Right.

I shove my phone into my pocket. "The first part of the assignment is due in a couple of weeks, which wouldn't be a big deal if I had the names of any of Mom's relatives. If there's anyone in her family you know of that I can contact. Maybe they can . . . I don't know . . . fill in some blanks." I shrug to keep it casual.

GP has one eyebrow cocked discouragingly, but I'm in too deep not to finish testing the water.

"I know you won't like this idea either, but if you don't have anything that might help me I could always ask *he-ain't-your-goddamn-Uncle-Phil* if he has anything I can use."

"You know I don't want you doing that."

GP lets out a barking cough.

"Are you sick? You've been coughing a bunch."

"I ain't sick," he snaps.

Okay fine. His gross cough says otherwise.

The coffeemaker sputters behind me and GP stands without saying another word. In three strides he's beside me again casually, but not so casually, reaching for the glass carafe behind my back. I jiggle my leg to work off my mounting anxiety until his eyes flick to my leg and I stop cold.

"You nervous about something?"

Sweat prickles my spine. "I'd like a decent grade on this project and don't have much to go on. Other than that I'm just waiting for coffee so I can go on my Saturday run."

"You oughta know that the fire isn't *sort of off-limits*. There's just not much left to say."

Sure there is. Loads.

I bite my lip as he hands me a mug of black coffee. I stare into the cup's dark abyss and imagine myself two inches tall, standing on the rim, ready to dive back into familiar avoidance.

"The only thing I ever said was off-limits was Phil Maddox," GP says. "I told you he ain't family. He was a kid I felt sorry for, which turned into a big mistake on my part."

"But you've never say why." I'm not keeping my distance from anyone just because GP says. Not without an explanation.

"You ever hear the saying the devil you know ain't always better than one you don't?"

"I have. But he was never a devil to me. And if he has pictures and stuff that would make up for what we lost in the fire . . ."

"Nothing that man could give you is ever gonna make up for what you lost in that fire," GP snaps. "I know the two of you got history. Hell, I got history with him, too, in spades. But I'm asking you to keep your distance because I'm done worrying about the people in this family."

Coffee splashes from his cup onto the local newspaper because his hands are shaking. But I'm too annoyed to help him clean it up this time. He takes a seat at the kitchen table, lowering himself slowly like he's in pain. Maybe he's getting the flu.

"Fine," I say, to avoid an argument.

I'm going to Uncle Phil's house today anyway, just like always, whether GP approves of it or not.

He stares at me and sighs, then reaches for the bourbon bottle that sits squarely on the table where most people keep a vase. He unscrews the black cap and replaces the coffee that sloshed from his mug with something stronger. Not like I didn't see that coming.

"How 'bout you just concentrate on the Mackey side for now," he says.

Great.

Everything I know about Dad's side of the family would fit on a square of toilet paper and is just as shitty. Dad was an only child, like me, one parent deceased, the other a drunk. Pretty grim family history if you ask me. But okay. I'll just put up a one-sided family tree, then field questions from my classmates. I can see it now.

*Wait. Both your parents died? At the same time?*

*Nope. I accidently set our house on fire and my mom got trapped inside. My dad had a heart attack three years later while driving and crashed, which was probably just a domino effect from my mom's death. I'm still working on her side of the tree, but thanks for asking.*

"You got your mother's distant look in your eye, kid," he says, shaking his head. "Make sure you're in control of whatever thoughts are haunting you right now and not the other way around, and I'll see what I can do to help you with the Rogan side."

He picks up the bottle of bourbon and walks away, conversation over. He pauses to examine me as he pulls his office keys from his pocket, his face soured by the thought that I'd go against his wishes.

GP hasn't stayed in that room for any length of time in months. But when he used to go in there and shut me out, he'd be gone for hours, sometimes days. That was sometimes better, sometimes worse, than when he started drinking openly around the house.

# NINE

**Forward Save:** Movement of the body in a forward somersaulting rotation after entry into the water on spinning dive to adjust a dive that is either short (under-rotated) or long (over-rotated).

**I GRAB** my running shoes from the foyer closet and lace up. Earbuds in, loud music on. Talking to GP put me a little behind my Saturday routine. There aren't many divers who actually like running. Doing the required cardio. But I do my best thinking when I'm running through the streets, around the center of town, feeding off the energy of people zipping through their weekend errands. I need this run today to clear my headspace and stop obsessing about the project and decide what dive I'm going to do at the demo later.

As I turn the front doorknob my phone vibrates like I touched a live buzzer and I flinch. I expect the text to be from Uncle Phil, a reminder for today, but it's Chip.

*Head okay? Mom's asking.*

*Better today,* I lie. *Took a bunch of Tylenol. Heading out for a run. Tell her thanks.*

*Will do. Hasta mañana.*

He means tonight, not tomorrow. I reply in all caps. *HASTA ESTA NOCHE.*

*Show-off,* Chip types. *El Capitan Show-Off.*

Let's hope that's true tonight, especially with Iris coming. Shit. And Les. I forgot about Les for a blissful minute.

As soon as my feet hit the sidewalk, I run. As far away from the house of empty memories as I can get. I stare straight ahead and let my instincts carry me. Not to the rotary, like usual, but to the cemetery.

My phone buzzes in my pocket, but I ignore it this time. I breathe deep, in through my nose, out through my mouth, trying to bring my focus back to choosing a dive. My feet land in rhythm with the bass pumping into my ears. Led Zeppelin and a ten-mile run on a fall day. I couldn't ask for a better fix outside the pool, but my focus is shot. The tempo of the song changes and I pick up my pace, matching the speed and power of John Bonham's drumbeats. The song carries me a mile—"Ramble On"—and then another. And another. Until I reach the intersection for Mount Pleasant Road.

The path into the cemetery is loaded with maple trees whose leaves have begun to change. Once I'm in the middle, it's like running inside a kaleidoscope full of jagged orange and gold flakes. Sunlight flickers across my face in rhythmic flashes through the breaks in the trees, completely out of sync with my music and disorients me. I take another deep breath, squinting through a large patch of sunlight, trying to keep one foot going in front of the other until there's a break in the line of trees. Maybe a Back 4½ Somersault would do the trick tonight. At least I'd have 4½ rotations to show on something.

"No. No. No. Stop."

I hear a distress call ringing in the distance that isn't part of the song and stop dead in my tracks, tugging my earbuds free with one pull. I glance behind me in case someone was calling after me to stop running, but I'm alone on the narrow asphalt road.

I'm either losing my mind, which is starting to feel like a real possibility, or the universe just objected to my thoughts on doing the 4½.

"Stop it!"

The female voice cries again from my right, full of alarm and panic seizes me. I sprint in the direction of the call, zipping between irregular headstones, forgetting my own troubles for the moment. The trees on this side of the path are densely planted, forcing me to twist my shoulders as I navigate between them. I brush against rough bark and trip over a gnarled root before the trees break open and hurl me onto a small clearing.

There's a girl halfway up a huge maple tree, her left arm clamped around a low branch to help balance her weight. I search the grounds for an animal that may have chased her, but there's only a notebook and army-green canvas bag. I scan the surrounding area for someone who may have pursued her but there's nobody visible in any direction.

"Let it go," she pleads. "Drop it." And I recognize her voice immediately.

I watch her swat at a bird high in the tree above her head before clearing my throat. "Iris. What are you doing in that tree?"

Her hood falls as she turns to the sound my voice and her long, dark ponytail swishes from side to side. Her face mirrors my surprise before she pushes free and drops to the ground, landing in a perfect ninja crouch at the tree's base. "I was trying to stop that vicious oriole from eating a monarch butterfly, but it's no use."

I raise my eyes to the orange-and-black bird happily munching its innocent victim. "I think you're gonna lose that battle. You can't mess with the food chain."

"Want to bet?" She brushes the dirt from her hands and jeans then writes something in a notebook that she jams into her bag with a huff. "Don't you think it's freakish how similar they are in color?" she asks, matter-of-fact. "You think he'd stop because it's like cannibalizing a tiny version of himself."

I'm around 80 percent sure her first question was rhetorical so I just nod in agreement. "Do birds see in color?"

"More than humans. They can even see ultraviolet light."

"That's trippy." I rock on my heels. "So do you come here and climb trees often?"

I refrain from closing my eyes, but in my mind I slap myself in the forehead because that sounded like the worst pickup line ever.

"Actually, I do." She clamps a pencil between her teeth and winds her long ponytail around the elastic band at the back of her head. When she reaches the end, she stabs the pencil through the mass to hold it in place, which is both badass and resourceful. She straightens her shirt like she's ready for anything and I'm legitimately positive I'm in over my head. No sideways look from Coach Porter needed.

"What brings *you* out here? Did you change your mind about visiting your dad yesterday?"

"I was out running," I tell her, dodging the truth.

"To or from something?"

Good question.

"A little of both. I usually stick to the same route through town, but I'm glad I went with my gut this time. It's not every day I find a girl climbing a tree."

"Maybe you hang out with the wrong girls."

"I'm sure I do."

"So being here today is just a coincidence? Not hoping to see anyone? Dead or alive?"

She winks and I catch the stalker innuendo just in time to return her crooked smile. "Total coincidence. I don't actually like coming here," I confess. "Inside the actual cemetery."

"There aren't many people who do."

Right.

"My parents are buried on the south side, but I don't go very often because I don't know what to say."

"Most people start with hi."

"Hi," I say, eyes locked on hers.

Iris blushes a little and I don't feel like as much of a dolt.

"I was on the hunt for birds today, not graves," she offers. "The Mass Audubon Society sent a newsletter out asking volunteers to record oriole sightings so they can monitor the species. They want to ensure orioles thrive in Massachusetts. But that one"—she points at the branch above her head without looking—"the one you saw me swatting he's a stone-cold murderer. I swear I've seen that same bird eat every butterfly in his path."

The offending bird flew away a few minutes ago, but I don't have the heart to tell her. "How do you know it's the same one?"

"I can tell," she says. "He sings a certain way and gets this look in his eye when I catch him. Old soul that bird." She digs through her canvas bag like it's bottomless. "Survival is a wacky trade-off, don't you think? The food chain, like you said. That poor monarch experienced the last moments of his short life in this cemetery." She finds the pack of gum she was rummaging for and stuffs a piece into her mouth. "Usually, the dead are brought here—you know—*after*." She pauses while offering me a stick of gum to run the package across her throat like a knife.

I drop a laugh that rings through the quiet cemetery. "So you're like an official bird-watcher?"

"Something like that." She smirks and hands me a stick of gum. "Do you have a few minutes or were you headed somewhere specific?"

"It can wait."

I follow Iris to a stone bench nearby and pop the gum into my mouth, thinking of how to ask the question I've let stonewall me since summer. I rephrase it in my head, and just when I think I've nailed my approach, after weeks of lead-ups, she gasps.

"I just had a thought. Are you staying at the carnival after your diving demo?"

"Yes," I answer. But it's the most cautious yes in the universe. If Iris asks me to hang out before I even get a chance Chip will have a field day. My phone buzzes again as I take a seat, but the only person I'm interested in talking to right now is sitting next to me.

"You should come see me at the psychic's tent so I can read

your cards. It'll give me a better chance to understand what kind of person Mr. Malone gave me for a partner."

"You believe in that stuff?"

"Of course. It's in my blood." Iris tilts her head. "Why do you look like I just told you I swallow swords for fun?"

"I don't know. What if you see something in my cards you don't like? Would you tell me?"

"Would you want me to?"

"If I believed in that sort of thing . . . Sure."

Iris rubs her palms together. "A nonbeliever. My favorite kind of customer. I can tell you this, right now. I'm the real deal. By the time I'm through with you, you might be a total convert to all thing mystical."

I have no right to judge, considering my own tripped-out mind. I just have doubts about whether or not the future can be predicted, even if my own mom did have had a knack for knowing the outcome of my meets or the success of dad's clients. There were other times, too, where she'd tell me not to eat something because I'd choke. And then I'd eat it anyway and choke. She had an eerie sixth sense. Maybe that's all the cards pick up on.

"What about fate?" she asks. "Do you believe in that?"

"I'm starting to warm up to the concept. I'm here. You're here. Could be considered fate."

"Could just be you got lucky this time."

"True. But I like the idea of it being fate better." I kick the dirt with the toe of my running shoe. "Can I ask you something else? Unrelated to what my future might hold?"

"Of course. Is it about the project?"

I shake my head. "Ever since I saw you at the quarry this summer, I've been wondering how often you go cliff jumping."

"As often as I can." Shock must register on my face because she smirks and says, "Why do you seem so surprised?"

"Because I don't know that many people who are willing to

jump from that height. Especially the girls who I've clearly mis-judged as worthy friends. In fact, I only remember seeing one other girl jump from the highest cliff. I was around ten years old, swimming with my mom. You kind of remind me of her."

"Your mom?"

"The girl who jumped."

"Is that why you were staring at me that day?"

I nod. "I didn't realize it at the time, but yeah, I guess so."

"Kind of like how little kids get obsessed with their babysit-ter, and then when they get older they realize one of the girls they're crushing on looks just like her?"

"Who said I'm crushing?"

Her cheeks flush again. "Just a hunch. My mom is the one who brought me to Pikes Falls too," she says. "She had a student who told her it was the best way for anyone to get over their fear of heights. You just let go and jump. Besides, don't you go out there all the time with your friends? From what I heard you'll be out there tonight. Is that right?"

I raise my eyebrows without comment and she leans a little closer. "I overheard some swimmers talking about it before my anthro class. They were practically glowing with excitement. Don't worry though. Your secret is safe with me. I won't list it as a public event in the *Monarch Monthly* calendar or anything."

"I am going out there with the team tonight," I confess. "And I have been jumping from that cliff for years. But there's some-thing different about doing it at night. Especially when you factor in the stories of the flooded valley beneath the water."

"That wouldn't scare me," she says. "There isn't anything down there at night that isn't there during the day."

"What about Blood Woods?" I slip another urban legend into the mix to see how she'll react.

"I've been around death my whole life, Theo. Old Quarry Road isn't where the monsters and ghosts reside in this town."

She looks down and pushes the toe of her shoe into mine. "I would never dive or do anything crazy out there, but jumping makes me feel alive. When I'm in that moment, throwing caution to the wind, I get the biggest rush. Executing that power is exhilarating. Don't you think?"

Jeezus.

It's like she can see inside my soul. Her eyes are as intense as her words, dark lake blue. I force myself to stop staring when my brain connects with the inference in her words for the second time in as many days. Pikes Falls is a harrowing 10-meter drop. I picture Iris hugging her books after her mom died, eyes hollowed, and wonder if that's the reason she jumps. To feel in control of her mortality.

"When you say your power, what do you mean? Like your superpower?" I ask cautiously. Hopefully. Because I also know what if feels like to want to die.

"No, of course not. I meant my personal power. I cliff jump because I want to, not because someone says I have to or tries to make me feel inferior if I don't."

"Oh, okay. That's a good philosophy." I realize a beat too late that I might be the person she means, the one who expects people to jump on Monarch Night. Ready or not.

"I have another philosophy," she says. "But it might color your perception of me."

I raise my eyes from the ground. "I seriously doubt that, Iris. But let's hear it."

"I think most people are afraid to take a stand against the norm because they're worried about being judged or excluded so they do nothing. Because it's easy."

Ouch.

"I take it you're one of those people who found about our team's tradition and thinks the whole thing is dumb?"

"I wasn't talking about Monarch Night, just the general belief that most people our age don't like to disrupt the status quo. Jocks over here. Nerds over there. Everyone staying inside their own boxes, so apparent they might as well be color-coded."

"So what makes you so different? As far as I can tell you don't fit into any one box. Not that I've seen."

Her mouth twists in a wry grin. "What, are you an unofficial shrink or something?"

"Something like that," I say, then lick my lips, which are suddenly, incredibly dry.

"If I had to pick one thing I'd say loss," Iris confesses. "That's what made me different. It's probably what makes you different too. For a long time, I didn't think I had anything left to lose. I was wrong, of course. Which I'm sure you understand."

I hide my discomfort with a smile. "I definitely do."

"Sorry," she says. "I didn't mean to lay a dark cloud over your normal blue skies."

"Normal blue skies. Is that how you see me?" I ask, even though I know that's what most people think. I've constructed it that way.

"Not always," Iris says. "But I see people differently than your average tree climber. Plus, I like when I see you as sky blue. Blue is good. It's peaceful." She shakes her head slightly. "Never mind. That sounds dumb." She sits up straight and folds her hands in her lap. "But you're the shrink, so, do you think this cliff-jumping malady of mine is curable?"

"I hope not. But if we spent more time together, I might be better equipped to evaluate the kind of person Malone matched me with for this project."

"Sounds like you need to come to the psychic's tent."

"Okay, Iris. Challenge accepted. I think I can put aside my skepticism for the greater good *if* you'll agree to come with me to Monarch Night."

"Okay, Theo. I think I can put aside my distrust of social norms for the greater good. Who knows? We might even reach a mutual conclusion by end of the night."

I can imagine reaching more than mutual conclusions with her, but try not to smirk. "Don't worry, Iris. Spending more time with me won't make you a social norms convert."

"Then it should be even easier to win you over."

"You already have."

"Trust me. You already have."

# TEN

Chuck It: Giving in and trying a new dive.

**I FINISH** my run at Uncle Phil's doorstep more than an hour behind schedule. I've been to his house loads of times. But today, when I hear "Mercy, Mercy" playing inside, I can't help but think, *For me or him?*

I take a deep breath and raise my fist to knock, but the heavy wooden door swings open before my hand makes contact. A tall woman with shoulder-length hair and smooth, brown skin startles at seeing me on the stoop. I get it. I've never seen Uncle Phil with a woman, and this one just caught me standing with my fist raised like a lawn jockey missing a lantern. She directs her face to the sunflower in her hand and rushes past me to her car. No introduction needed, I guess.

"I've been wondering when you might show up," Uncle Phil says evenly. He holds the door open for me with his eyes fixed to the curb. "I called to confirm your arrival, but it seems you missed my calls. Please. Come in."

"For a minute there, I thought you sensed me coming up the walkway," I tell him. "My mom had a habit of answering the door before visitors knocked."

"Your mother's intuition has always been unparalleled. Unfortunately for me, the ability to anticipate things before they transpire isn't a skill I possess."

"She's a tough act to follow in more ways than one."

"Indeed she is. But I have no doubt you'll make her proud."

Uncle Phil's woodsy aftershave hits me as I step past him into his huge foyer, making the pulse under my jawbone do a quick rat-a-tat-tat as I bend to remove my shoes. That smell used to be a normal part of our house. Now all I smell at home is booze and dirty dishes and the trash that needs to be taken out.

The heavy console table in the entryway holds an enormous vase of sunflowers that makes me stop short again. There were always flowers in this house, and anytime I came with Mom she would pluck one from the vase to keep for herself before leaving. But sunflowers were always her favorite. I guess seeing them in the hands of someone else leaving his house got to me.

"You look much like Sophia at the moment, lost in reverie, I'm loath to take you out. Is everything okay?"

"Yeah. I mean yes and no. That's sort of why I'm here. Sorry about being late. I ran into a friend while I was out running. I should have checked my phone." I pull it out and shake it like an Etch A Sketch before seeing I missed two calls from his number. "Nice choice of flowers," I say, flipping a glance at the vase. "You didn't happen to leave some at the cemetery earlier, did you? I'm asking for a friend."

"Any friend in particular?"

"I'll give you one guess."

"Bruce Mackey. I presume. Sunflowers weren't my choice for your father's grave, though I did notice some were left for your mother. Did I ever tell you that my affinity for flowers was passed to me from a very special patient who saw meaning in multiple symbols?"

"Is the woman who just left the very special patient?"

"Not quite. We work together. She was, however, delivering the bouquet along with some research materials she neglected to round up on my behalf. Generally, I don't allow staff to come to my home but the circumstances were extenuating. The patient I was referring to passed away unexpectedly, much like your father."

My eyes dart around the living room, first to the massive bookshelves, then the wall of glass doors that overlook the canyon, and finally the marble fireplace, lit with a small fire even though it's nearly seventy degrees today. When my mom was alive she'd leave or forget things here all the time. A cardigan sweater, her pill case, and most often her reading glasses. I do another quick scan for anything that might give away the presence of the woman who just left, but the place is spotless, not a bobby pin or glass stamped with lipstick that would suggest he's lying.

"You're looking around like you've never seen the place before."

"I was just thinking about the times Mom brought me here while you were in the middle of doing research. There were always books and stacks of papers everywhere. Remember how she was always losing her reading glasses?"

"I recall trying to remedy that situation by buying her several extra pairs for Christmas." He plucks a petal from a flower and rubs it between his fingers. "I suppose I've grown more fastidious over the years. Publishing my research still remains the crux of my career, of course. Without the recognition that comes from doing research, I'd just be another shrink without legacy."

Another shrink like Dad.

I don't say it, and neither does Uncle Phil.

Before they had their falling out he and Dad would joke about the difference in the paths they took in their field. Dad used to say Uncle Phil liked to read about himself in print. And Uncle Phil said Dad liked to hear his name during interviews with athletes. I don't see much difference. They both wanted recognition.

So do I. Maybe that has everything to do with nature *and* nurture.

"Are you feeling all right?" he asks.

I nod before realizing I've stepped into Uncle Phil's living room.

"It's perfectly normal to reflect on the past when presented with the anniversary of a loved one's death. But it is curious that the focus of your thinking today is on your mother and not your father."

"Mom brought me here more. Her vibe kind of hangs all over this place."

"Perhaps you bring that vibe with you." He tips his head slightly. "You know you're always welcome here, Theo. Especially if it makes you feel closer to your mother. We are family, regardless of contrary opinion. Let's have a seat so you can tell me more about this project you mentioned yesterday. I gather it has you thinking more about your own legacy, which could prove beneficial in the end if all goes according to plan."

"It's definitely bringing up questions about the nature of family."

"It's a concept that can't always be easily defined. Growing up in foster care, as your mother and I did, forced us to look for our families outside the parameters of the strictest definition. The result of those searches culminated in you considering me as your uncle. Not all families are as simple as mother, father, sister, brother."

Uncle Phil rolls up the sleeves on his light-blue button-down as I sink into a brown leather chair opposite him. He picks up his silver Zippo lighter from his glass side table and flips it around in his hand, tapping the edge against his thigh on each rotation. Waiting for me to speak again.

"I know you always carry that lighter, but I don't remember ever seeing you smoke."

I know it's a diversion. He does too. I see it in his eyes before he humors me with a response.

"I did smoke," he says. "Once upon a time. The lighter is more of a talisman now that represents an old friend, as well as an older more egregious habit."

"I guess the matches I keep under my mattress are sort of the same thing."

"Depends on whether or not you still light them."

I look away. Truth is, I have struck a few matches, in the shower or bathroom sink, but never near anything flammable.

"Have you tried speaking with your grandfather about the fire yet?"

"You mean have I told him it was my fault?" I shake my head.

"Is it better to continue holding onto the guilt?"

"If the truth ends up being the thing that kills him, too, then yes. I have enough Mackey blood on my hands."

"You started the fire, Theo. But you're hardly a killer. Telling him might be cathartic."

Uncle Phil and I have talked about this before, the fire being an accident. It doesn't change the facts.

"I'm curious," he says, "about your grandfather's health. I've heard, well, you're the best person to tell me how he's doing."

"I think he has a cold. Other than that he's as cranky as ever. More when he's been drinking a lot. The same old GP."

Uncle Phil taps the lighter under his chin. "Does he know you came to me for help with your family history?"

"I brought up the idea this morning and he sort of snapped. I got the feeling he might start locking himself in his office again. Remember when I told you he used to do that and ignore me completely? Sometimes for days."

"I recall you mentioning that behavior, yes. Alcohol abuse can sometimes come in waves, making a person more or less inclined to maintain normal behaviors, including eating and pursuing hobbies. It's a disease closely linked to depression."

"The only hobbies GP has that I know of are arguing with Curtis and fishing. I used to hear him tinkering behind his office, right after Dad died. It sounded like he was tearing and shuffling papers. I pictured him building model airplanes or something. Isn't that the kind of thing retired people do?"

"It's the kind of thing people with a collecting instinct do." Uncle Phil leans forward, elbows on his knees. "Do you mean to tell me in all this time you've never been inside your grandfather's office?"

"No, I have. Chip and I picked the lock once after Dad died. Once I saw the row of empty Jack Daniel's bottles on his desk, I figured I'd seen enough." Something tells me to leave out the part about seeing GP's gun in a drawer because that gave me nightmares too. "It's just a messy paneled office with a desk and chairs," I tell him. "His man cave or whatever. My whole situation with GP stresses me out. Can we talk about Mom instead?"

"Of course. Your mother has always been my favorite subject." He leans back in his chair and picks a piece of lint off his pants. "I haven't found anything concrete I can give you in the limited time I've had, but I'm happy to keep digging and share everything I know or can ascertain about the Rogans as soon as possible."

"Whatever you can give me will help. GP said he'd try to help out with the Rogan side. But even if he gets too drunk and forgets, my class is going to the county clerk's office on Monday. They should have something on file."

"This Monday?" he asks. "I'm not sure if you'll discover anything via that route. The files on foster and adopted kids are often sealed. But I'll be interested to hear what they can offer you."

"Me too."

I chew the inside of my cheek and stare at the golden flames flickering in the fireplace. It doesn't take long for me to become mesmerized. I should tell him the other stuff, right now. While the fire is hot (pun intended). But I don't.

"I don't need a degree in psychology to see there's something else on your mind," Uncle Phil says.

I sigh and let it rip. "I do need your help with something besides Mom," I tell him. "Something my dad wouldn't have been able to solve with affirmations and mantras."

"This is about diving?"

"I wish it were that simple."

# ELEVEN

**Voluntaries:** Basic dives selected by the diver with a capped degree of difficulty that demonstrate a diver has mastered basic techniques, such as balance, physical presence, grace, and form.

I KEEP my eyes on the dark wood, unsure which thing I should bring up first, the fucked-up dream where I try to bash him in the head or the choppy memories I've started to regain. I stall by chewing the swollen skin on my finger where I ripped out the hangnail.

"Sorry," I tell Uncle Phil, my throat tight. "I'm just trying to figure out how to explain this. Do you think I could get a glass of water?"

"Of course. I should have offered. Can I get you anything else? Are you hungry?"

"Just the water." Uncle Phil goes to the wet bar in the corner and brings back a water bottle and a banana.

"You were out running. You should eat something," he says. "Your mother would approve."

"Banana-mama. Yeah, you're right. She would." The inside joke makes us both grin. And surprisingly, now that the banana is in my hand, I'm ravenous for it. But I'm stalling, again.

"Whatever truth you're struggling to put into words, Theo, will stay between us. But I can't help you unless you say them out loud."

"Remember when I started having bizarre dreams after the fire?"

He gives a solemn nod and I gulp a piece of fruit without

chewing. Of course he remembers. He and my dad reconciled for a short time so he could treat me with hypnosis because I was such a wreck.

"I think they're starting up again."

He takes the banana peel from me and wraps it inside a cocktail napkin from his side table without emotion or concern. "Why haven't you mentioned this before?"

"Because it just happened. And it felt different from the ones I had before, not so much terrifying as strange. In this one I'm running down a deserted hallway, throwing open doors while dirt gets shoveled in alongside me. I'm trying to get to the last door but you slither around the corner like a snake and block me."

"What kind of hallway? One at your school, perhaps?"

"No. It's more sterile. White walls, gray doors, humming fluorescent lights."

"Carl Jung believed that everyone in your dream is, in fact, you. The person running down the hall, the image you perceive as me slithering like a snake, even who or whatever you think is behind the last door. He also theorized that snakes are a symbol of transcendence. Perhaps this dream is meant to show you that you're capable of surpassing your ordinary limitations. Your subconscious may be trying to help you make sense of your life in the wake of your parents' deaths. A different door for the many different versions of yourself you need to maintain on a daily basis."

I wonder what Carl Jung would think about me wanting to clobber Uncle Phil. Seems more like Freud's area of expertise.

"Would that still apply if I'm not actually asleep when it happens?"

Uncle Phil stops flipping his lighter against his pant leg to study me more intently before picking up a small legal pad. In two seconds flat he looks more like a shrink than the guy I grew up around and the instant shift makes hairs prickle on the back of my neck. I don't like when he goes into shrink mode. I just wanted to talk.

"Dreams, and dream states, can express hidden desires," he explains, while scribbling notes on his pad. "Whether they occur during waking hours or in slumber, they offer an escape from reality. The only exception is when they're maladaptive. Meaning they feel real to the point of interrupting day-to-day activities. Are they maladaptive, Theo?"

*Dream states.*

"Theo? Are you seeing something now?" Uncle Phil's deep voice brings me back around to the conversation.

"What? No. I'm not crazy. I was processing what you said about dream states. You know I hate it when you psychoanalyze me."

"It would be difficult for me not to, considering my position. And since you haven't offered to elaborate further on the things bothering you, I find myself at a loss both as your friend and as a therapist."

I decide to start at the beginning, with the memory that returned in the parking lot at school. The rest can wait. Otherwise I might actually sound as fucked up in the head as I feel.

"My memory is coming back too," I tell him. "Yesterday, a diver on my team left a note on my truck and it triggered this memory of a fight I overheard between my parents. Only it was more than a memory. I felt like I was in the room in real time, standing on the carpeted stairs. I could sense all the emotions of everyone in the room. Dad's disgust, Mom's worry. Dad always said if a person sees or hears things that aren't there, they probably need help because it means they're going insane. I'm not sure what they were fighting about, but I remembered him telling Mom she was addicted to her own mind, maybe even delusion. I don't know what he meant exactly, but I do know mental disorders are sometimes hereditary."

"What you experienced was a flashback. A completely normal

psychological phenomenon in a person with PTSD, such as yourself. Mental disorders *are* sometimes hereditary, but not always. And believe me, Theo, if you've inherited a fraction of your mother's mental acuity it's something to be lauded, not feared. The hypnosis I used to help you with the night terrors wasn't foolproof. Profound stress, like that brought on by the anniversary of a loved one's death, can bring PTSD symptoms rushing back to the surface. Including flashbacks, dream states, and nightmares, and in some cases hallucinations. Have you been under an unusual amount of stress?"

"I wasn't. Not until I showed up to practice and that diver I just told you about, Les Carter, ripped a perfect 4½ Twist dive right before telling Coach Porter he wants to go to Stanford. You should have seen the look that guy gave me, like he knew he was going to screw up my chance of getting a scholarship. The worst part is I have to work in a group with him on this family history project. I can't get a break from the guy. That was probably the undue final push for me mentally."

He smirks, knowing I just flipped a little psychobabble back at him with *undue*.

Nature versus nurture.

"Do you have reason to believe this other diver would purposely try to get under your skin? Not to sabotage you, but so you sabotage yourself?"

"He's never seemed the type before, but trying to get a scholarship to Stanford is a big deal. Everybody gets rejected from that place. Do you think I could be imagining a Stanford hallway in my dream state?"

"Perhaps. Only time will tell for sure. I'm reticent to try hypnosis again. But, considering your age and physical stature, I think increasing your Adderall dosage might help. As long as you don't double up again without consulting me."

"What if taking more *doesn't* help?"

"I doubt that will be true in your case, but there's only one way to know for sure. What's the worst thing that could happen?"

"I lose my mind."

"Let me be the judge of that. Are you taking any other medications or supplements I should know about?"

I shake my head.

"It's important for me to know what you put into your system, Theo, recreationally or otherwise. I'm not here to judge."

"Sometimes me and the guys drink and smoke a little weed."

Uncle Phil writes something on his legal pad and I swallow nervously.

"I know Dad used to smoke weed to chill. I wasn't blind. The guy went to the garage a lot at night, even though he kept his car in the driveway. But he never drank because of GP, you know? Guess he didn't want to manifest the whole like father, like son cliché."

Uncle Phil keeps his head down but lifts his eyes. "Is that manifestation something that worries you, as well?" he asks.

"Becoming like my father? The Mack Attack." I chuckle. "Not at all."

"There are worse people you could emulate," he says seriously. "We all have our vices so I'll caution you to use your best judgment. Mixing drugs is an unpredictable and dangerous game. Addiction is only fifty percent genetic, so you've got a fighting chance there. The other fifty percent is wired to coping skills. I'm sure watching your grandfather's downward spiral has helped you understand the consequences of that better than anyone. Of course, I'll have to draw a vial of blood to ensure—"

"You want to draw my blood now? Here?" My stomach twists faster than Les Carter doing his 5239D. I've a always hated needles more than anything. I'm just not sure why.

"I'd prefer we do it at Green Hill. I want to ascertain whether the Adderall has had any adverse effects on your liver. It's a fairly standard practice in prescribing amphetamines, I assure you. One vial should do." He pulls out his phone and flips through screens. "I'll give you a short supply today if you're available to come to the hospital on Tuesday. Say, four P.M.?"

"It might be more like six because of practice. Is that too late?"

"The most important thing I've ever learned is that it's never too late for anything important."

I grin at him and check my phone for the time. "I better head home and get ready for the carnival. I still need to come up with a dive for the demo tonight." I'm out of my chair, heading for his front door when I turn and say, "Maybe you should come watch. I know GP will be there, but last time I checked it was a free country. I'll be taking the board around seven."

"Seeing you dive tonight would be well worth the risk of running into Bruce Mackey." He tosses me his lighter. "Don't leave just yet. Let me get those Adderall capsules for you."

I flick the cover on the lighter open and closed and run through my dive list. Forward 3½, Inward 2½, Back 1½ with 2½ Twists. The flip cover gets stuck on the next strike against my thigh and nearly burns my leg. I should know better than to play with fire by now. My eyes flick reflexively to the fireplace in the living room and I migrate toward the mantel. Uncle Phil has never kept photos on display before, but today there's one of the three of us from the quarry: Mom, Uncle Phil, and me. I'm not 100 percent sure if it's from the same day, but Mom is the only one whose smile doesn't go all the way to her eyes. The same smile she gave me in the water.

"You look like your mother again. Perhaps you should do the 5337D for your performance tonight." Uncle Phil hands me an unlabeled prescription bottle. "That's enough for two weeks."

"Coach told me I wasn't allowed to chuck Mom's dive before the Andover meet. I have been working on it, though, visualizing myself ripping the entry. I just haven't nailed the final twist yet."

"I have no doubt you will," he says. "You're more like your mother than you know."

"I hope you're right."

As I turn to put the frame back on the mantel something stabs the bottom of my foot. I reach for what I assume will be a push-pin or a staple. Instead I find a small diamond earring in the shape of a triangle that I know belonged to my mom.

I hold it in my open palm for Uncle Phil to see without saying anything because I realize in that moment, with my heart skipping a beat, how much finding this tiny thing that belonged to her means to me. That maybe I didn't destroy everything after all and this trace of her confirms that there must be more, just like Coach Porter said.

"Incredible," Uncle Phil says. "I'm surprised the cleaning woman missed vacuuming that up after all this time." He goes to take the earring from me and I close my fist.

"Of course. It's yours. Take the photo, as well. It was meant for you. Something I had on my desk at Green Hill. I was so enthralled by our discussion I nearly forgot to mention it."

"Thanks, Uncle Phil." I head to the door for my shoes.

"Before you go, Theo, I'm curious to know what you think might be behind the unreachable door in your dream state?"

"If I had to guess—I'd say it's the thing I want most."

"Very perceptive. You may carry some of Mitch's traits, after all."

"Don't sell yourself short, Uncle Phil. Dad isn't the only shrink I've been around most of my life. I'm the perfect case of nature versus nurture."

"I'm rather inclined to agree."

# TWELVE

**Spotting:** Visual cues used by divers to pinpoint where they are in the air to determine when to come-out of a twist or somersault.

**I POPPED** another Adderall on my way to the demo since I still hadn't decided on a dive and my focus was pure shit. Twenty minutes later a wave of confidence and focus rolled through me like never before and I was ready to chuck whatever dive I thought of on the fly.

While I watch my teammates leave the board before me—Trey's perfect reverse, Sully's sublime Inward 3½, Les's uninspired but solid Forward Triple tuck—I remember everything Iris said about expressing personal power. I pick up my phone to text her, just to prove to myself that I can, and right there, spelled out in black and white on the screen, is the perfect dive. A Forward 2½ Somersault, 1 Twist in pike, otherwise known as the last four digits of Iris's phone number. It's not my Mom's dive, of course, but a 5152B is always impressive. It might even be showy enough to leave the crowd with the impression that we saved the best for last, even if I never did get around to sending her that text.

With only a few minutes to spare, I let the announcer know what dive I'm going to perform and rush back to the board. I scan the crowd for Iris as I climb the ladder and spot Uncle Phil slipping into the swim complex. He stays near the exit, far away from GP who has his arms crossed like this event is keeping him from another night with the bottle, which is true. But I should probably give the guy more credit since even when he's on a bender GP never misses a single meet or performance.

I shake out my limbs and breathe deep, bringing my focus back to the dive. The 5152B isn't one of the voluntaries on my list. If I'm going to chuck it in front of all these people, I have to visualize it perfectly. And I do. With more showboating and fanfare than accompanies most high school diving events, but it's how I get myself fired up for the challenge.

I nod at the announcer and he starts the song I picked to go with my dive. "Break On Through" by The Doors. Which is exactly what I'm about to do. There's a lot of chatter rising up from the stands. People who aren't used to watching springboard divers don't know silence is golden. Unless I'm just hearing them more clearly tonight. The Adderall has definitely sharpened my senses. Packing a punch that makes the lights seem extra bright and the smell of chlorine so sharp I can taste it. I search for the hum of the pools' filters and use that to find a quiet place in my head. Then I find the perfect spot in the rhythm of the song to unleash the dive.

I approach the end of the board, crow hop, and press down hard, letting the board spring me into my flight. I rotate into the 2½ somersaults and transition into the twist, right hand by my head, left hand on my chest, toes pointed. I come-out of the dive right as the song demands that I break on through to the other side and I punch the entry.

A round of applause rises from the crowd as I lose contact with a physical world that explodes with color, then disappears.

But the portal I've always loved transforms right before my eyes and I find myself surrounded by unfamiliar dark water. A shadowy form zips past me, pointing to the surface, screaming my name in waterlogged tones. I whirl in panicky circles, searching for something, someone, anything, nearly running out of air before I remember to frog-kick back to the surface.

The light changes as I rise, like a Polaroid developing in

reverse. The pool returning to its normal crystal blue state, lit by fluorescent bulbs overhead. I take a huge gulp of air as I break the surface and the series of camera flashes assaults me from all sides.

*I don't want my picture taken.*

The crowd is still applauding as I hoist myself out of the pool and wave. Keeping up the appearance of the Theo everyone expects, even though the smile I present them feels loosely tied to my face by the thread unraveling inside my head.

That didn't feel like a flashback to me. If anything, it was another dream state. But I can't really deal with that if it starts affecting my diving.

*Maladaptive.*

*Interrupting day-to-day activities.*

That's when Uncle Phil said it becomes a problem. I'm going to have to tell him if it keeps happening. But right now, I need to focus on getting through the rest of the night—Monarch Night.

The announcer taps his microphone and informs the crowd that my dive concludes the demo right as another camera flash hits my eyes, bright as a solar flare. Cameras aren't allowed at meets, but they don't ban them from the demo because we're seen as more of a circus act.

I look for Uncle Phil on instinct. The camera flash put blind spots in my vision but I still see him filing out with Rocco Bennett. Seeing them together shouldn't bother me, considering they've known each other since Rocco and I were in grade school, but it does. Actually, just seeing Rocco here makes me uneasy. The guy was once my buddy, a Monarch. Now that he's an Andover Shark co-captain the last thing I need is him snooping around our team taking note of our dives.

A towel smacks me square in the face as I round the corner into the locker room and I overreact to the hit.

"Jumpy much?" Chip says. He's sitting on the wooden bench between the lockers, tapping away at his phone.

"Yeah. I, um, Rocco was out there," I stammer. Diverting attention from what's really bothering me. "You don't think he was trying to get a preview of our dives before the meet, do you?"

"I doubt it. He knows we don't unleash new dives at the demo."

"He just came to watch, out of the blue?"

"Who cares? You guys didn't rip anything new."

That's not exactly true. I ripped a new dive along with a hole in my already questionable sanity. I know what Uncle Phil said about PTSD, but something about my flashbacks and dream states doesn't feel normal at all.

"Just be happy you didn't choke out there," Chip adds.

"You thought I would? Thanks for the vote of confidence." I shake my head and open my locker.

"Let's just say I wasn't placing any bets after seeing how much Les's dive got under your skin at practice."

I give him a what-the-fuck face and poke my head around the corner. "Are the guys still here?" The last thing I need is anyone else thinking I'm sweating Les's dive.

"Relax," Chip says. "You know I wouldn't do you like that. They all showered when you got on the board and split. Your buddy Les mumbled something about having to hurry so he could stop a friend from doing something stupid. I was only half listening to him, as usual. But you'll be happy to know I was paying full attention when Ace said he and Sully were going on a packie run with his brother. They're gonna meet us at the quarry."

"What about Trey?"

"Oh, this is classic," Chip says. "His mom told him he had to come home for dinner or he couldn't go back out because she doesn't want him eating junk at the fair. When he tried to protest, she started yelling at him in Korean loud enough for me to hear and he took off."

I wrap the towel around my neck and laugh. "Hopefully she'll let him out of the house."

"Whatever," Chip says. "I never feel bad for that guy. He's

going to Harvard. I'm pretty sure having a super-strict mom helped him get that early admission."

"I wouldn't mind my mom yelling at me if it meant she was around."

"If you stop kissing *my mom's* ass, for five minutes she might yell at you."

"And ruin my favorite-son status? Never."

"It's gross how much you two like each other."

"Are you gonna tell me what you thought of Les's new dive now that you called me out or sweat me about the love affair I have with your mom?"

"Honestly," Chip says. "I thought it was fucking poetic. Didn't you? Don't lie."

"No, I did. It was. I just wasn't expecting Les Carter to rip a dive like that in the eleventh hour. I never had to see him as competition for Stanford before."

"I don't think you need to sweat it," Chip says. "It's one dive. The scouts for that team already think you're the shit."

Let's hope it stays that way. I grab my deodorant and street clothes from my locker. "Give me ten minutes to rinse off and we can go."

"In case you didn't notice, you had a better audience watching on you than Rocco Bennett," Chip adds before I walk away. "Iris was out there, GP, I even saw Dr. Maddox near the door, wisely giving your grandfather some space. Haven't seen those two in the same room for a long time."

"I went to see him after my run and asked if he wanted to come."

"Brave. Did he give you anything for Malone's class?"

"He's still looking. But he did give me a higher dosage of Adderall."

"Nice. Now we don't have to take as many."

"Exactly."

Keeping up the façade of normal is getting harder, especially with Chip, but I feel a little better after hitting the shower and changing into jeans and a long-sleeve T-shirt. When I get back to my locker he's on his phone, fingers flying over the keyboard.

I kick the toe of his black Adidas and slide on my letterman's jacket. "You ready?"

"One sec."

"Is that Amy?"

Chip shoves his phone into his front pocket. "She wants us to meet her by the games."

"I think that means she wants you to win her a stuffed animal."

"Then it's a damn good thing I possess a variety of skills to please the ladies." Chip tugs at the front of his black-and-white plaid button-down and struts toward the door like a penguin headed to a mating ritual.

"Whatever you say. But at some point I have to go to the performance tents. I told Iris I'd let her give me a psychic reading."

Chip freezes and spins around extra slowly. "Hold up. You actually spoke to her? As in words came out of your normally idiotic mouth and went into her ears?"

"I invited her to Monarch Night. Guess I'm not as chickenshit as you think." I take a step forward and he throws up a block.

"Not so fast. On the phone or in person?"

"In person. Does it matter? I ran into her while I was out running."

"Hell, yes, it matters. It's about time too." Before Chip opens the door he says, "Get your game face on, Big Mack. The Monarch Night games begin five, four, three, two  "

"One. Showtime."

# THIRTEEN

**Optionals:** Free choice dives for competitions that have a higher degree of difficulty than voluntaries, which can result in higher total scores.

**WE BREEZE** into the school parking lot to find a tripped-out version of neo-carnival meets traveling circus has taken over the usual boring lot. I don't think I've ever seen so many colored lights in one place in my entire life. The dance team and cheerleaders are moving around at light speed, handing out glow sticks to students who are turning them into everything from hats, to necklaces, to whoa—bras.

Chip's brain must be more compromised than mine tonight because he tries to touch one of the cheerleader's glowing bras and promptly gets his hand slapped.

"Nice try," I say.

"Don't pretend you weren't thinking the same thing."

"Oh, I was. I just wasn't stupid enough to act on it."

"I couldn't help myself. She was right there and all I saw were glowing boobs."

"And I'm the one who needs Adderall to focus."

I scan the carnival setup. Rides are to the left, and food trucks sending enough sticky, salty, greasy aromas our way to make me salivate are stationed to the right. I take a deep whiff of kettle corn and my focus instantly shifts from glowing bras to food.

That is until Chip starts tapping away at my arm like a woodpecker. "Oh shit," he whispers. "Here comes trouble."

I follow his gaze to a set of girls dressed like the four musicians in Kiss. They're linked arm-in-arm, headed straight for us. The one dressed like Gene Simmons sticks her abnormally long tongue out at me and winks. Size doesn't matter, my ass. I don't have time to react before they're breaking around us, and her friend, the one whose face is painted like a cat—I can never remember that band member's name—licks my cheek. I stand there a little stunned. I've never been the victim of salacious all-girl drive-by before tonight, but I'd be lying if I said I didn't like it.

"Aw, Kitty," Chip says. "Don't be like that. Come back."

Cat-Face sticks two fingers up like she might give Chip the peace sign, then flickers her tongue between them and keeps walking, giggling with her friends.

"Who the hell was that?" I ask, wiping my cheek on my shoulder.

"That's Bliss. The school's all-girl Kiss tribute band. Those chicks are capital D dirty. I hooked up with the one dressed like Peter Criss after a show once, but I forgot her name and never called. My bad."

"I'm guessing her real name's not Kitty."

"Trish. She wrote it across the hood of my car in face paint."

I laugh loud enough to turn heads. "Does Amy know about you two?"

"I dunno," Chip says. "We never had the are-we-exclusive talk. She doesn't ask. I don't ask. No harm, no foul."

"Or so you think. Honestly, I don't know how you do it. I can only handle one girl at a time."

"Barely," Chip says. "But if you want to see my methods for enticing the ladies, Bliss is playing the sound stage later. Hot chicks, rock music—we could go check them out?"

"Can we get some food first? I'm starting to salivate like Pavlov's dog."

"Bliss will do that to you, bro. Those chicks know how to ring a guy's bells. But let's wait on food until we find Amy. Trust me. We'll all be starving soon enough."

Aerosmith is being pumped at maximum volume from the speakers at the Flying Bobs ride—"Walk This Way"—and we do. The music melds with the girlish shrieks erupting from a ride called the Freak Out a few feet away. If I closed my eyes, I bet it would sound like a live concert. Even the smells are similar: sweat, grease, metal. It's no wonder people puke on rides. They go from all the good cinnamon, popcorn, and cotton candy to the noxious smell of machinery.

"You see Amy anywhere?" Chip asks.

"Psst! Over here." Amy's white-blond head pops out from around the corner of a trailer emblazoned with the carnival company's logo.

I'm about to ask what she's doing back there when the skunky smell of weed hits me.

"What took you guys so long?" she asks. "I've been standing here for, like, forty minutes. Les was supposed to come wait with me, but he bailed." She hands Chip a half-burned joint and rolls her eyes. "He said something popped up. I can only imagine what that means." She pops her index finger straight up, in case we didn't get the picture.

I always forget Les and Amy are friends. Mostly because I can't wrap my head around it. Les is as straight edge as they come. I've never seen the guy so much as sip a beer. And Amy is . . . well, Amy. Always ready to party with the guys.

"Theo took forever to get out of the pool." Chip gives me his go-along-with-it face, then takes a hit from Amy's joint before passing it to me.

"I'm good for now," I say, remembering what Uncle Phil told me about mixing drugs. Not that it's ever been a problem before.

"You sure?" Chip asks. "This might help you chill before you go see Iris."

True.

"Iris Fiorello, huh?" Amy teases. "I heard about that."

"Oh yeah? What did you hear?"

"Just that you two are sociology partners."

The way Chip shrugs without looking at Amy tells me he blabbed.

"That's true," I tell her. "We are just sociology partners."

"Mm-hmm. I'm calling bullshit on that." Amy raises one eyebrow, but that's all the info she's getting out of me for now. She'll put her own spin on it when I bring Iris to the quarry later.

Smoke floats above Chip's head as he exhales a second hit and the look of nirvana on his face makes me reconsider. Normally I'd wait until the chance of running into parents or teachers has been minimized before I'll get lit in any capacity. But this week has been everything but normal.

"Okay," I tell Chip. "Hand it over. But keep an eye out. I don't need one of my grandfather's old buddies from the fire station snitching that they saw me smoking weed."

"He doesn't know about your dad?" Chip asks.

"It's not something we'd talk about even if he did."

He grins, passing me the joint. I use my thumb and first two fingers to cover the end and take a long hit, letting the vapors rise around my nose as I inhale the sweet smoke.

Amy leans forward with a smirk. "You better take it easy, Theo. My brother Ajay calls that his kind weed. That's not the schwag Sully usually gets for us."

"She's right," Chip says. "If that's the nitro Ajay got me high with over the summer, it's a chop to the head."

"I'm pretty sure living most of my life around pill pushers removes me from virginal drug status."

"I meant because you rammed your noggin in my pool yesterday. Remember?"

I remember. My short-term memory isn't the issue.

"I'm fine," I tell him then take another hit.

Better than fine actually. This might be the most relaxed I've felt in days. Months. Uncle Phil doesn't have it right about mixing weed with Adderall. Chip and I do it all the time and we're fine. An involuntary smile stretches the corners of my mouth wide enough to fit a wedge of cantaloupe.

Chip takes the joint from me and hands it to Amy before I take a third toke. "I'm doing you a favor, bro. A little goes a long way and we have to be ready to get out there later and . . . boom . . . show 'em how it's done." Chip gives me a fist bump.

"You're both ridiculous," Amy says, snuffing the roach under the toe of her green Doc Martens. "Maybe Les will show you both how it's done."

"What's that supposed to mean?" I ask.

"Nothing. I just heard he killed it at practice today."

"Seems like you've been hearing a lot things." I give Chip my best fuck-you-bro glare.

"Don't look at me," he says. "I didn't tell her."

A wailing screech of feedback from the sound stages makes us cringe. It also pops a no harm, no foul thought into my stoned head that might make Chip reconsider any future blabbing to Amy about me and Iris.

"Amy, have you ever seen the band Bliss?" I rock back on my heels.

Chip's eyes bore into mine, but he doesn't need to worry; I'm no snitch. I just want to test his exclusivity theory.

"Once," she says. "Last year. I'm not a big fan of the drummer."

"They're playing tonight," I say. "We should all go watch. Together. Chip said they're good."

"I'm sure he did." Amy tucks a section of platinum hair behind an ear loaded with piercings and shoots a sour glance at Chip that spills the truth.

"Actually. What I said was that we *could* check them out. If *Theo* wanted." Chip clamps a hand on the back of my neck and pulls me away from the trailer. "Let's get that food you wanted so bad. You dick," he whispers, slapping the back of my head.

"Serves you right for talking to her about me and Iris."

"Point made. My bad. Bros before hos and all that."

Chip was right about waiting to get food; I'm starving. But he was dead wrong about Amy. She knows about Cat-Face and wants Chip to herself.

We head over to the food trucks and get pizza for Amy, a Polish dog with the works for Chip, and a cheeseburger for me. After we're stuffed, I pull several rows of Admit One carnival tickets from my pocket. Amy snatches them from my hand before I can even dangle them in her face.

"Holy motherlode. Let's go win me something."

"Told you," I say to Chip.

"Yeah, yeah, yeah. And I told you. I got this."

Amy jogs to the Hi-Striker, a feat of strengths game. She turns with an open-mouthed smile that counts as a dare.

"Step right up, fellas, and test yer strength," the game operator shouts. "Even if you don't ring the bell, I'll give the little lady a prize." He winks at Amy, causing her to beam.

But the underlying message in his sales pitch irks the hell out of me. This is nature versus nurture too. My dad would be the guy telling me to give back the stuffed Rasta banana or whatever because I didn't earn it. And I agree. I'm not down with being just another diver at any university any more than Uncle Phil wants to be just another shrink. What's the point of being good, or even great, at anything if everyone wins?

"Which one of you is the strongest?" Amy asks.

Chip puffs out his chest. "Place your bet."

As fun as it would be to compete against Chip, I know we have less two hours before we have to leave for Monarch Night. "Why don't you win something for Amy while I go see Iris?" I suggest.

"You learned your lesson racing me, huh?" Chip says.

"Sure." I give him a few smart-alecky pats on the back. "Come find me when you're done proving your manhood."

The clang of the weight striking the bell from Chip's blow reaches me as I snake through the midway toward the sideshow tents. Hundreds of clear latex balloons, inflated around Mylar monarch butterflies hang like rows of chrysalis between each colorful tent. All the signs are painted like old-time circus posters, beckoning patrons to enter and experience the wonders inside.

The psychic's tent has purple scarves in multiple shades draped over the creases around the outside. The front flap is closed but doesn't stop the murmured voices inside from reaching my ears, especially the tone of the customer who sounds like he doesn't want to believe anything Iris is saying.

Chip's hand lands on my shoulder. "One and done."

I turn and see the stuffed monkey he won for Amy.

"Iris is in there with a customer," I tell them.

"I can tell you your future right now if you want. In five or ten minutes you're gonna go inside that dimly lit tent and punk out. That'll be five bucks." Chip holds a hand out for payment and I whale on it the way I should have hit the Hi-Striker.

He's still shaking out his hand when Amy says, "Look over there." Her normally raspy voice lilts as she points at a swarm of butterflies being released by one of the biology teachers.

She pulls Chip and me into the crowd where fluttering insects surround us in minutes. An involuntary response causes me to blink fast, mimicking their wings, and the effect is similar to how I felt running through the patches of sunlight by the cemetery this morning. Only this time, images flash on the backside of my eyelids.

*Sharks circling a body, red blood seeping into water, people running, yelling.*

They pass like flipbook animation, one morphing into the next, too fast for me to understand, and too mesmerizing to break away.

"Hey!" Amy shakes my arm. "You look like you're having a seizure."

I stop blinking, but my heart keeps hammering the same

wing-flapping tempo. There are people running and yelling, but it's normal for this crowd. If Amy didn't interrupt me I don't know what else I would have seen, but it didn't feel like a flashback. More like another dream state, which *is* starting to freak me the hell out. I don't need Uncle Phil to interpret the meaning of sharks for me this close to the meet against Andover. But blood seeping into water is not something any diver would categorize as a hidden desire.

"You okay?" Amy says. "You wigged."

"I'm fine," I say, shrugging it off. "I was just trying to interpret what I was seeing."

It's the truest thing I've said yet, at least to anyone beside Uncle Phil.

Amy laughs. "Like what, the significance of seeing so many monarchs in one place? Maybe Chip was right to cut you off earlier."

"I'm always right when it comes to this gigantic fool," Chip says.

I nod like that's true. Even though my dream state probably had nothing to do with Amy's kind weed, and everything to do with the fact that I might actually be starting to go off the rails. Despite what Uncle Phil said.

The majority of butterflies have dispersed throughout the carnival, but a pair lands to rest on Amy's arm. She tries shaking them off but they're persistent. Survivors.

"Don't." I steady Amy's arm, remembering how Iris tried to save one monarch this morning, even though dozens swarm the carnival tonight. "Let them break away on their own."

"I think they're having sex," Chip says.

"Play your cards right and they won't be the only ones," Amy says.

Jeezus. There's my cue to leave.

I look back at the psychic's tent and notice the flap is open.

"Looks like I'm up for getting my fortune told. I'll catch up with you guys when I'm done."

"Amy's going with the swimmers," Chip tells me. "But I'll be here waiting. Don't punk out."

"I got her number, didn't I?"

"By default."

That's true. But so far, I haven't punked out entirely when it mattered.

# FOURTEEN

**Balk:** A false start in which a diver makes an obvious attempt to begin the forward or backward approach but does not complete the dive, leading to a deduction in scores of up to two points per judge.

**I STOP** short when I catch sight of Iris, backed by the open doorway, her long dark hair loose and wavy under a twisted swath of orange and black fabric. She smiles and sways, making her multi-tiered skirt swish across the ground.

The fortune-teller of my freaking dreams.

"You look—Wow."

Her cheeks turn pink. "Thanks. The skirt belonged to my grandmother. I figured it couldn't hurt to represent."

Iris unties the cord holding the flap open and I follow her inside. The canvas flap whooshes shut and we're alone. I resist the impulse to touch her hair, wanting her to turn and face me, and she turns on her own. Saving me from balking. We stand there staring at each other underneath tiny lights strung in the highest reaches of the tent, but neither of us makes the first move. My pulse is thumping from head to toe and everywhere in between. This would be the wrong time to punk out, if I were going to, which I'm not.

"I'm really glad you showed up," she says. "I didn't want the guy who just left to be my last customer. It was like giving a reading to a flashing stop sign. Red, red, red intense. Those kinds of customers always give me the creeps, but this guy was extra pushy. He wouldn't stop insisting I was holding out on him."

"Were you?"

"Maybe a little. But sometimes that's the right thing to do."

I step closer, until the space that separates us is harder to keep open than closed. "Would it help if I told you I've been thinking about coming here all day? I even brought my normal blue skies with me to even things out."

"Actually, I'm getting more of an orange vibe from you tonight. With a little black seeping in around the edges."

"A Monarch can't really change its colors."

"You'd be surprised," she says.

My eyes follow the curve of her lips to the pearly buttons left open at the top of her ruffled shirt. I put my breathing in sync with hers and watch our chests rise and fall in time. If there was ever a time to kiss her, it's now. I bend my head toward hers and she places her palms flat against my chest stopping me mid-swoop before releasing a breath as long and slow as a train whistle.

"We should probably get started on your reading," she whispers. "The teachers are watching the tents to make sure we don't dawdle with our friends."

Damn.

Iris gestures to a small round table covered in thick black cloth. A single white candle flickers shadows across a well-worn deck of cards waiting to spill my fate. "Have a seat."

"No crystal ball?"

"Hardy har har."

"Black cat? Candelabra? Stevie Nicks music?"

"The cards are all I need, Theo. I'm *that* good." The way she smiles as she shuffles the deck doesn't leave much room for doubt.

"Are those tarot cards?"

"They're Romani fortune-telling cards. Different than tarot. They were my mother's. She brought them with her from the old country." Iris removes a well-worn pair of cards from a purple deck and puts them aside. "I'll start by telling you the same thing I tell every customer. If anything I say starts to make you feel uncomfortable, we can stop."

"Do we need a safe word?" I joke.

"Not for this." She gives me a look that sends a rush of heat to the deepest pit in my belly.

I tip the chair back on two legs and puff out a big breath, trying to regain some control over my lower body.

"You ready?" Iris chuckles lightly and places the deck in front of me. "I want you to cut the deck and ask a silent question you'd like answered. But only one, or you'll send a confusing vibe out."

I think we covered confusing vibe thirty seconds ago, but I'm game.

*Will I beat my biggest opponent?*

"Did you think of one?"

I nod and she deals the cards faceup in a pile, counting out loud. When she gets to the number fifteen a joker appears. She stops, leaving the counted cards on the table then shuffles the remaining deck hand over hand in a triple cut.

"What was that all about?" I ask.

"When the joker lands predicts whether your question will be answered or is doubtful."

"Which is it?"

"You have to wait and see. I'm going to keep shuffling. You tell me when to stop."

The cards make a zipping sound as Iris riffle shuffles from two stacks, bridging them together, over and over.

"Okay. Stop."

She picks up a card that's been sitting to her right and places it faceup in the middle of the table. Half the card looks like a normal two of hearts, but the other half has No. 19 in one corner next to a drawing of a man in a long coat.

"This card represents you," Iris says, anchoring the card to the table with one finger. "The man whose fortune is being read. Every male customer gets this as his grounding card. What I'm going to do next is deal two sets of cards around this one. The inner cards shape your destiny and the outer cards represent the forces surrounding you. Any card's significance can change depending on its proximity to your grounding card, or any of the other cards I deal for you. Do you have any questions before we start?"

"No, but I really feel like I'm laying my cards on the table here, Iris, and you haven't told me that much about yourself."

She winks at me and deals the two groups of cards. Each one has a numbered suit in one corner and an image in the other.

"Take time to look at all the cards, then choose the one that stands out to you most. That's where we'll start."

I peruse the spread, shifting my gaze a few times to see if there's one card Iris is drawn to, but she's not watching the deck. She's watching me. I hold her gaze and point to the card with a Cupid in the corner.

"This one. You said the inner cards shape my destiny, right? What does Cupid have to say about that?"

Iris shifts her eyes to the table. "Amor. Interesting choice. This card means someone is looking at you with love and longing. And because it's next to the Park, which represents new love, the meaning of both cards becomes intensified."

"But are they doubtful?"

"Patience, grasshopper."

I don't realize I'm tapping the edge of my phone on the table, turning it over and over until she says, "Are you thinking about deleting my number now that you've seen what I do for fun?"

I laugh so hard I blow the candle out. "Not at all. Your phone number actually helped me out at the demo earlier. I was about to send you a text when I saw the last four digits of your number were 5152. In diving a 5152B is a Forward 2½ Somersault, 1 Twist, so I decided to do that dive on the spot. Up until then, I wasn't sure what I was gonna do. I have you to thank for the inspiration."

"Glad I could help. Coach Porter was right about you by the way. Your performance was pretty amazing." She relights the candle from a long match and the addictive *snap-whoosh* it makes as it's struck steals my attention.

"Maybe you can teach me an easier one sometime," she says.

I narrow my eyes. "I thought you didn't dive or do anything crazy?"

"I don't. Not off the cliff. But I think I can handle a few mid-air somersaults from a diving board."

My eyebrows shoot skyward. "Oh, really! I'd love to see you try, Iris. Challenge accepted. Anytime. Any place."

"Ye of little faith," she says. "There's more to me than meets the eye, Theo. But right now this reading is all about you. Are you ready to hear more?"

"My destiny is literally in your hands. Go for it."

She gives me a quick smile and straightens a few cards. "See here, how the Cat and the Mouse are next to each other? Because they're beneath your grounding card it means they're working in tandem. The Cat, being this close to you, means you might suffer a personal injury. And very soon, because when I put that card down it slid, overlapping the corner of your grounding card Don't take that lightly. The Cat has been the most actualizing card in my deck. The Mouse, though, adds a level of trickery. It means you either lost or will lose something through strife. Together they're telling you to watch your back. Like that old saying, playing cat and mouse."

"Buckle my seat belt, wear a helmet, don't take candy from strangers. Got it."

"Exactly." Iris taps her fingers on her lips and studies the set. "Now this one, the Eye—my mom used to call it the Ever-Watching Eye—being this far away from your grounding card signifies that you feel suspicion or scrutiny about someone. And the Fox means an acquaintance may seek to betray you. But luckily the Dog right above that Fox means a true friend will be by your side."

"Chip is definitely a dog," I say. "No contest."

"The guy with the loud muffler?" She chuckles. "That makes sense. You two are inseparable."

"And as far as suspicion and scrutiny, I haven't been feeling much love for Les lately."

"That's not good, considering he's our project partner. Is there anything I need to know?"

"Nothing I want to talk about tonight."

"Okay then, let's see what the outer set of cards have to say since they represent the forces surrounding you. The people or situations you have little or no control over."

"I'm not sure I'll like these. Loss of control is the enemy of diving."

"It happens to the best of us. Usually at the worst times."

True enough.

Iris crosses her arms and leans forward on the table, examining my cards more closely, so I do the same. Our upper bodies hover above the cards at inward facing angles, forming a tighter tent. Shadows from the small flame dance across her sharp cheekbones, making her look more legit.

"The Snake." Iris flashes her brows at me and stamps her index finger on a card with a coiled snake in the lower right corner, rising up to snatch a small orange and black bird from a branch. Just like the oriole Iris was swatting in the tree.

"When the Snake is this far away from your ground card it suggests the presence of an unresolved calamity in your past."

I wouldn't necessarily say I had little or no control over that revelation. I chew the side of my middle finger and pump my knee up and down to quiet the bell that started ringing in my ears the minute she said *Snake*.

Iris tilts her head. "That card bothers you."

I drop a shrug. "A little." I could tell her about my parents, the fire, even my latest flashback if I actually knew how to bring up any of those things without making her run for the hills.

"The Snake shows up whenever I do my own readings too," she

confesses. "I think the reason it makes us uncomfortable is because it forces us to think about the past when we want to be told about the future. But the past and the future aren't mutually exclusive. You can't have one without having survived the other. The tricky part is remembering to hold onto the present when the past and future are pulling our thoughts in opposing directions."

Her interpretation of that card couldn't be more accurate.

"There's some stuff I should probably tell you."

"Okay. Me too. You go first."

The tent flap opens with a *whoosh* before I can utter another word and our heads turn like we're synchronized to face a middle-aged man with a tight-lipped mouth stepping inside the tent. I'm about to tell him to get lost when Iris stands up fast with a gasp and her chair tips over backward.

"Dad! What are you doing here?"

*Dad?*

I stand and straighten my shirt.

"I came by to see if my daughter had time for one more customer." He waves a row of Admit One tickets in the air.

"I'm *with* a customer," she scolds. "You can't just barge in while I'm in the middle of a reading."

Her dad waves the tickets again. "We all pay, one way or another."

I take that as a yes and reach into my pocket.

Iris touches my forearm, then turns her chair upright. "You don't have to pay, Theo. This was my treat."

Her dad narrows his eyes and gives me the once-over like I have kid-who-wants-to-make-out-with-your-daughter written all over my face. I was definitely thinking about it before he showed up.

"Does this *customer* have a name?" He asks, putting air quotes around "customer" so I know I'm under the microscope.

"Yes, he does. This is Theo Mackey. My partner for the sociology project. I told you about that, remember?"

"How could I forget?"

Iris flicks apologetic eyes to me. "Theo, this is my dad, Bert Fiorello."

"Nice to meet you." I extend my hand and he looks at it like it's barbed.

I keep my arm stretched out between us like a tollbooth gate, but I'm pretty sure her dad isn't giving me the green light.

"You're related to Dr. Maddox." It's not a question.

"He's my uncle. Sort of. It's complicated. My dad is—was— Dr. Mackey, the sports psychologist."

Mr. Fiorello locks onto my hand suddenly with an iron grip. His fingers are thick, bone dry, and rough. Iris must have gotten her intense blue eyes from her mother because her dad's are the same color as the mud he's slinging at me.

I pull my shoulders back along with my hand and try again. "Your daughter told me some interesting things in here that might change how I view people over the next few days."

"Runs in the family," he says. "But I'm guessing you already knew that."

"Only what Iris told me." The innate need to defend myself comes out stronger than I'd intended. Even if her dad's harsh reaction to me doesn't make sense.

"Okay then," Iris says. "Now that everyone has met . . ." She pushes her dad into my vacant seat. "Stay right there and I'll do one more reading. Just for you." She follows me through the tent flap. "I know you have to go soon. I'll try my best to meet you there."

"I lied to you," I blurt.

"About what?" She tilts her head, waiting for me to explain. And now that I've blurted there's no backing out.

"The other day, when you asked if I had everything I needed for the family history project. I lied. I barely have anything. Truth is, Malone couldn't have given you and Les a worse partner."

"Isn't that why he grouped people together in the first place," she says, "so we can help each other? You're not in this alone."

"Sure. But don't you think it's weird that he put two people whose parents died in the same group? If you look at the rest of my cards you'll probably find my influencers can't bring much to the table."

"No. I don't." Iris touches my arm and a jolt of static electricity sparks between us. "Sorry. That happens sometimes with flannel tablecloth."

"Maybe it's not the flannel."

"You'll have to wait and see about that, too, Theo Mackey. I can't show you all my cards at once. But for the record, Mr. Malone asked how I'd feel about being in the same group with you. I'm his student TA."

"Iris!" Her dad bellows impatiently.

"You better go, Theo. Before it gets too late. Just remember what I told you about the Cat."

The tent whooshes shut and I stand there, staring at the flap.

An old Clash song from the eighties floats over from the Flying Bobs—"Should I Stay or Should I Go."

Great question.

I hear Iris's dad say, "What are you doing hanging around with that boy?" and decide to stay a few minutes longer to find out what his deal is with me.

"You know he's my sociology partner," Iris says.

"And *you know* how I feel about them?"

"Them or that boy in particular?"

"Don't argue semantics with me. You know exactly who and what I mean. What you were doing in here wasn't about sociology."

There's an unnatural pause before her dad says, "Tell me what his cards said."

"No. That's private. Tell me why you don't like him."

"Young lady, you're playing a dangerous game."

"It's not a game. You know that as well as I do."

"Anyone involved with Phillip Maddox isn't someone to be toyed with."

"Theo is his own person. You don't even know him."

"I don't have to know him. I know enough."

What the—

I should go. It sounds like whatever problem Mr. Fiorello has with Uncle Phil makes me guilty by association, which is weird as hell. Plus, if he doesn't want his daughter dating me, he definitely sees me as the trouble that song is talking about and I'm not ready for whatever double might come from lurking around.

# FIFTEEN

**Judging:** Scoring each dive on a scale of 0 to 10 determined by the starting position, approach, take-off, flight, and entry into the water without applying preconceived prejudices.

**THE LONG,** V-shaped gate that blocks the access road to Smith's Quarry is usually locked in the evenings. But that hasn't stopped a Monarch Night in thirty years. We don't question how the gate gets opened, and we don't tell. Team policy.

I bounce my leg in time to the Drowning Pool song playing through Chip's audio system. It's a killer track for getting revved, but not the best for letting go of how colossally fucked-up my interaction was with Iris's dad.

Halfway down the long access road we catch sight of the bonfire's glow and Chip starts bouncing in his seat like a ten-year-old heading to Six Flags. He accelerates, forgetting this dirt road is nothing more than a long mound and the Dart rumbles and shimmies across the strip.

"Slow down before you hit a rock and swerve over the edge. I don't know why we took your car instead of Bumblebee."

"You think your foreign piece of crap can handle this dirt road better than my dragster?"

"Foreign has nothing to do with it, you dolt. I have four-wheel drive. And a warranty, which your piece of shit hasn't had since when—1972?"

"The Dart's a classic."

*The Dart* lumbers over a huge bump two seconds later and we swerve, coming within millimeters of the road's edge before Chip manages to straighten out.

"How much did you have to pay to have your sway bar replaced again?" I ask.

The reality of that number must register with him because he eases off the gas. "Is that better, Grandma? Hey. There you go. You can add me to your family tree."

"Good idea. But I think I'll put you in the slot for brother. Let gap-toothed Malone try to contest it."

"Aw, aren't you sentimental? Lasagna night at Chez Langford must have really gotten to you."

"Piss off," I say with a laugh.

The Dart's wheels crunch gravel as we pull into a spot alongside Sully's Honda. Time to put my game face on. Sully is reclining in his front seat, smoking a joint, waiting for us. We get out to see who's with him and Amy pops forward and snags the joint from his's lips.

"Hi again," she says, flirty-smiling past me at Chip.

"Jesus Christ," Sully gripes. "I think you pulled my skin off." He licks the raw spot on his lip and I stare at his thick scar, remembering how he once tried to cover it with a pitiful mustache in ninth grade. He calls it his Joaquin panty-dropper. I rub my finger across the pea-sized moles on my right cheek; doubtful they have the same effect.

"Serves you right for bogarting," Amy says. "Ace and I want some too."

I doubt that's true since Ace is curled on the backseat zoned out or passed out. It's hard to tell.

"What's wrong with The Flying Ace?" I ask.

"He started partying too early," Sully says. "He's already on the downswing."

"Jeezus. We just got here. When did he start?"

"The minute we left the packie." Sully takes the joint from

Amy and offers me what's left, a pathetic little roach likely to burn my fingers if I try to hold the thing.

"I'm good," I say. "I like to get amped up before I dive out here. Weed makes me mellow."

"More for me," he says with a shrug.

Trey walks up between Chip and me, scratching the little black soul patch on his chin. "Who brought the liquid provisions tonight, boys? Not all of us like to damage our lungs."

"Weren't you supposed to bring the booze this time?" I give Sully a furtive, wide-eyed nod so he'll play along. "It's alphabetical and Sully brought it last time, so . . ."

"Oh man," Sully chimes in. "We were counting on you. Does this mean there's nothing to drink?"

Trey's face goes slack and I stifle a laugh.

"T-H comes before T-R," he says. "So *technically*, wouldn't you be next, Mackey?"

"Relax Dumbass," Chip says. "They're messing with you. Ace and Sully took care of it."

"Not cool, man," Trey says. "Funny. But not cool."

For someone Chip likes to call *Dumbass*, Trey Dumas is pretty smart. Like valedictorian smart. But he's anal as hell. That's probably what makes him a good diver. *Technically.*

Sully tosses Chip his car keys. "Pop the trunk, Butterfly Stroke. Beverages are in a cooler."

Chip returns a few minutes later in a clatter as he shifts the weight of the cooler in his arms. When Amy hears the familiar jingle she squeals and hops out of Sully's car like he's carrying a crate of puppies.

"Down girl," Chip says, giving Amy a crooked smile as he places the cooler at his feet. "No need to lose your mind."

Most girls I know would freak over the dog reference. Not Amy. She flings her arms around Chip's neck and slobbers his cheek with kisses. "I always lose my mind around you. You know that?"

Sully rolls his eyes at me and shakes his head. The rest of us know those two are made for each other whether Chip is ready to admit monogamy or not.

Chip reaches into the cooler and tosses me an energy drink. "Give one of these to Ace."

I catch the red and gold can. Phoenix—*now with even more caffeine!*

This stuff has its place. Before intense meets. Early morning practice. Tests. But I can do Ace one better tonight. I pull two Adderall capsules from the baggie in my jacket and pop the tab on the can. I shake the contents of the capsules into the energy drink. Tiny performance-enhancing balls roll through the air in a mini-avalanche, sizzling upon contact.

"Wake up, Ace. I've got something special for you."

Ace bolts upright and stumbles from the car, dark red hair matted in the back, eyes half-moon slits. "Is that a Big Mack Attack?"

"Could be. You'll have to try it and find out."

He clamps onto my shoulders, giving me a little shake. "I can always count on you to bring it when it counts, Mackey."

*That's me. Expectation fulfiller. Strong finisher.*

We help collect the booze and head toward the bonfire to join the larger group. Monarch Night is a dive team ritual, but the swimmers and their dates, who are supposed to be sworn to secrecy, are always invited to join the festivities. We may score individually, but we're still one team. There are a bunch of girls hanging around some guys on the team, laughing at their jokes, and I wish Iris's dad hadn't shown up at the tent and screwed up our plans.

I grab a beer from the cooler and hang back looking at my phone, struggling over whether or not to send her a text. It's also a legit way for me to avoid being too near the raging fire without being conspicuous.

Chip walks up to me with his arms out like Frankenstein and

grunts. "Mmm. Fire bad." He backhands me in the chest with a smirk and hands me his beer. "Hook me up too, brainless."

He knows me too well.

I'm about to slip two Adderall capsules into our beers when I notice Les Carter standing slightly apart from the group, staring like he's keeping tabs on Chip and me. Maybe to rat us out to Coach; I'm not sure. But I know I can't trust the guy to have my back if he wants to go to Stanford. That's just a fact of competitive sports.

"Fucking Les is watching us," I mutter.

"Somebody should slip that guy a mickey," Chip says. "Just once, so he'll relax." Chip turns, angling his body to block me from Les's view. "Hey, Les Is More. You gonna rip that new dive of yours out here in the dark? Now *that* would be something worth staring at. I, for one, would love to pass judgment on that action. Not that anyone on our team would ever do that with Monarch Night being sacred and all."

Chip to the rescue.

"I probably could," Les says. "But I think playing it safe and clean is the way to go."

"To each his own," Chip says and turns his back on him.

It's better Chip said that to Les than me since I was standing here thinking that somebody should reintroduce Les to Amy, his pot-smoking BGF. A sudden high-pitched whistle blares from the path leading to the main road, making me accidently spill half the contents of an Adderall capsule on the ground. I throw an extra one into my drink for good measure, then look up to see who's coming. Hoping it's not the cops.

The whistle sounds again—caw-caw—and I pause. I know that signal.

But it's not until Chip says, "My man, Rocco Bennett," that it clicks into place.

"What the fuck is he doing here?" I ask.

"What do you mean? Rocco always comes," Chip says. "He's one of our boys."

"Not anymore. The Sharks made him co-captain."

Chip's face twists in confusion.

"Coach told me yesterday. Said he wanted to keep it on the QT."

Rocco steps into the light of the bonfire and gives a round of fist bumps and bro hugs to the team, saving me for last. "Theo Mackey, the myth, the man, what's up?"

"You forgot legend?"

"We'll have to see about that." We clasp hands and bump shoulders. "A little birdie reminded me you guys would be out here tonight so I thought I'd come by and make sure we were copacetic before our meet."

"We're good," I tell him. "But you know I can't let you stay."

"Come on," Rocco says. "You're really gonna make me cut out? It's not like I'm here to spy on you guys or anything. Just let me hang like old times. I don't like the way we left things, Big Mack."

And by left things he means telling me to go fuck myself when I made captain. Because, as he put it, things came to me too easily, which is total bullshit. Seems petty, I know. Because the real chasm between us started the night my mom died. Nobody knows this, but earlier that night Rocco and I stole some of my dad's weed and a bottle of GP's whiskey and got faded deep in the woods behind my house. We were so messed up he tried to kiss me. In retrospect, I may have overreacted when I pushed him to the ground, but I didn't see it coming. I love the guys on my team, just not in a romantic way. I don't know if Rocco was embarrassed or pissed, but he left, speed-walking through the woods to his house, and I snuck back into my room through the window where I lit matches until they almost burned my fingers, trying to forget the whole thing ever happened.

Except one of those matches got away from me that night.

It bugs me that I can remember all of this without a problem, but not other things leading up to the fire. At least not collectively, which makes what I am remembering confusing as hell.

"Are you gonna say something, man, or should I just leave?" Rocco is tugging on his ear, waiting on my response like I'm Judge Supreme, and I guess I am when it comes to Monarch Night.

"Is that what you were doing at the demo earlier?" I ask. "Hanging like old times?"

Rocco is about to explain himself when Chip, of all people, steps forward. "Don't be a jerk, Mackey. It's Rocco Raccoon. Let him stay for old-time's sake? We know Andover doesn't have any of our Monarch-type rituals."

"It's true," Rocco says. "They have after-parties, but—"

"They don't throw down like us, do they?" Chip says.

The answer is on Rocco's face. No response needed. But he made his choice.

All eyes are on me, waiting for me to make the final call. Rocco stares at me with the dark eyes of a wounded animal behind Clark Kent glasses and the raccoon label Chip pinned on him freshman year becomes funnier. I check out the statement on the T-shirt he's wearing under his pinstriped blazer—

MY

PEN IS

BIGGER THAN YOURS

It's hard stay mad at him, even after everything. And it's my bad for never telling him I didn't care if he's bi, gay, or whatever, just that I wasn't.

"Fine. You can stay on one condition, *Captain* Bennett."

"Cat's out of the bag, huh?" Rocco says sheepishly.

"It is now. I've got a little birdie of my own."

The collective murmur of disbelief rises up behind us on both sides. I know Coach didn't want the guys to know yet, but that's not fair to them or me. And with Rocco here, they were bound to find out. Why else would he come?

"You can stay, but only if my guys agree they won't rip dives they're planning for our meet against Andover. Otherwise, I'll make sure they're relegated to first-seeding bait, no matter how well they do tonight." A few guys laugh, but I'm not joking.

"Most of us rip the same dives," Rocco says. "What's the big deal?"

"Maybe we do, maybe we don't, defector. But that's the condition. Take it or leave it."

He raises his shoulders and surveys his old team to see if they'll agree and a bunch of grumbled "Yeahs" and "Okays" fill the air.

"Always by the book, eh, Mackey?" Rocco says.

"He wrote the book," Les says. "Good luck getting any new dives out of him."

I shift my eyes to Les so I can . . . I don't know, thank him or something, but he's already walking away. I haven't had any love for the guy recently, but he did just give me props.

"I guess we can do this one last time. You ready?"

Rocco rubs his palms together. "Yes I am, *comrade*. For old-time's sake."

A dozen flashlights click on and we hike up the wooded path to Pikes Falls. The September air is dank with the smell of wet pine needles and rotting mushrooms, but we lucked out as far a temperature goes. This afternoon hit in the mid-seventies, so it's still reasonably warm. But when the days are warm and sunny, and the nights call for a jacket, the only thing left to follow the farce is snow. Not a form of precipitation I'm down with since it can hit without much warning. New England weather at its finest. We'll still have weeks of undulating temperatures, but this will be our last outdoor swimming adventure. Monarch Night marks the end of one season and the beginning of another.

The swimming hole and cliffs are far enough from a main road that it's dark out here—dark and creepy as hell. But the real fear factor for most newcomers is the Old Stone Church, the only building left unharmed when the state elected to open the

Chance River, flooding four towns in the 1930s to create a reservoir. They annihilated homes and farms, forcing people to leave their livelihoods behind. The graves were exhumed from the cemeteries, and the bodies reburied elsewhere. Iris might not buy into the urban legends, but it's common knowledge that there are buildings and houses at the bottom of the reservoir and swimming hole—ghostly remains of a once thriving New England valley—and that the people who refused to leave still haunt the reservoir, the Old Stone Church, and nearby Blood Woods.

I trample over rocks and twigs thinking about being out here with Mom and Uncle Phil. I am like her when it comes to diving, but I'm still not sure what she meant by *"Don't blurt out everything you see. Not everyone will understand."* I didn't mention how I thought I saw her behind our old house to Uncle Phil because I'm pretty sure that was just wishful thinking. Brought on by the suffocating hope I felt that she'd make it out alive.

We're almost to the top of the hill when I hear distant voices on a nearby cliff. "We're alone out here," I mutter. Mostly to myself, but suddenly Amy latches onto my arm.

"What did you just say?"

"Nothing. Don't worry about it." The last thing I'm ready to admit to her—to anyone other than Uncle Phil—is that my mind's been playing tricks on me.

"Seriously. Did you hear something, Theo, because I can't find Chip? One minute he was right behind me, and then—"

There's a sudden hard snap behind us. Someone or something grabs Amy around the waist. She screams bloody murder as her hand is wrenched from my arm. I drop into a defensive stance as her shriek echoes through the trees before finally ending in Chip's hysterical laughter.

"You should have seen your face," he says.

"You're such an ass," Amy says. "Did you and Theo plan that whole stunt in advance?" She slaps Chip's arm, but at least she's laughing.

"Nope. The genius was all mine," Chip says.

"Well-played," Les says, holding a flashlight under his chin for ghoulish effect as he walks closer. "Don't you know she's a total chicken?"

"It's true," Rocco says. "Remember the time she got locked in the girls' bathroom in middle school? Seventh grade, I think. The whole school heard her wailing like a banshee."

"I remember Les was the only who let me out," Amy says. "And that's why he's my BGF." Les and Amy share a smile that makes my eyes roll back into my head. "Maybe I'll start my own band and call it Banshee's Scream. To hell with Bliss."

"You can be my banshee any day," Chip says, grabbing Amy in a bear hug. He spins her around in a circle. "Wail for me, baby."

"Oh. I will," Amy says. "After you impress me with a daring leap off the cliff."

"No problem, señora."

"Señorita," I say. "Unless you're ready to marry her."

Amy puts her hands on her hips, challenging Chip to answer. He kisses her instead, his wisest move to date, and they start making out. The rest of us know by now to ditch them. We keep trekking up the craggy hill, eager to see what level of daring we all have in store for the cliff tonight.

# SIXTEEN

**Dive Smack:** When a diver under or over rotates or twists on a dive, hitting the water with enough force to cause pain or physical injury.

**MONARCH NIGHT** has two hard and fast rules. One: if you don't dive—or at least jump—you don't get to party with the big boys. And two: underclassmen have to leave once they've shown the team they're not wussies. No exceptions. One inquisitive parent wondering why their kid is home late, maybe drunk, is all it would take to end this tradition forever.

By the time I've had my third beer, one freshmen and one sophomore have looked over the edge and chickened out. That's average loss. We power through the rest of the underclassmen without problems and sent them packing, ready to let the big boys play.

I crack my neck side-to-side and catch the flicker of flashlights coming from the nearby cliff out of the corner of my eye. At least the part about us not being alone out here wasn't in my head. But if Rocco is a decoy for his new friends at Andover, I'll kick his hipster ass this time and mean it. I spot him off to one side talking to Les whose arms are pumping like he's mad. Rocco has his hands tucked so deep into his pockets his shoulders are by his ears. Twice Les points away from the cliff, like he's telling Rocco to leave. Interesting. I don't remember those two ever being friends so it's strange to see them arguing.

I'm about to suggest that the upperclassmen start diving when Chip claps a hand on my shoulder.

"Mind if I go overboard first?"

Amy is biting her thumbnail behind him. She grins at me and I get his underlying urgency.

"You always go overboard. But yeah. Go for it. I'll just hang here without a date."

"And whose fault is that?" Chip says.

Mine. The fault is definitely mine on this one. I could have waited for her and the later it gets, the more doubtful it is Iris will show up.

As I turn away from the cliff's edge, I notice a couple of freshmen lurking by the trees, stragglers, trying to play it cool.

"What are you two still doing here?"

"You let a bunch of girls stay to watch," one of them whines, "so why can't we?"

Easy. They're girls.

I shine my flashlight at the whiny voice and the beam of light lands on the same pimple-faced freshman that stood in my path at practice yesterday. If I remember correctly, he actually pulled one of the only daring freshman dives tonight. He shadows his eyes with his hand.

"No freshmen. Them's the rules."

He points at Chip. "But that guy's not even a diver."

"You won't be one, either, if you don't haul your scrawny asses out of here."

"He's right." Pimple-Face's buddy says. "My mom will pitch a fit if I'm late. We should go."

"If my cousin was captain," Pimple-Face grumbles to his friend, "he'd let us stay. He doesn't care about girls."

Neither do half the guys on the team. That's not the point.

He mutters something else as they shuffle away, but it's too low for me to hear.

"Hey, tough-guy," I call out. He turns and I shine the flashlight on him again. "What's your name?"

"Miles Stone."

"You pulled a good dive tonight. I'll be watching you at practice."

"Big whoop," he says. "I'll be watching *you* too."

Chip cracks up. "That little punk's got balls."

"Yeah. I wasn't kidding about watching him. You ready to go?"

"Prepare to be awed, my friend."

Chip keeps a long arm pointed at Amy as he backs up several paces. He huffs out a few quick breaths, then runs for the edge and yells, "Bonzai," as he hits the air, then turns headfirst into a couple of somersaults and disappears.

*Bonzai* . . .

I never told Chip what I yelled at the quarry that day, but that one word gets my heart racing like I was the one flying through the air. Tonight would be the worst time to have a flashback. And the fact that I have no control over them puts me on edge (pun acknowledged, not intended).

I stare at the triangle of moonlight on the water until I see him swimming toward the rocks. Little flecks of color wave in peaks around him, striving to make order out of the chaos below the surface. It'll take Chip fifteen minutes to make his way to the top again.

I know it's too late now, but I probably should have assigned a few people to guide everyone back. Last year, a freshman got lost on his way back up and it took an hour to find him, slowing down the whole night. Another reason Pimple-Face and his much wiser friend needed to go home.

A few minutes pass before Chip shouts, "All good," signaling that it's clear for the next person to jump. But I'm not sure it is. Not for me, anyway.

Ace comes forward to take his crack at diving, but I grab his arm and pull him back.

"You sure you're okay to do this? You were wasted earlier.

Rules are rules, but I can bend a few for you. It's one of my only privileges."

"Would you give Les Carter a GET OUT OF JAIL FREE card if he was a little wasted?"

When I don't answer, he says, "Exactly. You don't need to worry about me. That Big Mack Attack has got me feeling first-rate."

I'm glad Ace is up to the task, but if he's picking up on my tension toward Les the other guys must sense it too. I need to watch out for that.

Ace leaves the cliff in a spectacular display of height, and everyone close by sucks in a breath of awe—he is the Flying Ace after all. He does a perfect pike that makes him look suspended by moonlight before he disappears into the darkness.

Sully and Les take turns after him, which means I'm up soon. I didn't expect Chip's dive to throw me off my game, but I'm feeling a little out of sorts. I move my flashlight around the group, looking for him. "Anybody seen Langford?"

"I'm right here." Chip steps out from behind a tree with Amy. "You up?"

I nod and set off for the spot where I'll begin my take-off.

"Make way for your captain," Sully says, doing his best impression of Coach Porter.

I flip him off with both hands as I shake out my limbs.

"Don't forget you have to say something," Chip says.

Right. I almost forgot it's tradition for the team captain to address the group. If anyone is expecting me to impart words of wisdom on the fly, they might be disappointed. But I'll give it my best shot by using something that's been weighing on me a lot lately.

The nature of family.

"Listen up," I say loudly. "Before I take a flying leap—something a few of you may have been hoping for anyway—I want to say something in honor of Monarch Night."

The team stares at me with serious expressions. I picture Sully and Ace and Rocco in recreational swim and my idea of family makes more sense to me.

"I don't believe family is defined by blood alone," I tell the group. "For me, family applies to the people in my life that support me and make my experiences memorable. By that measure, you guys have been the best family a guy could hope for, and that's made all the difference in how I think as a captain and a teammate."

Sully is the first to raise his beer. "Hear! Hear!" But the others quickly follow his lead.

I make sure to catch Chip's eye. Amy is rubbing his upper arm, her head resting on his shoulder. He raises his beer to me and nods. Definitely family. And definitely the best.

Whoops and hollers follow me as I run to the cliff's edge, but I stop short, flapping my arms to keep from falling over. Whenever I put on a show like this for the team a jolt of power surges through my veins like a live wire. But tonight, there's a battle in my gut-brain making me hesitant. I need another minute.

"Changed my mind," I say, stalling. "You want to see something with a little style. Am I right?"

There are a few whistles before they let their suggestions fly.

Sully says, "Just do an open pike, Captain Show-Off."

"A triple," Ace shouts.

"How 'bout a twister?"

That one was Les.

The 10-meter drop is high enough to pull it off.

"I don't know," I say. "How about an armstand?"

I take a few steps away from the edge and do a handstand. Holding perfectly still. The group goes silent. They know doing an armstand dive from this cliff would be suicide. You have to jump far away from the edge to hit the water, which means you need a running start. I just like calling their bluff. I stay that way until all the blood rushes from leaden feet to my head.

A big splash interrupts my theatrics, followed by a dog barking in the distance that puts me on high alert. I flip back to standing too quickly and a massive head rush hits me right as I lean over the edge of the cliff. My vision swims, momentarily blurring the water below.

Flashlight beams skim across the surface from the nearby cliff like searchlights until they conjoin, holding steady and illuminating a dark, motionless mass that looks like . . .

I search the group, my heart rattling the bones in my chest like a caged animal. "Where the hell is Rocco? Did anybody see him jump?"

People rush to the edge with flashlights, blindly following my lead.

"Um, dude, there's nobody down there," Sully says.

"I don't see anything either," Chip confesses, his brows pushed together.

"Didn't you hear Belly barking?" I ask Chip. "Move back. I'm going in."

I know what I saw.

"Whoa. I'm right here." Rocco yanks me backward. "I went into the bushes to take a leak."

Les appears right behind him and our eyes meet right before I drop a hand on Rocco's shoulder and sigh a breath of relief. "Jeezus, man. I thought you were hurt."

Actually, I thought he was dead.

I could have sworn . . .

"What's gotten into you?" Rocco asks. "I've never seen you this jumpy."

Chip is a few feet away, staring like he's waiting for an answer to the same question.

"Nothing," I say. "I'm good. I'm just a little lit."

But that's a lie. Everything from my head to my stomach feels out of whack.

I wipe the sweat from my brow. Real sweat. Even though I

make a show of it. "For a minute I was convinced one of you threw Rocco overboard for defecting to Andover. Not that I'd blame you."

They laugh and cut jokes I don't entirely hear because I'm trying to get my head on straight. And fast. 10-meters is thirty feet. And thirty feet is a big drop, whether it's the cliff or the pool.

I return to my take-off point, taking a deep breath in, deep breath out. Punking out isn't an option. I have to jump. Them's the rules.

Chip puts a hand on my chest. "Hold up. You sure you're okay?"

"I think going upside down after a few Big Mack Attacks sent too much blood rushing to my head. My eyes were playing tricks on me."

"And your ears," he whispers. "I know what hearing Belly bark means to both of us."

"I know. We can talk about it later. Go make out with Amy or something. I got this."

"If you say so. Don't do anything I wouldn't do."

I forcibly huff out a big breath and run to the edge with my heart and head thrumming. Convincing myself this time that *I got this*. Once I'm airborne, I make a split decision to do an easy 1½ Somersault. But as I come-out to spot my entry, I lose my layout. My knees bend like door hinges, yielding to the hard pull of gravity, throwing off my alignment. My back hits the water. Hard. So fucking hard a whip-crack of pain shoots through to my lungs and I gulp half the reservoir.

*Jeezus. Motherfuck. That hurt.*

I can barely move.

Light skims the top of the water.

*Get to the surface.* That's all I can think. But my stunned muscles refuse to obey.

The need to take a clean breath becomes excruciating.

A tiny voice in my head yells, *Kick to the surface, you imbecile, or you'll drown.*

Buzzing fear takes over as I sink deeper.

The water becomes darker and darker until I'm part of the reservoir's flooded city, inside one of its many hidden rooms where everything is awash in shades of black and blue.

A woman sits alone in a chair facing a window that faces nothing. Her blond hair waves around her like weeds made of shadows. I open my mouth to speak and only gulp more water, but she turns her face to the small bubbling sound of my lungs filling.

Jeezus.

*Mom?*

*"You found me."*

I flail in a series of backward strokes, my heart a pulsating vessel on the verge of bursting. She rises from the chair and floats past me, so close there's no denying what I'm seeing. She points to something behind me and I blink, trying to sharpen my vision, but I'm too immobilized by shock to move.

*"You're running out of time."*

I sink deeper.

Mom screams my name.

And everything goes black.

An arm loops under mine, small but strong, and pulls me upward. I take a huge breath as we breach the surface and cough up the water in my lungs, sputtering as I run a hand over my eyes to clear my vision.

"I got you. Just breathe."

"Iris?" I croak. "You're here."

She tugs me toward the flat rocks where girls like to sunbathe. The spot where I stood and watched her jump a couple of weeks ago. I climb out on my hands and knees and take a few ragged breaths, then collapse and roll onto my back.

Iris leans over me, her long hair dripping water onto my chest, eyes wild with fear. "I saw the whole thing from the other cliff."

I stare into her eyes, wondering whether I made it out alive or if this is some near-death wish fulfillment. And to be honest, I'm not sure which one I'd prefer.

"Are you okay? Can you talk?"

I nod, open my mouth to speak, but my lungs have a different plan, and I spew more water. I sit up and my nose drains in a flash flood. I throw my head back, pinching my nostrils, sucking the fishy water down my throat.

"Oh God. Can I do anything to help?"

"You just did," I say, raspy and waterlogged. I struggle to prop myself up enough that I can shout to the group. "All good." But my voice is so weak Iris yells it for me again.

"Someone else jumped in right after you," she says.

*Chip. He must have stayed by the edge to watch.*

The obvious logic barely forms before Rocco climbs onto the rocks beside me.

"What the hell happened?" He swipes water from his eyes. "I've seen you do that dive from this cliff dozens of times. It's basic."

"I broke form," I tell him. Wrapping the truth in a lie because two maladaptive events in the span of a few hours is a kick to my head and my ego. "Thanks for coming in after me."

"I didn't. Not at first. I mean, I did jump in after you for kicks. Because you were so freaked out before. Then I heard you smack, right before my own feet hit the water. I'm glad you're okay, but that one's definitely gonna leave a mark."

I already feel it forming. A long patch on my back stings like I've been branded.

"I dropped my flashlight in the water and couldn't see his coloring when I pulled him out," Iris says. "I thought he was going to need CPR."

I wouldn't have objected.

She extends her arm in front of me to Rocco. "I'm Iris."

"Rocco." He shakes her hand. "You look familiar. Are you on the Ellis Hollow swim team?"

"No. I write for the school newspaper."

"With Les?" He studies her for a long minute. "Interesting. Their loss on the swim team, though. You've got mad jumping skills."

"It wasn't my first time." Iris winks at me and gathers her hair in a long bunch. She wrings the dark tendrils, drizzling water onto the ground at her feet. Every curve of her body is being hugged tight by a sleeveless wetsuit, making it hard not to stare.

Iris flips her hair behind one shoulder. "I need to grab my towel and flashlight. My friends and I always leave extra stuff at the bottom before we hike up. Be right back."

As soon as she's out of earshot, I turn on Rocco like a viper. "Dude, you gotta go. For real. Get the fuck outta here."

"What?" He looks startled for a millisecond.

"Don't get me wrong. If you two didn't jump in I'd probably be . . ."

"Dead," he says. "Yeah, no shit."

"It's just . . ." I flick my eyes to Iris.

Rocco looks in the same direction and a lightbulb clicks on in his eyes. "Gotcha. You like the jumper. Okay, I'll go. But just for the record, I didn't go to the demo *or* come out here to spy on you. I want to make sure we're clear on that."

"Crystal. Now go."

Iris returns and hands me her towel so I can wipe my face. It smells like something flowery and mint and I take a deeper whiff, pressing it against my face to hide how much pain I'm in. I don't want her to see that Im struggling, so I give her my best grin, crooked and full of confidence.

"It looks like you're in good hands here," Rocco says, pushing off my shoulder as he stands. "I'll let the guys know you'll be topside in a few. It was nice meeting you, Iris."

"Same. I'm sure I'll see you at a meet. The editor has me covering sports now."

"If you come next Friday that's a guarantee."

"Hey, do me a solid when you get up there, will you?" I say. "Don't tell the guys I smacked."

"Sure. *No Worries, Mr. Perfection. I'm good at keeping secrets.* But you're gonna owe me one."

"Fine. Deal."

I don't know if the gleam in his eyes means that's a joke, but owing Rocco is the least of my problems.

Iris plops down on the rock beside me and we watch him scramble up the rocks into the night. She leans back on straight arms and sighs, telling me I'm not the only one whose heart went berserk in the water.

I stare at her profile, the slope of her nose. Both of us still and silent after-the-fact, which is quickly becoming awkward seeing as I'm the rescuee. And the girl I like is the one who saved me.

"So Iris," I start, "do you come out here and save springboard divers often?"

She tips her head back and laughs. "Only about as often as I climb trees to save monarchs."

"I wasn't sure if I should text you or just leave and hope you'd show up. I sort of overheard your dad tell you to stay away from me before I left, so I'm glad you came, but why were you on the other cliff?"

"I got a few friends to drive out here with me then realized I never asked which cliff you'd be on. I just assumed it would be the same one we use. I'm sorry you overheard that conversation, though. My dad is way too overprotective of me. He'd be furious if he knew where I was right now." She grabs her flashlight and signals to her friends with a series of long and short flashes. "Right before I jumped in I told them I might be a while."

In less than a minute someone from her group signals back. It's brilliant. I should use that for the team.

"I don't usually smack that hard. It's kind of embarrassing. But I'm glad you were here."

"I couldn't let the captain of the diving team drown now, could I?" She smiles at me the same way she did when we ran into each other here over the summer and I can't stop staring at her eyes. They're big as pool balls and rimmed in a million lashes. Tiny drops of water cling to the ends like sparkling stars. Jeezus. Maybe I am a goner, after all.

Iris clears her throat and I resuscitate all over again.

"If you hadn't come, who knows what might have happened. The ghosts that haunt the quarry could have gotten me."

"I'm sure Rocco would have saved you."

"I'm telling you, Iris, I saw things down there." I laugh it off, even though it's true.

Because I bet telling the girl you like you've been seeing things that aren't there ranks as a top red flag warning in every how-to-lose-the-girl-fast handbook.

Iris gives me a wry grin. "Would it make you feel better if you knew I came here against explicit orders not to because of your card reading? I know it's not an urban legend, but the Cat gave me a sketchy feeling."

"Didn't my cards also say something might happen in the midst of a new and mutual love?" A sharp pain twinges my back when I try to sit up, making me wince in a way I can't hide.

"You're hurt," she says.

"A smack from 10-meters packs a big punch."

"Mind if I take a look?"

Damn.

I was hoping she'd give me more to work with in the cupid Amor card department. Iris clicks on her flashlight and lays a hand on my back. Her warmth seeps through my skin into my bones so deep I shiver.

"You have a nasty welt. From here to here." She runs her hand down the length of my back making it impossible for me to gauge my current pain level since her touch has me near frenzied.

Nothing like nearly drowning after seeing your dead mom to make a guy feel horny.

Her friends flash their lights again.

"Looks like they want to get going." Iris starts to stand.

I grab her hand to make her to stay. I feel better when she's around me. More sane.

"Do you have to leave with them? Come back to Monarch Night with me. I can walk you to the other cliff to get your stuff. Chip and I can drive you home."

A smile flits across her face. "All the way out here I kept wondering how much my appearance would disrupt the status quo. Are you sure you're ready to dismantle that box?"

"How can I not be? A beautiful fortune-teller told me it's in my cards."

# SEVENTEEN

**Punching the Entry:** Flattening the hands prior to entering the water to create zero to little splash.

**FIVE HOURS** later I sneak into my grandfather's house and fling my coat over a kitchen chair so I can hit the bathroom and check out the damage left by my smack. Grabbing my T-shirt at the back of my neck sends a dull pain shooting through the middle of my back, but I don't wince. Not until I yank the shirt over my head and see the swollen red patch, running from the top of my shoulder blades to my waist. There are a few white patches where my skin didn't make contact. But the edges around those places will be purple by morning. Nothing hits as hard as water. And for a few days, it'll be a challenge to see the pool in the same inviting way.

I take two pain relievers from the medicine cabinet and swing the bathroom door open. GP is standing on the other side with his arms crossed over his chest. I think it says something really shitty about both of us that my first inclination is to sniff the air between us for traces of booze. But I've learned to read the level of pungency coming off him like a barometer for his mood. To-night it's hitting all the notes of looking-for-a-fight.

"Where've you been all night?" he asks without flinching.

"Out with the guys." I walk past him to the fridge and look inside for something to eat. "It was Monarch Night." I pull out the ham and cheese and start making the sandwich I missed out on earlier.

GP's eyes narrow.

"You want one?" I ask.

"What I want is for you to explain what Phil Maddox was doing at your diving demo?"

Shit.

I reanimate some of the bravado I felt when I invited Uncle Phil in the first place and give GP the straightest answer I can, killing two birds with one stone. Sometimes it's better to rip a Band-Aid off and beg thin-skinned forgiveness.

"I invited him," I say, my mouth full of the first satisfying bite of my sandwich.

"You went to see him about this project of yours, even after I told you to stay away?"

This is starting to feel like an interrogation. The former Ellis Hollow fire chief in action.

I plead the fifth with tight lips and a tilt of my head.

"I see," he says. "You've been going to see him all along, is that it?"

This is what Uncle Phil wanted, for me to be open, but having everyone riding my jock over Uncle Phil this week makes me snap.

"I don't get what's with you parents. Grandparents. *Whatever*. I'm almost eighteen. I think I can make my own decisions about the people I want in my life. It's not like I can count on you for anything. Not with the way you're always drinking."

The minute the words leave my mouth I feel like an asshole. Living with GP is no picnic, but he is my only biological family left. He used to be fun when I was a kid, taking me to the fire station, letting me ride in the trucks.

"I don't know which *parents* you're talking about, but you might wanna watch where you're stepping, kid. A lot of convoluted shit could get dug up." He starts coughing like his throat can't handle when he raises his voice.

I meant Iris's dad of course. But I don't feel like adding Mr. Fiorello's obvious issues with Uncle Phil into the mix right now.

"I'm just saying. I need information and photos, and even when you're sober you avoid the topic of family like it's a land mine."

"That's because it is one." I see the need for a drink rising in GP's eyes. "If you have half the brains your father gave you, for better or worse, you'll end your relationship with Phil Maddox before it blows up in your face. You're a Mackey. If you need information, I'll get it for you. Stop looking for something real where you won't find it."

"Why?"

"Because you're not eighteen yet. Until then you're my goddamn responsibility."

"I get that. I know he's not my real uncle, but I need his help right now with more than just this stupid project. You don't have to get involved."

GP swipes a hand across his mouth. "Actually, kid, if this is how it's gonna be you ain't leaving me much choice."

He walks away. End of discussion. There's a hitch in his step as he passes the Jack Daniel's bottle on the coffee table. I get that too. Hell, I'm ready to go upstairs and light matches until I feel better. But tonight, GP does something unexpected. Tonight, he keeps walking without taking a drink.

I wolf down the rest of my sandwich in three bites and head to my room. Next time I see Uncle Phil, I'll warn him GP's pissed. Hopefully by then he'll have some information for me, but that's not the point. My gut is telling me to remember what Coach Porter said about people leaving traces behind. I felt more than traces of Mom when I stood at the site of our old house and it has me determined to prove that theory with or without help from GP or Uncle Phil. I still have the county clerk's office field trip, and the internet.

What I really need help with is what Mom meant at the quarry about not blurting and what Uncle Phil meant by "Do it" the night of the fire. Not that I'll be getting answers to those questions tonight.

I flop onto the bed, exhausted, but check my phone before setting my alarm in case one of the guys on the team had a problem after we left.

There's a text from Les sent during the carnival that I ignore. And one from Iris, time stamped at 11:30 P.M.

*Thanks for inviting me into your color-coded box. I had a great time.*

*Me too. Looking forward to our "date" on Monday.*

She responds immediately. *Doesn't that make us a throuple?*

*I'd rather go as a couple.*

She sends an emoji of a Cupid and it makes me feel a little better about almost drowning in front of her, even if Rocco did spend half the night talking to her once we rejoined the group. Probably because he knew it would bug me. Not that it mattered in the end. I worked up the balls to kiss Iris by the end of the night and I'm pretty sure that changed everything.

I look at the text from Les. *Can we talk before Monday?*

Jeezus. He won't quit. The guy might want an A more than I do.

*I have a shitload of homework. We can talk on the field trip.*

I reach between my mattress and box spring to touch the book of matches I keep hidden there before closing my eyes on this seriously strange day. I steady my breathing, willing sleep, but I can't relax. The musty smell of the reservoir is stuck to my skin, blending with the stink of bonfire and the tinge of chlorine that always hangs on me in varying degrees. I don't want to sleep at all if it only brings me back to that deserted hallways full of doors. Not to mention the murderous intention to clobber my uncle. But if the itch I'm getting under my skin is any indication, that's exactly where my restlessness night is headed.

I get up to take a hot shower like washing away the smells

from Monarch Night will undo the fact that I freaked out in front of the team, then smacked and saw Mom in that secret place beneath the reservoir where people who refused to leave their homes got trapped and died.

I press the top of my head against the white tiles and let the hottest water I can stand run into my open mouth and over my sore muscles. I picture Rocco coming out of the water right after Iris saved me from drowning. The set smile he gave me when he said, "I'm good at keeping secrets. But you're gonna owe me one," like he knew exactly what that meant.

The smell of bonfire and musty water intensifies for the first few seconds, then starts to fade away. I fucked everything up for my family. And Rocco, for better or worse, was there right before it all happened. Sneaking around with me in the woods behind our house when we should have just stayed home.

*I'll keep your secret.*

That's what I whisper-yelled to Rocco as he took off through the woods that night.

Maybe I owe him more than one.

I recognize the sensation of a memory tugging at me this time and relax, letting it rise with the steam pulling away from skin.

*I flinched when I recognized the sound of Dad's fist slamming onto the dining room table. I'm surprised to learn my parents fight the same way whether I'm home or not. Their voices are muffled. I can't make out what they're saying, but I stay in my room. Thinking about what just happened between Rocco and me in the woods.*

*I struck another match and watched it burn.*

*My parents thought Rocco and I were sleeping over at Chip's. They don't know Chip had to cancel, or that I stole a few pinches of Dad's weed from the garage, or that Rocco and me snuck into GP's and took a bottle of Wild Turkey from the liquor cabinet while he was sleeping. They definitely wouldn't like to hear I* pushed one of my best friends on the ground before I came home and crawled into my room through the window by way of the trellis. I reached for one of the small boxes of matches I kept under my mattress, then laid there, lighting them one by one until I felt calm again. Watching the flames devour the wooden matchsticks until there was nothing left but charred worms always made me feel better. I wouldn't flick them out until the flames were so close to my fingers I felt the threat of being burned.

I stopped lighting the matches when I heard a few faint ticks on my bedroom window. When I pulled back the blue plaid curtains I saw Rocco in the middle of the trellis. I wasn't sure if he was climbing up or down. When he saw me, his face folded in an apology, but I didn't open the window to hear what he had to say, or let him in. I just shut the curtains, hoping he'd go away and forget the whole thing.

I went back to lighting matches until my eyelids grew too heavy to keep open.

Mom and Dad were quiet. I hoped that meant they'd made up and their argument wouldn't spill over into the morning. I imagined a big pancake breakfast waiting for me. Mom would smile as she poured syrup over melting butter on a triple stack with a side of bacon.

I love the smell of bacon, fried to a well-done crisp.

I was jolted awake by my bedroom door bursting open. A heavy blanket was thrown over me like a net before someone wrapped me tight and lifted me from my bed.

"Let me go," I groaned. Thirteen felt too old to be carried, and the blanket made it hard for me to breathe.

The temperature dropped suddenly and whoever had me started to run. I got bounced around like a rag doll and tried to fight my way free, but the arms clamped around me tighter.

"It's okay. You're safe."

I didn't know who or what I was safe from until my butt was plunked down on a slab of freezing metal and I punched away the *blankets. A woman dressed in official blue was leaning away to avoid being struck. When I stopped swinging she helped me rewrap the blanket around my shoulders.*

*I looked past her and saw a burly fireman jogging away in the snow. He must have been the one who carried me outside. I stared at the neon-yellow stripes stretching across the back of his canvas coat as he rushed back toward our house.*

**I'M SHIVERING** under the spray of water that's run cold. This time, my flashback lines up with some stuff I already remembered, making it a little easier to start putting the whole night back in order.

I'm stepping into a pair of sweats when a sharp ping taps against the windowpane in my bedroom. I jump into the legs quickly and open the blinds, then the window. The cold blast of air that hits my face doesn't convince me this isn't still part of the same flashback; the similarities are too real.

I lean out farther and scan the empty yard. I'm about to shut the window when I think I catch a glimpse of movement along the edge of the woods. Rocco is the only person who's ever knocked on my window in the middle of the night. So whether or not this is real, I owe it to the guy to hear him out this time. I grab my E.H.H.S. hoodie from the hook behind my door and head downstairs as quietly as possible, snatching my running shoes from the foyer before heading outside.

I want to call his name, but I'm afraid to wake GP so I slip into my shoes and jog toward the trees, my eyes slowly adjusting to the darkness.

"Rocco!" I whisper-shout and wait.

But there's nobody out here.

I trudge back to the house, worried I'm starting to hear things too.

New information from the night of the fire swims in my fully conscious mind: the paramedic, the fireman who carried me from my room.

I stop short when I spot something flapping on Bumblebee's windshield.

Maybe all the bats haven't left the belfry after all.

I'm expecting it to be another E.H.H.S. school paper. Maybe an article Iris wrote. We dropped her off over an hour ago. That's enough time for her to hop in a car and drive over here to leave me a surprise. But the *Monarch Monthly* is just that, monthly. I doubt she would have written an article about our team before coming to one of our meets.

What I don't expect to find is my own photo above a photocopied article from the *Ellis Hollow Gazette*. It's a profile shot, but mostly the back of my head and a bit of my cheek and nose. I'm wrapped in the blanket that got thrown over me. Our house ablaze in the background.

### SUSPICIOUS FIRE PROMPTS INVESTIGATION

Ellis Hollow Fire Chief Bruce Mackey found himself in for quite a surprise when he and his crew were called to the scene of a fire at his son's home on Eight Moon Hill. The fire, originally listed as accidental in a report filed by the chief and county fire marshal, Curtis Jacobs, has come under investigation after an anonymous tip was received, claiming the veteran fire chief may have falsified reports to dissuade an investigation into this and a correlating fire that devastated his own home several years ago. Fire Marshal Jacobs and Chief Mackey were unreachable for comment. However, a source close to the family tells us that his daughter-in-law Sophia Mackey, a former championship springboard diver who has been the subject of headlines herself over the years, died in the unfortunate house fire in question. She is survived by her son Theo, a promising young springboard diver in his own right, and her husband Mitch Mackey, a revered sports psychologist known as The Mack Attack.

What the—

Is it possible GP knew I started the fire this whole time and covered for me? That's almost worse than me not telling him, because it means he knows I'm a liar. I search the photo for any trace of my mom near the tree line for Blood Woods, but she isn't there. Which means whatever I thought I saw when I went back to the empty lot was all in my head.

The only person who might leave this for me is Les if he really is trying to get inside my head so I'll sabotage myself, like Uncle Phil said.

"Les," I whisper-yell his name, once, twice. "Are you out here watching? You want to talk to me so bad. Here I am."

My only answer comes as a car engine starting, at least a block away.

It's a hard to believe anyone on the team would do something this shitty. Then again, it's hard to believe Les had it in him to rip 4½ Twists in the first place, which makes me wonder if we can really know another person at their core. For all I know, *this is the real Les Carter* and everything else is just an act. It's not like I don't know a thing or two about façades.

# EIGHTEEN

**Fail Dive:** Zero points are given to dives if a diver gets help via call-out during the dive, steps off the board after assuming the starting position, takes more than one minute to begin the dive after a warning, performs a dive other than what was announced, or refuses to execute a dive.

MR. MALONE has us line up with our project partners at the county clerk's office on Monday afternoon. I'm standing with Iris talking about Monarch Night, trying to ignore Les who's been on his phone texting someone and smiling the whole time. I imagine he's bragging about the stunt he pulled with the article Saturday night and I have to fight a full-blown urge to throw him up against a wall and shout: *What's your goddamn problem?*

But I don't.

*Because I'm Theo Mackey, fulfiller of expectations.*

We move forward two steps as one of the groups ahead of us gets their information and leaves.

"You ready?" Iris asks, leaning into me. "We're almost up."

"Ready as I'll ever be."

I'm eager for anything I can add to the photo Uncle Phil gave me after listening to everyone chatter-bragging for the last hour about the all information they already have.

"Next," the woman behind the counter calls.

"You guys can go first," Les tells us. "I've already got more than I need for this thing."

Of course he does.

I look down the line behind me for Chip so he can see how annoyed I am by Les and he gives me the most sarcastic thumbs-up

I've ever seen. And then we step forward, all three of us in tandem, like we are in fact a throuple.

The clerk gives us a limp smile, examining us over half-moon glasses secured by a beaded chain.

"Parents' names?" Her eyes are on me.

"Sophia and Mitch Mackey."

"Maiden name?"

"Rogan."

The clerk writes that down, then looks at Iris.

"Bert Fiorello and Ioana Dalca."

"That's a mouthful," the clerk says. "Mind writing that on this slip of paper?" She slides a phone memo pad to Iris.

"My mom was off-the-boat Romanian. Fiorello is Italian," Iris whispers to me.

"Hence the cards," I say. "We're Irish. At least on the Mackey side."

"Hence your obsession with rainbows and leprechauns and pots of gold."

"More observation than obsession."

The clerk gives us a slight eye roll and continues typing at warp speed, pausing only long enough to whack the return key as hard as humanly possible. Her wispy eyebrows are knit so tightly they're almost overlapping.

"I've got Mitch Mackey's birth certificate and, oh." She looks up. "We have his death certificate, as well. I'll print that stuff up for you straightaway, but I can't seem to find anything in our database for a Sophia Mackey or Rogan. Do I have the spelling right?" She states each letter of my mom's maiden name like I'm hard of hearing.

"That's correct." I rub the back of my neck where it's heating to a low boil.

"Don't sweat it, Mackey," Les says, leaning forward. "I'm sure you've already got the important stuff. This is just perfunctory. It doesn't really tell us anything about our families that matters."

I give him a dismissive nod, even though my hackles shot up with his backhanded jibe.

"Let me try yours," the clerk says to Iris, sliding her pink memo pad closer to her keyboard. As she types Iris's mom's name she repeats it long and slow. "I-o-a-na Dal-ca. Well, there you go. I have a marriage certificate and a . . ." She stops midsentence and meets Iris's deep blue eyes. "I'm sorry, dear. Her death certificate is here, as well, but no birth record."

The clerk looks between us, trying to conceal her horror as it dawns on her that three out of our four parents are dead.

Because it's weird, like I said.

"Thank you," Iris says. "My mom wasn't born in the United States."

"I can check immigration records as well."

"That would be great. What about Theo's mother? Sophia Rogan. Do you think you'll be able to find something for him, too?"

I'm thankful Iris took over for me, but have a feeling I'm shit outta luck.

"There may be something in physical storage, or on microfiche. Would you like to fill out a form so someone can look into that?" She slides a clipboard across the counter to me. "Just put Rogan-Mackey at the top, and unless the records are sealed, we should be able to find something for you by the end of the week."

A different clerk, unable to mind his own small lipped business, creeps up behind the woman that's helping us and says, "Not to eavesdrop or anything, but someone else came in here early Saturday morning asking about those records." He studies me with dark beady eyes above a crooked nose underscored by a cop 'stache.

"Tall guy, dark hair?" I ask. Uncle Phil is the only person who would have come here on my behalf.

"No. This was a lady that came asking," he says. "Southern. Polite. Told her the same thing we tell everyone about sealed records. Excuse me now while I get back to my group."

I shrug at the clerk assigned to us. I don't have a clue about who the lady that came asking might be.

"What do you mean by sealed?" Iris asks. But I already know.

I lean closer to the clerk so only she and Iris can hear the little bit of truth I'm about to rip. "My mom was in the foster care system before she was adopted. Could that be the problem?"

The clerk gives me a sad smile, the exact brand of short-lived sympathy I've been trying to avoid for years. "Could be. We only carry public records: birth, death, and marriage certificates. The foster care system keeps their own records. But there are other sources of directory information you could try. Addresses, phone numbers, and place of birth can often be obtained from school records. You'd have to prove you're a relative, of course. They won't hand the information to just anyone."

Andover Prep.

They'll probably have a copy of the photo missing from Coach Porter's trophy case too.

"I'm sorry I couldn't be of more help," she says. "Sometimes family members are the best source of information for these things."

Sometimes, but not always.

"You have helped," I tell her. "More than you know."

"How about you, young man?" she says to Les.

"Karen and Andy Carter. Maiden name: LaFace."

That's my cue to leave. Les and Iris have already heard more about my family business than I'm comfortable sharing. Watching Les get his family records handed to him without a hitch is more than I can tolerate today.

Les makes a grab for my arm as I walk away. "Don't go yet. I need to talk to you before practice."

I clamp my lips and keep walking. I don't even wait for Iris. I just take the stuff they had on my dad and leave, before I say or do something I'll regret.

# NINETEEN

**Lost:** The loss of body control during flight that ends with a bad entry, dive smack, or the sensation of not knowing where you are during a dive.

**I KNOW** now that the dive Mom did at the cliffs that day was a Front Dive Straight. A Swan Dive. I've replayed it a dozen times since the quarry flashback. The simplicity. The grace. But it was more like a black swan dive. Because after that outing, something between my parents changed.

I climb the ladder to the board, bringing myself back to that place in time before giving that Swan Dive a go. No holding back. Chest open, arms holding wide until I angle past the horizontal tipping point, then straight and purposeful to cut through the water.

I use the underwater silence to piece together every memory that's come back to me so far: the quarry, the girl with the tattoos, the fight between my parents. There has to be more.

The fire is another story. One that got printed in the *Ellis Hollow Gazette* that's currently burning a hole in my practice duffle until I figure out a way to bring it up with GP.

Thanks to Les.

Coach Porter isn't smiling when I surface. "Try again."

"It wasn't good?" It felt pretty good, considering.

"I'm looking for great. Ramp it up a little. I'm counting on you for the Andover meet."

"Yes, Coach. I was just warming up."

I pull myself out of the pool and back to the ladder, studying the other guys on the team along the way. I imagine how easy it might be for them to go home and ask what their great-grandmothers or uncles did for a living, where they were born, or how and when they died.

Coach grabs my arm before I make it up the first rung and spins me around so fast it whirls me out of self-pity. I've been so tripped up by everything that's happened since Monarch Night, I forgot about the bruise left by my smack.

"What in God's name happened to you? I told you to play it safe out there," he says through gritted teeth.

"I did. It wasn't that. I tried to do Daley's Twister dive at Chip's yesterday."

All lies.

I've never attempted that dive in my life, but I know it's impressive enough to throw Coach off the scent. The advanced dive, a Backward 2½ Somersault, 2½ Twist in pike, has a high degree of difficulty. Leon Taylor, the inventor, is a former Olympic silver medalist. The only person my age I've ever seen rip it successfully was his mentee, Tom Daley, another Olympic medalist. And even he claimed the dive freaked him out.

Coach gives me a strange look, a combination of awe and disappointment. "Don't try that one on your own again. Understand? You need to work on your dryland and lead-ups if you want to spin a dive like that into gold, Rumpelstiltskin."

"Yes, Coach."

An Inward 3½ Somersault has a lower degree of difficulty, but it should satisfy Coach's thirst today.

I take a deep breath at the end of the board, turn, and then execute a nearly perfect backward press and take-off, rotating toward the board I left behind. But right before I come-out for entry, I over-rotate and blow it. I smack again. Not nearly as hard as Monarch Night, but it stings more than it would on unwounded flesh.

This time, Coach is even less impressed.

"Maybe I wasn't clear. Show me the progress you've made on the dive you did last Friday."

Shit.

My muscles are super tight today, making Mom's 5337D a tall order. Uncle Phil said the higher dose of Adderall would help me focus, but on what? I've got more on my mind today than Mom's dive, too much more. Add that to the people running around the halls outside the swim complex and it's a mental formula for disaster. But they aren't the reason I've been diving like crap. I need to get in control. Acknowledge my fear of smacking again and do it anyway.

I take three big steps and start my hurdle, counting through the process of gaining height. One: *I'm in the air. I got this.* Two: *getting higher. I know this dive inside out.* Three. The last hurdle gives me great height. I throw my arms hard, rotating backward, and a sharp pain shoots through the middle of my back. I lose sight of the board as I enter the twists and the crystalline pool fills with pointed fins, swimming in my vision. *Sharks again.* I'm twisting at incredible velocity with little control. The water turns bloodred. I need to come-out and line up my entry before it's too—

*Fuck!*

I smack the water hard and everything behind my lids goes dark, pulsing with lightning strikes, neurons firing like an electric storm.

I scramble beneath the surface like a fish caught in a net. Each twist of my torso reminds me once again of the bruise darkening my back in grotesque shades of purple and charcoal. Bringing pain as sharp and red as the dots still swimming in my eyes. The ringing in my ears is deafening as I frog-kick to the surface and take a breath.

But the alarm is real, shrieking in long pulses, warning of my worst nightmare. Fire.

Everyone is scrambling to collect their things before heading to the exit. Everyone except Miles, the pimple-faced freshman from Monarch Night. He's standing at the edge of the pool, watching me with a smile that's hard to explain. At first, I think he's relieved I'm not hurt. But when he doesn't break away with everyone else, I realize he's trying to provoke me. Like he wanted to make sure I saw him first. That's a hefty grudge to hold for sending him home early on Monarch Night.

Chip throws me a shammy. "That was bad, but you have to shake it off. Some asswipe started a fire in one of the labs. We gotta go."

People in the hallways are shouting and slamming lockers. Combined with the intermittent screech of the fire alarm, and the shock of screwing up my dive again, it's sensory overload. We join the herd of students rushing the exit, and when they push through the double doors a blast of cold air assaults the artificial warmth inside the building. Heavy wafts of smoke swirl and blend with the sharp smell of chlorine, creating a nauseating stench. But that's not the worst part.

Outside, it's snowing.

Huge flakes whirl around me as I scuff and shimmy through the dusting on the ground in the flip-flops I keep by the pool. I wrap my arms around myself to contain my body heat, but it's fleeing fast, rising like steam from a lake.

Given any other situation, I'd be game. Looking skyward to try and catch one of the massive flakes on my tongue the way Trey and Chip are doing. But right now I'm more interested in catching one of the blankets Coach Porter is throwing. As one of the last divers outside, I didn't have time to grab my dive team windbreaker, but I'd give anything to have that fleece-lined jacket because I'm shivering and sweating simultaneously. When I finally do catch one of the blankets my teeth are chattering like a wind-up toy.

Siren blare, growing louder and closer. I want to cover my head and ears. Not only to stay warm but to hide from anyone whipping out a cell phone to take photos, because the last time I was shrouded in one of these scratchy fire department blankets our house was burning to the ground.

A fireman jogs past me to enter the building. The broad, neon stripes shimmering against his canvas coat rivet me until all I can do is stare and wait for these flames to take over like they did once before.

Coach Porter and the chemistry teacher start to argue within earshot, their voices mixing with the wailing sirens like a swan song.

"That's preposterous," Coach Porter barks. "My entire team was in the swim complex."

"If you say so. I know what I saw."

I flinch.

*Preposterous* . . .

That one word, spit above the blaring sirens, spins me back in time.


*"What's the matter, Sophia, cat got your tongue?" Dad said in a bitter tone.*

*"In retrospect, I suppose, I knew how this would play out, Mitch. Long before I met either one of you. But sometimes the things I see aren't always absolute."*

*"Thank you, Madame Balanchuk. But this outcome you think you saw coming takes the fucking prize."*

*"I'm sorry," Mom said.*

*"No, you're not. But you will be, Sophia. When the time is right. You'll see it before anyone."*

*"Pun intended," Uncle Phil said sarcastically. Joining their argument. "Nobody did this to hurt you, Mitch. But we thought it was your right to know. Blood doesn't lie."*

*"Blood." Dad chuckled. "I thought that's what we were, Phil. You were like a brother to me."*

"Even Cain and Abel had their differences," Uncle Phil fired back.

"Do you really think that's the best example, considering one of them was a jealous asshole that bludgeoned the other to death?"

"Our story doesn't have to end so savagely."

Dad's fist slammed onto the dining room table. "She's my wife, you son of a bitch."

"Come on now, Mitch. You know my lineage can't be confirmed or denied. We don't even know who my mother was. She may have been a saint."

"I doubt that, considering the devious prick you turned out to be."

"What can I tell you; the heart wants . . ."

"That's preposterous. We both know you don't have a heart."

"I thought you would appreciate the platitude."

"Think again. Preferably on your way out the door."

"Mitch," my mom pleaded.

"Get out, both of you," Dad yelled. "Before I do something I'll regret."

"Not without my son."

THE FIRE department announces it's safe for us to reenter the building and I shift back to the freezing parking lot. Away from the argument I was never meant to hear, because I was supposed to be sleeping over at Chip's. But I did hear, and their voices weren't muffled at all.

Twenty minutes later I'm in the locker room. Trying to ignore the smell of burning plastic that hangs in the air while I add the truth of my latest flashback to what I already know.

Mom and Uncle Phil were having a fucking affair. Are you kidding? How the hell am I supposed to feel about that? Being mad at her makes no sense. She's gone. But Uncle Phil . . .

Jeezus-fucking-Christ.

I must be a fucking idiot for not noticing what was going on right under my nose, thinking it was my fault. Now I understand what my dad saw as all harm, all foul. Why there was no room for mercy. For all I know the argument my parents had after the quarry wasn't about me at all.

Chip closes the locker beside mine with a clang that makes me jump out of my skin. "What's up with you, man? You look like you saw a ghost."

That's not too far off base. I press my head against my locker and take a deep breath that reminds me how sore I am. Mentally and physically.

He doesn't press me again until I rotate my head and give him a look that's as agonized as I feel.

"What? The dive smack?" he asks. "The fire alarm rang. That would have happened to anyone."

"That's only part of it."

My eyes dart around the crowded locker room. Les-freaking-Carter is watching us again. I clench my fists, ready to ask if he got a good look at me smacking. But I don't. I'm supposed to stay in control and set the example, whether I'm losing my shit in and out of the pool or not. Ace already noticed. Everyone at the quarry noticed too. So I do the only thing I can to avoid creating another spectacle. I grab my duffle and split.

"Wait. You're *leaving*?" Chip grabs his stuff and chases me into the hallway, grabbing my arm before I round the corner. "Whoa. What gives?"

I pace in front of him, rubbing a hand over the spiky ends of my wet hair. I should have filled him in sooner.

"Stop moving, man. You're freakin' me out."

"I think there's something wrong with me," I blurt.

"You just figured that out?" Chip raises his eyebrows, trying to keep it light.

"I mean more than normal. I've been regaining all these

memories, flashbacks from around the fire. That's why I keep smacking. It happened today, at Monarch Night, at your house while we were racing in the pool. That's why I hit my head."

"Rocco said you were on the lower cliffs hitting on Iris."

"I was. *After* she saved me from almost drowning. I asked him not to tell you guys about me smacking. But before that, I honestly thought I saw him facedown in the water. I've seen my mom a couple of times, too, like she's actually there."

"Like hallucinations?" Chip looks worried. "I was wondering what was up when you said you heard my dog barking on Monarch Night."

"Uncle Phil called them dream states and flashbacks. All I know is they're intense enough to make me think I'm losing my mind." I rub a hand over my head and almost laugh. "Consider the irony there, Chip. The shrink's kid goes loony."

"Everybody has freak-outs," Chip says. "That doesn't mean you've flown the cuckoo's nest. You didn't hit your head hard enough to see dead people, either, so slow down. My mind goes to some strange places when I'm swimming. We have to gauge it on a scale. Like if Amy's freak-out when I scared her at the quarry was, let's say a four, then yours would be . . . ?"

"A fifty." No contest. "And freak-out is the perfect name for it."

"Didn't I say your memories were locked in your mind castle?"

"Palace. You were right. Which is why I need to go talk to Uncle Phil again."

"You want me to go with? *Me casa es* you *casa*."

I get what he means, but there's plenty of other stuff I haven't told him yet. Stuff I'm not ready to get into right now.

"I can handle going to see him alone. But I could use a wingman at Andover Prep. The clerk said they might have my mom's school records."

"Whatever you need. A bet's a bet, right? I got you."

Yeah. *A bet's a bet.*

"It's probably too late for Andover now. I was thinking Wednesday. We don't have practice because of the district-wide coaches meeting."

"Good idea. What about Iris?"

"What about her?"

"You gonna ask her to come along? She is your project partner."

So is Les.

"I figured I'd give her a break from watching me run into Mackey brick walls. But maybe I'm being dumb. Avoiding things like you always say."

"You got her number, you asked her to come to Monarch Night. Lead-ups, bro. One step at a time. You gonna go see Dr. Maddox's now?"

"That's my plan."

My only problem is where to start. How the hell am I going to tell Uncle Phil about the incriminating flashback I had of him today without sounding completely paranoid and nuts? It's not as simple as walking into his house and saying, *Hey, Uncle Phil. Were you by any chance boning my mom behind Dad's back? Oh, you were? How long was that going on—since that day we went to the quarry? Is that the real reason you and Dad had a falling-out? You said you had that picture of the three of us on your desk at work. Old habits die hard, huh? Yeah, that's cool. Do you think I could get some more Adderall from you while I'm here?*

Jeezus.

I don't know that much about hypnosis other than my own experience, but I do know I can't trust my own returning memories. Not with such big chunks missing.

*Are you seeing something now, Theo?*

That's what Uncle Phil asked me, like he was probing for the nascent insanity, which I'm betting must feel something like my own maladaptive uncertainty.

# TWENTY

**Getting Paid:** Receiving a higher score for a dive than it may be worth.

**I CAN'T** get out of school fast enough. If running were an option, I'd hightail my ass to my truck and squeal out of the parking lot straight to Uncle Phil's. But seeing as there's an inch of snow on the ground and more than a few people still cleaning off their cars, I slow my roll. Pretending to be the Theo everyone expects. A springboard diver under full control.

And then I see Iris, leaning against my truck in a puffy white parka. She stops biting the lid on her disposable cup to smile at me when she sees us coming and some of the weight on my back lifts for real. Until I remember the way I ditched her at the county clerk's office.

Chip elbows me. "Looks like your plans for a lobotomy just changed. Good luck with that next round of lead-ups." He gives Iris an upward nod with a grin and treks to his car.

"What are you doing out here in the snow? You're not stalking me or anything since the field trip, are you?"

I give her a crooked grin, trying to save face. I haven't exactly let Iris in on anything that's been going on with me, even after she saved my life on Monarch Night, because guy-that's-losing-his-gourd isn't really the message I want to send this early in the game.

"I've never stalked anyone before. I might be. Do you have

somewhere you need to be right now? You two were coming in fast and furious for a minute there."

"I was heading over to my Uncle Phil's to interview him for the project, but it can wait."

It's not a total lie. If it weren't for the family history project, I probably wouldn't be remembering so much in the first place.

"I was hoping you and I could go somewhere private and talk."

My guilt returns. "About the project or why I hauled ass out of the county clerk's office?"

"Aren't they the same thing?"

"Yeah. I guess they are. You never miss a trick, do you?"

"Not if I can help it."

I give the edge of her fur-trimmed hood a tug. "I take it you knew about today's weather too. Was that in the cards?"

"They've been predicting this squall for a week," Iris says. "Don't tell me you don't read the *Monarch Monthly?*"

"Uh." The back of my neck starts to get warm. "I should. I mean, plan to. It's sort of a juggling act just to keep up with homework when we're in season."

"Don't worry. You're not alone. *We're* not alone, actually." She throws an informative glance over her shoulder and I scan the parking lot.

More than a few gaping looks are being cast our way. This was bound to happen. When Iris and I showed up together at the bonfire on Monarch Night the expressions on everyone's faces—priceless—like I plucked her straight out of the flooded town beneath the water. Nothing like shocking the shit out of your friends while they're buzzing. Once the initial shock wore off the rest of the night went great. Iris fit right in. Making Chip right once again. The people gawking today, though, aren't my friends. I barely know most of them, which makes their fascination more ridiculous.

"They've been staring at me the whole time, like I broke a

force field to get near your truck." She blocks her mouth with the side of her cup and leans closer. *"I mean, what are those two even doing together? He's like, a jock. And she's like a library nerd or a hippie or something."* She grins and eases back against my truck with a shrug. "I like to imagine them struggling to find the right box for me."

Classic.

Plus bonus points for inflection.

"Weren't you the one who said people were afraid of disrupting the status quo?"

"Yes. Because it's true."

"So what bothers you most, their judgment or the idea of exclusion?"

"Neither. I'm not the captain of anything."

"Well, I am. And I think you should consider writing an anonymous article about breaking the status quo. From the front lines to the front page."

Her eyes widen agreeably. "An undercover infiltration piece. Nice I like it."

I open the passenger door and hand Iris my keys. "You mind starting the engine while I clean off Bumblebee?"

"Who?"

"My truck," I explain, shaking my head. "Chip named him."

"After the Transformer?" She laughs. "I can see that."

"You and the rest of the team. Nicknames and tags are a thing we do. Sully, The Flying Ace, Dumbass for Trey Dumas. Chip just applied the name game to my truck."

"What do they call you?"

"Big Mack." Her eyebrows shoot up and I clear my throat. "Because I'm tall for a diver."

"Uh-huh." She smirks so hard this time my head gets hot (pun acknowledged, not intended).

"What do you think my nickname would be if I were on the team?" She asks.

"You're on my team now so I guess I better get to work on that." I try to think up a few nicknames on the fly. Something that means lifesaver: buoy, lifeguard. Those sound dumb and don't fit the awesome that is Iris Fiorello.

I dig around in my trunk for my knitted beanie and snow scraper, then clean off my truck as fast as possible, smiling at Iris through breaks in the slushy snow that whoomph onto the ground in big swaths as I sweep them away. I jump into the cabin and crank the heat, holding my hands in front of the blast of warm air.

"That dark hat brings out the moles on your cheek." She uses her peace fingers to touch one mole at the outer corner of my eye, and the other at the top of my cheekbone.

I'm not sure my moles are quite the panty-dropper Sully has with his lip, but I'll take it. I'll take all the normal I can get for the moment.

I'm thinking about kissing her when Chip rolls up and sounds his mutant duck horn. I lower my window and lean out.

"I see you two are keeping the latest E.H.H.S. gossip afloat?"

Iris leans across my lap to get closer to my window. "That's right, loud muffler. It's a good thing you stopped or my nerdy, newspaper-loving rep may have been destroyed."

I run through a bunch of dive combinations in my head, struggling to ignore how much of Iris is touching me. There's definitely boob on my arm. *Breathe in, breathe out.*

Chip cuts me a look. "Good thing for *you*, maybe. I can't say the same for Theo. But I like the way you roll, French Fry."

"French Fry?" Iris scoffs.

"Who doesn't love a Big Mack and fries?"

I look at Iris and shrug. "He beat me to it. It's done."

"Go easy on him, Iris," Chip says. "My boy's had a shit day. The last thing he needs piled on is a case of blue balls."

Jeezus.

"Thanks for the tip," Iris says. "I'll keep it in mind."

Chip gets a shit-eating grin, like he wants to riff off her usage of *tip,* and I think he would if I wasn't giving him a death glare.

"All right, you two." Chip shifts his Dart into drive with a thunk. "I've got a tip of my own that needs minding. I'll catch you later." He rumbles away through the parking lot.

As usual, I thought-spoke on his perverted behalf too soon.

"Don't mind him," I tell Iris. "He doesn't have a filter."

"Filters are overrated. Not having one makes Chip easy to read than most."

I lower the temperature in the truck to compensate for another round of guilty heat rising to my cheeks. I don't have a filter so much as a shield.

"So where to, *French Fry?*"

"Can I drive? There's something I'd like to show you."

"My *truck?*" I feel my eyes pop. "I've never let anyone drive Bumblebee. Not even Chip. Plus, I don't think I've ever seen you behind the wheel of a car before."

"That's because it got totaled." Her hands shoot up in surrender when my eyes widen more. "I wasn't the one driving it at the time. I swear."

She crosses her arms, nearly hugging herself, and I know there's more to her story. I take a deep breath in through my nose. Trusting the person that saved your life should probably be a given. Which is why I drop my guard and surrender control of the driver's seat to Iris for a little while.

# TWENTY-ONE

**Fade:** To fall slightly off the board backward.

**UNLIKE CHIP,** Iris is a great driver. Even in snow, which is falling more like rain now, making a mess of the roads. I show her how to disengage the four-wheel drive and she snakes along Route 12 and onto Wampanoag Road. The late-afternoon sun is glinting off every reflective surface it touches, blinding me. I avert my eyes and listen to the rush of water being expelled by my tires because I'm worried the flashes might cause another one of my level-fifty freak-outs.

When Iris turns onto Mount Pleasant Road, I realize she's heading to the cemetery. Not my favorite place, but I have to admit it's sort of beautiful right now. The blitz of salt trucks and traffic is absent, leaving the isolated sound of my tires laying fresh tracks in the untouched snow.

I look at Iris and she smiles like she's aware of my eyes.

"Do we have unfinished business here?"

"More like new business." Iris cuts me a quick glance before turning onto a new road. "I couldn't stop thinking about the county clerk's office. Your face when that lady said she couldn't find anything about your mom; I get it. I really do. You're not the only one having a hard time with this project. So in a way, I guess I lied to you too."

Iris parks my truck in front of an engraved monument.

A life-sized marble angel is weeping over the slab of granite; the tips of her unfurled wings swoop to the base, taut and primed.

"That's my mom's grave," Iris says without looking my way.

"I . . . I'm sorry," I say, my tact rivaling a donkey's. Rejecting all the sympathy handed to me taught me nothing about how to behave when the situation is reversed.

"I appreciate that, especially coming from you. It's been a year now, so it's getting a little easier to talk about." She looks down and picks at one of her thumbnails. "She was driving my car when she got in the accident. That's how it got totaled."

"Oh," I say. Then *Oh. Shit.* She means that's how she died.

"I don't want you to think she was a kook or anything but before the accident I heard her telling my dad she felt like someone was following her, watching her. Maybe I'm just being paranoid, but I get that feeling, too, sometimes, like I'm being watched." Iris shakes her head. "I don't know. She was intuitive, always reading her friends' fortunes from the deck I use now, but so much more accurate than me. The last time she read my cards, she told me an unexpected peril in the near future would change my life. And unfortunately, she was right. That dang Cat card was prominent in my reading too. Just like yours. I laughed it off. Which was pretty stupid of me, in retrospect."

"It's not stupid," I say. "I wasn't sure about the card reading until you showed up at Monarch Night and saved my life. But that's because I was raised by a shrink who fed me science and skeptic's milk even though my mom had phenomenal intuition. She once told me not to ride my new skateboard on my eighth birthday, because she had a hunch. I figured she was just being a worrywart so I didn't listen. Broke my arm in two places at Sully's house three hours later."

"Actually," she says, "that kind of intuition is part of the reason I wanted to talk to you today."

"Um, okay. We can do that." I guess. I swallow hard wondering if there was something in my cards she didn't tell me. "I'm glad you brought me here, Iris. Your friendship means a lot to me."

She chuckles. "That's what my name means. Almost verbatim. *Your friendship means so much to me.*"

"No, it doesn't. You're making that up."

"Look it up sometime. All the women in my family were named after flowers. My mom's name, Ioana, means violet. Even Fiorello means little flower in Italian."

That explains the pens.

Iris grins but it's short-lived. "I've never told anyone this, but on the day of the accident my mom was on her way to pick me up at school because I was being a jerk about taking the bus. She was late getting out of a doctor's appointment, rushing. She called my cell to say she would be there in twenty minutes, but she never made it. A truck hit my crappy, old Pinto from behind and my mom crashed into the ravine. The car caught fire, they say, in minutes."

I know the ravine she means. It's at the intersection of Cutter's Cross, one of the scariest roads in town because there are breaks in the guardrail and nothing but drop on the other side.

"I knew about your mom's accident because my dad died around the same time, I just . . ." I look at my lap, regret sinking me lower. "When I saw how much it hurt you to be at school last year, I didn't know what to say."

"It's okay, Theo. It's not like you didn't have your own bag of grief to carry around."

True enough.

She leans against the door, twisting a silver spoon ring around her right thumb. "I think I need to explain why my dad had such a strong reaction to you at the carnival. We got into an argument about it when I got home from Monarch Night and he saw you and Chip driving away."

"Shit. Sorry about that, Iris. I didn't mean to cause problems for you at home. If you can't hang out, just tell me. It's okay." I try to hide my disappointment but my mouth twists to the side involuntarily.

"It's not you, Theo. It's your uncle. Apparently, my mom's appointment on the day of her accident was with Dr. Maddox. I knew she was having scary dreams and paranoia. I didn't know she was seeing a psychiatrist. But somehow my dad has himself convinced your uncle was negligent in letting her drive away from his office that day. It seemed like there was other stuff tangled up in what happened, but he got all aggravated and wouldn't answer any of my questions." Iris against the door. "Anyway, I thought you should probably know."

"Dr. Maddox isn't really my uncle, if that helps. He was my dad's best friend. Their relationship was sort of complicated."

For a second I can't help but wonder whether I made that delineation for her or me, like corroborating something about their longtime friendship might make the cheating easier to take.

"It's okay, Theo," Iris says. "Dr. Maddox was her shrink, not her babysitter."

I chew the inside of my cheek to keep from telling Iris about the affair since I haven't fully processed it myself. I know it would feel like shit if she and Chip hooked up. I'd hate it. But would I hate *him*? I don't know for sure, but I'm positive I have to tamp my anger down to a simmer before Uncle Phil and I talk. He's never been one to react in the face of strong emotions, so I'll need to be smart about my approach.

Iris touches my knee, snapping me out of my headspace. "You want to hear something kind of cool?"

"Definitely. Tell me something cool."

"After the funeral, my dad pulled me aside and told me that my mom named me Iris because of her love for the flower. But my dad went along with it because in mythology Iris was the personification of the rainbow, a psychopomp who escorted the newly deceased into the afterlife. He liked that, being a cemetery sexton and all. And I know this might sound crazy, but I hope, in some way, that means I was with my mom when she crossed over."

A lump lodges in the hollow of my throat. Her reaction to me bringing up rainbows makes more sense now.

"It doesn't sound crazy at all."

"Good. Because doing readings with my mom's fortune-telling cards makes me feel close to her, even when it makes me sad."

"I understand that completely. It's the same for me with diving."

The ring she's been non-stop twisting around her thumb drops onto the floor mat, and our conversation stalls while she bends beneath my steering wheel to retrieve it. I make a move to help her, but freeze fast when I spy the inky lines of a tattoo, peeking between the space where her shirt and jacket meet her jeans.

"Got it," she says, slipping the ring back on her right thumb as she leans back into the seat. "Why are you looking at me like that?"

"You have a *tattoo?*"

She nods, pulling her shirt down in the back even though she's up against the seat. "Don't ask me about it."

"Can I at least see it?" I ask. Because there's only one other cliff-jumping girl with dark hair and body tattoos that's ever left an impression on me, and right now the similarities are too real.

Iris closes one eye, lips pursed. "How about we answer one-for-one questions, since we're supposed to be working on our projects, and we'll see if we get to the tattoo? I'll go first. Tell me something that bothers you about your everyday life."

Easy.

"My grandfather started drinking after my dad died and being around him is like babysitting a grizzly bear. Can I see your tattoo?"

"It's sort of intense. Tell me something nobody knows about your mom?"

She's cheating, but I take a deep breath and let a bigger truth rip. "When I was thirteen our house burned down and my mom got trapped inside. My parents were fighting a lot before that happened, and afterward, my dad, shut everyone out. He stopped talking to my Uncle Phil, for the most part, and to me about anything important."

"I didn't know your mom died in a fire," she says.

"It's not something I like to talk about. Can I see your tattoo now?"

Iris narrows her eyes.

"It's important. Just for a second."

She sighs deeply, conceding, then turns and lifts the back of her shirt.

"Holy crap."

Iris glances over her shoulder to read my face. "It told you. It's intense."

"It's not that, Iris. It's you. You're, um . . ."

"Not what you expected?"

"More than I expected, actually."

Because what if she's her? The girl with the dark hair and body tattoos who made me believe it was okay to jump when I was ten years old. She was too far away for me to see any detail. But that's impossible. It was three years before I saw Iris jump from the same spot wearing a yellow one-piece, her torso fully covered. It has to be a coincidence. They can't be the same person. Iris was ten years old at that time, same as me. The girl I saw was a teenager even if nobody saw her but me. Not even Mom. Unless it was a dream state, way back then and I just didn't know.

But did Mom? I remember her looking around nervously.

*"You're so much more like me than I ever imagined,"* she said, *"and that makes me incredibly happy. But you have to be careful what you say to anyone but me. Don't blurt out everything you see, okay? Not everyone will understand."*

*". . . sometimes the things I see aren't always absolute."*

*"Dreams, and dream states, can express hidden desires,"* Uncle Phil said.

My heart starts beating so hard I'm sure it's audible. I keep staring at her indigo tattoo. Barbed wire wrapping around her hips likes she's bound, every spiky strand run through with flowers.

Iris looks at me again. "Whoa. You're completely gray."

I feel gray. Numb. "Do you ever wear a two-piece bathing suit?"

"Sometimes. I was wearing one on Monarch Night, but it was so chilly my friend loaned me one of her wetsuits. Why?"

My palms are sweating. I rub them on my jeans. "Um, do you think people can have certain abilities like fortune-telling but without cards?"

"Of course I do. I come from a long line of women with preternatural abilities. What are you getting at, Theo? You keep . . . Your face keeps changing color."

"Remember that girl I told you about, the one I saw jump from the cliffs when I was ten?"

"Babysitter crush girl?"

"Yeah. She had tattoos on her torso too. Maybe it was a sign. Like I knew we'd meet someday."

"Now *you're* the one making stuff up."

"I'm not," I say, but laugh it off like a joke. Just in case my mom was right about blurting out everything I see. "Can I ask why barbed wire?"

"Because I felt—still feel, actually— somewhat responsible for my mom's death. The flowers are irises and violets, which represent my mom and me, obviously. And the barbed wire is meant to cut as deep as the pain I felt when she died. But most of all, the tattoo reminds me not to be selfish. Not that I'd ever forget."

I'm so used to her being the brave girl who jumps off cliffs and climbs trees, unafraid of anything, that seeing her with caution signs inked over her body makes me want to pull her close and rub the barbs until they're smooth. Taking away the sadness and pain that's represented by her tattoo.

But I don't.

I knew how I felt about Iris the minute I saw her soar past the edge of the cliff so I leave the situation wide open for her to tell me what she wants, if *I'm* what she wants, especially if there's history between our families.

"I think it's really beautiful," I tell her. "Intense and beautiful, like you."

I ask myself again if I'd hate Chip if he hooked up with Iris. I might. I think I honestly might. But *her*? I don't know if I could ever hate her.

She stops spinning her ring and without another word climbs over the console into my lap, straddling me. I recline the passenger seat back as far as it will go as her mouth crashes onto mine. Her grief gathers up my own in an avalanche. Our bodies, pressed this close, makes me swell with want and Iris responds with a small moan that might make me lose my mind completely. Willingly.

She pulls the knitted beanie off my head and kisses me again, then unzips her puffy coat and slides free, tossing our outerwear in the backseat. I slide my hands inside her shirt, over smooth skin, warm enough to melt the snow on the roof. I caress the lines of her tattoo with careful hands, tracing the barbs from memory before inching higher, watching her face. She smiles and nods. All systems go.

After we've touched every inch of each other, we lay there, her head on my chest rising and falling with my breath. I lean forward and search for a song on my sound system, then lean back. I stroke her hair, listening to "Wild Horses" by The Rolling Stones as her dark strands slip between my fingers, and I think about how intertwined we are by members of our families. Barbed.

And I wonder if I'll ever feel the same way about another girl.

Iris turns her head to look at the display. "I love this song." She bolts up suddenly, pushing off my chest. "Is that the right time? Theo, we have to go." She starts buttoning her shirt, climbing back into the driver's seat. "I need to get home before eight. You should probably drive."

We dash around my truck like a game of musical chairs and I start the engine. The rain has stopped, but everything including my brain is a slushy mess as I pull away from her mom's gravestone.

Iris reaches into the backseat for her coat and pulls forward the newspaper that was left on my windshield. "For someone who doesn't read the *Monarch Monthly,* you sure took care of this one."

"Someone left that on my truck a few days ago. I think it was the PTA."

"Theo, this paper is from 1994. Whoever left this for you removed it from the school's newspaper archives. They're all wrapped in this same plastic."

"I bet it was Les. He left me a note saying we needed to talk. I didn't put the two things together."

"He could be trying to help you with the project." She snaps the paper open and starts flipping pages. "Or not."

"Why? What's it say?" I shoot her a quick glance while driving and notice the furrow of her brow.

"There's a Post-it Note pointing to an article about your mom. Maybe you should pull over."

"Just tell me."

"It says, 'Former Andover Prep Star Athlete Suspended from Stanford University Swim and Dive Team.'"

What the—

I jerk the wheel and pull over to the side of the road. "Can I see that?"

Iris passes me the newspaper and I read the rest out loud.

"'Championship springboard diver Sophia Rogan maintains she was prescribed stimulant medication for focus by a licensed psychiatrist that in no way enhanced her performance, but was either unable or unwilling to supply a medical exceptions report to the reviewing board. The Division I athlete was last seen leaving a training session in Ellis Hollow, Massachusetts with Mitch Mackey, a highly sought-after local sport's psychologist, and famed gymnastic coach—Ioana Dalca—known simply to her students as JoJo.'"

"*What?*" Iris grabs the edge of the paper when she hears her mom's name and reads the rest. "'The springboard diver refused to answers questions on whether or not she will be filing for appeal. For now, the NCAA has ruled out prior knowledge by the Stanford Cardinal's swim and dive coaching staff, but additional routine drug tests have been scheduled for every member of the team.' Did you know about this?" Iris asks.

"No. Did you? I knew my mom did some dryland training there during college breaks, but I didn't know your mom was JoJo of JoJo's gym. I mean, I wouldn't have because she goes by her maiden name, right?" I manage to take a breath before a different realization dawns on me. "You're a *gymnast?*"

"I *was* a gymnast when I was younger, but I hated everything about it: the training, the pressure, the early mornings. My mom and I fought about that sometimes."

My world feels like it's tipping on its axis. Tripping on its axis with my mind.

Iris squeezes my arm. "Oh my gosh, Theo. *That's* why I recognized your mom's name when we were talking to Coach Porter. Sophia Rogan was the name of the student who taught my mom about jumping from Pikes Falls. Why on earth would Les leave this for you? It doesn't add anything to your family history project."

I stare straight ahead through windshield. My parents told me Mom left school because she was pregnant with me, unless the two aren't mutually exclusive. That's a shitty thought. Even shittier than the idea of Les dropping off these articles to get arise out of me.

"He's fucking with me," I blurt. "Les wants to go to Stanford and I'm his competition."

"That doesn't sound like the Les I know. Plus, this photo is of the 1988 team. Isn't that the same photo that was missing from Coach Porter's trophy case? Les works on photography and design, not editorial. Maybe he was trying to get you a copy."

"I didn't tell him it was missing. Did you?"

Iris shakes her head. "You think your coach may have gone to the archives looking for a replacement photo?"

"Coach Porter wouldn't leave me something like this. He'd bring it to me privately."

Iris bites her lip, trying to figure it out, but I'm one step ahead of her this time.

"Les was throwing around a few self-righteous slings on Monarch Night when he saw Chip and me putting Adderall in our beers. And later that night, after I got home, someone left an article on my windshield about the fire that burned my house down. It said my mom had been the subject of headlines over the years. You really don't think it's possible that Les would try to get inside my head and mess me up so he can get ahead with diving? I didn't see this drug-related article until today so I never reacted to it. Maybe he was upping his ante."

"Okay," Iris says, "Adderall and ante aside. It still doesn't explain why the arrow on *this article* is pointing at the diver *next to* your mom."

Iris the journalist in true form hands the article back to me so I'll take another look.

The photo is on newsprint that's over twenty years old so it's far from perfect, but my mom is front and center. 1988 Individual Springboard Diving First Place Winner: Sophia Rogan, Andover Preparatory Academy. Everyone on the team is wearing wide, cheesy grins, except the girl standing next to my mom, giving her the stink-eye. Second Place Winner: Luanne Cole, Ellis Hollow High School. She's black. Her hair is pulled back tight like all the other divers, and she's tall like Mom. Almost too tall for a diver. I resurrect images of every person I've met, flipping faces in and out of my consciousness in search of a match, but come up empty-handed.

"I don't know. Maybe the Post-it moved. I don't remember ever meeting anyone named Luanne Cole."

And yet something is nagging at the back of my mind, telling me I'm wrong.

"You have to be in journalism or part of the school newspaper staff to get access to the archives, but I can poke around for any follow-up articles about your mom's suspension if you want? Maybe the claims were unsubstantiated."

I put my truck back in gear. "That would be good to know. I'll ask my grandfather and uncle about the articles, and find out if they know anything about this Luanne person."

"What about Les?"

"Don't say anything to him," I tell Iris. "If he is doing this to mess me up, I'm not gonna give him the satisfaction."

# TWENTY-TWO

**False Start:** Attempting to start a dive, then stopping motion before the take-off.

IRIS'S DAD flies out of their house the minute we pull onto her long driveway. If I thought there was a chill in the air earlier, the sensation pales in comparison to the unwelcome reception I see in her dad's eyes. A brand-new storm front headed straight for me that I should have seen coming.

"Shoot," Iris says. "I had a feeling we might not beat him home. But don't take off too fast. That'll make it worse. You and I were out working on our projects. No big deal."

A hollow feeling sinks into my stomach as I open the truck door for Iris and face her dad. Because even though he's maintaining eye contact with me, he speaks directly and only to her.

"I think I left the kettle on the stove, Iris. Why don't you go inside and turn it off for me while I talk to your friend?"

Iris shoots me an apologetic look and gives me the one-minute finger before rushing inside.

Sure. No big deal. I swallow hard.

The second Iris is gone her dad's eyes go hawk-like. "Why are you hanging around my daughter? Do you think this is some kind of game?"

"I don't know what you mean, Mr. Fiorello. I'm only—"

"Trying to screw with her head?" he interjects. "I know. But you can forget it. Find yourself another filly to toy with, young man. I've paid my dues to your family. We don't need any more freebie psych treatments. Iris is off-limits. To you *and* that uncle of yours."

I go into temporary shit shock, but manage to pull it together enough to defend myself. "I'm not sure what you're talking about, Mr. Fiorello. Iris and I are working on a project together, and I do like your daughter, but I'm not playing any game."

"I don't believe that for a second." He stares at me like there's something I should know. "Just remember at the end of the game the king and the pawns go into the same box together, no matter who wins."

What the—

Iris comes out of the house, sees my face, and gives her father a scolding look. "Dad, you never even turned the gas on for the kettle."

"I must have imagined I did. You know how the mind can play tricks." Mr. Fiorello pulls Iris forward and kisses the top of her head, all the while staring into my eyes. "Make it quick, Iris. You have homework and chores." He walks away, leaving me confused. I definitely know how the mind can play tricks. But how would he?

"Sorry about that," Iris says once he's gone inside. "He's been a little overprotective since my mom died."

Mr. Fiorello's face pops up in a window behind her and that old Clash song runs through my head again. I'd say more than a little.

"It's cool. But I should go. It was pretty clear your dad lumps me in with his feelings about my uncle. I'll see you at school tomorrow."

I turn to leave and she catches me by my sleeve. "Theo, wait. I had a really good time today. Don't let my dad scare you away, okay? He's all bark."

That might be true. But if Chip's mom taught me anything it's that a barking dog can be more than just a warning.

"I had fun too," I tell Iris. "It was great. But maybe we should—"

"Do whatever makes us happy? Great idea." She pulls me closer and kisses me, once and fast. "I'll let you know if I find anything else in the archives."

As she jogs up the front steps to her house a tiny voice inside my head finishes my original thought—*maybe we should heed your father's warning and cool it for a while.*

The problem is staying away from Iris is the opposite of what I want to do, and it's clear she feels the same.

# TWENTY-THREE

**Rushing:** Missing the timing of the board by anticipating the spring too early, or moving too quickly in a hurdle or back press, usually due to anxiety.

**UNCLE PHIL** is leaning on the roof of a Passat talking to the driver when I pull up behind the white sedan. It's hours later than I intended to show up here, a lot has happened, but my purpose is the same. When Uncle Phil sees me his expression flashes from surprised to composed, much faster than my own reaction to learning he had an affair with Mom. He says something to the driver, taps the rim of the open window twice, and she shifts her car into drive. Our eyes meet in the driver's side mirror before she pulls away and I see the woman who was leaving his house last Saturday.

"Theo." Uncle Phil's surprise carries into his voice as he meets me halfway on the sidewalk. "It's late. I wasn't expecting you."

"Should I have called first?"

"Of course not. You know you're always welcome here. Come in."

My head spins as I follow Uncle Phil to his enormous kitchen, a room that could easily contain GP's foyer, kitchen, and half his living room.

"Have you eaten? You look a little peaked."

"Not yet," I tell him. "I was busy. Diving, homework, you know how it is."

"I was concerned the higher dosage of Adderall might suppress your appetite."

"Nah. I'm a springboard diver. I can always eat. I was just a little preoccupied today."

I never thought I'd feel the need to manipulate the truth out of Uncle Phil. But right now, as he pushes an aluminum swan across the granite island, I see a different person. Someone who was capable of cheating with my mom behind Dad's back, the kind of guy who made Iris's dad so suspicious he told me to stay away from her without explanation.

"Leftovers from Davios," he says. Assuming my hesitation has anything to do with his dinner scraps and not my conflicted feelings.

I unwrap the foil, exposing a steak dinner with creamed spinach. "Thanks."

"Is the new dosage helping your focus?"

"Yes and no. Everything seems heightened if that makes sense: sound, smells. But I'm smacking on dives I should have a better handle on by now."

"Because of the stress you feel about the project." He tip-nods his head like that's understandable. But he's wrong. Dead wrong. "How did it go for you at the county clerk's office?"

I shrug and he takes an empty pint glass to the stainless steel refrigerator, watching me closely as water bubbles noisily into the vessel, like he senses something's up. My throat dries up more by the second. Not to mention my brass because he's got that look in his eye. Shrink-mode.

"You were right about the sealed files," I tell him. "Total bust. I was just talking to Iris Fiorello about the other sources of information available and whether or not they might be reliable. School records, newspaper clippings, stuff like that."

There's an unmistakable pause in his movements before he slides the water glass across the granite island. "The cemetery sexton's daughter is helping you with this, along with that other diver you mentioned, the one who left you the note?" He snaps his finger three times like he's trying to remember.

"Les."

"Les," he repeats. "Les *Carter*? Is Iris the girl Chip was referring to you when he said you were stalking someone?"

I nod and try not to gulp the bite of steak I'm grinding between my teeth. I wait. Swallow. Breathe. "Iris is our other project partner. I take it you know her dad."

"My two best friends died within a few years of each other, leaving my nephew an orphan. You could say he and I have had some dealings."

"Right. That makes sense. So what's your take on him? I only talked to the man for a few minutes but it was pretty clear he wasn't too keen on his daughter spending time with me."

Uncle Phil gives a tiny grimace. "Bert Fiorello is, in a word, observant. In fact, the only other person I've ever known to be more vigilant was Mitch."

"It was definitely hard to slip anything past my dad."

"Sometimes to his own detriment."

True. But he didn't even flinch. That's not anywhere close to a confession of guilt.

Uncle Phil removes his tie, unbuttons the top button on his gray shirt, and pours two fingers of scotch from the decanter on the counter behind him. "I can't speak from personal experience, of course, but I imagine any decent father is protective of his child. Speaking of which, I have a few more photos for you that will help with your project. I'll get them while you finish eating dinner."

I scarf the last two bites and get up to put my dish in the sink. "I'm done, actually. I'll come with you."

"I hardly think that's necessary, Theo. Have a seat in the living room. I'll be right back." He stops to light the gas fireplace before heading down the hallway toward his bedroom.

I head for the set of leather chairs we always sit in but can't settle down so I traipse over to the bookshelves lining one of wall. I don't know what I'm looking for exactly but I scan the titles: *Acid Dreams, Hallucinations, Mycology, On the Origin of Species, Manifesting Minds.* Not exactly what you'd call light reading. Our shelves at home were filled with sports biographies, mysteries, and thrillers, exciting stories about real lives or families with problems. Uncle Phil's books are mostly clinical.

I pull the mycology book off the shelf and fan through a few highlighted pages that outline the uses of psilocybin in psychiatry. Specifically how combining magic mushrooms with meditation or hypnosis can awaken the subconscious and free the mind from negative thought patterns.

"You'll either never eat mushrooms again after reading that book or decide they're just the thing you need." He takes the book from me and hands me four photos: my mom, my mom and me, and two more of the three of us. "Do you have any with my dad?"

"Sadly, I don't. I know it's not much, but I'll keep digging for photos and official documents on the Rogans."

The Rogans. Jeezus. I nearly forgot.

"I didn't come here tonight because of my project," I confess.

The real reasons tap away at my consciousness like insects trapped under glass. But acknowledging the affair, asking what he knows about Mom's suspension from Stanford, even telling him my dream states are becoming maladaptive is harder than I thought.

"Why did you come?" Uncle Phil slides his hands into his pockets and waits.

I don't know where to start. I wrestle with my most recent *freak-outs* and pick the easiest one first. "Do you think . . . This is gonna sound crazy . . . But is it possible Mom was outside of the house at one point during the fire?"

"An interesting concept. What makes you ask?"

"I went back to the site of our old house and thought I saw her standing near the tree line, just for a second."

"The mind has a way of protecting us from certain truths. The jarring realism of the flashbacks you've experienced can make it difficult to accept what's come to pass. Have you experienced other flashbacks that make you think your mother was safe from harm at one point that evening?"

"No. Not flashbacks, exactly. But there have been more dream states. I saw Mom underneath the water when I went cliff jumping on Monarch Night. She was sitting in one of the rooms in the flooded town beneath the surface. She said, 'You found me' and told me I was running out of time."

"Has anyone else ever spoken to you during one of your dream states?"

"Never. But I thought I saw Rocco Bennett floating facedown on the water the same night. And before that, at the carnival, the wings of some butterflies fluttering near me had me seeing sharks circling a body, red blood seeping into water."

"Sharks represent deeply buried emotions about situations in which you feel threatened. You have a swim meet coming up against the Andover Sharks and you said you felt threatened by Les Carter's diving performance. It could be that the dream-ego is trying to prepare you for that situation in your subconscious mind."

"How did you know we had a meet coming up against Andover?"

"The team schedule is hardly a secret, Theo."

"Right."

I'm being weird.

He straightens the books on the shelf next to my head. "I'm wondering if you'd be opposed to spending a few days at Green Hill with me? An overnight or weekend, perhaps. Just to give you the opportunity to relax in a supported environment, undisturbed. If I could observe and record your dream states via EEG to look for disturbances in your REM and non-REM sleep cycles—"

"I don't think GP would go for that. Plus, you said this was all PTSD."

"It may very well be, but I'm concerned that the additional stress from diving is inhibiting your recovery, for better or worse. Believe me. I've put people under observation for far less. You'd be in capable hands."

"I'll come to Green Hill tomorrow so you can check my blood or whatever, but there's no way I'm asking GP if I can stay at that place. It gives me the creeps."

"Would you prefer to stay here, with me?"

"I don't think GP would go for *that* either."

"Yes. I doubt he would."

It's the first time I've ever been thankful to have GP as an excuse. There was a time I would have said yes to Uncle Phil's offer without hesitation, but now I'm torn. I still need his help with Adderall for diving and understanding the dream states, which puts me in a tough spot. But that doesn't mean I'm looking for a temporary pass to Green Hill.

I reach for the book on his shelf titled *Manifesting Minds.* Uncle Phil makes a quick jerky move like he might stop me, but runs his hand down the front of his shirt instead.

"Theo, why don't you put that down and have a seat so you can tell me more about the room you saw underwater."

I'm too fidgety to sit now. Too interested in why he lurched forward. I pull the book off the shelf, flip it open, and a photo drops to the floor.

I swoop to catch it and stand slowly, staring in disbelief at the missing photo from Coach Porter's trophy case.

"How did you get this?"

"I suppose your mother gave it to me."

"When?"

"I can't be sure," he says. "You seem bothered that it's in my possession."

I see through the question-statement, know he's leading the conversation like a shrink.

"Not bothered. Just curious. I don't have any of Mom's diving photos."

I flip it over, knowing she used to label the backs. The initials SR are written in the lower right corner, but the tail on the R is so small it could be a P for Steve Porter. There's only one way to know for sure if Uncle Phil is lying.

"Can I have it?" I ask.

"Of course. What's mine is yours."

I check my phone for the time so I can make my escape. "This is great, Uncle Phil. Really helpful. But I should probably get going before GP sends out a search party. See you at Green Hill tomorrow?"

"Indeed you will. Try to arrive on schedule. I have a staff member staying late to help me with your blood work."

"Six o'clock. I'll be there. I'd say with bells on, but you know I have an irrational fear of needles."

I DRIVE to the end of the block and pull over. My adrenaline is making my hands numb. I don't know why Uncle Phil would lie to me but something doesn't feel right. Not the photo, or the way Iris's dad treated me, or the newspaper articles.

I reach into my front pocket for my phone to call Iris and the post of the earring I found last Saturday jabs me under my middle fingernail, drawing blood, which is fitting.

"Miss me already?" she answers.

"My uncle had Coach Porter's photo at his house," I blurt.

"Wait. *What?* How? *Why?*"

"You forgot *when,* but I have no freaking idea. He said he got it from my mom. I'm gonna run it by Coach Porter after practice. Are you doing anything tomorrow around six P.M.?"

"Homework. Searching the archives for you. You want to meet me after practice and help me search?"

"I was actually hoping you'd come Green Hill with me?"

"The park or the psychiatric hospital?"

"The hospital. I have an appointment with my Uncle Phil. Not as a shrink. I can explain on the way there, but I'd rather not go alone."

"You want me to lie to my dad so I can spend time with you and the man he thinks is partially responsible for my mom's death?"

"When you put it like that it sounds—"

"Like a terrible idea. I know. Count me in. I've always had a morbid curiosity about that place."

# TWENTY-FOUR

**Lost Move Syndrome:** A psychological condition in which athletes find themselves unable to perform a skill that was previously automatic.

**COACH PORTER** isn't smiling when he calls me over at practice the next day. "What's going on out there? You guys look worse than the JV."

"Honestly, I don't know, Coach. I wasn't paying attention to what the guys were doing. But I can take a step back and help out more if you want."

He stops glaring at me to do a double take. "You feeling all right, Mackey?"

"You mean beside crimping, stomping, or killing the spring on every dive?"

Coach narrow his eyes and pulls me farther away from the team by my elbow. "Normally, I don't mind a little sarcasm, but today I have to ask . . . Are you on something?"

*"What?"* The headline from the article about my mom moves across my mind like a running news ticker. "Did you go into the school newspaper archives?"

*"Archives?* What in the hell are you getting on about, Mackey? I asked you a simple question. Are you on something? I don't have time for this crap. Not from you."

"Nothing. Just the Adderall my uncle prescribes me. Why?"

"Because you're all pupils, like a cat. There's hardly any green left."

"I didn't get a lot of sleep last night and drank a ton of coffee."

(Or Phoenix—*now with even more caffeine.*) "Other than that I'm fine, I swear."

Total lie. I haven't been fine since I left Uncle Phil's last night, and took two Adderalls with that Phoenix before practice.

Coach considers this excuse for half a second. "Maybe it's the lighting. I told maintenance we had bulbs out a week ago. But pull it together out there, would you? We have a meet coming up. You're running out of time."

A clammy sweat rises on my skin. Of all the things Coach could have said—

"You listening to me, Mackey?"

"Yes, Coach."

He blows his silver whistle next to my ear and it pierces my brain with such lobotomy-like sharpness I swear I can taste metal. The guys stop in their tracks and rotate toward the sound like a group of synchronized swimmers.

"You have five minutes to remove your heads from your behinds," he yells. "Or we might as well wrap up practice and forfeit the Andover meet." He turns to me. "Unless you're still having trouble with whatever complex put that bruise on your back, get up there and show me something that will save this sorry excuse for a team on Friday."

Actually, I am. More than trouble but I say, "How about a Reverse 3½ Tuck?"

"307C. Good. Let's see it."

Les is waiting at the base of the ladder. "You want to go first?" he says. "I'm feeling pretty good about the meet."

"Nah. Go ahead, Les. Ladies first."

"Do you enjoy being such a jerk?" he asks.

"Not really. I think you just bring it out in me."

Les expels an irritated puff through his nose, then climbs the ladder and does a perfect repeat of his new dive.

I try to refocus once I'm on the board, but it's tough. I'm sick of having to play nice with him and my frustration surges through me like a live wire. I crack my neck, roll my shoulders, even the chlorine smells too strong today and stings the insides of my nostrils.

I take extra time preparing for my dive, cracking my neck, touching my toes. Coach gives me a puzzled glance from the floor and taps his watch. Time's up. A diver can get points deducted from his scores for hesitating. I move to the end of the board quickly and use my irritation with Les to get the best height of my diving career. I stretch higher than ever while reaching back, one with the air, and grab my knees yanking them to my chest into a tuck, rotating, once, twice, here come's the third. Centripetal force out of control. I should be spotting my entry.

Coach yells, "Kick-out."

But I can't stop spinning.

The water below turns as red as all the anger I've been holding back over the last five days. I'm in my fourth or fifth rotation, heading straight for a gory, blood-filled bath, when I finally pull my shit together and come-out of my tuck to slow down. But it's too late. My arms and legs splay, like a cartoon character falling from a building and I smack the water with the side of my face and body. The last thing I hear is the wicked crack of the impact.

Immeasurable time passes in dreamlike darkness: seeping red blood on the water, sharks circling my limp body, the whip-crack of punishment hitting me over and over. My true vision telescopes in and out of focus. Blurred faces stir around me like a circle of aliens, moving closer to examine my body before retreating. Their muffled voices rise and fall, drifting to me from a different dimension. I shut my eyes to make them go away, and I return to darkness.

Someone says my name.

"Theo. Wake up."

My head jerks to one side with a stinging slap. Sharp ammonia stings my nostrils. My eyelids struggle against substantial weight. I force them open in protest to a flood of light. Coach Porter's wizened face is inches from mine, flashlight primed to blast me again. My teammates form a human halo around him. As my focus returns relief claims their faces. One by one they straighten up and leave my line of vision.

Coach Porter hangs his head, huffing a gust of relief. "He's okay." He puts his hand flat on my chest and pats twice.

I squeeze my eyes to combat the residual haze and the first thing I feel is the throbbing, unilateral pain in my face.

My failed dive rushes back to me.

Fuck. Not again.

I try to sit up and reel.

"Easy," Coach Porter says. "Your nose is bleeding."

Chip rushes up and hands me a water bottle. "Here, have a drink."

"A *drink*? Christ, Langford. He drank half the pool," Coach says. "What happened, Mackey? Weren't your eyes open?"

"I'm not sure. Everything went wonky in the rotation and I lost control."

"Help him up and take him over to the bench," Coach orders.

Chip and Sully link their arms under mine and help me to my feet. "How bad did I mess up my money maker," I ask Sully. "I've got a hot date tonight. Think it'll earn me some extra love?"

"You gotta go Joaquin Phoenix big if you want to impress the ladies."

"I'll keep that in mind for next time."

"There better not be a next time," Coach barks. "You damn near gave me a coronary."

The guys deposit me on the bench where I have to watch Coach put Les-freaking-Carter in charge before taking a seat beside me.

"You're not gonna call my grandfather about this, are you?"

"You lost consciousness, Mackey. I have to fill out an incident report."

"But I'm okay. Still breathing. I think I can get back out

there . . ." I start to stand and Coach puts a hand on my shoulder, pressing me back down.

"Don't even think about it. You're sitting out for the remainder of practice. Stay here while I'll go grab you an ice pack for that cheek. It's already starting to bruise."

Not as much as my ego, watching Les lead the team from my position on the bench.

**AFTER PRACTICE,** I slide into a vinyl chair across from Coach Porter's desk with the sloshy ice pack pressed against my cheek.

"You think you'll be okay to dive Friday?" he asks. "The last thing I want to do is bench you for the Andover meet, but you've had a run of bad dives this week." He slides an incident report across his desk, and I sign the bottom. "Do you know what it's called when a skilled diver suddenly can't perform?"

"Lost move syndrome. But Coach, I don't have LMS. I'm just dealing with a massive amount of sh . . . stuff, and it's messing with my concentration."

"Normally, I'd recommend a sports psychologist. But in your case, it might be better to avoid an LMS blemish on your athletic record. Did your dad have any colleagues you might be able to talk to on the sly?"

Jeezus.

"Yeah. I can think of one."

"Don't look so depressed, Mackey. Once you flush the shit that's bogging you down, it'll be gone forever. It's all up here." Coach taps his temple. "And get some sleep, for goodness' sake. You look awful."

"Yes, Coach."

"Yes, Coach what?"

"I'll get some sleep and make sure that shit gets flushed before the meet."

I don't bother reminding Coach what happens when you have so much shit it clogs the pipes. *That shit* usually returns with a vengeance.

I place the photo I found at Uncle Phil's house on his desk as casually as possible while he searches for an incident report.

"Isn't this the photo that went missing from your case? It was on the floor under your desk." It's only a half-lie. I check the clock on his wall, playing it cool, but my right leg is jittering.

"I'll be doggoned." He flips it over. "I searched the whole room for this."

"Guess it took a younger eye." I give him a lopsided grin hoping he'll change his mind about calling GP. Because I am a strong finisher. I got this. Something's just off with me.

*And with Uncle Phil* since it's clear he had Coach Porter's photo.

"Don't get smart, Mackey, or I'll drag you back out to the pool and show you what that dive is supposed to look like."

"Yes, Coach."

I leave the swim complex late to pick up Iris and paranoid as hell about what's happening to me, in and out of the pool.

I'm halfway to the exit door when I hear, "Theo. Hey, Theo! Wait up."

I pinch the bridge of my nose before turning around. Les couldn't have picked a worse time to come at me.

"I'm glad I caught you," Les says then notices my cheek. "Wow. That looks bad. Nothing gives a bitch slap quite like water. But hey, I was thinking—if you wanted—we could do some extra training together before the weekend. I have some stuff I've been meaning to talk to you about. Maybe we could—"

Miles skidders around the corner, but stops short when he sees Les and me talking.

"What do *you* want?" I ask, feeling a quick flare of anger.

"I was trying to catch up to my ride," Miles says. "Excuse me for breathing, Captain Smackypants."

"Jesus, Miles," Les says, looking over his shoulder. "Meet me at my car. I'm almost done here."

Miles huffs and leaves, but the sound of his footsteps stop too soon. He's listening, but I don't care.

"What I was saying," Les continues, "was maybe we could grab a cup of coffee and—"

"I appreciate the offer, Les. But my routine and schedule are set."

"I know. Mine are too. I'd have to squeeze it in. But I thought we should have each other's backs. I learned some stuff at Masters that I'd like to talk to you about. Especially after I heard about your smack on Monarch Night."

My jaw clenches. "Listen, I think it's cool you went to Masters; it's great for the team. But what you learned there applies to your skills. Not mine. Just because we have to work together on the sociology project doesn't mean I want or need your help with diving. I got this."

"Why do you always snub me?" he asks earnestly. "Is it because of what happened at regionals last year? I had the flu." He tips his head after a pause like he just caught on. "Is it because I told Coach I want to go to Stanford?"

Yes and no. I can't believe how good he is at pretending.

"I just like to keep my private training—private."

"I get that. And it's not like I don't know what you say behind my back. Les is *less*." He gives a quick shrug. "But I'm not less, Mackey. I've been loyal to this team and a little more appreciation and support from you, as captain, might be nice. Especially since Coach Porter thinks it could be this season's big take."

Jeezus.

I rub my eyebrow to keep from losing my shit.

"Les is less is a *joke*," I tell him. "A play on words. If your last name were Moore, I'd do the same thing. But you're right. Your one new dive is killer. I'm sure the Stanford scouts will be all over it. But right now, I've got somewhere to be. So if there's anything else you need to tell me, just find another article and leave it on my truck. So far, that's been working for you. Messages received. Loud and clear."

"What are you talking about?"

"Don't play dumb, Les. It's not helping your game."

"Whatever you say, Mackey. Don't say I didn't try."

He makes no additional apologies before lumbering away and the restraint it takes to not punch the nearest locker kills me.

# TWENTY-FIVE

**Free Position:** A combination of straight, pike, and tuck positions used only in twisting dives where multiple positions are required during different parts of a dive.

IF GREEN Hill were capable of generating sound it would be the lowest tone audible by human ears—a warning knell. And its flavor would be ash. Uncle Phil once told me it was an architectural legacy bequeathed to Ellis Hollow by its founders, which must account for the sharp intake of breath I hear from Iris as we pull closer. But awe is nowhere close to the feeling this place gives me.

She sticks her head out the passenger window, rotating at an extreme angle to get a better look at the clock tower whose time is permanently frozen at 6:50. Day or night is anyone's guess.

Iris jumps out of my truck the second we're parked to marvel at the imposing stone building. "Look at the portico."

"The porta-what?"

"The columns supporting that brick overhang."

"Looks like a giant mousetrap."

"Not to me. I'm torn between majoring in journalism or architecture," she explains. "I love to relay people's stories, but buildings also fascinate me because they tell stories too. Etchings in cement, leaded windows. Victorian-Gothic. They don't design public structures like this anymore."

"Don't get too excited, Iris. It's still a mental hospital. Once we check in, we might not check out." I take her hand and lead us up the stairs under the portico.

Heavy medicinal air greets us as soon as we open the heavy wooden doors. I squeeze her fingers involuntarily.

"You really hate needles that much?" She studies my face like one of her cards.

"More. My dad told me all people are born with only two innate fears. Falling and loud sounds. I'm almost positive I was born with three."

We approach a rail-thin receptionist with skin as transparent as a jellyfish. "I'm Theo Mackey. I'm here to see Dr. Maddox."

She stares at me blankly for too long before checking the appointment calendar. "Do you happen to know whether we have all your current information on file?" she asks, her tone freakishly robotic. She doesn't wait for me to answer before handing me a clipboard with shaky hands. "You should probably fill out the intake forms anyway."

"That's probably not necessary. I'm not a patient. Dr. Maddox is my uncle."

"Oh." Her eyelids flutter, finally flashing a tangible emotion. "I'll let him know you're here right away." She falters, jerking back and forth like a broken windup doll deciding which way she should go. "You can take a seat in the lobby."

Iris tugs me toward the waiting area. "Does she seem okay to you?"

"They probably have patients work the front desk as part of their therapy."

"She reminds me of the doppelganger mom from *Coraline*. The Other Mother."

"I only saw the movie trailer. But I'll take your word for it."

Iris crosses and uncrosses her legs while we wait, swinging her foot as she flips through psychology journals. I can't stop glancing at her dark hair, or the thick fringe of lashes casting spidery shadows on her cheek as she reads. I swallow nervously and keep my hands on my lap, fingers laced, trying to steady my pulse under the deep nagging feeling that bringing her here may have been selfish.

The receptionist reappears, flitting her eyes around the room like she's watching a fly that never lands. "Sorry about the wait. An orderly will be here shortly to escort you. Sorry about that."

"Is it me or is she a nervous wreck?"

"No, I caught it too."

A minute later a guy the size of a Mack truck enters the lobby. "You Theo?" His baritone voice booms through the chilly reception area.

I stand, facing the twenty something orderly who looks official enough in his green scrubs, despite the tattoos across his knuckles that read GAME OVER. I'd hate to be the patient that pisses him off. One punch and your eyelids would probably read K.O.

"Come with me. Dr. Maddox asked me to put you in room two-twelve."

We start following him to a door with a wired rectangular window, and he says, "So you're Sophia's kid, huh? What was it like growing up around shrinks?" He stops abruptly when he notices Iris walking quietly beside me. "I don't have clearance for both of you. Snow White's gonna have to wait in the lobby."

Iris looks at me, eyes wide.

"I'm not leaving her out there with the creepy mom from *Coraline.*"

The orderly fixes me with a stare, unsure how to handle his boss's nephew, so I add, "And since you asked, growing up with shrinks sucked. Do something right, get psychoanalyzed. Do something wrong, it's your mom's fault."

"Hmph. I bet. What's with the shiner? You mouth off to someone?"

"Springboard diving mishap."

"An athlete. That makes sense." He takes a moment to reassess Iris's threat level. "Did you bring a handbag with you, princess?"

She shakes her head. "I left it in the car."

"Anything in your pockets?"

As she turns her pockets inside out he gives her the once-over like a creeper. Iris shows him a cherry lip gloss and Life Savers and he flicks her a suggestive grin.

"You look like you could do more good than harm with those, Snow White. Let's go."

He swipes a badge that opens the door to the wards.

"Are you drawing my blood today?" I ask. Because this guy looks like he'd crush the needle, and my bones, in his club-like hands.

"Nope. I'm damage control." The door clicks behind us and locks with a series of beeps.

Iris looks around the hallway like she's curious where all the doors lead. I know exactly how she feels, even if the checkered linoleum floor, dull yellow cement walls, and curved ceiling aren't what I saw in my dream state.

"Still glad you came?" I ask, swaying into her.

She nods then leans closer and takes my hand when a patient shuffling toward us starts muttering to herself. The elderly woman stops infront of Iris and tilts her head.

"How you came back?" she asks in a thick European accent. "They say you dead."

"What are *you* doing up here?" The troll-like orderly asks her. "That's the bigger question." He tries to grab her arm but she jerks away faster than I imagined possible for someone her age.

"I curse you." She spits at him, waving a crooked finger. "*Te ćernol ćo mas pa tu!* The flesh shall rot off you."

The orderly picks up the walkie-talkie on his hip. "Valentina is loose on two again. Come round her up."

The receiver crackles before a male voice on the other end whines, "You-know-who keeps letting her out. Be right there."

"I've never been here before," Iris tells the patient kindly. "You must have me confused with someone else."

"No. It's you. The gypsy girl. Just like the ones they run from

211

my village. You see things. I know. Leave this place before it's too late." The woman shuffles away, murmuring unintelligibly in a foreign language.

"She's Romanian," Iris whispers.

"She's a pain in the ass," the orderly replies, leading us along.

I watch the way Iris looks at every door with her brow furrowed. She scans left and right then over her shoulder to take in one or two she's missed along the way, analyzing some bit of information about the rooms.

"If this is the first floor," she asks openly, "why are all the rooms labeled in the two hundreds?"

"Observant little thing, aren't you?" The orderly scans Iris in a way I don't like again. "The floor beneath us is ward one. It's where Dr. Maddox and his team do research."

"What kind of research?" Iris asks. "Not on animals, I hope."

"That depends on your definition of animal."

Iris scowls disapprovingly.

"See this?" he says, showing Iris the employee access badge attached to a retractable clip. He extends it all the way out for her. "Floors two through seven only. The research lab requires a backstage pass, and I'm no VIP. But maybe your boyfriend here can fill you in on the secret workings of Dr. Maddox." Iris passes the badge to me and I read his name: Derek Smalls.

A serious misnomer, considering his size.

Derek opens room 212 for us. "I'd say you two lovebirds have ten minutes tops before the nurse shows up. Don't do anything I wouldn't do."

Total creeper.

We step inside the empty exam room and Derek closes the door. There's a phlebotomist's chair, an examination table, cabinets. Everything you'd expect to find in a physician's office. Plus a phrenology model, which is straight-up shrink.

Iris slinks through the room opening drawers and cabinets.

"What are you hoping to find?"

"I don't know," she says. "This whole place feels like a mystery. It's so historic. Can't you feel it?"

"A little. But it's being overpowered by my desire to leave."

There's a soft rap on the door. Universal hospital code for: *are you decent?*

"Yep," I say. "Come on in."

Iris hops onto the examination table and plays with the velcro blood pressure cuff.

A tall nurse with dark hair slicked into a tight bun enters and makes brief eye contact. She gives Iris a quick scan before setting up her tray. "Who's this?"

"She's my um . . ."

"Friend-slash date-slash-project partner," Iris explains.

That sums it up, I guess.

The nurse slides translucent amber eyeglasses down her nose, pouting burgundy lips as she considers the predicament that is Iris, sitting cross-legged and doe-eyed on the examination table.

"Bringing a guest isn't usually allowed. But apparently we're bending a few rules around here lately." She flips my chart open. "I see here you're not a fan of needles."

"I'm not a fan of a lot of things. Needles are just way up there on the list."

The nurse puts my chart on the examination table next to Iris and pulls three collection tubes from her pocket.

"My uncle said he only needed one vial."

"The order says three."

"What else is he checking if one was for my liver panel?"

"You'd have to ask Dr. Maddox that question," she says. "I'm not at liberty to say." She snaps a pair of latex gloves over her hands. "I'll try to make this quick and painless. You just sit back and let me take care of you, 'kay, darlin'? Straighten your arm and make a fist."

I suck in a breath. It's the *'kay, darlin'* that throws me, even more than the needle in her hand. The hint of Southern accent detectable in those two words. I could swear I've heard someone say that exact phrase to me with the same Southern regionalism before.

She swabs the inside of my elbow with alcohol and looks at me, really looks at me this time, and her haloed green-hazel eyes take me by surprise. The catlike luminescence is unnatural.

"Are you wearing contacts?" I ask.

She gives me a flimsy smile and ties a rubber tourniquet around my bicep that becomes uncomfortably tight within seconds. "A lady never reveals her secrets. Isn't that right?" She hastens a glance at Iris.

"It's true," Iris agrees, pumping the blood pressure cuff on her own arm. "We're all about smoke and mirrors."

"Have we met before?" I ask, watching my largest vein rise to the surface like an eel. "You seem crazy familiar to me. Your accent."

"I don't believe so." The nurse clears her throat and taps my vein. "Relax your hand, darlin,' so I can insert the needle. If that part bothers you, look away."

I turn my head when the cold syringe is resting against my skin, ready to break the surface. I meet Iris's eyes and hold her gaze until—

"It's just a little pinch," the nurse says.

My seat turns cold as metal when the needle slips into my vein. *Just a little pinch—*


*"It's okay. You're safe."*

*I didn't know who or what I was safe from until my butt plunked down on a slab of freezing metal and I punched away the blankets. A woman dressed in official blue was leaning away to avoid being struck. When I stopped swinging she helped me rewrap the blank around my shoulders.*

214

I looked past her and saw a burly fireman jogging away in the snow. He must have been the one who carried me outside. I stared at the neon-yellow stripes stretching across the back of his canvas coat as he rushed back toward our house.

The woman in blue turned my chin to look me in the eyes. And for a minute, it felt like we were alone inside a snow globe. "You're okay," she said. "There's been a fire. I need to take a listen to your lungs, 'kay?" She had traces of a Southern accent and spoke slowly.

She pulled out a stethoscope while I stared at her smooth, brown skin. "Are you a nurse?"

"I'm a paramedic. But I'm gonna be a nurse real soon." She listened to my chest as I watched flames rise behind her on the hill. Shooting out of the windows, licking the yellow siding, threatening to swallow our house whole. A dozen firefighters were working on putting out the fire with powerful sprays of water extending from mile-long hoses being dragged through the snow. But even I could tell they were fighting a losing battle. I gaped at the blaze, mesmerized, until a blast of heat reached us on a gust of wind and snapped me to attention.

Cameras flashed behind me. I turned my head to see a few news camera crews.

"I don't want my picture taken," I shouted. "Where are my parents?"

"I don't know," the paramedic answered. "Just sit back and let me take care of you, 'kay, darlin'?" She gave me a forced smile and clamped a tiny machine on my index finger. A blue light began blinking on the top, reading something I didn't care about. All I wanted to know was that my parents were safe.

I stretched my neck to look over her shoulder, my heart beating fast.

"I'm a little dizzy."

The paramedic pulled a purple juice box from a cooler and unwrapped the straw. "Drink this." She nudged the drink box toward me, her eyes stern. "Otherwise I have to put it in your arm. Doctor's orders." She pointed to a plastic pouch hanging in the truck, filled with clear liquid. I was about to take a sip of juice when I saw Uncle Phil marching toward us.

I ripped the little machine off my finger and dashed forward, throwing the juice box on the ground.

"Where are my parents?" I tried to dash around Uncle Phil, but he held me back by the arm. "Where's Mom?"

"I don't know. They'll find them."

"Mom!" I yelled for her but my voice cracked and I coughed up a lung. I tried to jerk out of his grasp. "Let me go! I'll find her myself. This is all my fault."

"Do it," Uncle Phil hissed.

But he never let me go. He wasn't giving permission to me.

I turned my head as the paramedic said, "It's just a little pinch," piercing the skin on my upper arm with a needle.

I winced. "What was that?"

She hurried away without answering as a warm tingle spread over me from limb to limb. Her form shrinking as my eyes grew heavier and I swayed on my feet. Someone picked me up and I relaxed my head on their shoulder.

"I'm too big to be carried."

"Take it easy, son."

"Dad?" I whispered.

"That's right. Get some rest. Everything is going to be fine."


"YOU DOING okay?" The nurse's voice jolts me back to the present.

We have met before. She's the paramedic who was working the night of the fire. Same brown skin, same vocal distinctions. My fear of needles isn't so irrational after all. I blink my overly dry eyes and I replay her words. "You just sit back and let me take care of you, 'kay, darlin'?" Uncle Phil hissed "Do it" to her, not me. And she injected me with something that made me sleepy.

I stare at the nurse and imagine her less refined, dressed in navy blue, without the colored contacts that hide her brown eyes. Her hair is pulled back, same as that night. Only this time, she's missing an earring, and the one still in place is a diamond stud in the shape of a triangle, just like Mom's.

What the—

My throat tightens. "Were you at my Uncle Phil's house last Saturday?"

She nods. "I was dropping off a few things."

Taking a few things, too, I think.

I stop myself from demanding why she's wearing my mom's earring by fixating on the syringe in my arm. I freaking knew it was weird to see her at his house more than once. He lied. The cleaning crew at Uncle Phil's didn't miss vacuuming the earring up. He gave them to her. Unless she stole them. Mom was always leaving stuff there.

She twists the first collection tube loose and rocks the dark blood back and forth to incorporate the contents before placing it on a metal rolling cart for safekeeping. I tense, averting my eyes, as she inserts the second tube. My pulse is racing, causing my blood to gush into the tube faster.

"Relax." Her voice is smooth as coffee with cream.

There something else about her, scratching at the deepest recesses of my mind. I look for an access badge similar to the one Derek the orderly was wearing. There isn't one, at least not visible. I adjust my position on the hard seat and duck my head, but she doesn't catch my eye again.

I try a different tack. "I just realized I didn't introduce you to my new friend-slash-date-slash-project partner. Must be the needle. Or the loss of blood. This is Iris."

"Nice to meet you, Iris," she says politely but keeps her eyes on task.

I clench my jaw to keep from scowling. "So, how long have you been working here with Uncle Phil?"

"A few years."

"So what's that, three? Four?"

"Mm-hmm." She rubs my arm with her free hand. "Try not to clench your fist. We're almost done."

Most professionals would have introduced themselves. Not that we bothered to ask the orderly when he escorted us to the room, but we saw it on his badge.

I take a deep breath in through my nose and watch her twist out the second tube. "Where did you work before Green Hill? Have you always been a nurse?"

"No. I had a few jobs before this." She pulls out the second tube and inserts the third. "What about you? Do you have a part-time job after school?"

"My schedule doesn't leave much time for anything but—" I stiffen and clench my fist again "—I springboard diving."

Holy shit.

I didn't recognize her from the team photo because we didn't meet the night of the fire. Not officially. Why the hell would we while the house was burning down? My blood starts gushing into the tube. What the hell does this nurse, this paramedic-slash-springboard-diver, have to do with my mom?

"Dr. Maddox mentioned you were a diver," she says. "The team captain. Relax your arm. Last one."

Sweat leaches from my pores as I assess her build: broad shoulders, muscular arms, small waist. A body built by hours of training. She releases the tourniquet on my arm in one swift move, allowing blood to rush back to my brain.

"It didn't go so well for me at practice today," I tell her. "Sometimes the pool likes to give you a slap to remind you of your place in the universe. Know what I mean?"

"Sometimes the universe likes to give you a slap without a pool," she says. "Luckily, small surface wounds heal easily."

She removes the last tube and places a wad of gauze over the needle before sliding it from my arm. She adheres a strip of surgical tape over a folded square of gauze and drops the last collection tube in her pocket.

"All done. Bend your elbow. That wasn't so bad, was it?"

"Not at all. I'll make sure to tell my uncle what a great job you did. What did you say your name was?"

Her face folds into an expressionless mask. "L . . . anne."

"L'anne," Iris says. "That's different. Is it an old family name? French? You've got a little bit of a Creole accent."

"It's Anne. Just Anne," she says, correcting herself. "My family moved here from New Orleans when I was in grade school." She peels off her latex gloves, then grabs my chart on her way to the door. "Dr. Maddox wants to see you before you leave. I'll send Derek to escort you and get you something to drink while you wait. Doctor's orders."

I reel from the increasing similarities and go for a final test. "Do you have any juice boxes?" I ask. "Another nurse gave me a purple juice box once. Before she stuck me with a needle, though not after."

She stops dead in her tracks, hand resting on the door handle. I take the opportunity to pull out Mom's earring.

"Oh hey, did you drop this?"

She turns and I hold up the diamond stud. The pause in her expression and movements is undeniable when she sees the earring. She turns slowly to face me and the mask is off.

I hold up the diamond stud. "Is this yours?"

"I've been wondering where that went to." She tugs her earlobe. "Funny. I haven't been in this room for weeks."

"Sometimes missing things pop up when you least expect it."

"That's true," she says. "But I should probably be more careful. Stay put while I go hunt down Derek and that juice box."

# TWENTY-SIX

**Late:** Movement by a diver that is not made in time to obtain the intended objective.

**I BOLT** from the chair the minute she leaves and charge the door. "We need to get out of here before she comes back with that juice box."

Iris wraps her hand around my wrist to keep me from walking out. "What's going on? Why were you drilling that nurse with questions? You went totally gray. And not because she was drawing your blood."

"I think that nurse is Luanne Cole."

"From the photo in the newspaper?"

"The same photo that was missing from Coach Porter's trophy case. Did you hear the way she said her name? L'anne."

"How did you figure it out?"

"It's a long story. The short version is a bunch of stuff has been coming back to me in bits and flashes. Luanne Cole isn't just some nurse or springboard diver that competed against my mom. I think she was the paramedic on duty the night my house burned down. While she was drawing my blood I had a flashback of her injecting something into my arm the night of the fire that made me sleepy. And my uncle was the one who told her to do it."

"They sedated you? Were you freaking out or something?"

"A little. But none of that explains why Les Carter, of all people, would leave me those articles."

"It doesn't explain why your uncle had the team photo from Coach Porter's trophy case either."

"Exactly. So I want to go out to my truck and get the article to see if I'm right before I have to go talk to him."

"Okay," Iris says. "Let's go."

I crack the door open, peek into the hallway, and extend my hand to Iris. "Nobody's coming."

We slink down the hallway quickly, looking for Derek over our shoulders, but when we reach the end we find the exit door locked. There isn't even a handle. Swipe card only.

"Shit. We're trapped."

"Mousetrapped," Iris whispers. "Like your card reading. The Cat and Mouse."

"You think that's what this is?"

"You don't?" she asks, completely serious. "The cards don't mean anything unless you pay attention to the signs."

"I don't know. But I'll keep it in mind from now on." I peer down the hallway. "Any minute now, Derek will be coming back for us. Maybe we can persuade him to let us back out for a little while."

We're fifty paces from reentering room 212 when Derek exits another patient's room and intercepts us.

"What are you two doing wandering the hallways?"

"I was starving," I say. "I thought there might be a snack machine near the lobby. It felt like that nurse took a gallon of my blood."

Derek presses his tongue around the inside of his cheek then hands me a small carton of orange juice. "This should do the trick." He glances at a camera mounted on the ceiling before opening the door for us. I didn't think about there being surveillance.

"Why don't you step back into my office, junior, so we can talk." He takes a seat in the phlebotomist's chair and clasps his hands behind his head. A mermaid tattoo dances across his right bicep as the muscle flexes. "Where were you two going, really? Teen ward? Research facility to rescue *the animals?*"

"Outside," I say. "I was hoping to get some air before I had to deal with my uncle's psychobabble. Like I said, growing up around people who are always trying to get inside your head sucks. Makes you paranoid."

Derek chuckles. "Especially if you're not telling them the truth, junior. But here's a news flash. Trust issues and paranoia are the reason half the patients are holed up in this place."

"You think you can cut us loose for twenty minutes?"

"I'm not supposed to let you off the ward."

"I swear we'll come back so fast you'll barely notice we were gone."

Derek flicks his eyes to Iris and licks his bottom lip. "We might be able to work something out. What's twenty minutes of freedom worth to you?"

"Seriously?" I can't believe this guy is going for a shakedown.

"Maybe I read you wrong, junior. I assumed what you really wanted was to hit your car and I dunno"—Derek makes a double clicking sound inside his cheek—"I know what I'd be thinking about doing with Snow White if I had twenty minutes to kill."

Iris's face is a mix of shock and fascination. I don't know whether to be turned on or worried.

"How much are we talking about?" she asks, joining in the negotiations. "Would twenty bucks do it?"

"Twenty bucks and Snow White shows me her tits for more than a flash." Derek rakes his eyes over Iris, but keeps the negotiation going with me like I'm her pimp.

"Leave her out of this and I'll give you forty bucks if you let us borrow your badge so we can reenter the building on our own." I open my wallet and riffle through the contents. I have sixty bucks and a free movie pass to my name.

"Fifty bucks for Snow White's tits *and* the badge. Take it or leave it."

"I'll leave it," I say. "And stop looking at her like that. Jeezus."

"Fifty bucks, huh?" Iris grabs my wallet. She removes two twenties and a ten from her back pocket and winks at me. I hope that means she's calling his bluff.

Derek's eyes glint with smug victory. "Remember, Snow, more than a flash or no dice."

"Fine." Iris keeps the bills clenched in her hand. "Give me the badge first?"

Derek digs into his front pocket, ignoring me now that bargaining with Iris has become more interesting. "I just happen to have an extra one right here, with full VIP access." He hands the badge to Iris, but doesn't let go.

"One last thing," Iris says, holding the extra badge in a tug-of-war. "What can you tell us about the nurse who drew Theo's blood today?"

"Psht. Easy." Derek releases the card. "Luanne Cole is Dr. Maddox's favorite pet. She's part of his research team and does whatever he says. Secretly, I get the feeling he hates her. The guy's not too big with the emotions if you haven't noticed, but he seems to prefer women with a little fight in them. He'd get a kick out of you, Snow, that's for sure."

*Fuuuccck.* I lean into the examination table as a wave of nausea runs chills over my body. I was right.

"Now you really do look like you need some air," Iris says.

More than she knows.

"Show 'em if you got 'em," Derek says. He relaxes in the chair, one hand resting on his lap near his crotch. If he touches himself, I swear to God . . .

"Back off, Derek. How about I show you *my tits* and give you sixty bucks for the badge? I just need to get some air. You're being a dick."

"Comments like that are the real reason guys like you get a black eye. Eighty. You're not that pretty, junior."

"Sixty," Iris says. "And we won't tell your employer what happened here."

"Well, well, well. Looks like I read you right from the jump, princess. Deal."

Iris trades out the money in my wallet and slaps the bills into Derek's palm with a satisfied grin. He wraps his huge hand around her wrist and pulls her close enough to kiss and my hackles go up. I'm primed to pounce if I have to, knowing he'd fucking clobber me.

"Some other time, eh, Snow?" he says.

Iris jerks her hand from his grasp. "In your dreams, Shrek. And the name isn't Snow White or princess; it's French Fry."

Derek smirks with amusement and shoves the cash into his front pocket. "Go left to the exit and keep your eye on the sky. When the light's flashing on the camera Big Brother is watching."

This time, we make it outside in less than five minutes. I squeeze my eyes shut and inhale, purging my nostrils of the hospital's ancient, medicinal stench, never feeling this reborn outside of the water. I don't know whether to bolt or go ask Uncle Phil what's up. Derek confirmed that nurse was Luanne Cole, but I still want another look at the article in my truck.

I take a step forward, Iris's hand in mine, but she doesn't budge.

She's riveted in place, mouth gaping like she just stepped into something from *The Twilight Zone* instead of the neglected grounds behind the hospital.

"Holy cow, Theo, Do you know what this place is?" Her face is pure fascination as she shuffles her feet over the wet lawn. She stops to kick into a spot with the toe of a brown lace-up boot, then kneels and unearths a wet clump of dirt, still rooted with grass. "Look."

A rectangular stone is embedded in the ground with the number 167 carved into its surface. "Is that a mile marker?"

Iris looks at me with huge eyes. "It's a *grave* marker. This is Ward Hill Cemetery. I overheard my parents talking about it once. Mount Pleasant and Ward Hill Cemetery are both run by the state. A few years ago they gave my dad the added responsibility of burying patients on these grounds that didn't have families to claim the bodies. There were so many my parents were wondering if they'd have to start cremating bodies once they ran out of space."

"How many are there?" I kick at the ground a few feet away, looking for another grave.

"Hundreds. Maybe thousands, according to my parents."

Jeezus.

"They buried them like hamsters in shoe boxes and your dad was okay with that?"

"Not at all. He was furious. But what could he do?" Iris tosses the clump of dirt, then stands, brushing her hands on her shirt. "It's his job."

I wonder what else Derek the orderly does for his state job. Uncle Phil said everyone that works for him has to get their hands dirty. Derek seems like the kind of guy that would enjoy that, literally and figuratively.

"You weren't really gonna show Derek your . . ." I motion toward her chest. "Were you?"

"Not if I could help it. I was just trying to sweeten the deal for you so we could call his bluff."

"Pretty dangerous bluff."

"I know that, Theo. And Derek Smalls is probably the exception to what I'm about to say—another one of my philosophies—but most people aren't who they appear to be on the surface. Everybody has something they're dealing with or feel they need to hide from people. It was obvious to me that whatever got under your skin in there is a big deal, and I'm guessing it has nothing to do with the Theo you let people see at school. It's something you keep hidden."

Somewhere deep inside my sense of self-preservation deflates. "Trust me, Iris. If you were me you'd keep some stuff hidden too."

# TWENTY-SEVEN

**Approach:** Three or more steps forward to the end of the board before hurdle and take-off.

"**DOES IT** have something to do with Luanne Cole?"

"Yes and no."

"You can trust me, Theo. We're partners, remember? Big Mack and French Fry."

"I do trust you. It's not every day a girl commits to giving a peep show on my behalf." I give her a lopsided grin.

"I know. I was on the verge of pulling out the big guns." Iris glances at her chest. "Medium guns. A girl can only work with what she's got."

"You're—they're—um . . ." Heat rises to my ears.

Iris smirks "It's okay, Theo. I can appreciate where you were going with that."

I rub the back of my neck. "How about we get that article from my truck and I tell you the long version?"

"Sounds good."

We walk over markers for hundreds of graves, people forgotten or abandoned by their families, on the way to Bumblebee, and I think about what a jerk I am for not visiting my parents' graves. I chew the inside of my cheek raw as I search for the right lead-up before diving straight into my most painful memory.

And then I chuck it. I just let it rip. Starting with the night our house burned to the ground in front of my eyes with my mom trapped inside.

I describe how the flames shot through the darkened windows turning our house into a demonic jack-o'-lantern against the midnight sky. Thirteen-year-old me being carried out by a fireman, then watching him return to the blaze in a heavy coat with neon stripes. Luanne the paramedic who took my vital signs, gave me a juice box, and then injected me with something that made me sleep for hours. The Southern accent I heard today when she said *'kay* and *darlin'* that tripped extras in my memory. I describe her uniform, the sirens and flashing cameras, the gusts of heat, smoke, even cold. And then I confess to the guilt I feel over having a grandfather who was the Ellis Hollow fire chief but knows nothing about the box of matches I lit that night. At least as far as I can tell since we've read the article.

By the time we get to Bumblebee I'm segueing into the affair that caused the fallout between my dad and Uncle Phil, and how dumb I was to think it was because of me. I fill her in on the night terrors that started after the fire and how my dad had to call on Uncle Phil to help, even when they weren't on speaking terms. I even reveal a few things about the dream states and freak-outs that are making me smack, including a repeat description of the girl with dark hair and tattoos who showed me it was okay to jump.

Iris listens through all of it without asking questions.

I pull the article out of my practice duffle and hand it to her without looking myself. She doesn't look as horrified as I thought she would. She looks sad. For me. And this time, I accept the pity being offered without feeling ashamed. Because maybe everything isn't always as it seems.

I rip off the tape and gauze stuck to my inner elbow and stare at the puncture. "I keep trying to convince myself the entire night was a dream—a nightmare—but that won't justify what I did, or fill the hole that fire left in my life. And I think holding all of that in was making me lose my grip."

Iris touches the swollen side of my face where I hit the water, her eyes red-rimmed. Then she pulls me in for a hug so tight and unexpected I worry my protective shell might crack. I haven't cried since my mom died. I won't. Guilt tells me I'm not allowed. I focus on the scent of her hair. Floral and minty, same as the beach towel she gave me on Monarch Night, and it helps clear away the darkness that's been swirling in me as grotesque as the bruise on my back that everyone can see.

She pulls away and takes my hand, folding and unfolding my fingers like she's counting my options until she's only flipping my index finger. Down to one.

"I think you should go in there and ask your uncle why he had that nurse drug you. Or better yet why that nurse was being so sketchy."

I shake my head, lips pressed tight.

"Why not?"

"Because I found that earring I gave her at Uncle Phil's house. It used to belong to my mom. You heard Derek say Luanne was my uncle's favorite pet. If he gave them to her, then maybe they're both lying, about something. It might be better to ask my grandfather about it first. He knows the most about what happened during the fire."

"So what's your plan? You're not thinking of taking off, are you?"

"No. I want to go back in there and feel him out."

"Okay. Good. I think you should. Is there anything I can I do to help?"

"Just keep looking through the archives for a follow-up article about my mom's suspension." I check the time on my phone. "Shit. We have to get back."

We race to the building and let ourselves inside. Derek is pacing the floor in exam room 212, biting his nails.

"You gotta be kidding me," he moans. "I almost came look-ing for you two. Dr. Maddox called five minutes ago, asking about the holdup."

"What did you tell him?"

"That I went to the kitchen to get you a bagel because you felt sick after having your blood drawn."

"Did he buy it?"

"Hard to tell. He paused for a long time, then told me to move you along. So move along, junior." He flaps his hand to rush us through the door and we follow him to the fifth floor where Uncle Phil and his staff have offices. He waits while I sign in at the receptionist desk.

"Dr. Maddox is the third door down on the left." He gives Iris a wink. "Pleasure doing business with you, French Fry. Come back real soon."

"Don't count on it, Shrek," Iris says.

He turns with a chuckle and leaves through the stairwell.

Iris and I only take a few steps before Uncle Phil's voice spills into the hallway from his office. I hold my index finger over my lips, hoping he's with Luanne, then take Iris by the hand and inch us closer to the open door.

Uncle Phil says, "How is this time different?"

"She nearly escaped our secure ward," a man with a nasal voice replies. "She even set one of her favorite cohorts loose to prove her beliefs. They took a new orderly down in the process, which is neither here nor there. The real news is that under a measurable amount of prodding our inpatient divulged a few things that suggest she may be developing a variation in her abil-ity we didn't anticipate, one that further connects her to the out-patient in our study. A form of remote messaging."

There's a pause that makes me hold my breath.

"I have some recent revelations to add to that discovery, as well. I'll come find you when I through here," Uncle Phil says. "Let's increase her dosage of Philomax. In the last month alone the drug has proved its ability to raise levels of perception. If we see another jump we'll know we're really onto something."

Iris is squeezing my arm so hard her nails are biting into my skin through my shirt.

"I'll do that then," the other doctor says. "But only slightly. We don't want to eradicate our progress by having her cross over into phantasm."

"In the meantime, I'll see what else I can squeeze out of our outpatient."

The other doctor shows his rat-like face a moment later, his steps arresting when his beady eyes land on Iris and me, caught in the act of eavesdropping. My choices are to make an excuse or turn and leave. But we don't have to do either because he tugs an earlobe and nods nervously at us then walks away with his eyes on the floor. When he reaches the exit door, he turns his head to consider Iris and me one more time before leaving.

Untimely awkward detection averted.

Uncle Phil's voice stops me from taking my next step forward.

"Sorry about the intrusion," he says. "Dr. Aldridge may be brilliant, but he lacks boundaries when it comes to our research. You were saying?"

"I was saying, your nephew thought he recognized me when I drew his blood."

Luanne was in the room the whole time. I squeeze Iris's hand, wondering if her heart is beating as hard as mine.

"The boy merely asked for some juice. Perhaps to deflect his attention from the needle you were putting in his arm; I can't be sure."

"He asked specifically for a *purple juice box*," Luanne injects. "After asking questions about my contact lenses and my life before Green Hill. I hope sending me in there wasn't your way of testing your theories. I didn't sign up to be a pawn in your memory game."

"Didn't you?" Uncle Phil snaps. "Maybe I can refresh *your* memory. You were offered a position as head research RN, knowing who my patients were, and jumped at the opportunity. Not to mention the handsome salary. Do I have cause for concern here as your employer? This is the second time your past has influenced your judgment. Theo was bound to meet you, eventually. But I can't help but wonder now, based on your wary expression, if I suddenly strike you as a man who hasn't thought through his endgame."

There's another pause in the conversation that lasts three blinks.

"Not usually. But you might want to keep a closer eye on your little rook. I felt something from him."

"You *felt* something?" Uncle Phil makes a sound like a laugh, a chortle. "The patients must be rubbing off on you. Theo's questions sound like standard abreaction. I am the leading authority on posthypnotic amnesia and can assure you any memories that are resurfacing are intentional on my part. Cancellation of hypnotic assignment is specific to certain triggers."

*Triggers. Like something in a person's mind palace?* Jeezus. Chip was right.

"His simple questions may have yielded simpler answers had you handled them more deftly," Uncle Phil adds. "Instead of panicking like a schoolgirl."

"I think you're underestimating that kid. He's sharper than any tack I've ever seen. And the girl he brought with him was just as wily."

"Enough," Uncle Phil says tersely. "Perhaps it's you whom I've underestimated. I have Theo under excellent care and control. As for the girl who accompanied him here today, that's another matter entirely. One I intend to deal with separately and resourcefully. Now, if you don't mind, I am expecting him to enter this office any minute. And I believe you have the afternoon rigmarole to oversee."

"Yes, sir. Right away, sir." The subservient Southern sarcasm she flings at Uncle Phil isn't lost on me. "But let me leave you with this." There's a blip of silence. "*Your nephew* thought I dropped it."

I hear her coming and pull Iris back to the reception desk where we tuck into a small waiting area, listening to the click-clack of the nurse's shoes. The sound grows faint enough for me to chance a peek around the corner and I see Luanne disappear into the same stairwell as Derek.

"No fucking way am I going in there."

My annoyance with Uncle Phil starts to roll across my skin like a bad rash. I thought he'd keep our conversations out of his workplace since I'm not his patient but I guess I was wrong about him on that too.

I pinch the bridge of my nose. "I can't fake not knowing who she is or what I overheard. If she and I were bound to meet anyway, then why the hell is she being so cagey?"

Iris has her hand wrapped around her throat like she's choking. "Theo, *Philomax* is the name of the drug my mom was taking."

"Are you sure?"

"I found them in her coat after she died. I didn't know what they were and couldn't find anything on the internet so I threw them out."

I rewind the conversation we heard between Dr. Aldridge and Uncle Phil. "They said the drug raised a patient's levels of perception. Do you know what they meant by that?"

Iris shakes her head.

"I'm sorry, Iris. I shouldn't have brought you here. I wasn't thinking—about your mom, and the stuff you told me about Uncle Phil."

"I agreed to come," Iris says. "I wanted to, but now—I think I'd like to leave."

I scan the waiting room, forging an exit plan, then approach the receptionist's desk. "Excuse me. Can I borrow a piece of notepaper?"

"Sure thing. Give me one sec." The receptionist pushes her clear pink eyeglasses up with one finger, spins her office chair to a set of drawers, and riffles through her supplies. She glides back with exactly what I need and I write a note to Uncle Phil saying something came up and I had to cruise. Then I take Iris by the hand and we get the hell out of Dodge, using the badge we bought from Derek the Creeper.

# TWENTY-EIGHT

**Come-Out:** Coming out or kicking out of a rotation to stop a dive's momentum to ensure vertical entry into the water.

GP IS carrying an overflowing recycling bin to the curb when I get home. The necks of at least a dozen liquor bottles stick up in all directions like the back of a dinosaur. If he didn't drink them all today, I might have a chance at getting some answers about the fire, at best. At worst, he'll confirm my beliefs about Luanne Cole. Any answers will be better than none.

"Thought I might have to send the dumb dog out after you," he says.

I'm not sure who he means until I spot Belly sitting on the stoop, tongue lolling like she's run a million miles.

"How long has she been here?" I grab my duffle from the truck and follow GP into the house with Chip's dog on my heels.

"She showed up about twenty minutes before you, barkin' and whinin' like a baby. I called Chip to let him know. Said his Mom would come by and get her later. I think he called her your girl-friend, unless he was talkin' about someone else."

"He was talking about the dog."

Belly starts licking the hurt side of my face the minute I drop my duffle and crouch to unlace my shoes. I pick up a weird pine aroma and sniff her fur, but she smells the way she always does, like chlorine and wet dog. I stand and look for a new air fresh-ener and notice our kitchen is clean. Not two guys living to-gether clean, but shiny sink and mopped floors clean.

But that's not the weirdest part.

Dinners is on the table. Roast chicken with potatoes and green beans. GP is watching me, his rough hands folded around a cup of coffee. I realize for the first time in months he's freshly shaven, wearing a clean polo shirt, but neither of those things mask the discomfort on his face.

"Whatcha starin' at? Ain't you seen a man without a drink in his hand before?"

"Plenty. But their names never started with Bruce and ended in Mackey. You cooked?"

"Of course I cooked. A man can't spend thirty years in a firehouse without learnin' to cook a thing or two."

"Why?"

"*Why?* Christ. You like it better when I'm drinkin'?"

"No. It's good. I'm just asking why the sudden change."

"Not to get too sentimental or anything, but I got the feelin' my grandson needed me to clean it up a little. That and Curtis might have given me a hard kick in the ass with an old boot labeled reality."

There's something GP's not telling me. Something that finally convinced him to give up his beloved Jack Daniel's, which I doubt has anything to do with me asking for help with our family history.

"You gonna eat?" he says. "I ain't got all night. Curtis is on his way to bring me to an appointment."

"What kind of appointment?"

"The none-of-your-business kind."

Nice to know the lack of drinks hasn't taken the cranky out of him. I take a bite of the chicken and close my eyes, surprised by how good it tastes.

"Your coach called. Said you got into a slap fight with the pool." He wiggles a finger at his cheek and takes a bite of his dinner.

"Guess you can see who won."

"You wanna talk about it?"

"Not really. I'd rather talk about Luanne Cole."

GP's fork hovers near his mouth. "Luanne Cole?" He questions her name like he can't put his finger on whether he knows her.

I leave the table to dig into my duffle for the newspaper articles then toss them onto the table in front of GP.

He coughs uncomfortably for a few minutes, then clears his throat and pores over each one, getting the gist of everything I know.

"*This* is what you came up with for your project?" His voice is reserved calm behind clenched teeth.

"No. Should it be?" He adjusts my curiosity with a stern look. "Someone left them on my truck." I don't go into detail about Les because it doesn't change anything.

GP places everything on the table with shaking hands and leans back. "Kid, you better take a seat."

"Just rip the bandage off, GP. I've had a weird freaking day."

"It's about to get weirder so strap your ass back in that seat. You said you needed a goddamn interview for your project. Wanted to know about your mom and her side of the family, right? Well, here it is."

I blow out a noisy breath. I'm way past giving a shit about this project. But I sit, fingers laced on top of my head.

"You got your own ideas about any of this?" GP asks.

"Yep. And they're not mutually exclusive," I tell him. "I'm pretty sure Luanne Cole was the paramedic on duty the night our house burned down."

"Could be." GP covers his mouth and gets a faraway look in his eye. "I can have Curtis look into that to be sure."

"And I think she's in a relationship with *he-ain't-your-goddamn-Uncle-Phil*. I saw her leaving his house wearing a pair of mom's earrings."

I slip him the half-lie knowing he'd probably go ape-shit if he knew I went to Green Hill.

"I ain't too happy about you going over there. But the news about him and her don't surprise me one bit. The question you oughta be asking yourself is why, because Phil Maddox only clings to people that can get him what he wants till he don't need 'em anymore. He was always strangely ambitious, even as a kid, but motivated by the wrong things. Control. Jealousy. Recognition."

I think about the way Uncle Phil said, *I am the leading authority on posthypnotic amnesia.* Like it wasn't up for debate. Did he just like the idea of being able to do something Dad couldn't? Up until I figured out he was messing around with Mom, I only ever saw him as good.

"I need to be in control as a diver," I press. "And sometimes I get jealous of other guys on my team. Those things aren't necessarily bad motivators, are they?" Even after everything I've learned, part of me still wants to justify his actions.

"Phil always took his jealousy and ambition to a different level. He was willing to do things most normal people wouldn't."

My patience snaps. "Is that it? You're just gonna give me a bunch of anecdotes about why you don't like Uncle Phil?"

"No, that ain't it, smarty-pants. But there's no such thing as black and white when it comes to the stuff you just slapped on my table. So you might want to cool your jets. As much as you favor your mother in the looks department, that fire in your eyes—the one that says you're gonna burn it all to the ground and ask questions later—you picked that up from someone else. And it ain't conducive to getting what you want."

"I don't even know what that is anymore." I jiggle my leg to keep from exploding. "A few weeks ago, all I wanted was to ask a girl on a date, uncover enough about my family to get a decent grade on a school assignment, and dive well enough to get to states. Now, I'm pretty sure I'm shit-out-of-luck for a scholarship from the school that suspended Mom. Not that seeing stuff that isn't there will help my case, since I'm smacking almost every time I dive. So I don't care if I resemble the queen of England right now as long as you tell me something that makes sense."

"What do you mean *seeing* stuff that ain't there?" GP goes paler than the napkin he's using to wipe the table.

Shit.

I pinch the bridge of my nose and think fast. "I went back to the site of our old house and had this flashback of seeing Mom outside the house the night of the fire. I know it wasn't real, but for a second, and I mean a literal second, it felt like she was standing there."

"And you're not wondering if maybe she went into the house after you?"

My heart leaps into my throat like a giant frog and lodges there. "Did she?" I croak.

"I don't know. But your dad asked me the same thing once." He fills his lips with air so tight the philtrum under his nose puffs. "We can figure out how Luanne Cole fits into all this. But you need to understand a thing or two about who your mother is first."

"Is?" I raise my eyebrows.

"Jesus Christ. *Was.* You're just like Mitch. Drop your damn guard and keep quiet for a minute. I want to tell you a story."

"A true story?"

"The truest one I know."

In the small gap of silence, the normal noises in the kitchen amplify: the hum of the fridge, the clank of the ice-maker. But the closest, most audible sound is my own pulse, pumping in my ears.

"Your parents met when your mother was in college," GP begins. "Did you know that?"

I nod, mouth held tight.

"She made an appointment with your dad, hoping he could help her overcome some performance anxiety and he prescribed some attention-deficit disorder drugs. Turned out she needed more than that. Much more. She saw Mitch privately for two years before they got hitched." He takes a swig of coffee, then clears his throat. "Sophia and Mitch. That girl was an answer to a prayer. I don't think she ever wanted to hide the fact that she was special. And she didn't, not from us. But your mother was something different all right. Beautiful and fierce, but different. She'd come visit me 'bout once a month or so, tell me all the things she saw in the future. Bad things. Good things. At first I thought she was just prone to storytellin'. But it turned out she needed to talk about it or she'd go insane holdin' the truth inside."

"Things in the future like predictions or her fears?"

"Both. Your mother knew things before they'd happen. Outta the blue. And she was usually right."

"Right. She used to help Dad with his clients."

"That was a good way to tame her anxiety," GP says. "But she knew other things too."

The room expands around me, pulled by the little threads of memory I've regained.

*Broke my arm in two places at Sully's house three hours later.*

*"Don't blurt out everything you see, okay? Not everyone will understand."*

*"What won't they understand?" I asked.*

*"You." Mom ruffled my hair. "If you see that girl again, promise you'll let me know, okay? I'll be looking for her too."*

I've been feeling anxious about my own flashbacks and freak-outs lately. Especially the similarities between the girl with dark hair and body tattoos and Iris. But Rocco wasn't dead in the water. My mom wasn't really sitting in an empty room underwater.

"You listenin' to me?" GP asks. "Where the hell did you go?"

"I'm listening." I bounce my knee, trying to wake my legs, which have drained of blood.

"Anyway, your mother had a rough start in life. Her adoptive parents discovered early on that their little girl wasn't all sugar and spice. Especially after she came home from a diving lesson and told them her coach was gonna die. Now, to hear Sophia tell it, this coach was healthy as a horse, an exercise enthusiast who had no intention of becoming ill, let alone dying. But within a few weeks . . ." He snaps his fingers. "Dead and gone. Pulmonary embolism. Your mother was ten years old the first time her parents admitted her to a psychiatric hospital. They released Sophia after a six-month stint. Once your mother learned to keep her mouth shut about things. She managed to keep that sham going till she was fifteen. Told me she put all her energy into gymnastics and diving, but the restraint nearly ate her alive. Then later that year, right before she turned sixteen, she was hiking with some friends and fell into a river. Said when she hit the water—bang—she had a vision of another diver she knew laying dead on a patch of grass. The girl's face swollen and distorted. Sophia had to force herself not to tell a single soul. Can you imagine living with that?"

Yes and no.

"Did her vision or whatever come true?" I swallow the bone-dry lump forming in my throat.

"Not right away. Not for another three months. Enough time for your poor mother to believe maybe they cured her in that hospital. But that girl she saw was home alone one afternoon. Went into the garden to pick flowers and stepped on a wasps' nest. Got stung a bunch. Bad. She died before she ever made it inside for help. When they broke the news to your mother, she nearly lost her mind. Because she knew, you see, and never told. Well, it was straight back to the hospital for Sophia. Worst part is the Rogans washed their hands of her after that. Just up and abandoned her at the hospital like some unwanted pet."

I think of the people buried on the grounds at Green Hill and take a sip of water to keep the lump in my throat from rising in my throat again.

"Your mother was made a ward of the state and sent into the foster care system. She never mentioned her visions, or what have you, again. But at twenty-two-years-old the pressure from school and collegiate-level diving piled on. She felt like she might have a psychotic break. But the truth was she had predicted terrible tragedies before they happened and couldn't handle the guilt."

Jeezus.

"She had your dad's full attention after that, not to mention that of his best friend. For different reasons. Phil was whisperin' in your dad's ear about potential research in psychiatry. But your father maintained that Sophia was a victim of trauma and needed help redirecting her focus to the right things. Shortly after, Phil was offered a residency at the hospital here in Ellis Hollow with a group that specialized in abnormal psychiatry. He jumped at that opportunity, quickly leading one of their research teams and moving up the ranks. It was clear Sophia admired Phil's drive and success. Mitch was workin' with student athletes at the time and offered her what a workaholic like Phil couldn't, the promise of stability. But it wasn't for lack of pursuit on Phil's part. It might be hard for you to understand this, but it is possible for a person to love two people at the same time. After you do some growin' up, though, you realize you can't have it all. At the end of the day, choices need to be made. And your mother chose Mitch. Everything seemed hunky-dory until she got pregnant with you and predicted your gender, your hair and eye color . . ." A clouded look settles into his eyes.

"And?"

"And you arrived exactly as she predicted. All the way down to those moles on your cheek."

"What the hell?" I slump against the back of the chair. "I thought she left school because she was pregnant. But now, with that article . . . Are the two related?"

"I can't be sure. But at least now we're gettin' somewhere," he says.

I think about Luanne saying she *felt* something from me. And that other doctor saying Philomax raised levels of perception.

"Do you think maybe Luanne Cole can predict things like Mom and that's why Uncle Phil likes her?"

"That ain't really the million-dollar question here, is it?"

"No."

The million-dollar question is: can I?

Thanks to Mr. Malone.

Muffled bird tweets come up from under the table two seconds before a knock at the door sends Belly rushing to investigate.

My grandfather pulls out his phone and his nostrils flare beneath hard eyes. "You expectin' someone?"

"No. I figured it was Curtis."

His face darkens. "Phil Maddox is on the stoop." GP shoves the articles under a fishing magazine. "Tell him I ain't home if he asks."

I move with the same jerky motions as the receptionist at Green Hill, unsure which way to go.

"You're the one who opened this can worms," GP says. "Time for you to learn how to play a little game called business as usual. 'Cause I doubt he's gonna go away if you don't, seeing as he ain't had the nerve to show his face here in years."

"Are you gonna leave?"

"I'm gonna go to my appointment, like I said."

He walks away, leaving me to open the door like everything is normal.

When I see Uncle Phil my arms and legs go numb. It takes serious effort to pull my shit together and present the Theo who's good at fulfilling expectations.

"You left the hospital without coming to see me," he says.

"Yeah, sorry about that. I had my friend Iris with me, and her dad called and told her she needed to get home ASAP." I look over my shoulder for GP.

"I should have told you bringing friends to Green Hill isn't something we normally allow. There are strict visitation policies. Not to mention the issues of liability we have to consider."

"Understood. I won't let it happen again." He looks past me like a vampire waiting to be invited inside.

"Is your grandfather home?"

Every instinct in my body has me primed to lie. "I just got here. He could be holed up in his office, but I haven't heard him banging around in there or anything."

"I couldn't help noticing the plethora of empty bottles at the curb. It's always interesting to me how some people feel safest behind locked doors when others want to be free. Regardless of whether those doors are physical or the ones we construct in our minds."

"Did you come all the way over here just to tell me not to bring friends with me?" I ask. "Isn't that kind of risky, considering how GP feels?"

"Actually, I was hoping we might initiate a reunion. I'd like the opportunity to speak with him about your treatment and the possibility of you coming to stay at Green Hill. Seeing as he isn't here, though, I think it's safe to give you these." He reaches into his pocket and hands me a new prescription bottle. "I wanted to ensure you had enough for the Andover meet on Friday."

"Are you coming to that?"

"I'd be a fool to miss it. But Theo, as pleased as I am that the Adderall is helping, I'm afraid my resources for acquiring information about your mother's family have run out. The photos I gave you seem to be the best I can do."

"No worries," I say. "GP filled me in on all things Rogan. Plus, Chip and I are going over to Andover Prep tomorrow to ask about her school records. I'll figure it out in the end. Adapt or perish."

The slightest curve of amusement lifts one corner of his mouth. "I have no doubt. The ability to adapt to a change in conditions is sometimes all it takes to succeed. My research colleague often reminds me of his affinity for Darwinism. Survival of the fittest."

"Dr. Aldridge?"

The name spills out of my mouth before I can think fast enough to stop myself.

Uncle Phil studies me for a long beat, his face an expressionless mask, and I start sweating bullets.

"Have you two met?"

"No. I think I remember you mentioning him, though."

"Yes, well, I should probably get back to the hospital," he says. "Dr. Aldridge and I have a big research project on the verge of breaking, and much to discuss." He makes a move to leave and stops. "There is one other thing. The nurse who took your blood today said she found your behavior somewhat erratic. Is there anything you want to tell me? Anything you'd like to ask?"

Loads. But I do what GP said and keep up business as usual, with a twist.

"Not really," I lie. And then drop another lure just to see if he'll bite. "I thought she was top-notch at her job. Once she stuck that needle into my arm my mind went to everything other than what was happening in that room at the time."

Uncle Phil tilts his head. "Perhaps having Iris with you was a comfort. Some women wield an incomprehensible power. Especially those who possess a certain magic." He reaches into his trench coat pocket for his keys. Tell your grandfather I'm eager to speak with him about your treatment."

"I'd rather not, Uncle Phil. I don't think it'll go over the way you think."

"Very well then. You and I can continue meeting privately untill you're ready to discuss it with him yourself."

When Uncle Phil reaches his Escalade he pauses to look back at GP's house like he knows I'm lying. But he does a good job faking it with a wave.

I lean against the back of the door and exhale every bit of air in my lungs. Then I head back to the kitchen with the intention of sending GP a text, but see he got to me first.

*Won't be home till late. Keep up business as usual until I can hunt down some answers on Luanne Cole.*

I'm good at fulfilling expectations but I can't wait that long.

I grab my laptop and search as many keywords as I can think of that might pull up something about my mom's suspension from the Stanford team. Nothing. I switch to googling Luanne Cole + diver, Luanne Cole + paramedic, looking for a connection to Uncle Phil. Nada. I try Philomax. Zilch. I search Dr. Phillip Maddox and the page fills with returns but every topic is in praise of his excellence. I stare at the blinking cursor trying to come up with different sets of search parameters until I fall asleep.

# TWENTY-NINE

**Hurdle:** The jump to the end of the springboard taken from one foot following the approach or walk down the length of the board.

**THE COLOR** red is everywhere—Sharks, Sharks, Sharks. The extreme display of Andover spirit pulsing in every corner is fueling my red-hot frustration with their front office staff.

"You've got to be kidding me." Disbelief sputters from my lips as I shove the newspaper article in the school secretary's face. "She was a student here from 1984 to 1988. Look!"

She gives it another cursory glance and turns up her nose. Probably because all she sees is the part about Mom being suspended for drug use.

"There's nothing in the system, which means there's nothing I can do to help." She eyes my Ellis Hollow jacket before handing back my birth certificate, flashing a quick grin that displays an irregular row of large teeth. Fitting for a Shark.

"So that's it?" I ask. "As far as this school is concerned Sophia Rogan was never a student here? That's great. Awesome."

"Even if there were anything on file, I couldn't give it to you without the student's written consent. You can file a request with the Family Policy Compliance Office of the U.S. Department of Education."

Jeezus.

I spent my entire day in a daze. Waiting to get here so I could find some shred of evidence that my mom was a living, breathing human being who left traces behind only to be met with this crap.

I flip an apologetic look at Chip for wasting his only afternoon off from practice to help me chase another dead end.

He's leaning on the counter, eyes steady, index finger hooked around his mouth, thumb under his chin. Thinking this through in full Watson-mode. I start to open my mouth and he kicks me with the side of his foot to shut me up.

"We understand it's not your fault the record was misplaced. But there must be some way we can verify Ms. Rogan's time as a student here." He gives the school secretary a smile I've only seen him wield around girls he wants to bone: dimples deep enough to hide a marble, a single cocked eyebrow.

The woman cuts me a disapproving glance and turns her attention to Chip, patting her over-dyed blond hair. "You could try the district office," she says. "But if you're merely after unofficial proof, our library should have the yearbooks from the eighties."

"Great idea," Chip says. "I knew an intelligent, and may I add beautiful, woman like yourself might suggest a suitable solution. Which way is the library?" He moves his arms, pointing in multiple directions.

"Go back through this door and take a left, dear. Then go to the end, take a right, and you'll see a sign for the library pointing you in the right direction." Her eyes flick to the clock on the wall. "It's highly unlikely you'll find anyone there. We're a bit short staffed after school."

"We'll give it a try," Chip says. "Left, end, right, sign. Thanks for your help." He winks at the middle-aged woman and makes a clicking sound with his cheek.

"Are you for real?" I ask once we're in the hallway. "You called *me* the Eddie Haskell?"

"Watching you kiss my mom's ass taught me a thing or two. Plus, haven't you ever heard you'll catch more flies with honey?"

"Yes. But the only thing I've been getting from office flies lately is shit. Loads of freaking shit. I can't believe they don't have her records. What the hell is that? The county clerk didn't have anything. The school doesn't have anything. Jeezus! It's like she . . ." I stop walking.

"It's like she what?" Chip asks.

"Nothing."

"It's like she *what*? Say it."

"Got erased from existence."

"That's bullshit," Chip says. "We're gonna find something in this dumb school and lay that hang-up of yours to rest."

I raise my brows. "You think it's gonna be that easy?"

"I didn't say it was gonna be easy, bro. But you and I both know this has fuck-all to do with Malone's project at this point."

"True."

"You didn't come this far to only come this far, did you?"

"Now you sound like my dad."

Chip shrugs, giving my dad more credit than I ever did.

The smell of chlorine hits us as we round the second corner. Shimmering waves of light seep under the swinging doors leading to the Andover pool.

Chip says, "If I were a bigger dick I might be inclined to take a leak in their pool."

"Since when are you not the biggest dick?"

"True. Maybe I'll execute project golden shower on the way out," he says. "Right now we're on a mission."

We find Andover's massive library at the end of the dark corridor, but the doors are locked, lights off.

"Crap. Why is it always hallways and locked doors?"

"What do you mean?"

I shake my head. "Nothing. It doesn't matter. I'm screwed. Let's get out of here before I decide to piss in the pool with you."

"Now you're talking. Drain the main vein. Point Percy at the pool. Take a Wiz Khalifa."

"I got it, Chip. Don't hurt yourself."

We pass a janitor mopping the floor as we backtrack to the front of the building, followed by a few students still here after school for clubs or sports. Their eyes rove over our black and orange Ellis Hollow jackets suspiciously, but nobody questions our presence.

I stop short as we pass Coach McGee's office with a change of plan.

"If Coach Porter keeps files on every diver, wouldn't McGee do the same?"

"It stands to reason," Chip says. "Go on."

"If that's standard practice, then there may be an old folder on my mom in there." I try the doorknob. Locked. "Shit."

"Try this," Chip says, handing me a nail clipper.

"Why do you have a nail clipper in your pocket?"

"I was clipping my nails in the parking lot while waiting for you because sometimes that's the only opportunity I get between practice and homework and chores. Are you gonna sweat me on my grooming habits or are you gonna pick that lock?"

Good point.

"What about the janitor?"

"He was going the other way. If he turns back, we'll hear him coming. I'll stay out here."

I chew the inside of my cheek and review my options.

"Fuck it." I crouch and start working on the lock. Heat steams up from my chest as I jiggle the tiny metal file in the lock and feel for the catch. The click is almost imperceptible, but it's there, and once it catches I turn the knob slowly to the right, keeping the metal shim steady as the lock gives way.

"Holy shit, Sherlock," Chip whispers. "Go."

I enter Coach McGee's dark office with a sideways gait and walk straight into his desk. I curse in a groan as I reach for the light switch on the wall behind me. The first thing I see is a huge white board emblazoned with the names of Andover divers. His seed list. The red dry-erase scrawl mocks me, testing my capacity for doing what's right. Even though being in here automatically puts me in the wrong. I'm only after one thing, so I avert my eyes. Coach McGee's desk is strewn with files and paperwork. His silver whistle and red lanyard left in a heap in the center. The tiny office leaves little room for more than his desk and two chairs. But there's a storage nook recessed into the opposite wall. That's where I begin my search. Filing cabinets line one wall. Shelves stacked with storage boxes line the other with four feet of space separating them. I open a drawer at random, but the files are too recent. I leave it open and crouch to try another, thinking I'll find the chronological order that'll point me to the right set of drawers.

"You find anything?"

Chip's voice startles me and I stand too quickly, slamming the top of my head into a drawer I left open. The clang gnashes my teeth. "Jeezus! I thought you were keeping watch?"

"I thought it would be quicker if I helped." He turns the light off.

"We need that. There's no overhead in here."

"Chill, bro. This is less conspicuous." He clicks the small LED flashlight he keeps on his key chain and shines it over the cabinets. "What year was she? What am I looking for?"

"Anything from 1984 to 1988. These cabinets are from the last decade. We should try the boxes."

"On it." Chip shines his light over the labels. "Up there. Look: 1987 to 1990."

Finally.

I stretch high and grab the cardboard file box, missing Chip's head by an inch when gravity rushes the box downward with a cloud of dust. The onslaught clings to our lungs with the sticky persistence of spiderwebs, making us cough. I lift one knee, balancing the box against the shelf, and remove the lid. Chip shines his flashlight inside and we scan the folders.

"Rogan, Sophia." Chip says, "Boom! There it is."

My heart goes ape-shit, pounding hard enough to bust through its bony cage.

I'm pulling out the file when the lights snap on in Coach McGee's office.

"What the hell are you two doing in here?"

I stumble backward into the filing cabinets, the weight of the file box giving me an extra push, and the bruise on my back takes a wallop from one of the U-shaped handles.

Rocco is standing in the open doorway. "I can't believe what I'm seeing. After you accused me of coming to Monarch Night to spy."

"It's not what it looks like."

"It looks like you came here to steal shit," Rocco says. His eyes shoot to the white board. "Why are you guys in the storage closet?"

"Theo's mom used to dive for Andover," Chip says with a huff. "He's been running all over looking for information on her for a school project but can't find anything, so we came here. The front office lady was useless, but we realized Coach McGee might have something."

"Your mom was a Shark?" Rocco says in disbelief. "As in you've been diving with Andover blood in your veins this whole time? Ever think you might be diving for the wrong team?"

"Not even for a second." I hoist the file box back into the gap on the top shelf.

Rocco points at his cheek. "What happened there? Another dive get away from you, Big Mack?"

"Bite me."

"Ouch. Looks like somebody needs a Happy Meal." He scans the boxes. "Why didn't you just ask Coach Porter to call McGee for what you needed? Or talk to McGee yourself for that matter."

"It's complicated."

"Seems pretty simple to me."

"Imagine how that might look," Chip says. "I can see the bo-

252

gus headline in the school paper now: 'ELLIS HOLLOW DIVING CAPTAIN IN TALKS WITH ANDOVER HEAD COACH.' Everyone would assume Theo was a traitor." Soon as the words leave Chip's mouth, we all realize what they imply about Rocco, all defector jokes aside. Everyone avoids eye contact for a few seconds.

"If we're talking headlines, it would look a lot better than 'ELLIS HOLLOW DIVING CAPTAIN CAUGHT BREAKING INTO ANDOVER COACH'S OFFICE.' You're lucky one of the assistant coaches didn't catch you in here. You'd be toast. Good-bye scholarships. Good-bye swim team."

"What are you doing in here?" Chip asks. "You guys don't have practice."

"No. District coaches' meeting, same as you. But I have a hookup for the pool after hours. I'm here working on a new dive."

"Alone? Are you stupid?" I ask. Because I'm picturing Rocco the way I saw him at the quarry, facedown in the swimming hole, motionless.

"I have a training partner with me." Rocco presses his tongue inside his cheek, scratching his jaw as he walks all the way into the storage closet. He raises his eyes to the one file box protruding a fraction more than the others. "Did you find what you were looking for?"

"Not exactly," I say. "But if you're willing to turn your back for five minutes . . ."

"You know I can't let you take anything out of the office. But I'll tell you what. I'll keep my mouth shut about all this"—Rocco waves his index fingers around the closet—"*and* I'll make a copy of that file for you. But I want something in return. You still owe me from Monarch Night."

"Not that you kept your mouth shut about my smack, but what do you have in mind?"

"I'm not sure." Rocco cuts a quick glance at Chip, even though his satisfied smirk tells me he knows exactly what he wants. He's gone from copacetic sympathizer to full-fledged turncoat in a flash.

So much for old times.

"Chip, can you go keep an eye out while I talk to Rocco alone for a minute?"

He looks a little offended but says, "Yeah. Okay. Sure. I'll make some noise if anyone is coming."

As soon as Chip is out of earshot Rocco says, "A little birdie told me someone on your team is rolling out a big dive on Friday."

"So?"

"So, that's what I want."

"Come on. I can't give you my mom's favorite dive. Especially since I barely glanced at McGee's white board."

"See, I think you can. And after you give it some thought, I think you will. Because there's only one optional dive I'm after and it's not yours. One dive that if given to a captain on another team might keep you at your current ranking at E.H.H.S. Scholarship to Stanford secured."

Rocco adjusts his glasses, but I'm the one starting to see things clearly.

If I give him Les's dive, Rocco can come out as Andover's sleeper. Making Les look like *less*.

I chew the inside of my cheek. "Does it have to be Les's dive? What if I give you something equally as solid? I'd even be willing to come train with you at night on a new dive combination."

"It has to be that one. I have my reasons."

Part of me wants to give it to him and make Les's dive this season's big give instead of its big take. The other part needs to decide what the information on my mom is worth to me. It's not like Rocco doesn't know that optional dives are sacred, or that diving is as much about who will perform the dive as the combinations themselves; he just doesn't seem to care.

"Are you mad at him or something?" I ask. "I saw you two arguing on Monarch Night."

"Or something."

I shake my head and chew the inside of my cheek. "This is a bad idea."

"Oh, man!" Rocco's face broadens into an ear-to-ear grin. "You don't think I can pull it off."

"I don't think *I* can pull it off. I need to think it through."

"Don't take too long, Mackey. The clock's ticking."

"Chip and I will be at the diner tomorrow night around seven. Can you meet us there?"

"Can you throw in a couple Big Mack Attacks? I missed out on Monarch Night."

"That's prescribed to me. If you got caught . . ."

"It's not prescribed to Chip, is it? Or Ace Coburn. You don't seem to have a problem giving *them* an edge."

Shit.

"Bring me my mom's file and we'll take it from there."

"Does that mean we have a deal?"

"That's depends on whether or not you follow through."

"I feel like we should kiss on it," he says. "To seal your deal with the devil properly."

"Still a hard pass, Rocco. But thanks for asking this time."

He shrugs. "We all live and learn."

That's the most either of us has ever said about that subject. Maybe that's all that ever needed to be said.

That ease is short-lived once I file out of Coach McGee's office and see Chip waiting.

"*Hasta el viernes, muchachos,*" Rocco says. "I've got a date with the pool."

"*Buenos nachos.*" Chip gives him a bro-hug, totally clueless about what went down in McGee's office.

And something tells me to protect his plausible deniability in case there's any blowback.

We go our separate ways. Rocco heading to the shimmering light of the pool, Chip and me into the nearly empty Andover parking lot. Neither of us looks back.

"What did he want?" Chip asks as we climb into my truck.

"He was looking to settle an old beef between us."

"Did he hook you up with your mom's file?"

"Not yet, but he will. He's gonna meet us at the diner tomorrow night." I start Bumblebee's engine and let Chip pick the music.

"See. I told you he was one of our boys," Chip says.

*Was* is right.

# THIRTY

**Suspension of the Hurdle:** The peak of height before landing on the end of the board for take-off.

**THE ONLY** way to approach the Blue Belle Diner is by driving through the rotary at Buzzard's Corner. I don't think a single driver in this town understands when to yield, including me, but at least I passed my driver's test on the first try. Unlike Chip who failed because of this rotary. Twice. I merge with oncoming traffic and an overly aggressive SUV driver drafts my bumper, forcing me to continue circling the rotary like Clark Griswold in *European Vacation*.

I crank the volume on my sound system, grip the steering wheel, and speed up, singing two corresponding lines from a Them Crooked Vultures' song that tells me I won't make it out. But I do. Cutting my wheel to take the turnoff whether I'm ready or not. The other driver blares his horn long and loud, announcing my arrival as I whip into a space beside the 1950s railroad-style dining car.

I take a minute to catch my breath. The Blue Belle has always been a ritual for Chip and me. We come here the night before every meet to load up on out-of-this-world burgers and fries. Not to mention shakes so thick your cheeks hurt from sucking on the straws. But tonight is the exact opposite of business as usual. I invited Iris, for one. And the envelope meant for Rocco is sitting on my passenger seat like a troublemaking accomplice. My decision to trade Les's dive has more to do with what Coach Porter said about people leaving traces behind than finding something for Malone's class. At least that's what I tell myself as I slip the envelope into my pocket.

The smell of grilled onions and hot grease welcomes me as I step under the sky-blue awning and through the door. Followed by Aggie, the diner's oldest and best waitress. She may be all of four-foot-eleven, but she wields herself like an Amazonian aunt.

"Well, I'll be. Ray, look who else the cat dragged in," Aggie yells over her shoulder, addressing the short-order-cook-slash-owner and me simultaneously.

Ray ducks his balding head under a row of order tickets to wave a spatula at me, toothpick clenched between his teeth.

I open my arms as wide as my smile. "You are a sight for sore eyes, lady."

She wipes her hands on a ruffled apron and tucks her boney frame into mine, hugging me tight and quick. "And you, young man, are the same wicked flirt you've always been. But I'm gonna keep lettin' you get away with it 'cause it makes my old bones feel young. Your buddy Chip is at the VIP table. Go on back." She taps me in the ass with a plastic menu, then goes about her business.

And for a moment I feel like I can do the same. Pretending this is just another night at the diner before a meet.

As I head to the booth at the farthest end of the diner, I see Amy cutting over to our table in her ultra-short Blue Belle uniform. She puts a strawberry shake in front of Chip in a perfunctory way, then stalks off with her nose in the air.

Chip leans across the table to grab her hand with a look in his eyes that betrays his usual front. When I'm close enough for them to notice me, Amy pulls away from him to give me a hug. "Just so you know," she whispers, "I don't blame you." Then she retreats into the kitchen, untying her powder blue apron.

I give Chip a puzzled look. "What was that about? Did you test your theory on coming too fast?"

"Very funny. I forgot Amy and I had plans when I went to Andover with you. I didn't mean to blow her off," he says, "but it's always bros before hos. Probably shouldn't have said that to *her*, of course."

I can't help but laugh in his face. "That's definitely something that's meant to stay between bros. But she'll get over it. Amy knew you were a bonehead before you started dating."

"That's what I said. Maybe I'll tell her that bruise on your cheek is from me punching you in the face for screwing up our plans."

"I'll go along with that. My love life isn't going much better these days." I take a long pull from his strawberry shake and wipe my bottom lip with my thumb.

"That's right," Chip says, leaning forward on the table. "You never told me if you at least made it to second base with Iris before you brought her to the nuthouse."

"There wasn't really a time. The whole trip was colossally fucked up."

"There's always time for yabos, bro. Always." Chip says this flat, and with all seriousness. Like he's reciting a verse from his personal manifesto.

"We got past second base days before that," I tell him. "But after Green Hill she might be rethinking the whole Big Mack and French Fry combo. She wasn't in Malone's class and hasn't responded to my text messages. I left her a message anyway inviting her to meet us tonight. We'll see if she shows."

"Past second, though. Not too shabby. I'm impressed."

"How pathetic do you really think I am?"

"On a scale of one to ten, bro? Fifty."

"Fuck off," I say and laugh. Chip's great at twisting my problems into jokes, which is exactly what I need right now.

"Did I miss something funny?" Rocco's voice precedes the two shadows stretching across the table.

"What the hell are you doing here?" Chip asks.

"Theo invited me," Rocco says. "Didn't he tell you?" He drops his messenger bag on the seat and sits, nudging me so I'll make room for him and Miles, the pimple-faced freshman I scolded on Monarch Night.

"He means the freshman sidekick."

"He's my cousin. Miles Bennett Stone. He's on your team, guys. Look alive."

Jeezus.

*He's* the promising Bennett Coach Porter was talking about. Rocco's little birdie. I study the glower on Miles's face and it all makes sense.

"Funny," I say. "He never said a word about you to any of us. But now that you mention it, he does have the same know-it-all attitude."

"It's part of the Bennett family charm." Rocco shrugs out of his blazer and hands it to his cousin to hang up. "Actually, my mom made me bring him with me tonight."

"I told you he has it in for me," Miles tells Rocco. "You should have dropped me off at the mall like I asked."

"I don't have it in for anyone," I tell him. "I was following the rules, which you and your cousin were too happy to break."

"Not *anyone*?" Rocco says. "You sure about that?"

His sly grin puts my conscience back on the envelope in my pocket. But I have one stipulation up my sleeve that might not make this decision as bad as it could be. For Les, and for me as captain if anyone found out.

"You're an underclassman," Chip tells Miles. "You can't expect a higher place in the pecking order."

"I thought my awesome diving skills might matter," Miles says.

"Don't we all," Rocco says. "But everyone has to pay their dues one way or another. Isn't that right, Big Mack?"

I give him a tight upward nod that might as well be a fuck-you.

"Do me a favor," Rocco tells Miles. "Go grab me some of those mint toothpicks they keep by the register."

Miles grumbles but goes, giving Rocco a chance to pull a manila folder from his messenger bag. He slides it onto my lap under the table. "Your mom's file from McGee's office. We can take care of that other thing whenever you're ready."

Chip is smiling like he's glad something is going my way, but he's only witnessing half the exchange. He'd freak if he knew what I plan to give Rocco in return.

I channel some of my resentment about the whole thing at Miles when he returns from fetching toothpicks. "So what's stopping you from joining your cousin at Andover?"

Miles shrugs. "Maybe I'm waiting to see how I'll do at E.H.H.S. If I leave I wanna go out with a bang."

I'm about to tell him to go bang nails when Chip elbows me in the ribs. "Look who's here."

My irritation wanes when I see Iris. She saunters closer, giving me an all-knowing smile as our eyes connect. Looks like Green Hill didn't scare her away, after all.

"Sorry I'm late," she says. "I had to wait for my ride to finish writing her article on the nutrition center."

"Welcome to the Monarchs' lair," Chip says. "Where unhealthy eats abound." He gets out of the booth so Iris can sit between us.

Her leg bumps against mine and she keeps it there, fusing our limbs, and I have to remind myself to breathe.

Rocco's face morphs into perplexity. "Iris. I almost didn't recognize you in street clothes."

"Same here. You're wearing glasses."

"They used to call me Rocco Raccoon."

"I'm French Fry."

Rocco laughs. "Does that mean you and the Big Mack are an official thing since Monarch Night?"

Iris bobbles her head like she doesn't know how to answer, then mercifully says, "Yes. I guess it does," and I breathe a sigh of relief.

"Glad I could help with that." Rocco flips a look at me, like I owe him again.

Aggie approaches our table before either of us is forced into giving Rocco more information. "You boys ready to order?" She notices Iris a second later. "Sorry, hon, didn't see you there. I'm guessin' you're the reason Amy went barnstormin' outta here. Honestly, Chip," Aggie scolds. "You should know better than to bring another girl here."

"She's with Theo," Chip says.

"Not that Chip didn't offend Amy in an equally boneheaded way," I add.

Aggie's scolding eyes soften on me, but that doesn't mean she's through with Chip. "Whatever you *did* do has Amy madder than a hellcat. She punched clock and tore outta here with another fella. Curly brown hair. Fancy car. I won't tell you what she muttered on her way through the back door, but it was unsavory."

Les Carter. Always there whether you want him to be or not.

Chip slinks down and hides his face with the menu. "Thanks for the warning, Aggie."

"Young love's not what it used to be," she says. "So, what can I get you kids tonight?"

We give Aggie our order and she taps her pencil on her pad before repeating it back to us, simultaneously yelling it to Ray in the kitchen. "Ray, gimme a Jack Tommy for the lady. Then burn four. Run three of 'em through the garden and make 'em hemorrhage. Make one of 'em cry. Take away the tears on two, and make one a melt. And put 'em on the rails. Chip's gotta go see his girl and make good." She bops him on the head with her order pad and walks to the kitchen.

Hearing Aggie give our order to Ray is the highlight of coming to the Blue Belle. She's been trying to teach diner lingo to the other waitresses, but they don't give it the same flair.

"Wow," Iris says, "That's a whole other language. Her energy is ultraviolet."

"That's one way to put it," Chip says.

"Haven't you been here before?" I ask. "Aggie's the best."

"Not since—it's been a long time." Iris smiles at me, but it doesn't reach her eyes and I understand. "So what brought this group together tonight?" she asks. "I'm sensing a greater purpose at work."

"That's perceptive," Chip says. "For a fortune-teller. The truth is, Iris, the Big Mack needs our help hatching a plan to discover whether he was dropped here on earth via alien spacecraft, or really had a human family. I don't know what the freshman is doing here, but I think we're planning to use him for alien bait."

Iris's laughter is infectious. "Better him than me."

"Screw you guys," Miles says, dampening the mood.

"Does anyone beside Chip know your mom was an Andover diver?" Rocco asks. "That must feel alien to your Monarch pride."

"Coach Porter knows. Iris knows. And now, thanks to you, so does Miles."

"He doesn't care," Rocco says, then turns his attention to Iris. "I think your boyfriend might be diving for the wrong school."

"I disagree," Iris says. "In fact, I just finished writing up an article about the diving demo for the school paper, and Theo is a Monarch, through and through. He's not the Methuselah generation."

"I'm not the what?"

Iris shakes her head "Monarchs normally only live about four weeks. Kind of how we go to high school for four years," she explains. "But every autumn, a special generation of monarchs is born called the Methuselah generation. They have ten times the life span of their counterparts, making it feasible for them to migrate all the way to Mexico to hibernate, then return to ensure the continuation of the species. They live a little longer, but in order to get where they need to go they have to leave everything behind. Like you did, Rocco. Maybe underneath your red Shark suit you're still a Monarch, after all."

"Survivors," I say, picturing the swarms of butterflies at the carnival.

"Adaption," Iris adds. "Remember when Mr. Malone was quoting Darwin in class. He said, 'It's not the strongest of the species that survives, nor the most intelligent, but the one most responsive to change.'"

Adapt or perish.

"I think I'm that too," Miles says. "The Methuselah generation."

"Actually," Iris says, "I get the impression you're a viceroy."

"What's that?" Miles's voice is rife with anticipation.

"A viceroy wears a special costume that looks like a monarch, but it's mostly to ensure its own survival. Look it up. It's very cool stuff."

Miles opens his mouth like he's going to ask something, then shreds a paper napkin instead, his ears reddening.

Iris gives me a closemouthed grin and squeezes my knee. I'm not sure what the hell she's talking about, Methuselah and viceroy, but I think she just burned Miles in her nerdy, nature-loving way, without provocation from me. Almost like she doesn't need her cards to read people at all.

Aggie returns to our table with a huge tray of food. She doles out the shakes before putting a cherry Coke in front of Iris, making a point of catching her eye. "A Coke with virtue for the lady," she says, then proceeds to distribute the plates of burgers and Iris's grilled cheese. When she's done, Aggie tucks the tray under arm to waggle a finger at Iris. "I never forget a face, but yours took me an extra minute. I must be gettin' old. Older by the second these days, 'cause I could swear you're the spitting image of—are you Bert and JoJo's daughter, by chance?"

Iris nods with a small smile and takes a sip of her cherry Coke.

"I'm sorry for your loss, hon," Aggie says, patting her arm. "Your mother was real good people. Read my cards once in this exact same booth. Accurate as all get out too."

"Thanks," Iris says. "I appreciate hearing that."

"You got yourself a keeper, Theo. Don't screw it up like your buddy Chip."

"Hey," Chip moans. "It wasn't entirely my fault."

I lean closer to Iris as she picks up her first french fry. "If you eat that, won't you be cannibalizing a tiny a version of yourself? I wouldn't want you to end up in the same murderous category as that oriole munching on that monarch butterfly."

"Maybe *you* should eat her french fry," Chip says casually.

The entire table goes quiet. Chip shrugs and takes a bite of his burger. "You left yourself wide open for that one," he says, mouth full.

"I told you, Iris. No filter."

"Your Dog is true to his colors. I like it." She gives me a wicked grin, then stuffs the fry in her mouth.

Actually, my dog is a poonhound. But I keep that to myself.

Once the ketchup is flowing, conversation around the booth becomes less about who's a Monarch and who's a Shark and more about what's going right for everyone, making the envelope in my pocket feel like a bigger burden. If I'm going to do this it has to be now or never.

"Can you guys let me out," I say. "I have to hit the restroom." I kick Rocco under the table so he gets my meaning.

"Me too. Scoot." He gives his cousin a nudge.

We slide out of the booth to hit the john and before the door even closes behind us Rocco starts in on me.

"You gonna give me the dive or what?" He removes his black

glasses and cleans them with the bottom of his RESPECT YOUR MOTHER T-shirt.

*Subtle, Rocco. Real subtle.*

I reach into my pocket and hand him the envelope. Inside is a slip of paper that explains Les's dive, what I'd do for lead-ups, and two of the Adderall capsules Uncle Phil gave me on Tuesday, for old time's sake.

"This makes us square; I was never in Coach McGee's office."

"Who was in McGee's office?" He smirks, then tears the envelope open. "Nice. This should help me amp things up."

"Listen, Rocco, that dive hasn't been performed at any of our meets to date. It's advanced. So don't go for it until you're ready. I think it'd be safer if you practiced first and used it against a different school."

He cocks an eyebrow and I drop my hands on his shoulders. "I'm serious. I don't even think I could pull it off without a lot of work. Les got private training for that dive. He's perfected it." Admitting all of that leaves a bitter taste in my mouth.

"I know. That's part of its appeal."

The restroom door swings open and in strolls Miles.

I take my hands off Rocco's shoulders fast and he stuffs the envelope into his back pocket. But our actions are clumsy, at best, and one of the capsules drops to the floor.

Rocco lunges for it as I growl, "What the hell are you doing in here?"

"What do you think? I have to take a leak."

"Tough. Go use the ladies'."

"No way."

I'm in his face in two strides. "Get. Out."

"No. What were you doing in here?" He looks past me at his cousin. "Are you being secretly gay with him now or something?"

What the—

I want to smack this kid in the head. "We're not *being* gay, whatever the hell that means, you narrow-minded twerp. And it wouldn't be any of your freaking business if we were."

"Just go," Rocco tells him. "We'll be out in a minute."

Miles storms out in a huff.

"Thanks for that," Rocco says. "You defending my honor actually means a lot to me. But I can see why he hates you."

"I don't need him to like me," I say. "Haven't you taught him anything? Respect the team captain and listen. That's the only way he's gonna learn and get better."

"In case you haven't noticed, Miles tends to go off half-cocked."

"Just make sure that isn't a Bennett thing too. Think about what I said. You should take your time with that dive."

He gives me an exaggerated salute and clicks his heels. "Aye-aye, Cap-i-tan!"

And I understand how Iris felt trying to warn me about my cards.

# THIRTY-ONE

**Crow Hop:** Lifting one or both feet from the board before jumping on a backward or inward take-off.

**THERE'S THIS** awkward moment in the Blue Belle parking lot where everyone stands around, wondering who's going to break off for the night first. Chip checks his phone and a huge grin breaks across his face. "Yes. I'm back in with Amy. Guess I'll see you jerkwads later." He gives me a bro hug, then grins at Iris. "Maybe we can get a do-over-double-date sometime. I'll talk to Amy." Chip throws Rocco an upward nod. "I'd say break a leg, man, but—yanno." Then he punches Miles lightly on the arm. "I'll definitely see your punk-ass tomorrow. Try to remember you're one of us. When it comes to the team, water is thicker than blood."

Chip struts to his car, giving us a final wave. His glorified I'm-gonna-get-laid swagger is legendary in our circle. Today, he's probably right.

Rocco says, "Guess I'll catch up with you tomorrow night. May the best team win and all that jive."

"In that case, let me offer you my condolences in advance?"

Rocco's laugh is a loud, put-on guffaw. "Don't be so quick to jump the gun, Big Mack. I'm packing something special to go." He points both hands at Iris. "See you there?"

"Definitely. I'm looking forward to seeing *all of you* dive." She tries to make eye contact with Miles, but he scowls and looks away.

Rocco grabs his cousin by the scruff of the neck. "Come on, cuz. I think we need to have a little talk."

I wave to him with the folder he gave me as he drags Miles away.

"What's that?" Iris asks, pointing at the folder.

"Rocco brought it for me. I think it's my mom's school records, but I haven't opened it yet."

"What are you waiting for?"

"Everyone else to leave."

"Me too, actually."

I let the cover fall open and we see a note from Rocco that reads: *Sorry. It's the best I could do.* My mom's transcripts are inside, but all the information I need—guardians' names, address, phone number—has been crossed out in black Sharpie.

"Fuck." I scan the parking lot, hoping to catch Rocco before he leaves and see him pulling onto Main Street in his mom's Prius.

"Why is everything redacted?" Iris asks.

"That's a great question." I give her an abbreviated version of what happened at Andover, including the deal I made with Rocco. "But maybe they do that for all past students to protect their information?"

Iris takes the top sheet from the folder and smells it.

"What are you doing?"

"Seeing if it smells like fresh marker. It doesn't."

"It doesn't make sense for Rocco to do this," I tell her. "It has to be a policy. Do you have to get home or can you go someplace and talk about what happened at Green Hill?"

"I'd love to, but my dad is on his way to pick me up. He's being abnormally clingy."

"Does he know you're with me right now?"

"No. And I'm super sorry about not texting you back. My dad took my phone."

"Because of me?"

"It doesn't matter, Theo. But I need to tell you something before he shows up. I wasn't late getting to the diner because

I was waiting for a ride. I was late because I was searching the archives at school. The article about your mom *was* signed out by Les weeks ago."

My nostrils flare reflexively.

"Hold on." Iris touches my arm. "That's not all. I searched printed and microfiche looking for a follow-up article. But there weren't any. High school journalists aren't great at sequels. There's too much turnover. But I did find an article about Luanne Cole."

"Let me guess. Luanne Cole had to flee from New Orleans after being arrested for drugging kids under her care?"

"Worse. The Luanne Cole that was standing next to your mom in the photo died when she was sixteen."

"That's impossible. We just saw her at Green Hill."

"I think we met Lianne Cole. Both girls were divers for E.H.H.S." Iris continues explaining as she reaches into her bag and hands me a printout of an article. "Luanne Cole stepped on a wasp nest in her backyard and was stung to death when she was sixteen. Her twin sister *Lianne Cole* was also a springboard diver and listed as one of the grieving family members."

My arms and legs fill with pins and needles until they're uncomfortably numb. "It's even stranger than just that, Iris. I think my mom predicted that girl's death before it happened. My grandfather told me the same story last night. I guess my mom had the ability to see things before they happened. Sort of like you and your mom, but without the cards. Maybe the same way I saw the girl on the cliffs with dark hair and tattoos before I met you."

"You think that girl and I are the same person, like you saw me jump before you ever met me?"

"It sounds crazy when I say it out loud."

"No, it doesn't, Theo. Not to me."

I FIND GP walking out of his office with Curtis and I blow right past them to take a peek inside without explanation. Before they close and lock the door. I'm not sure what I'm expecting to find but there's nothing extraordinary inside. Same heavy desk, a few dirty dishes, a couple of easy chairs, but not a single model airplane in sight.

GP straightens up like everything is normal but his face is ashen, punctuated by dark purple crescents under each eye that give me pause.

"Are you feeling okay?" I ask, dropping my own agenda. "You look terrible."

"Chemo has that effect on a person. Not that you've been looking so hot yourself lately."

*Chemo?*

It takes a minute for that word to sink in.

"You're *sick?*"

"You spend your whole life fighting fires and in the end you find out those fires kept fighting back long after they got put out," GP says. "Ain't that right, Curtis?"

"Karma truly is a bitch," Curtis says.

A sense of vertigo hits me so fast I could swear the floor just dropped out beneath my feet. The way he's been coughing, but not blowing his nose. Jeezus. It's in his lungs. I can't believe I didn't see. He's all I've got left.

"How bad is it?" I direct the question at Curtis.

"Not as good as we hoped."

"That's the appointment you didn't want to tell me about?"

GP doesn't answer as he takes a seat in his favorite armchair. He looks out the window, away from me, and my eyes start to sting. I wipe a hand under my nose and try to keep it together.

"Why didn't you tell me?"

"I just did."

"Before. When I asked if you were sick. I could have done something. Been home more."

"He didn't want that for you," Curtis says. "I've been looking out for him. And you. Especially when he has to hole up in his office after treatments and can't leave the house. But the chemo is starting to take its toll on him. It was time for you to know."

"Is that why the office is always locked? I assumed you just went in there to pay bills and drink."

"I did a little of that too," he says. "Gotta keep a balance between the truth and lies."

"Cancer is a big fucking lie to keep."

"Look who's talkin'. You want to tell me how long you been takin' pills from Phil Maddox?"

Curtis tosses my prescription bottle at me without warning and it bangs against my chest like a maraca.

Shit.

I sit on the couch and drop the truth. "Since Dad died. Uncle . . . I mean, Phil's been refilling the Adderall prescription Dad gave me. I go to see him a couple of times a month and we talk about my issues with focusing at school and diving. But I've only been to Green Hill once since Mom died."

"What the hell were you doing *there*?" GP coughs in a croupy series that makes me cringe.

"He asked me to come in for blood work so he could check for adverse effects on my liver. I didn't go alone. Iris Fiorello came with me."

"That explains the angry voicemail I got from Bert," Curtis says solemnly.

"Your liver ain't the thing that needs watchin', kid. It's your head. Didn't you read the article you showed me?"

"They're just Adderall. Same as Dad prescribed, just a little stronger now that I'm older."

"*Just Adderall* just got opened up for debate."

GP flips Curtis a wary, conspiratorial look.

"I'm already on it," Curtis says.

"On what? You're being ridiculous. I need those to focus. Don't you think I'd be able to tell if they were different?"

GP takes the prescription bottle out of my hand. "That's the question you should have been asking when you told me you've been seeing things. And seeing as you're still a minor, taking prescription drugs ain't really up to you. Or him, since I'm the one who's your guardian."

"Come on," I moan. "I have a meet coming up."

"Then I suggest you take up meditating. 'Cause you ain't allowed to go back up on that hill. Understand?"

"If I didn't go to Green Hill I would have never found out about Luanne Cole."

"We know she was the paramedic working that night," GP says. "Curtis told me right before you came home."

"Did he also tell you Luanne Cole is dead?" GP looks at me like I'm nuts until I hand over the article Iris pulled from the E.H.H.S. archives. "We think her twin sister, Lianne, is working as a nurse at Green Hill posing as Luanne. We just don't know why. But, do you think Luanne could be the same girl Mom told you about in that story?"

"Christ almighty," GP says slowly, skimming the article before handing it to Curtis. "You think Mitch was actually onto something?"

"Onto what?" I ask.

"Kinda makes you feel bad for blowing him off, huh?" Curtis says.

"I was tryin' to help him move on."

"Onto *what?*" I ask more forcefully.

GP sighs. "I think your father may have been looking into the Cole girl after your mother died. Said he thought there was something fishy going on with her and Phil. He became obsessed with everyone who worked the night of the fire."

"Fishy like injecting me with something that made me sleepy? I remember Uncle Phil telling her to do it, like he was angry."

Curtis and GP turn their heads to look at each other in slo-mo.

"I felt a sharp pinch right here." I point to my deltoid. "It was her, Lu . . . Lianne Cole. I remembered while I was at Green Hill. How I felt myself slipping out of consciousness. Dad had to lift me up. Next thing I knew I was waking up in a hotel and both Mom and our house were gone."

"Theo," Curtis says quietly, "your dad wasn't there during the fire."

"Sure he was. I remember him carrying me away."

"That was Phil."

"Your mother wouldn't leave the house without you. That's what he told me, at least. So your dad got a hotel room. He found out about the fire after *we* got there." GP whips a flinty look at Curtis. "Can you pull the files for that fire from the station?"

"Yep. And I'll pull the boxes Mitch left behind in storage," Curtis says. "I'm with you."

"So that's not something a paramedic would do then?"

"Not usually."

I lean forward. "When I was at Green Hill she was acting nervous while she drew my blood. Afterward, I overheard her talking to *he-ain't-your-goddamn-Uncle-Phil,* telling him she thought I recognized her from the night of the fire."

GP raises an eyebrow. "Did you say or do anything that might have raised that suspicion?"

"I asked her to get me a purple juice box because that's what she gave me that night. I was testing her to see if she was the same person."

"That might explain why Phil Maddox showed up at our house." GP rubs his balding head.

Balding because of the chemo.

"We need to look through Mitch's things and play it cool. If he thinks we're suspicious of him for any reason—" Curtis cuts himself off. "You realize what he's capable of?" he asks GP with thirty-plus years of friendship coloring his worry.

"I know better than anyone," GP says. "But he's messed with this family for the last time. We need to make this right. For Theo and for Mitch."

"Make what right? What's he capable of?"

My grandfather swipes a hand over his mouth and sighs. "Arson, for one."

The skin all over my body feels like it might shed and leave me raw, exposed, because this is where I'm supposed to tell GP the truth. I started the fire. But I can't find the words or the sack to 'fess up.

"What are we trying to make right?" I ask, swallowing hard.

"I'm not a hundred percent sure so I don't want to say just yet, but your father was looking into a bunch of stuff trying to figure out why your mother . . ." He stops and looks at me cautiously. "Why Sophia wanted to leave him for Phil after all these years. He wanted to show her Phil wasn't quite the man she thought. And it looks like he may have been right. Maybe he even got more than he bargained for, kid. That's something we may never know. But the truth always comes out. Even when it takes longer than expected."

"I already figured out something was going on between Mom and Phil."

All three of us go hush quiet for a minute.

"None of us are perfect, kid," GP says. "But your mother was a good person. I don't want you thinking poorly of her."

"I don't. She's not the one I blame."

"Now you're seeing things like a Mackey." He looks at Curtis. "It's risky. But I could go talk to Phil. Tell him I heard he stopped by the house. Do you know if he's coming to your meet tomorrow?"

"He said he was."

"If I can catch him alone in the parking lot before—"

"Alone?" Curtis interjects, sounding worried GP is diving into something that requires a spotter.

GP ignores him and turns to me. "I never missed one of your meets before, but if I skip this one, it'll give Curtis and me a chance to put together some old documents of your father's we put in storage. But if anything should happen to me between now and then, I want you to call Curtis right away. You understand me? He's the only person I trust with my life. And yours."

"If anything happens? You mean if you die, from the cancer?"

"It ain't the goddamn cancer I'm worried about. It's Phil's compromised morals. Promise me you'll call Curtis."

"I promise."

"I don't like this," Curtis says.

Neither do I. "Maybe I should go with you," I tell GP.

"No. You gotta go to that meet of yours tomorrow like normal so Phil sees you there, then come home. If any of the conspiracy theories your father was spewing are true, you might get what you need for your family history project and more. You have to trust me on that."

And I do. Suddenly, I trust him more than anyone. All the way to my core.

# THIRTY-TWO

**Adjusting the Fulcrum:** Adjusting the moveable wheel beneath the diving board to control the amount of spring the diver will receive for a forward or backward take-off.

**MONARCHS VS. SHARKS.** That's what the sign says outside the swim complex. Not the most logical pairing since it means taking bets on cute vs. ferocious. Ladybug vs. Grizzly Bear. Crickets vs. Tornadoes. Nobody wants to bet on cute, which is usually to our advantage. But tonight, I might get swallowed alive because my head is not where it should be before taking the board.

It doesn't help that every season, without fail, some ringleading jerk from an opposing school tries to fluster our team by flapping their *wings* and calling us the Butterflies. Tonight's wannabe champion of snark was Andover Co-Captain Rick Shay, a scrawny prick that never grew into his enormous teeth. No big surprise there since *Ricochet,* as Chip likes to call him, has been a bootlicking asshat since recreational swim.

But once Chip dove into the pool and kicked their asses, the taunting stopped. That's how a Monarch does it. Silent as a butterfly.

The same is expected of me.

The locker room is explosive with swimmers keyed up by how many heats they won, making it hard for the springboard divers to prepare. But there are only a few minutes left before the moment of truth. Mine, and Rocco's.

Chip taps me on the shoulder. "You ready?" He's bouncing on his toes, amped by how hard he crushed it out there.

"Almost. I need a little extra edge." I open my locker and pop the tab on a can of Phoenix.

"Can't say I blame you." Chip grabs the can and takes a few sips off the top.

When he hands it back I chug the whole thing.

The team is gathered in the common area, waiting for me to lead them to the pool. When I round the corner the whooping and hollering gets louder and echoes in my head, matching the beat of the vein throbbing in my temple.

Ace claps me on the back. "We're gonna slaughter those Sharks and leave them bleeding on the dock."

"Andover might need to rethink the food chain," Trey adds.

Coach Porter enters the locker room and we fall into a hush. "You guys ready to rumble?"

"Yes, Coach," we say in unison.

He puts a hand to his ear. "I couldn't hear you, ladies. I asked if you were ready to rumble?"

"Yes, Coach!"

"That's more like it."

He stops me on my way through the door. "What about you, Mackey? You ready?"

I give him a quick nod and smile. I better be.

Coach taps my arm with his clipboard. "Attaboy. Show 'em how it's done."

We enter the swim complex with "Hells Bells" roaring through the speakers—captain's choice. I scan the stands for Iris then remember she's grounded. I go take a seat between Ace and Sully. I need to focus on my first dive, visualize the rotations and twists.

Before I sit, I catch sight of Phil Maddox in the stands. A pit forms in my stomach as I wonder whether or not he already spoke to GP and what was said.

Ace bumps me from the right. "Where are we celebrating after?"

Before I can answer Sully leans in from the opposite side, rubbing the scar under his nose with his index finger. "I heard Les Carter is throwing a party."

"I'm not going to that," I say.

"Why not?" Ace chimes in. "You don't have to like the guy to drink his booze."

"Let's focus on diving. Then we can worry about celebrating."

I watch the first two divers prep their fulcrums and prepare to dive, thinking: *speed it up, guys. Points off for stalling.* I lean forward with my arms resting on my knees and look for Rocco on the Andover bench. He's crouched forward in the same position, staring straight at me. The left side of his mouth curves in a grin before he bites his tongue and flips me the rock-on symbol.

I wonder if Rocco knows that hand gesture is also the sign of the devil. Exactly what he should feel like right now for giving me bogus info. I start pumping my knee up and down so fast I could churn butter. Maybe there's still time to talk to him before he dives. I head to their bench but Coach McGee throws up a block.

"You can't be over here right now, son."

"I just want to wish an old teammate good luck."

"You'll have to wait and congratulate him after the meet." He flips me an arrogant grin and I spy a grayish wad of chewing gum wedged between his teeth and cheek.

Apparently he missed the part where we whooped their ass in swimming.

"Hold on. You're Theo Mackey, right?" he asks. "Rocco told me you came by looking for some information about your mom. I was set to pull her files for you over the weekend, but someone trashed the coaches' offices last night. It'll take weeks to straighten out the mess. You wouldn't happen to know anything about that, would you?"

My eyes zero in on the shark embroidered on the breast pocket of his red polo shirt. "No, sir. But I'm sorry to hear about it."

Rocco is waving his arms, fighting for my attention in the background. He gives me a questioning look over his coach's shoulder. All I have time to do is shake my head and mouth, "Don't do it."

But it's no use.

Rocco is nodding back at me in exaggerated movements, pointing with both hands stretched all the way out. He mouths back, "Oh yeah! It's on."

"Son," the Andover coach says. "It's time to go."

I trudge back to my team as the announcer starts reading the latest scores. Our guys are already ahead. There's nothing left to do now but wait. When Sully's name hits the board I know I'm almost up. Unfortunately, this is when Uncle Phil chooses to come over to the bench to talk to me. Something he's never done before.

"Why were you talking to the Andover coach?" he asks, eyes fixed on Coach McGee.

I steal a glance at Coach McGee before I look back at Uncle Phil, straightening his collar, his knuckles scraped red-raw.

*"Someone trashed the coaches' offices last night. You wouldn't happen to know anything about that, would you?"*

I feed him a half-lie, looking for the truth with an alarm ringing in my head. "I went to wish Rocco luck. What happened to your hand?"

"Flat tire." He spills the excuse easily. Maybe too easily.

But I don't have time to harp on it because I need to prep for the board. "I'm on a first-name basis with roadside assistance," I say, feeding him an equally easy lie. "But I'm about to dive so . . ." I rock back on my heels.

"Yes. Right," he says. "Break a leg."

Wrong thing to say to a diver but I let the smell of chlorine refresh my senses on the way to the ladder. Breathing in, out, in, out. Ready or not.

The din of the crowd has an echo-like quality tonight. I give myself a minute to pull my shit together. Then it's go time. Mom's dive for the win.

I get good height and enter my first rotation. So far so good. But then the water turns bloodred again, right before my eyes. I shut them tight—a major diving no-no. Not because points can be deducted, but because I'm basically flying blind and a danger to myself. I go on instinct alone, coming out of the rotations to start my first twist, counting the spirals—one, two, three—and a half. I straighten out and enter the pool like an arrow, hand over hand. Boom. Water rushes past me. I nailed it.

*Para mi madre.*

The crowd goes nuts when I break the surface. I climb out and wait for my scores. Our school uses a three-judge panel and scores between 1–10, totaled, then multiplied by the degree of difficulty. I hold my breath until my scores illuminate the board, one at a time: 8.5, 9.0, 8.5. Not too shabby.

I'm so pumped about my scores that when Trey starts nudging me I get annoyed.

Until I see why he's so hell-bent on elbowing me to death.

Rocco is on the three-meter facing backward.

My eyes shoot back to the scoreboard where it says Bennett 5239D.

Sully mutters, "What the fuck?"

Les stands, hands clasped on top of his head, chest visibly heaving. His panicky reaction compels me to look for Miles who's sitting nearby biting his nails to the quick as his cousin prepares for a dive way beyond his skill set.

When the Andover coach jumps from his seat and starts berating his assistant coaches, I realize Rocco didn't tell anyone. I doubt he even practiced. There wasn't enough time. I don't understand what he's trying to prove. Coach McGee starts yelling so furiously at his assistants he chokes on his chewing gum and starts coughing. Barking like a dog. I think about hearing Belly barking at the cliff on Monarch Night, making it the last warning I need to know something is going to go wrong.

Chip comes and crouches in front of me. "Can you believe this shit?" His face is a mask of disbelief.

Yes. I totally believe it.

Rocco rises up on his toes. You don't have to be an expert judge to see how much he's shaking. He pushes down on the board to start his backward press, but doesn't let the board come all the way to the top and it kills the spring. He throws his arms hard like he knows he needs the height, and takes flight, a little too close to the board for comfort. He gets in one good rotation and his head hits the board. Hard. The thunderous crack of his skull making contact is only outdone by the piercing screams from the audience.

The room whirls around me, then telescopes in and out. Everyone is rushing to the side of the pool. Everyone but me. People bump into my stupefied form to reach Rocco. Where blood, red fucking blood, is spilling into the water from Rocco's head. His teammates dive into the pool from all sides and circle his lifeless body, like—

*Sharks.*

Just like I saw.

Jeezus.

What the fuck did I do?

Chip dives in, followed by Ace, and Sully, and Trey. But by the time they surface, the Andover Sharks are pulling Rocco's lifeless body out of the water. Coach McGee starts CPR while people rush around on cell phones, calling for paramedics, sobbing. The commotion roars in my ears like a storm.

And then the strangest thing happens. The room becomes unnervingly quiet as everyone waits for help to arrive. The minutes stretching as emergency sirens whine in the distance, growing louder and closer, building into the wailing screech of banshees.

I press my palms to my temples, holding my head together as action resumes around me.

But I can't move.

I can't fucking move.

"This is your fault." Miles points in my face. Two of his fingernails are chewed to bloody nubs. "I know you gave him that dive *and* those pills."

I stare at him, mute. Because he's right. This all my fault.

I lit the match on this disaster too.

"Why are you accusing him?" Chip asks. "Theo would never . . . He and Rocco were friends."

*Were.*

"He did this," Miles says. "And I'm gonna prove it." Then he walks away to watch his cousin being lifted onto a stretcher and rushed from the building.

# THIRTY-THREE

**Degree of Difficulty:** A numeric value assigned to each dive indicating how hard a particular dive is to execute. Also known as a dive's tariff.

**I SQUEEZE** the steering wheel and adjust my sitting position. Chip and I have been driving around for an hour, drinking coffee and rehashing the meet. Mostly I've been listening to Chip spew theories on why Rocco would perform Les's dive. Or even try a dive that's beyond his ability in the first place. In between his understandable bouts of confusion, I've been trying to get ahold of GP and Iris. I'm nodding in response to Chip so much at this point my neck hurts.

But I'm a goddamn liar, and I can't take anymore.

"I knew." My whisper roars into a shout. "I fucking knew, goddammit." I slam my palm against the steering wheel repeatedly, then pull to the side of the road and snap the shifter into park.

"Fuck!" To hell with constant control.

Yelling feels good.

"What do you mean *you knew*?" Chip asks.

"I gave Les's dive to Rocco. That's the deal we made after he caught us in McGee's office. And I think I knew he was gonna get hurt before it happened."

No—not think—I knew. I saw. I just didn't see.

"That's what Rocco wanted when he said you owed him one?" Chip's voice is hushed by disbelief and confusion.

"Give him Les's dive or he'd tell the Andover coaches we broke into their office. He asked me for Adderall too. Jeezus. Monarch Night. Rocco floating facedown on the water. I saw this coming before it happened." I hang my head, but it doesn't stop my heart-pounding panic.

"Whoa. Slow down," Chip says. "You're not making any sense."

I run through everything I know in greater detail starting with the newspaper articles all the way through Monarch Night and GP's cancer. He listens without a peep when I say it's possible I have a genetic propensity toward level-fifty freak-outs. And then I tell him what else has come true. The water turning red before my eyes, bloody Andover Shark-infested waters. I recount what Iris and I overheard at Green Hill, and everything we know about Luanne Cole and her sister, the story about Mom's past, even a little about Iris's mom. All of it. Every deplorable word up to Rocco's accident.

It sounds bat-shit crazy and unreal to my own ears. Except it is real. I just watched it unfold.

Chip exhales loudly. "I'm not gonna lie, bro. I'm kind of pissed you didn't tell me about this stuff sooner. But now that I'm in, I'm in. What's plan B?"

"I didn't have a plan A. Everything's so screwed up, and all I can think is that I'm some sort of freak. And nobody wanted to tell me. Not even my own mom."

"You're not a *freak*, bro. You've got a freaking superpower. And from now on I'm your sidekick on all things freak-out. But I have to ask, have you been able to tell when I'd win a race?" His eyes go wide. "Or when I'm gonna get laid?"

"Since when have those things needed to be predicted in advance?"

"True," Chip says. "Too true. But if you were to see something about me, you'd tell me, right?"

I can't help but think of Iris. "Would you want me to?"

"Hell yes."

I chew the inside of my cheek and stare through the windshield at nothing in particular. "You think Rocco's gonna be okay?"

"Shit. I hope so." Chip runs his hands over his head. "That freaked me out."

I raise an eyebrow. "No pun intended. Call your mom and tell her you're gonna be out late tonight." I restart my engine. "We're going to the hospital to check on Rocco. Then we're gonna go find Iris and talk to my grandfather about what just happened."

AMY'S PANICKY voice meets us at the entrance to the emergency waiting room. "Chip! Oh my God. Where were you guys? I got your message over an hour ago."

I watch them hug. Amy's white-blond hair, pulled high and tight in a ponytail, swooshes behind her studded ears when they collide. She makes eye contact with me over Chip's shoulder, then wipes away mascara-streaked tears.

"You okay?" she asks.

I'm the opposite of okay.

The sterile smell of the hospital causes tension to mount inside me like a pressure cooker. We take adjoining seats. Amy is sandwiched between Chip and me. We all hold hands, staring at our dull reflections in the hospital's darkened windows. Hear no, see no, speak no evil.

I stare at the hairline cracks in the dingy linoleum beneath my feet. There isn't enough disinfectant in the world to make this floor appear clean. And I'm just as tainted inside. Drinking a bottle of disinfectant wouldn't change the fact that Rocco is in here in part because of me.

The attending physician rounds a corner, grim-faced, running a hand through his dark wavy hair. The set of his mouth makes my chest tighten.

"Is one of you kids Theo Mackey?"

I untangle my hand from Amy's. "I'm Theo."

"I'm Dr. Bloomquist. I have a few questions to ask regarding your friend Rocco."

"How is he?"

"Alive, but his skull is fractured."

Amy sucks in a gasp.

"The question I have for you is in regard to the drugs we found in his system. There's a family member claiming you provided Rocco with performance-enhancing drugs. Drugs that he took before diving tonight. Is that true?"

I spot the cop watching us and try not to hurl.

"Rocco asked me for some of my Adderall capsules," I say.

"You shouldn't share prescription drugs with people to whom they aren't prescribed. That being said, what we found in Rocco's system were traces of amphetamines, neuroleptics and psychotropics. In order to treat your friend effectively, Theo, I need to ask you again if you gave him anything else?"

"Nothing. I swear."

"Can we see him?" Chip asks.

"Not yet, I'm afraid. Family only. But you're welcome to wait here." The physician gives me a dubious look. "We also put a call in to"—he scans Rocco's medical chart—"Dr. Maddox over at Green Hill. Rocco's cousin informed us that your uncle was treating Rocco for a separate, personal issue. He's on his way. But in the interim we're trying to gain as much information as possible in order to help your friend."

Through all of this I hear four things running like a background track on repeat: Dr. Maddox, on his way, neuroleptics, and psychotropics.

The doctor's voice sucks me out of my black hole and I think he may have been talking the whole time.

"If there's anything else I should know, now would be the best time to tell me." The doctor waits several seconds before I shake my head, "Okay. We're keeping Rocco in a coma until the swelling in his brain goes down. We'll keep doing everything we can, but if you think of anything else don't hesitate to come forward."

"Coma," Amy whispers. "Oh my God."

"That's a good thing," Dr. Bloomquist says, patting Amy's shoulder before he leaves.

Pressure and guilt push at me from all sides but I barely have time to take a breath before Les-freaking-Carter struts into the waiting room. He stops short when he catches the grave look on all our faces, but if our expressions serve as warning it doesn't stop him from running his mouth.

"What's going on? Miles just told me Rocco's in a coma because Theo gave him drugs before the meet that messed him up."

*That's it—*

I fly from my seat and pin Les against a wall, pressing my forearm against his throat. He tries to speak, but I'm crushing his windpipe. His face reddens and I keep pressing, hoping his head turns purple and bursts so I can be rid of him for good. Chip rips me away, leaving Les gasping for air.

"What the hell are you thinking?" Chip asks between gritted teeth. "Control yourself, bro. There's a freaking cop walking around and you're suspect numero uno."

I jerk away from Chip and walk to the windows.

But then Les says, "What's his problem?" and I lose it again.

Spinning back, so pissed I could spit blood. If it weren't for Chip, jumping between us, I'd strangle him again.

"You're my fucking problem," I tell Les. "Why are you even here right now? Aren't you supposed to be throwing some stupid victory party?"

"Les drove *me* here. Sheesh," Amy says. "What's gotten into you? I was at his house trying to get everyone out who wasn't at the meet when I got Chip's call."

*What's gotten into me?* That's the question of the hour, maybe the year.

"I have as much right to be here as you," Les says. "More actually."

"*More?* Are you fucking joking? You and your stupid 4½ twists are partially responsible for this."

"Christ, Mackey. Is that what this is about? My dive? Fine. It was Rocco who trained with me over the summer. But at one point, I asked to train alone because I knew the 4½ Twist would be a kick-ass dive for our team. I could have given Rocco the dive myself anytime. He and I are *together.* There. I said it. Even if he didn't want you to know." Les swallows uncomfortably. "I've been trying to talk to you for weeks, about a lot of stuff, but you always blow me off. But I tried, man. I really did. And I hate to say this, because I'm really into the guy, but Rocco played you."

"Just Rocco? You're the one who left those articles on my truck."

"I didn't leave you any articles. I left you a note on my way into school once because I dropped my phone in the pool at practice."

"Then who did?"

Les drops a hand on top of his head as he nails the truth. "Miles. That little shit asked me to pull an old newspaper from the archives. Said he needed it for homework. I pulled the edition but I didn't look at the content."

Rocco's little birdie.

He's—what did Iris call him—a viceroy in a monarch suit?

"I've been trying to warn you that Rocco wanted to know what dive I had up my sleeve. He was so pissed about it his parents sent him to see Dr. Maddox to help him with the pressure of diving at a new school. But I don't think your uncle helped him all that much because whenever Rocco would come back from his appointments he'd go off about how you weren't God's gift to diving and you needed someone to knock you off your pedestal."

"So why didn't Miles give him the dive if Rocco wanted it so bad? Rocco's been harping on me since I made captain."

"I'm guessing he wanted to see if he could get you to betray your own team."

To sabotage me. Rocco, not Les.

*"No Worries, Mr. Perfection. I'm good at keeping secrets. But you're gonna owe me one."*

"Shit," I mutter. Then add a few more choice words because even after everything I did see, I was blind.

"Miles snitched on me for trying to talk to you." Les. says. "Rocco and I got into a huge fight about it. He was convinced I told you we were together. I still don't get why that's such a big deal."

"Maybe because Rocco tried to kiss me once when we were freshmen and I sort of freaked," I tell Les. That's my best guess. "Not because I have a problem with him being gay. I just wasn't expecting it and he took be by surprise."

"You kissed him?" Les asks. I see the hurt in eyes.

I shake my head. "No. I pushed him, which is worse."

"Hold up," Chip says, looking at Les. "You and Rocco are together? Like *together* together? Didn't you go to prom junior year with that chick Carly Whatsername with the huge—" He holds two invisible basketballs in front of his chest.

"Chip!" Amy scolds. "Why does that matter?"

"The guy just took the term come-out as a diver to a new level. I was merely making an observation."

I get Chip's diving joke, but can only think about what Les just said. *Together. He played you. Miles.* I'm a fucking idiot. That's why Miles asked if we were *secretly being gay.* Rocco's presence at the dive demo wasn't about me at all. He was watching Les. I should have figured out they were together by the way they were acting at Monarch Night.

I wasn't paying attention to the damn signs.

"Les, man. I'm sorry. I screwed up. Rocco had me over a barrel on something and I thought giving him your dive was my only way out."

"And the drugs?" Les asks.

"He asked me for some Adderall to give him an edge. That's it. I swear. I don't know what that doctor's talking about."

Unless . . .

*Acid Dreams, Hallucinations, Mycology, Manifesting Minds.*

Holy fuck. The books on Uncle Phil's shelves said it all. He had Coach Porter's picture inside *Manifesting Minds*. His knuckles looked scraped, maybe from trashing Coach McGee's office. He's the one who told me he didn't think I'd find anything at the county clerk's office. My body goes rigid. *This was a lady that came asking. Southern. Polite.*

Lianne-fucking-Cole. His favorite pet.

"I know how pushy Rocco can get when he wants something," Les is saying. "As long as he's okay, that's what matters."

"Listen, Les." I cut him off. "I know this might sound insensitive, but I have to go find my grandfather before Dr. Maddox shows up."

"I get it," Les says "Rocco's parents are pissed and they're blaming you."

He doesn't get it. Not entirely. But that's okay because I think I do.

"I have to go with Theo," Chip tells Amy. "Are you okay catching a ride with Les?"

"Of course. You're not the only one with bros."

I look at Les with remorse and he says, "It's okay, Mackey. Go. I got this." And I know it's true.

THE AUTOMATIC doors of the Ellis Hollow Medical Center split open from the center, freeing me from the fluorescent guilt chamber. The harsh wind beyond the doors whips across my face, forcing its way into my mouth and nose. I gulp the air before it enters my lungs like it's some sort of elixir sent to cool the blistering thoughts suffocating me.

"Rocco tried to kiss you when we were freshmen?" Chip asks. "Really?"

"The night of the fire."

His eyes are growing wide with shock, too wide for the confession, and before I know what's happening I walk straight into Phil Maddox.

"Theo." He grabs my arms to steady me. "I thought you might be here checking on your friend."

I twist out of his grasp. "More like covering your mess."

Sometimes blurting is warranted. Despite what my mom said.

"Excuse me?"

"You heard me. What the hell have you been giving me because I'm not sure it's Adderall."

"Even if that were true, no drug can enhance what isn't already there. You have your mother's gift, the ability to see in your mind what you haven't yet observed. I merely gave that ability a nudge."

I feel a new surge of anger. "Is it a gift or were you *manifesting my mind* for your own agenda? Maybe I should go piss in a cup for the doctor who's working on Rocco to be sure?"

"If you think they'd be able to explain your gift, be my guest. But you might want to know what's at stake first." He gives Chip a dismissive glance. "If you wait here we can discuss this privately when I'm through. The middle of the sidewalk is hardly the time or place to—"

"We don't have anything else to discuss. But good luck in there with Rocco's family. You're gonna need it when you explain why he has mind-tripping drugs in his system."

"He got those from you, didn't he? That's what the doctor insinuated when he called."

"Lucky for me GP and Curtis are already working on whether or not that's true."

I turn and pull a stunned Chip away from the hospital knowing I have more explaining to do.

"Theo, come back here. You're making a serious mistake. We're family."

"No, we're not. You're not my goddamn uncle. And you were never my dad's friend."

I keep walking and don't look back, even when he says, "This won't end the way you think. We're not through here."

# THIRTY-FOUR

**Rocking the Board:** Excessive rocking of the board by rising up on the toes to get the board moving and create more spring merely increases the diver's chance of losing balance.

I CUT the lights and engine when we approach Iris's house, letting Bumblebee roll down the gravel driveway until I have to apply the squeaking brakes. There aren't many lights on this road and her broad, imposing house emerges like a mountain in the pitch darkness.

"Are you sure about this?" Chip asks. "It's past midnight."

"Trust me. She needs to come with us. I know what I'm doing." I get out of my truck and shut the door as quietly as possible, shifting my eyes to the house. "But listen, if Iris's dad walks out here with a shotgun, we might want to haul ass."

"Are you for real?"

I nod and pick some gravel from the driveway, weighing the stones in my hand against the insanity of my actions. If I pick the wrong window, and her dad comes out here and finds me flinging rocks, I'll probably never see Iris again.

"Which one is it?" Chip asks.

"Your guess is as good as mine."

He gives me his you've-got-to-be-shitting-me face. "How do you know she's even home? I'm not down with getting shot just because you're being an impulsive jerk-off."

"We're here now, so let's do this. I'm tired of questioning and explaining everything, to her, to you, to GP. I want the truth out in the open."

I slink up to the house thinking about which room I'd give my daughter if I were an overprotective dad. I wave for Chip to follow and we move along the side yard to the back, dead leaves crunching beneath our feet.

"Do those curtains look purple to you?"

"They look dark," Chip says. "Could be purple. Could be old-man navy blue. Fuck if I know. Just don't get me shot, bro."

We keep moving farther around the house until we're almost all the way around. And there, on the far corner, is a room with Christmas lights strung around the window.

"I bet that's it." I hold my breath and throw the first rock, hitting the house with a dull thud.

"You're a lousy shot," Chip says. "Here, let me." He takes the smallest rock from my hand and hauls off, hitting the glass with a sharp peck. "Want me to do another one?"

"No, I got it." I pull my arm back and throw, hitting the window this time.

I elbow Chip when the curtains part and Iris appears. She points to the front of the house and we retrace our steps. Three-quarters of the way around we hear a screen door creak. I stop moving and throw my arm in front of Chip, just in case her dad heard us and is coming out first. Shotgun at the ready.

Chip clenches the back of my jacket in his hand. I don't need to see his face to know he's scared. Hell, so am I. Her dad's warning to stay away was clear as day. But the figure coming around the corner is wispy, and moving on light feet.

"Are you out of your minds?" Iris whisper-yells. She throws a quick glance at the house.

"Can you come with us to my grandfather's house?"

"I can't leave. My dad flipped out after he picked me up from the Blue Belle and double-grounded me, which was bad enough. But then Curtis Jacobs and your grandfather showed up and told him they're trying to help you sort some stuff out about your parents and that my dad should keep me out of it. It sounded like there was way more to the story about my mom than I ever imagined. I overheard my dad telling them he thinks Dr. Maddox caused my mom's car accident. I mean, intentionally caused it."

A pang of pure horror stabs my chest. And then, like a fucking dog that's been conditioned to trust, I slip into sad disbelief. "That's insane. Phil Maddox isn't who I thought he was, not by a long shot, *but murder?* Jeezus, Iris. Please, just come with us."

"It's not that I don't want to," Iris says. "It's just my family's involvement with Dr. Maddox is complicated. I'm not even sure I understand it. My dad made it sound like he was obsessed with my mom. Not in a sexual way, but as his patient. He wanted to include her in some paper he was writing, and she refused."

"Because she was gifted?" I ask.

Iris nods.

"All the more reason for you to come. We can find out the whole truth together." I offer her my hand in the darkness, but she hesitates. Sneaking off with me in the middle of the night is guaranteed to land her in a heap of trouble. Infinitely grounded.

She stares at her house; conflicted by the truths she's already heard.

I inch closer, looking into her midnight-blue eyes. "Please, Iris."

She flicks a glance at Chip, standing a few feet away.

"Don't look at me," he says. "I'm out here ready to take a bullet for the guy. This goes way beyond the *no matter what* of our original bet, by the way, Theo."

Chip's loyalty gives me an idea that puts me short of begging. "We're partners in this Iris, remember? Big Mack and French Fry. I need you beside me on this."

Iris takes me by the arms and spins me a quarter turn so she can see me better in the light from the porch. "You're afraid."

"I am," I tell her. "But I have to do this anyway."

Iris throws a quick glance at her house and sighs. "Okay. I'll go. I gave you my word." She spins me toward my truck. "Please don't make me regret this."

# THIRTY-FIVE

**Twist:** Any movement during a dive that occurs when the diver rotates around an imaginary vertical axis that runs from the head to the toes of a diver.

I USE the fifteen-minute drive over to GP's to fill Iris in on what happened at the meet and hospital. I finish up with the confrontation I had with Phil Maddox right before I march through the front door, calling out to let him know I'm home.

"Maybe he's in his office." I knock on the locked door. "GP, you in there? I've got Chip and Iris with me." I try the door knob. Nothing.

"Where's the key?" Iris asks. "Can't you just walk in there?"

"My grandfather keeps it on him. He's been sick and goes in there for privacy. He hasn't been looking so great the last few days. I'm supposed to call Curtis if something happens to him."

"Sick with the flu?" Iris asks cautiously.

"Cancer." It's incredible how fast and easy it is to hate that word.

"Oh." Iris makes a pained expression. "Maybe he fell asleep. Pick the lock. That's what I'd do if it were my grandfather."

"She has a point," Chip says. "It wouldn't be the first time. I'll go hunt down a nail clipper."

"Wait. Try this first." Iris removes the bobby pin holding back the front of her hair and hands it to me.

I bend the end so it has a little handle for me to wrap my fingers under, then pause with my hand on the doorknob, dreading what I might find. I blow the air in my lungs at the door and insert the bobby pin, jiggling and pushing the lock until I hear an almost imperceptible click. The bobby pin inserts farther, but the lock isn't giving way. I repeat the jiggling and it clicks again, and then a third time. The pin is all the way inserted when the knob gives way.

"Holy shit," Chip says. "You should have been a cat burglar."

"The Cat and Mouse are working in tandem," Iris says. "Those are the cards you were dealt together."

"I remember. But losing anyone else isn't an option for me. That's never gonna be in my cards again."

She gives me a sad smile and I push the door open. I let it bang against the wall with a thud, and stand silent at the threshold before snapping on the light. GP isn't inside.

Seconds pass in silence as we take in the room: desk, recliner, crappy TV and VCR. This time, there isn't a single Jack Daniel's bottle in sight. But the room has transformed. Tacked to the paneled surface of my grandfather's office is an assemblage of information: pictures, maps, notes torn from random sheets of paper, articles. And at the nexus of everything sits a bulging photo of Phil Maddox. Lines are drawn in red Sharpie making connections across documents and photos, creating a web of connections.

"Looks like your grandfather's been working on your family tree."

"Not my grandfather," I tell Iris. "This is my dad's handiwork."

I pull the pushpins holding Phil's photo in place to see what's causing it to bulge and find a press release from a psych journal, dated March 7, 1997, boasting his succession to head psychiatrist at Green Hill Psychiatric Hospital. Along with the board of directors' praise and '*high hopes Dr. Phillip Maddox will produce breakthrough research in the area of abnormal psychology. Putting Green Hill on the Map.*'

As I pin the release back on the board, I notice clippings from local newspapers reporting on the fire that claimed my grandmother's life when Dad was a senior in high school. Morbid curiosity moves me to flip the newsprint and I find an arson report attached. I scan the page quickly, picking up bits and pieces, enough to get the gist: juvenile firebug, name withheld, willful and malicious intent, arson in the first degree, juvenile detention. I flip again and discover a duplicate report for the same fire, same date, same dwelling, same everything. Except the cause of fire: ACCIDENTAL. This is the other suspicious fire.

My hands and neck leach sweat as I keep flipping, only to find the report from the night my own house burned to the ground. I'm looking for one thing: cause of fire. And here, in black and white, I find the parallel: ACCIDENTAL. The asterisk drawn in Sharpie on this report matches the one on the picture of Phil Maddox. I flip the pages and compare official signatures. Bruce Mackey, Fire Chief, and Curtis Jacobs, Fire Marshal signed off on all three.

Jeezus.

These are cover-ups. I'm the reason GP lost his job. Heat rises from my chest to face, building until my head feels like it might detonate.

I place a flat palm on the wall and glance behind me with no set focal point. "You guys should see this."

They don't answer and I turn more fully.

Iris and Chip are on their own islands of intrigue. Chip is riffling through a box on the floor. And Iris is engrossed by a stack of papers on my grandfather's desk to the point of deafness.

I refocus on the collage. Mom's adoptive parents—the Rogans—are haphazardly tacked together on the far left of everything else. A sad pair of parental specimens, tossed aside like trash and disregarded by big black X's drawn over their faces. After everything GP told me, it's more than they deserve. I barely give the Rogans a second's glance, because Mom's biological parents, Bohden and Lena Dudyk, catch my eye. I follow their photos to a handwritten note:

*Lena Dudyk is a descendant of famed Ukrainian psychic Elena Balanchuk. E.B. was accused of witchcraft in the late seventeenth century, tried, and hanged. Historical research shows possible multigeneration link to psychic ability throughout the Balanchuk line. Children in the Balanchuk family, particularly those with light hair and eyes, are given up for adoption, even today, due to fear of religious or social persecution.*

Whoa.

*"Thank you, Madame Balanchuk," Dad said. "But this outcome you think you saw coming takes the fucking prize."*

GP was right. My dad had unintentionally gathered everything I'd ever need for a stellar family history project including psychics, crazies, and European witch hunts. Give or take a few blows to my psyche.

I join Iris at GP's desk to look for more information. There are two folders labeled PATIENTS and OTHER sitting under the heavy clay elephant I made my grandfather in third grade. Inside there are more labeled photos. Not all of them familiar, but the few that are include Lianne and Luanne Cole, one as a young girl, the other almost the same as I saw her at Green Hill; and Valentina Gabor, the old woman at the hospital who claimed to recognize Iris. I come across a photo of a woman with dark hair and light eyes like Iris and flip it over. Ioana Dalca. Iris and her mom look so much alike you'd think she time traveled.

"Um, Theo," Chip says hesitantly. "I found your birth certificate."

"I already have that," I mutter.

"Not this one, you don't." He swallows uncomfortably and hands it over.

I put the photos down and take it from his hands, my eyes lingering on his anxious face before I read the pertinent information. Mother: Sophia Mackey. Father: Phillip Christopher Maddox.

Reality clicks like the cock of a gun and I stumble backward into the desk. I want to say something, react, but the truth is creating a wailing chorus in my head that erases external sound and motion.

*"Nobody did this to hurt you, Mitch. But we thought it was your right to know."*

*"What can I tell you; the heart wants . . ."*

*"Blood doesn't lie."*

*"Get out, both of you, before I do something I'll regret."*

*"It is possible for a person to love two people at the same time,"* GP said. *"After you do some growin' up, though, you realize you can't have both. At the end of the day, choices need to be made."*

No wonder my dad was angry.

Chip shakes me. "Say something, man. You're freaking me out."

"Phil Maddox *is my father?*" I laugh, even though my stomach is clenched. "Tall, green eyes, same build, the similarity in our smiles. You said that yourself, Chip. And it's true. Maybe I never noticed because of his dark hair, but I look nothing like the Mackeys. Jeezus."

Iris gasps but it's not from my news.

She's holding the file labeled PATIENTS, opened to the photo of her mom. "I don't know why I'm so surprised. I mean, I know now, but . . ." She looks over at the stuff tacked on the wall like she might make another connection to her own family. And then she gasps again. "Do you know what that is?" she says, pulling me toward a map tacked to GP's wall. Two rectangles are circled in red pen.

I shake my head.

"It's a burial plot map. Each rectangle represents a grave. Usually the last names of the deceased are written on them, as well. But these are just numbered." She takes a pen and writes 856+857 on the inside of her wrist. "In case I need to ask my dad."

"Maybe they're family plots. Don't people do that sometimes, in advance?" I wonder if GP was making provisional plans, if things go south.

"They do," she says. "But these numbers are too high for Mount Pleasant. There's only one place in town with this many plots, Theo. Ward Hill Cemetery."

"Why would my dad care about a couple of unmarked graves?"

Her eyes dart to a thick bundle of paper on the seat of GP's recliner. "Shit."

It's the first time I've heard Iris swear.

"I swore I wouldn't tell," she says. "I wasn't even supposed to know, but I overhead my dad talking to your grandfather and Curtis Jacobs, and I made him tell me everything, including what he said to you the day you came to my house about the whole 'freebie psych treatments' thing. Do you remember that?"

"He said a lot of crazy stuff that day."

"And I know why. After my mom died, Dr. Maddox agreed to forgive her steep psychiatry treatment bills if my dad was willing to find him two private burial plots he could use at his discretion."

"To bury someone?"

"Or some*thing*," Iris says. "I'd like to believe my dad wouldn't let him bury a person. But it might explain why your grandfather has a brand new shovel next to the door."

I follow her eyes to the door.

Jeezus.

"GP was gonna see what he could dig up." Literally and figuratively.

Iris goes to GP's chair and picks up a bundle of papers.

"What is that?" I ask uncomfortably.

She gives me the same wary look I saw when she read the article about my mom. "A research paper written by Dr. Maddox about the effects of Philomax. At first I thought it was about my mom, because the names are redacted, but now it makes more sense that it might be about you and *your mom*."

I take the bundle from Iris, watching her closely as I stretch off the rubber band binding, wondering what she's already read. The first few sheets are typical: title, subject, patient information. Then I start reading.

Removing the Roadblock Between Traditional and
Parapsychology
A Gene Mutation Study

*By Phillip C. Maddox, PhD, PsyD*

**Female Subject A, Inpatient [BL-08]**
Inpatient [BL-08] erroneously presents with psychosis, current episode [F31.2], characterized by remaining presence of strong delusions and hallucinations, with a seemingly psychic connection to Male Subject B, Outpatient BL-09 [BL-09], due to genetic connection and parental bond. Administration of Philomax in BL-08 with addition of amphetamine salts and increasing microdoses of psilocybin shows a significant increase in precognitive abilities, as well as shortened time span between precognition and proof of vision.

**Male Subject B, Outpatient [BL-09]**
Beginning trials of Philomax in combination with amphetamine salts and psilocybin to test precognitive ability increasing with age and final maturation stage out of puberty thus far successful. Subject B presents as unawares, as yet, of chemical changes in compound and has not made connection to pharmaceutical and his own precognitive ability.

Revisit research paper. Maddox, Phillip. Parapsychology and Athleticism: A Case for Believing in Mystery. *Journal of Psychiatric Phenomenon.* (1994).

I skim a few more pages to grasp the central point and the one thing absolutely clear is that the paper *is* about Mom and me. Not only that, the sonofabitch has been giving us Philomax, some experimental *Doors of Perception* shit. The same psilocybin-based drug Iris said her mom was taking.

*"Are they maladaptive, Theo?"*

*"Are you seeing something now?"*

*"Believe me, I've put people under observation for far less."*

I'm sure you have, you motherfucker.

(Pun definitely intended this time).

There is some humor to it, though, because I'm a complete idiot. GP warned me. Les tried to warn me. Even Coach Porter saw it in my eyes. I'm the only one that didn't see.

The irony in that is a fucking joke.

I keep scanning pages of psychobabble until I get closer to the end and find a patient transcription that makes my blood freeze.

080103 102

---

**Onset:** Age ten. Patient involuntarily committed, by parent/ guardian. BL-08 to Boston Public Psychiatric Hospital for inpatient care, 11/12/79. Patient believes she predicted the death of her teacher. Estimated stay, one month.

**Second admittance:** Age sixteen Recommended by parent and physician, Dr. Charles Aldridge. BL-08 involuntarily recommitted to Boston Public Psychiatric Hospital for inpatient care. 8/13/84. Patient believes she predicted the death of a friend.

I swallow hard and turn the page, skimming pertinent patient information to read a transcription.

**MED-SCRIBE 1.3**
**MED-SCRIBE TRANSCRIPTION SERVICES**

---

**SYSTEM PARAMETERS:** Language detection: English. Delay 3.2 seconds. Silence threshold: -6. Frequency Rate: 20–22kHz.
**TRANSCRIPTION PARAMETERS PER [GHPH]:** ↑Raised

Voice, Anger. ↓Soft Voice, Whisper. Verbatim w/ omit Patient
Names. Format: MS Word

---

CLIENT: GREEN HILL PSYCHIATRIC HOSPITAL
THERAPIST (TH): DR. PHILLIP C. MADDOX
OTHER PERSONNEL (OP1): Nurse, Janice Fletcher
OTHER PERSONNEL (OP2): Psych Technician, Darrell
  Banks
PATIENT (PT): BL-08 | ADMIT DATE: 8/1/15
DOB: 7/11/71 | S: Female | W: 135 | H: 5'10" | Age: 32
HAIR: Blond | EYES: Green
DATE OF RECORDED SESSION: 8/6/15
DSM-IV AXIS: 296.43, 296.44, 296.65

---

[BEGIN TRANSCRIPT]

[SHUFFLING PAPERS]

TH: You've been involuntary committed for recurring
    hallucinatory episodes.

[PAUSE]

TH: [PATIENT NAME REDACTED], do you understand
    what I'm telling you?

[SCRAPING SOUND]

PT: No. I don't understand. You have to let me out of here,
    right now.↑ I have to know if [NAME REDACTED] is
    okay.

[PAUSE]

[FOOTSTEPS]

[JANGLING]

TH: He is. Please, sit down, [PATIENT NAME REDACTED].
    The door is locked.

[POUNDING]

PT: Let me out.↑

[JANGLING]

PT: You have to let me see him. He's going to have night-mares, horrible nightmares, because of you. I know. I saw. Can't you see what you're doing?↑

TH: If you don't take a seat and gain control of yourself, I'll be forced to have you restrained. Is that how you want to do this?

[PAUSE]

[FOOTSTEPS]

TH: I brought you here because a seventy-two-hour obser-vation is the best course of treatment until you're well enough to exercise sound judgment.

PT: You sonofabitch.↓

TH: I'm trying to keep [NAME REDACTED] safe from knowledge until it's time. Isn't that what you and [NAME REDACTED] ultimately want for him?

[SIGH]

PT: No. Not this.↑ Oh, God. I should have seen this coming.

TH: Seen what coming?

[PAUSE]

PT: This. Are you crazy? [INDISCERNIBLE].↓

TH: I'm not the one on seventy-two-hour psych observa-tion, [PATIENT NAME REDACTED].

TH: Let's go back to [NAME REDACTED] that first time he jumped from the cliff. Weren't you concerned for his safety?

PT: No.

[PAUSE]

PT: But I am now. Is that why you brought me back to this hellhole? [INDISCERNIBLE]↓ Have you just been waiting for [NAME REDACTED] to show his ability? You bastard. You promised I'd never see the inside of a hospital again.

TH: You made promises too.

PT:   Tell me if he's the real reason you brought me here?

[PAUSE]

PT:   Answer me, Phillip.↑

TH:   I must insist that you call me Dr. Maddox during our sessions.

[PAUSE]

[SINGLE LOUD BANGING SOUND]

PT:   Answer me, damn it.↑ Is he the reason?↑

[SCRAPING SOUND]

[FOOTSTEPS]

[SHUFFLING PAPERS]

[SINGLE BUZZING SOUND]

TH:   Nurse, I need a restraint in room 301 five two one cocktail.

PT:   Don't you dare. You bastard.↑

TH:   [PATIENT NAME REDACTED], the pot shouldn't call the kettle black. Now let go of me and sit down, or I'll make it so you never see [NAME REDACTED] again. That is within my power.

PT:   You wouldn't. I thought you loved me. Us?↓

TH:   I could say the same thing until you turned the other cheek.

PT:   [NAME REDACTED] is smarter than you think. He'll figure it all out. You'll see. Or he will. I didn't raise a weakling. I raised a champion.

TH:   [NAME REDACTED] will see what I help him see, when I want him to see it. So will you. I'm trying to help us all. You do understand that, don't you? I only want what's best for him.

[PAUSE]

[DOOR OPENS]

OP:   We're here, Doctor.

PT:   No.↑ Don't. Get that away from me.↑

[SCREAM FEMALE]

[OP]:     This will be much easier if you cooperate, Miss. Other-
          wise Darrell here will have to use physical restraints.
[OP2]:    Your choice, Miss.
[PT]:     Ouch. No. For God's sake, Phillip. He's your son.↑
[PAUSE]
TH:       Bring her to her room once she's sedated. Then bring
          me the file on Outpatient BL-09 [BL-09]. I'll speak to
          her again once she's calm.
[CLICK]
[END TRANSCRIPT]

I flip back to the title of his paper. "I can't fucking believe it. He's working on proving a link between traditional and parapsychology, saying my mom and I share some gene mutation that predisposes us to precognition that reads like—fucking hallucinations."

"You mean like your freak-outs?" Chip asks.

"I mean exactly like my freak-outs. I thought everything ended the night of the fire, but that's when all of this began."

*"The most important thing I've learned as a psychiatrist is that it's never too late for anything."*

Seeing Iris on the cliff when I was a kid was the kickoff, which means adding the Philomax after Dad died was his long-awaited rocket booster. I go back and look at the date on the footer of the research paper and my breath hitches. "Jeezus-fucking-Christ. My mom might still be alive."

"At Green Hill?" Iris's eyes grow wide as she registers what that means.

She reaches a hand out to comfort me, but the voice of a child fills the room and startles us. We turn to see Chip kneeling in front of an old TV and VCR.

"Sorry," he says. "The label said PHILLIP CHARLES MADDOX, EASTER, AGE SEVEN. DEPARTMENT OF CHILDCARE SERVICES. I pushed the tape into the machine at the same time I heard what you said about your mom and it started to play. Give me a sec to stop this stupid thing."

The face of seven-year-old Phil Maddox fills the screen, and despite the sickness growing in my stomach over the revelation that my mom may still be alive, I say, "Don't. Let it play."

"Whatcha doing there, Phil?" says a man with a deep voice whose face we don't see. Only his acid-washed jeans and work boots. A foster parent, I assume.

"Killing spiders."

"Why on earth would you do that, son?"

"I'm not your son. Spiders are gross-terrible-evil. They have to die."

"Who told you that?"

The video zooms in on Phil Maddox's childhood fingers as he reaches behind him and presents a book of matches, igniting a spider excised of its legs before the man realizes what's happening.

"Oh, hey, hey, hey, wait a second." The video shakes around as the man stomps on the flame with a heavy boot. "Whoa now. Where did you find those matches?"

"I keep them under my mattress."

The video cuts to static and the white noise fills my head like a hundred matches struck at once. I keep them under my mattress too. Another secret. Too many to count.

A wave of headlights cuts across the doorway and we all freeze like scared rabbits.

"Maybe that's my grandfather. He said he was gonna try to talk to Phil in the parking lot before the meet, but then all that stuff happened with Rocco. Maybe he decided to go to his house or something."

I go to the kitchen and split the blinds. Phil's charcoal Escalade is pulling up to the curb across the street. My moment of hope explodes into frenzy.

"It's Dr. Maddox. We gotta go."

"We can't just run out there and let him see us," Chip says. "Look around you."

"Take everything you can. Tapes, the research paper, whatever you can carry and we'll sneak out the back through the garage." I rip articles and photos off the pinboard, shuffling them into a messy pile. Iris dashes next to me and grabs whatever she can.

"Wait!" Iris stops abruptly and touches my arm. "Do you smell that?"

It's not until I hear a *splash* that the smell of gasoline hits me. "Shit! Take whatever you've got. We have to move."

I peek through several windows before leading us to the living room, hoping we can sneak past Phil but it's too late. He's walking inside from the back deck, holding a red gas canister. Normal buttoned-up attire swapped for jeans, a pullover, and gloves.

When he sees us barrel into the room, arms loaded with as much as we can carry, an acid grin claims his face.

"Oh my God," Iris yelps. "It's you."

"Was this not in the cards?" he asks.

I don't remember mentioning Iris's card reading to him.

Chip tugs my sleeve and nudges his head behind us, but I don't look. I don't even move because I'm too busy watching Phil Maddox toss the contents of the canister around the room with his steely gaze locked on mine.

GP's gruff voice booms behind me and I jump out of my skin before stepping aside.

"You don't have to do this, Phil. We can still let bygones be bygones," GP says.

"I don't think we can, but you are tenacious. Following me from the parking lot to the hospital. It's a wonder you didn't get here first."

"Nice trick with the battery."

"An oldie but goodie," Phil says.

I narrow my eyes, thinking of Bumblebee sitting with a dead battery in the parking lot at school.

"I honestly can't decide what impresses me more. The fact that you climbed your way out of a bottle to finish what Mitch started so many years ago, or how quickly Theo caught on to the triggers I dropped like breadcrumbs along the way."

"Had to," GP says. "He's my grandson."

"Is he?" Phil's eyes land on me. "You should have listened when I said you were making a serious mistake. Don't you know blood is thicker than water?"

"Not always," I say. "Nature versus nurture."

"The oldest and most debated argument in the history of psychology." He pulls the Zippo lighter Dad gave him from his pocket and strikes the flint. "Which side of that argument do you think your propensity for starting fires comes from, nature or nurture?"

I see Phil Maddox for what he is, what he's always been, and hold my ground next to GP. It isn't until Phil fixates on the pointed yellow flame, and I recognize myself in his gaze, that I realize the true danger.

"Stop." GP barrels forward to tackle him before he drops the lighter, but he's too weak from his cancer treatments, making it easy for Phil to put him in a stranglehold.

"Clearly I didn't give Mitch enough credit considering the amount of information in your possession."

"Let him go." I push the documents in my arms on Iris and Phil glares at me, challenging me to make a move.

"Go!" GP demands of me. "I ain't the one that needs saving, kid. My clock's already punched. Take what you got and get outta here."

"No!" Iris roars.

And she's right.

"You're all the family I've got."

"We both know that ain't true now, don't we? Go *now*," he says. "Before you get us all killed."

I spin against a heavy conscience, pushing my friends toward the door. "You heard the man. Go! Get to my truck."

"You could stay," Phil proposes. "There's still time for you to make the right choice, son. Let your friends go. We can work something out."

Hearing Phil Maddox call me *son* puts a hitch in my step. I wheel around with so much fury in my eyes he tightens his grip on GP.

"You made me a promise, Theo," GP says. "You know who to call. And you know what you gotta do. Go, goddammit. Make me proud."

I nod. I've never made a promise I couldn't keep. Maybe that's nature versus nurture too.

# THIRTY-SIX

**Rip Entry:** Entering the water with zero to little splash producing the sound of ripping paper.

WE MAKE a beeline for the front door and I grab the shovel while running past GP's office. I jump the concrete stoop and race to my truck, turning my head to see Iris lagging behind, struggling to hang on to everything she took from the house. I grab most of her stack and pull her along. There isn't time for being gentle; we have to move.

"Chip." I release my grip on Iris to toss him my keys. "Drive."

"You sure?"

We duck for cover as the whoosh of an angry rip current bellows through the air. The fire has taken its first angry gulp, opening wide to devour everything in its path. Flames are already starting to lick the shake-shingles of the house, mesmerizing me. Fire. Always fire. I toss the shovel into the backseat beside Iris and hand her my dad's evidence.

We hear a loud pop, almost like a firework, an explosion.

"Was that a gun?" Chip asks. His eyes are as wide as the circles on my instrument panel.

"Maybe. Yes. Fuck! I don't know." I hit the dashboard twice. "Go. Drive." My heart is beating so hard it hurts. I think of my dad, his heart attack while driving. I don't know if GP will get out but I can't let anyone else get hurt because of me.

Chip throws an arm behind the passenger seat and nails the

gas, burning rubber as he peels out of the driveway, then takes off going the wrong way.

"Holy fuck. Where to?" he asks.

"Bang a U-ey, then head for the rotary and take Route twelve." I turn to Iris in the backseat. "You okay?"

She nods, trembling.

"What the hell's on Route twelve?"

"Green Hill. We're going after my mom."

"*Now?* What the fuck, Theo? Maybe we should go to the police."

"I'm not waiting around for Ellis Hollow's finest if my mom is rotting in that place. Because if we *don't* get my mom out of there—or worse if I'm fucking wrong—then that asshole becomes my legal guardian."

Chip torques the wheel, careening my truck to the right as we squeal in a semicircle and speed in the opposite direction. The perfect Masshole driver for the job.

I rubberneck to look at the flames rising above the gabled roof of my grandfather's house. Phil's Escalade tears out of the long driveway after us. Speeding to within an inch of my truck's bumper, flooding our interior with his brights.

Father of the fucking year.

Chip flips the tab on the rearview to deflect the glare and spots the Escalade in the mirror. "Holy shit! I can't believe he's chasing us."

"Forget everything I've ever said about your shitty driving and punch it."

He grips the steering wheel tighter and floors the gas pedal, pushing his full weight into the seat.

Iris gasps and grips the edge of the driver's seat. "Oh God, Theo. I don't want to die in a car." Her panic is as palpable as her biggest fear, history repeating itself.

"My dad doesn't even know where I am," she says. "What if—"

"It's okay, Iris. Breathe. I'm gonna call Curtis and have him meet us at Green Hill. Being the fire marshal also makes him a statie. He'll know what to do."

"You don't understand," she says. "Dr. Maddox came to see me at the carnival. He was the intense customer I had right before you. I didn't know." Her voice is shaking. "I don't usually tell people this because . . . I'm not supposed to, but I have this thing where sometimes I can see people's colors, like their auras. In the tent, he was putting off all ego, and angry red. I've learned to associate colors with different personalities. Chip is often happy yellow or blue unless he's talking about girls. And, Theo, you're almost always orange and blue, but lately you've been going a little gray and ultraviolet. But your grandfather—I'm so sorry."

She's nervous, speaking faster than usual, but so many things she's said, *an orange vibe, normal blue skies, muddy,* make sense now.

"What about my grandfather?" I ask.

"His aura was almost black when he and Curtis came to my house. I've only seen that once before, around my mom a few days before she died."

She doesn't have to say anything else. I get it. Death was already coming for him.

I rub my sweaty palms on my jeans and dig into my pocket for my phone. But trying to do anything other than panic while racing at breakneck speed around the world's worst rotary is easier said than done. I arch against the restraint of the seat belt and dig until I pull it free. With it comes several dollar bills and the access badge for Green Hill. My eyes pop. We never gave it back to Derek.

"I still have the VIP access badge," I tell Iris.

Chip cuts me a glace and I brief him on how we got it at Green Hill.

I slide the badge into my back pocket, then dial Curtis. I speed talk when I get his voicemail, watching Iris wring her hands and take glances out the rear window.

"Curtis, it's Theo. Listen, Phil Maddox just set fire to GPs house while we were inside. I don't know if GP got out, but Phil is chasing us to Green Hill. I'm with Iris and Chip. We grabbed whatever we could from the house and we're going after my mom. Go to the house or meet us at Green Hill as soon as you get this."

"We're almost there," Chip says.

Phil must make the same assessment because he races alongside us and jerks his wheel, ramming his Escalade into the driver's side of my truck. Iris screams as Chip swerves to avoid getting hit a second time. But Phil comes up alongside us again, forcing us into the breakdown lane. Chip speeds ahead for several yards, then tries to pull onto the main road, but he's forced back into the narrow lane. Phil's Escalade keeps inching us to the right until Chip has no choice but to ride against the guardrail. Bumblebee's passenger door squeals in protest, scraping in one continuous shriek of metal on metal that grinds my nerves raw. I press my feet into the floor and push against the seat, cringing away from the door.

"Fuck," Chip says. "He's got me pinned."

I look out the windshield and realize the guardrail ends up ahead. "Jeezus. Do you think he's trying to run us off the road at Cutter's Cross?"

"No, no, no. Not the ravine," Iris says. "My God. Not like my mom."

"Fuck that." Chip cuts hard to the left into Phil's truck. But I'm iffy on whether Phil Maddox will give up if Chip keeps nailing him. And I'm right, because he comes at us again.

"Hit the brakes!" I yell.

Chip slams the pedal, fishtailing and screeching to a stop, burning long strips of rubber in his wake. We momentarily outwit Phil who speeds ahead, tail lights glowing fiery red in the darkness.

"Go back and cut around to Prospect before he spins on us."

Chip whips us around and punches the gas.

I face a panic-stricken Iris in the backseat. "We're gonna be fine. You're one of the bravest people I've ever met, but right now, I need you to help me scour the papers we took from the house. Look for anything that says where my mom is at Green Hill: a room number, a ward, anything." She nods, and I swallow hard. "Iris, we're gonna be okay. I promise. I won't let anything bad happen to you . . . I—" I don't finish the sentiment, but the words linger in my mind. *I freaking love you.* "Don't be afraid."

Iris nods again and gets to work.

"Uh, Captain Quint," Chip says. "I think he's coming back around for his noon feeding." His eyes are fixed on the rearview.

"All you can do is try to outrun him."

"I have a better idea."

Chip makes a hairpin turn onto a side street, tossing me against the door. "Amy lives around here," he says. "There's a defunct service road where we go to park. It cuts straight through to Monarch Drive and back to Route twelve."

Chip to the rescue.

"Theo," Iris says hesitantly. "I can't find anything, but do you remember what Derek told us about where they do research?"

I don't have a chance to answer because Chip hits a thick tree branch in the road. My truck bounces high, hitting down with a thud that slams my head against the window. I grab the gearshift knob and zigzag Bumblebee into 4-D, engaging instant traction for the next mile of mud and fallen debris.

I make sure Iris is okay before I nod and say, "I remember. I thought the same thing."

We squeal into the parking lot at Green Hill Psychiatric Hospital five minutes later and file out of the truck. The damage to Bumblebee's side panel is monstrous. I can't believe we made it here alive. Chip's driving usually scares the shit out of me, but we needed Speed Racer to come through strong in the finish.

There's no good way to start looking. There's also no time. Just because we haven't seen Phil Maddox since the service road, doesn't mean he isn't coming, and that has every nerve in my body taut with tension.

"I'm going in," I say.

"Alone? What about the graves?" Iris says. "What if your mom is . . . ?" She doesn't voice her suspicion, and neither do I.

"I think it's better if we split up. I'll be faster on my own. I don't think he knows I have an access card."

"No. I'm going with you," she says, hands on her hips. The girl who jumped down from a tree after trying to save a single monarch.

"I'll dig," Chip says. "You two go."

"Grab the shovel from the backseat," I tell him. "There's a flashlight in the hatch. Don't get spotted. Just because we haven't seen him, doesn't make this a breather. "Ready?" I ask Iris.

"Point me in the right direction first," Chip says. "This is a big-ass cemetery."

"Maybe you should stay with Chip. You're the only one who knows how to read the map and find the markers."

Iris looks at her wrist where she wrote the plot numbers, then turns to Chip. "You're going to the south side. That way." She points Chip in the right direction. "The graves are in waves of hundreds. Here's where you need to be." She punches a small hole in the map with her finger. Walk halfway and find a stone in the ground and check the number. Keep going until you get to the eight hundreds. You're looking for eight fifty-six and eight fifty-seven."

"Go," Chip says. "I got this."

Ready or not.

I expel a big breath with a short "Whoo." Then rally and throw my hood forward, jogging straight for the employee entrance with Iris by my side. I swipe the badge without hesitation.

The little green Go light flashes and we forge ahead on pure adrenaline. Once we're in the stairwell our only option is to go up. We take the stairs two at a time and stand at the next door. I start thinking of this whole search-and-rescue like the game Chip and I used to play as kids: Red Light, Green Light. Then I swipe the badge again.

Green light. Go.

I open the door and peek into an empty hallway.

Red light. Freeze.

The camera in the corner is blinking. Someone, somewhere, could be watching us and be on their way. But we have to find our way to the basement. My pulse quickens. Screw it. We're out of options. I press myself flat against the wall on the camera side and tell Iris to do the same, and then we sidestep-run to the stairwell at the end.

Swipe.

Green light. Go.

I jump several sets of stairs that wind down to the basement. To my astonishment, Iris does the same. The gymnast's daughter. I hold my breath and swipe the card again, but nothing happens. I repeat the swipe. Nothing.

"Didn't Derek say this was a full-access badge?"

Iris nods. "He must have lied."

"Fuck. Of course he did." I kick the door. "We have to find another way."

We make it up a half-flight when we hear the door to the basement open, and then a whistle that sounds like *yoo-hoo*. Followed by, "Eh, gypsy girl? You there?"

Iris's eyes bug out before she walks down the stairs ultra slowly. "Valentina Gabor. Is that your name?"

The elderly woman nods. "I see you coming. You need inside?"

"Yes," Iris says. "We do."

"You see things?" she asks Iris with more scrutiny.

"Yes, I do."

"Everybody here sees things." Valentina steps aside, granting us access, then walks up the stairs to a different floor humming a song.

Iris draws a sharp breath. "That's the lullaby my mom used to sing."

The subterranean level is a far cry from the hospital upstairs. The lights are brighter, the walls and furniture newer, and the weighty vibe of whatever scientific work is happening here increases the antiseptic stench tenfold.

When we reach the halfway point, we find a circular room surrounded by glass. Walking around the perimeter is a single-file-only option, like a subway trench for rats. We survey the desks and workstations. The only things not following the room's shape are the two examination tables in the center.

Two tables, two graves, each lying side by side.

I can't help but think disposing of Mom and me like the forgotten patients in the unmarked graves outside has been Phil's endgame all along.

We walk into the arena-like lab, surprised there isn't some sleeping-on-the-job-night-shift asswipe nodding off at a desk. But aside from the hum of fluorescent lights, the ward is unnervingly quiet and empty.

I hold my breath and swipe the card.

Green light. Go.

If I can find my mom's name in the system I can find her room. I pick a random desk and tap the Enter key on the computer keyboard, waking an internal network that groans from sleep and offers me a blinking cursor. I type Mom's name into the blank field.

Name/ID: **Mackey**
SEARCH NOT FOUND
*Blink. Blink. Blink.*
Name/ID: **Rogan**

```
SEARCH NOT FOUND
Name/ID: Balanchuk
Blink. Blink. Blink
SEARCH NOT FOUND
Shit. Think.
Name/ID: Dudyk
```

Iris checks the door and windows as the timer wheel spins. I chew my thumbnail and bounce my knees. The circle goes around, searching the database. Then the screen blinks to life from top to bottom, filling in the data fields.

"Got it."

Iris is back at my side in a flash. I scan for relevant information, skipping over things that beg to be read. But there isn't time.

```
Name/ID: Dudyk, Sophia
Client #: BL-08
Doctor #: Maddox
DSM-IV Axis: 296.43, 296.44, 296.65
Ward: SecSub1
Room: 110
```

"Room one-ten. Let's go." I push the chair away from the desk, ready to find Mom and spring her from this hellhole, when my cell phone shatters the silence.

Shit.

I pull it from my pocket and swipe-to-answer fast, hoping I can stop the phone from ringing a second time.

"Looking for something?"

I know that voice. I lower my phone and turn slowly. Derek the orderly is standing behind us, arms crossed over his barrel chest. Band-Aids on his chin, cheek, and forehead make him seem like less of a threat, which isn't true. The bandage on his cheek doesn't fully cover the festering sore underneath. I remember the way Valentina cursed him with rotting flesh and can't help wondering if it came true.

"What are you two doing down here?" he asks. "Don't tell me; let me guess. You came back to save *the animals?*"

Curtis's voice rips through my phone's speaker. "Theo? Is that you? Where are you?"

"What about *you?*" I ask Derek. "You told us you didn't have full access to the wards AT GREEN HILL." I give our location in the loudest voice possible without shouting, hoping Curtis catches on.

"Dr. Maddox felt the need to beef up his security on this ward. Especially after I told him you were asking about Luanne."

"On my way," Curtis says faintly from my phone. "Don't do anything stupid."

Too late. I'm facing Green Hill's resident Mountain Troll.

Derek cocks an eyebrow when he catches sight of my phone. He lunges and Iris trips him, buying us a few seconds. We dash through the door and down a hallway, reading room numbers out loud to each other in search of 110.

"Get back here, you little shits," Derek thunders behind us.

We race to a corner that hopefully turns in the right direction. The door at the end of this new hallway swings inward and we find ourselves face-to-face with Lianne Cole, wielding a black pistol.

We screech to a halt.

Derek rounds the corner behind us in hot pursuit, and I know we're out of options. I knew Iris should have stayed outside with Chip. I vacillate left and right, trying to decide which of the two is the lesser threat.

"Gotcha in a game of pickle," Derek says. "Don't bother trying to escape this time, junior. *Uncle-Daddy* will be here any minute."

I narrow my eyes, glaring, seething disgust.

"Theo," Lianne says calmly, "take Iris and run past me."

I don't know what kind of twisted person tells their prey to keep running so they can shoot a moving target, but I'm not budging.

"Fuck you, Lianne."

Her eyes go round.

"Yeah. I know who you are. Lianne Cole, paramedic, sister to Luanne Cole, the 1988 second place springboard diver who died when she was sixteen. You blame my mom for that, don't you, because she never told anyone what she saw? Is that why you were okay drugging me? Her son for your sister. Go ahead and shoot then. Just know it might be the last thing you do as a free woman."

Her eyes twitch and behind us Derek laughs. "Don't look at me, doll," he says. "I would have blasted the little fuckers by now."

For a brief second, when my anger was telling me to call Lianne's bluff, I thought challenging her was the way to go. Now that she's taking aim, all I can do is squeeze Iris's hand, close my eyes, and surrender to the inevitable. Knowing full well and good that standing at the wrong end of a point-blank range weapon is a ballistics no-brainer.

Game. Over.

There's a loud pop, but the jolt and searing pain that should follow never comes. Instead, a heavy thud sounds behind us, making me spin. Derek is convulsing on the ground, pissing his scrubs. And Lianne Cole is on the right end of a long line, Tasering the shit out of him.

"Run," Lianne says. "There's no time for me to explain."

"Make time. I'm not gonna let you Taser us from behind."

"I won't. Dr. Maddox doesn't even know I'm here. Your mother told me what he has planned for me. She saw you coming here. You're not the only ones he preyed upon. We're all his pawns. But I'm your only hope for getting you two out of here."

"Does he know you're not Luanne? Was that part of the plan?"

She nods. "The colored contacts were my idea, though. I wanted your mother to see me every day and be reminded of what she'd done. Neglected to do. My sister Luanne had hazel eyes. Mine are brown."

"For how long?"

"Years. Since the fire. But then I saw you again, all grown up, and I felt so much remorse for what I was helping him do. None of this will bring back my sister. I'm sorry about everything, but I'm not lying to you."

Iris shakes my arm. "She's not lying, Theo. Her aura is as blue as Chip's. Come on. Let's go."

Iris pulls me past Lianne Cole, but my own distrust still makes me cringe as I wait to be hit from behind. When nothing happens, I take off like a bullet, reading room numbers: 101, 102, 103. The electricity in the lights crackles, then hums loudly and I'm jolted by the similarities. The deserted hallway, white walls, gray doors. Everything but the dirt being shoveled in beside me. The numbered doors run in reverse order and bend around another corner: 108, 109, 110. We found it. I'm so mind-blown and fixated on our goal that I don't see Phil Maddox slither around the corner until Iris screams.

He walks toward us slowly, deliberately controlling every move like this is a game of chess. Too bad I'm no longer one of his rooks.

"This is the hallway I saw in my vision."

"I'm impressed," he says. "It took your father—a term I'm willing to use loosely for all intents and purposes—much longer to figure it out with his more pedestrian methods. Nature versus nurture at play once again."

"What do you know about nurture?" I spit. "You lied to me. We had a funeral. We put a casket in the ground. You let me believe I might be to blame."

"A casket. But not a body. In your defense, I worked very hard to mislead you. But I never lied. Not if you think about every word. It may surprise you to know your mother came with me willingly, at first, once I guaranteed your safety."

"Because you were having an affair or because you had her addicted to her own mind, like Dad said?"

"That's a matter of perspective."

"Not really. Mom tried to warn me, didn't she? I overheard Dr. Aldridge say she seemed to be developing a variation in her ability. Remote messaging. That's what I saw behind the house and while I was underwater. Christ, she was pointing at Iris. She knew I was going to smack and someone was going to save me. Not someone. The girl with the tattoos from the cliff. You bastard. You've known since then, haven't you?" I look at Iris and almost laugh. "He's the goddamn Snake from my card reading."

She grips my arm tighter. "And the Mouse."

"All those things are more or less true," Phil says to me. "I was curious to see how you might react. I still am. Curious. You have so much potential, Theo. I can help you. All you have to do is decide which type of person you'd rather be, mundane or extraordinary."

"I can be both," I say, taking long purposeful strides toward him. "Step aside. I'm not leaving here without Mom."

"You know I can't let you get to that unreachable door. There's more at stake here than the thing you want most."

I spot the syringe he's trying to hide behind his back and know he'll jab me without giving it a second thought.

"Do it," I hiss, hoping he gets the double-pointed barb.

Phil shifts his steely gaze to Iris. "What color am I now?" he asks.

And to my surprise she answers.

"Mostly black with shots of red and muddy brown when you should be nothing but shades of golden orange and blue, like your son. Someone who cares about people. Someone loyal and ambitious instead of egotistical and greedy."

"Finally. An honest answer from the little fortune-teller," he says.

Phil takes a step forward and we take a step back. Then we do it again, an excruciatingly slow waltz with Iris moving as my shadow.

"You can still do the right thing," I say, stepping backward. "GP was right. Let Mom go with me and continue writing your research paper. I'm willing to help you. I'll tell you everything about my dream states."

"Precognition," he says. "It's time to call your gift by its proper name."

"You don't need her anymore," I say, ignoring him. "Do you?"

He cocks a grin. "I needed Sophia Rogan from the moment I laid eyes on her. And *you,* if you care to believe it."

He lunges at me with the syringe raised, aiming for my neck.

I jump out of the way and catch his arm, clamping my hand around his wrist. He grabs the back of my neck with his free hand and pushes my head forward, trying to fold me like a human accordion toward a needle that will make me lose everything all over again. Including Iris.

Phil Maddox is stronger than he looks. Matched to me in height and build. I'm tired from the horror of the swim meet, going to the hospital, the chase. The needle is inching closer. A bead of sweat runs down his temple, his teeth are clenched, veins bulging in his neck. But all of it pales against the determination in his eyes. If I want to win, normal rules don't apply.

I opt for dirty fighting, nailing him in the groin with my knee. He releases an animalistic groan, but doesn't cease his hold. I slam my forehead into the bridge of his nose and he flies backward, releasing his grip, stunned by pain I can only imagine. He recovers quickly, but I'm ready for him. "Come on," I yell, wanting to hurt him the way he's hurt me.

He lunges for Iris instead but freezes midstep and convulses, dropping to the floor at our feet with the whack of a plank of wood. Lianne Cole is standing behind him, holding the Taser.

"Run," she says. "I can keep him down, but not for long."

"Not without my mom."

"Derek is going to show up any minute and remorse is not part of his vocabulary." Lianne's natural brown eyes are imploring. Without the contacts, I see the paramedic I remember more clearly.

"You don't understand. I can't leave this building without getting to the last door."

Lianne takes a deep breath and picks up the syringe. "I'll do what I can. I owe it to Sophia. Hurry."

We take off at a run as Derek comes storming back toward Lianne.

"Fucking bitch," he growls. "I knew you couldn't be trusted."

Lianne lifts her Taser and shoots Derek in the chest again. I watch her go after him while he's still convulsing on the floor. The syringe she took from Phil Maddox primed in her hand.

I swipe the badge on room 110. Green light. Go.

Mom is sitting in a chair facing a window. The moonlight shining into the room gives it a bluish underwater quality. Just like I saw.

She turns with a smile like she was expecting me, and all the air leaves my lungs.

"You found me."

She's thinner than I've ever seen her. Heavy bags circle her eyes, but she's here. Alive.

I start with, "Hi Mom," because it's the easiest thing to say before blinking hard to be sure what I'm seeing is real.

"I saw you at the house," she says, in the same matter-of-fact way she's always spoken. "And one time when you were underwater. I tried to help."

I see Iris slip out of the room in my peripheral vision. I hear her release a strangled sob. I'm fighting back a few of my own.

"You did help," I tell her. "I'm sorry it took me so long to figure out. But we have to go. We need to get you out of here fast because . . ."

"I know," she says. "You're running out of time."

# THIRTY-SEVEN

**Fast:** When a dive is moving or rotating very quickly, sometimes too quickly to control.

**WE RUN** like hell across Ward Hill Cemetery, straight toward Chip's moving flashlight. Driven by adrenaline mixed with punch-drunk exhaustion, I could either run for days or pass out cold. When we reach Chip, I throw myself on hands on knees, sweating, panting so hard I can't form words. He's four-feet-deep in the ground, covered in dirt. Iris is a little farther behind me, going as fast as she can with Mom who's been locked up for the last four years to aid Phil Maddox's human vivisection.

"Holy shit," Chip says. "You found her. What happened in there?"

I don't know whether to laugh or cry. I manage to answer in one word. "Everything."

"I haven't found anything out here yet." He chucks the shovel into the earth like a spear and we hear the clang of the cutting edge hitting pay dirt.

Chip's eyes pop wider before he starts digging again, faster, unearthing a metal box too small to be a coffin for anything more than a pet. I jump into the grave to help and the dankness of the grave seeps outward from all sides and coats my skin with the earthy stench of manure and wild mushrooms. I won't forget that smell for as long as I live. Iris gets on her knees and pulls the box from the top while Chip and I hoist it onto the grass. We crawl out of the grave and I take the shovel from

Chip. I direct all my rage into slamming the lock until it springs open then drop to my knees in the freshly lifted soil and push back the lid.

Inside are Mom's admittance papers to Boston Public Hospital from when she was a kid, my parents' marriage license, Mom's birth certificate, her school records, even her passport—everything needed to erase a person from existence, buried inside this sarcophagus. Another folder is stuffed with page after page of psychological analysis on Phillip Maddox from his childhood as a ward of the state. It's hard to resist: childhood neglect, higher than average intelligence, conduct disorder, narcissism, fascination with fire, antisocial personality disorder.

"Why would he bury these? Why not just burn everything if that's his M.O.?"

"They're his trophies." Hearing Mom say this, knowing what he did to us, is chilling.

"He's a psychopath."

"And he's heading this way," Chip says.

I jump to my feet and grab the shovel. "Iris, take my cell phone and my mom and make a run for my truck."

They try but Phil fades left and intercepts them. He catches Mom by the arm and Iris by a fistful of her long hair. She yelps as Phil yanks her closer, her face pure terror.

"I could never discern whether this fortune-teller was as real as her mother or a little charlatan," Phil says, staring straight at me.

Iris whimpers and he wraps his arm across her shoulders to keep her close, leaning to whisper in her ear. "Shh. I know you're the real deal now. It's just a little too late."

"Let her go," Mom says. "She's not part of this."

"But she is. She always has been. Our son merely made her a bigger part of it when he brought her to Green Hill. I suppose I should thank Dave Malone for that. Pity she's not an athlete, though. I can always use new subjects."

Chip takes the dirty shovel out of my hand and steps forward, primed to strike, and I know my visions were clear, even if they weren't always absolute.

"Don't make another move, Langford," Phil says. "There won't be 'Mercy, Mercy' for anyone here tonight."

I put an arm out so Chip will lower the shovel. "Was it worth all this?" I ask. "Using us? Alienating your only real family? Is this the legacy you intended to leave behind?"

"It will be," he says. "When I'm the most well-respected psychiatrist of my time."

Sirens rip through the quiet night. Phil stiffens.

"Those sirens aren't for me," I tell him. "You can either cut and run now, or . . ."

He doesn't give any indication before throwing Iris to the ground like a rag doll. But when he dives for the metal box on the ground, I field goal–kick him so hard he flips onto his back. I pounce and start punching, blinded by rage and years of mistrust. Phil's cheekbone splits open, then his lip, but I can't stop. I don't care. I'll kill him. I'll fucking kill him for this.

Chip jumps on my back and pulls me off while I'm still swinging. "He's out, man. Stop."

I swipe the back of my hand across my mouth and taste blood. My knuckles ache. But when I look at the guy I once thought of as my uncle, laying unconscious on the ground, a bloody mess, I feel nothing. "That was for Mom." I haul off and kick him in the ribs one more time for good measure. "That's for Dad and GP and Iris and every other person whose life you corrupted."

Checkmate.

I reach into Phil's pockets until I find the Zippo my dad gave him. I look at the inscription. *My best man. My brother. My friend.* Every word is a lie. I glance at Chip as I slip the lighter into my front pocket, knowing someday he'll be the person that makes Dad's sentiments ring true.

The sun is beginning to rise, lifting this nightmare from

darkness with the wailing of sirens growing louder in the distance with each passing second.

Three state trooper vehicles pull onto the grounds, closely followed by Curtis in his black sedan. The staties jump out of their cars, reaching instinctively for their weapons, then relaxing when they see the perpetrator is down for the count. They check Phil's vitals, then call for an ambulance.

Curtis takes inventory of Iris first. She whispers something to him, then rushes at me, flying into my arms. I run my hand over her hair while her tears soak the front of my shirt.

"We're okay."

"He killed my mom," she sobs.

"I know." My heart shatters into pieces beneath her cheek.

Curtis approaches us with a stack of frown lines creasing his forehead.

"GP?" I ask, my question loaded.

He shakes his head and the weight of every lie crushes me.

Iris squeezes me tighter. "I'm so sorry."

"So am I." Sorry enough to finally put something else to rest.

"Did I start the fire?" I ask Curtis. "The one at my old house. I was lighting matches in my room that night and—I just need confirmation of the truth."

"That couldn't have been you," Curtis says. "That fire originated in the basement."

"Is that what you put in your report to protect me or is that what really happened?"

He gets a chagrined look when he realizes I know the truth. "That's what we put in the report, because that's the truth. At the time, we were worried it was your father, trying to get back at your mother and Phil. I think we know now it was Phil." He clamps a hand on my shoulder to reassure me.

Chip comes over and we fill Curtis in on the details of what happened tonight, while Mom gets checked over by a paramedic.

Curtis keeps shaking his head, not so much surprised by what transpired as astonished we made it out alive.

One of the staties interrupts our conference to ask if we know the woman walking across the lawn toward the scene. I turn and see Lianne Cole.

When she sees me, she smiles and nods, and a new wave of relief surges through me. Without her help, Mom would have been trapped inside that place forever.

"Well?" the statie asks.

"Her name is Lianne Cole," I say. "A nurse who works here. She knows everything there is to know about why my mom has been locked in this hospital against her will, by this man." I point at Phil, who's starting to rouse from unconsciousness. "I think there are others being held against their will inside. On the basement level."

The state trooper narrows his eyes at Phil, still in handcuffs on the ground. "Do you know this man, son?"

Phil turns his head and bores his green eyes into mine without a shred of mercy.

"He's my biological father," I tell the statie. "Dr. Phillip Maddox. But I never really knew him at all."

I leave Curtis to explain the rest and go to my Mom.

"Are you still glad I'm like you?" I ask.

"More than ever." She pulls me close.

Relief and happiness rock me so hard, I'm almost glad I didn't learn the whole truth until now. Almost.

"Remember our day at the cliff, when I promised to tell you if I saw that girl again?" I point to Iris. "Do you see her this time?"

"JoJo's daughter," Mom says and smiles. "I should have known."

Deep down I think I always did.

# THIRTY-EIGHT

**Gainer:** The diver faces the end of the board and rotates backward toward the diving board while moving forward and away. Also called reverse.

**PHIL MADDOX** was immediately remanded into custody, pending investigation. Locked away in a small cell, like the victims of his crimes.

Rocco is working toward a full recovery since coming out of his coma a month ago. His prognosis is excellent. And we are 100 percent copasetic.

Mom's road to recovery is only beginning. She doesn't talk about Phil Maddox or Green Hill, at least not with me. But every so often, late at night, I overhear her telling Curtis things like she used to tell GP. She has good days and bad days. Night terrors she insists on keeping because they help her understand what's real. We visit Dad and GP at the cemetery every few weeks and we always start with "Hi." But the best days so far have been the ones where she wants to go to the pool or she laughs and her smile goes all the way to her eyes. That smile reaffirms that she'll be okay.

Part of her therapy involves writing down all the things that happened in a journal, starting at the beginning with the Rogans, her adoptive parents. Last night, she announced she's planning to write a book about her experience. Which is a pretty nice way of describing what she went through, considering. I know it's a story I'm interested in reading myself someday.

I haven't told her this, but I had another one of my level-fifty freak-out visions while diving, a few weeks after Phil Maddox got hauled off and locked away. Before she made her announcement. I saw Mom sitting at a long table, smiling, signing books with her name emblazoned on the cover. Time without Philomax will tell for sure if what I've inherited from the Balanchuk family line makes me extraordinary.

For now, I'm fine doing mundane stuff, hanging out with Chip and Iris and the guys from the team at the Langfords' pool. Iris has been giving them readings but none are as accurate as the one she gave me at the carnival. Thankfully, I've learned to pay attention to the signs. The three of us don't talk about what happened too much. But now, when Chip lights the gas fire pit, or we go out to the quarry for a bonfire, I don't cringe. The dancing flames still mesmerize me. I can't help but see destruction every time they whip in the wind or make that low whooshing sound, like a living beast, ready to be unleashed at anytime. Which is why I finally threw away the book of matches under my mattress.

Not a day goes by that I'm not grateful GP put his life on the line for me. My only regret is that we didn't have more time. Because I finally understand the scope of protection he was trying to provide me. Not to mention the unconditional love. Rough as it was around the edges.

But I have Mom, my friends, Iris, and most of all, the truth. The scholarship I did end up getting from Stanford, along with the A+ on my family history project were just a bonus.

In the end, I suppose Phil Maddox got what he always wanted. Notoriety. He may have robbed us of the past and screwed with the present. But our futures remain to be seen (pun intended).